the rossiter file

an inspector stride mystery

THOMAS RENDELL CURRAN

the rossiter file

an inspector stride mystery

THOMAS RENDELL CURRAN

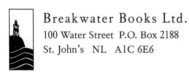

Breakwater Books Ltd.
100 Water Street P.O. Box 2188
St. John's NL A1C 6E6

Library and Archives Canada Cataloguing in Publication

Curran, Thomas Rendell, 1939-
        The Rossiter file / Thomas Rendell Curran.
(An Inspector Stride mystery)

ISBN 1-55081-212-2

I. Title. II. Series: Curran, Thomas Rendell, 1939- . Inspector Stride mystery.

PS8555.U68R68 2005   C813'.6   C2005-902613-8

Layout Design: Rhonda Molloy
Cover Design: Adam Freake
Editor: Tamara Reynish
Author Photo: Kristina Curren

The Canada Council | Le Conseil des Arts
for the Arts | du Canada
We acknowledge the financial support of
he Canada Council for the Arts for our publishing activities.

We acknowledge the financial support of the Government of Canada through the Book Publishing Industry Development Program (BPIDP) for our publishing activities.

Printed in Canada.

for

Arthur James Rendell
Newfoundland Regiment, Number 204
Killed in Action, Beaumont Hamel, France
July 1, 1916

acknowledgements

Few books are written in isolation, and *The Rossiter File* is no exception. Many people helped along the way, with information, support, and criticism both honest and constructive. Sergeant (retired) Bob Morgan of the Royal Newfoundland Constabulary provided information on the Newfoundland Constabulary, and on the Newfoundland court system in the post-war period. Wilfred Thomas was ever willing to set out on foot, bicycle, or automobile to obtain detailed local information on the various places in St. John's cited in the book. Paul O'Neill responded quickly and with great detail to my requests for information on aspects of the history of St. John's. Constance Auclair once again rendered invaluable assistance with manuscript preparation. Friends and family members reviewed drafts of the text and offered many helpful comments: sincere thanks to Meredith Stroud Curren, Kristina Curren, Anna M. Curren, Janet Martin, Terry Thomas, Alex Brett, Bridget McNeill, Betty and Michael Corlett, Margaret Young, Christine Jannasch, Stephen Knowles, and Bonnie Preston. I am indebted to them all. I am grateful to Clyde and Rebecca Rose and the staff at Breakwater Books, to Rhonda Molloy for the layout design, Adam Freake for the cover design, and to my editor Tamara Reynish for her enthusiastic work during the final stages of manuscript revision.

O N e

Constable Jack Corrigan liked walking the night beat, it suited his temperament and his personality. He liked the isolation and the quiet that came with the fall of night. It was a time when the streets were mostly empty and the rough edges of the city were softened by moonlight and shadows. He was especially happy to be on the night beat now because St. John's had been suffering under a heat wave for more than a week. Corrigan didn't like the heat. That was the beginning, the middle, and the end of it. The fact that a heat wave was a rare event in this corner of the North Atlantic didn't soften his discomfort one bit.

Corrigan was also something of a loner. He didn't dislike people, not really, but for the most part he had learned to do without them. He lived alone. He liked cats. And like the cats he lived with, Jack Corrigan had a great disdain for clatter and disruption.

So he wasn't at all happy when a car tire came hurtling down the steep incline of Cathedral Street at one o'clock in the morning, caromed off a telephone pole near the bottom of the hill, and sailed past his face, close enough that it almost swiped the cigarette from his lips. The tire bounced once in the middle of Duckworth Street, then thudded into a parked car, buckling the door and shattering the window.

In the wake of the tire, three young men sprinted down Cathedral and onto Duckworth. They came to a halt by the car and inspected the results of their enterprise. Corrigan thought the young bastards looked happy enough, but his sudden and unexpected appearance behind them changed that. He took hold of the one closest to him, securing him with a combination choke-hold and hammerlock. The other two took off, casting frightened glances behind them as they ran. Corrigan watched them turn right, over the sidewalk and into Scanlon's Lane which would take them down flights of concrete steps and out onto Water Street. Corrigan didn't care that they were getting away. The one he was holding would sooner or later lead him to the other two.

The young man struggled against Corrigan's choking grip trying to break free. He said a lot of bad words, some of which cast doubts upon the legality of Corrigan's birth, and the morality of his parents. Corrigan only smiled. He pulled his forearm tighter across the young man's throat and leaned backwards, lifting him clear of the ground. That brought the struggling to an abrupt end, and there were no more bad words. Corrigan took his handcuffs from his belt and with practised efficiency, he secured the young man's hands behind his back. Then, he bundled his prisoner across Duckworth, removed one cuff, and locked him into an embrace with the same telephone pole the tire had bounced off. He took a wallet from the young man's pocket, checked the identification, then tucked the wallet into a pocket of his own jacket.

They were close enough to the Court House that Corrigan could walk his prisoner to the lockup without having to call for assistance or transportation. But first he wanted to do a quick check of the laneway. He didn't really expect to find either of the two who had run away, but you never knew. Scanlon's Lane was poorly lit, and the steps leading down to Water Street were steep and twisting. One or both of the fugitives might have fallen and been hurt. That possibility didn't cause Jack Corrigan a lot of grief.

When Corrigan reached the entrance to Scanlon's Lane, he snapped on his flashlight and followed the narrow beam down the steps, casting it from side to side, walking slowly and with care. A third of the way down he came to a sudden stop. He moved the light back and forth, picking out the details of the scene before him.

"God damn them to hell," he said. The words were barely audible in the enclosed space.

The body of an old man lay on the steps. His shoulders and head were slumped against the concrete wall of the building on the west side of the laneway. His cloth cap was perched on his head at an odd angle, the peak pulled off to one side. Sightless eyes stared at the wall opposite. The old man's mouth lolled partway open, showing a row of ragged teeth in the lower jaw, discoloured by blood and age. A dental plate, grotesquely pink and white in the oval of light, lay on the step near his left hand. It looked almost as though he had been trying to recover the denture, and his dignity, before death took over.

Corrigan looked at the scene a moment longer, then made his way back up to Duckworth and the Court House to call for assistance.

t w o

Does anyone know

"Does anyone know who Scanlon was?" It was the sort of thing Eric Stride was interested in, the names of streets and places in the old city.

"I think it was named after a fellow named Michael Scanlon," Harry Phelan said. "I read something about him one time. He was a wine merchant. He had a business on Water Street, sometime back in the last century, on the corner of a footpath running from Water up to Duckworth."

"And this was the footpath?"

"I think so, yes."

Four of them were gathered now in Scanlon's Lane. Stride and Phelan, Jack Corrigan, and Detective Constable Kevin Noseworthy. It was going on for two o'clock, and the day ahead looked like it was going to be a long and tiring one.

Stride didn't think the old man had been dead for very long. The body was still warm and rigor mortis had not yet set in. He wondered, though, if the warm air had helped to keep the chill of death at bay for a little longer than normal. He chased the thought away. He would wait until the coroner, Thomas Butcher, arrived and rendered an expert opinion.

When Stride had finished looking at the body and had stepped away, Phelan moved closer.

"I'll make a guess that he's about seventy-five years old," Phelan said. "Maybe even a bit older than that." He crouched down, sitting on his heels, looking into the old man's face.

14

That was odd. Phelan usually had an acute reaction to the recently and violently dead. Twice in the not so distant past, he had literally keeled over when confronted with an especially grisly scene. 'Swooned' was the word Kevin Noseworthy liked to use for it. Noseworthy and Phelan enjoyed – Stride was certain that was the word for it – an ongoing rivalry. Noseworthy was the Constabulary's self-styled wizard of the evidence room, the essential third person at any major crime scene. Tall, pale, and often irreverent, Noseworthy masked his expertise with a talent for burrowing under Harry Phelan's skin. But always in a nice way.

Noseworthy had arrived in the laneway in the Constabulary's Black Maria a few minutes before Stride and Phelan made it there in Stride's MG-TA. He had already done his preliminary survey of the area and now he was well along in his picture-taking.

Scanlon's Lane, steep and winding with flights of concrete steps leading down to a dirt path that swung sharply to the left before exiting onto Water Street, was a useful shortcut during the day, but more likely to be avoided after dark. There were deep shadows then, and sometimes odd characters hanging about. Like tonight, probably.

Harry Phelan had taken the call at his home on Victoria Street from the desk constable at Fort Townshend, the Constabulary headquarters. Then, he called Stride. It was a routine they set up long ago. They alternated evenings and weekends as point man for an investigation, the one who would take the first call from headquarters, or "The Fort," as they called it, although no one else on the Force did.

Noseworthy took a final photograph and returned his camera to its leather satchel.

Stride spoke to Corrigan. "Give it to us once more, Jack. What do you think happened here?"

Corrigan recounted the incident of the tire sailing down Cathedral Street and slamming into the parked car, as well as his capture of one of the three youths.

"The other two, they took off and ran into the laneway here. I didn't give chase right away because I had to look after the one I had hold of." Corrigan laughed. "Not that I had a chance in hell of catching them. It's about twenty years too late for that. Anyway, when I had the young bucko secure, I came down the lane to have a look, in case one of them might have taken a spill on the steps. It's dark down here and that light up there on the wall doesn't help much." Corrigan pointed to a fixture high on the building on the right. It painted the scene on the ground in a dull yellow glow. Corrigan looked at the body again, then back at Stride. "I think what happened was that the old fella was here in the laneway, making friendly with a bottle." He gestured with his head. "You've noticed the smell of cheap booze, sir. I'm guessing one or both of the young fuckers ran into him and sent him arse-over-teakettle down the steps."

"Accidentally."

"It might have been an accident. Or maybe they gave him a shove just for the hell of it, to see how high he would bounce. We won't know that until we catch them."

"And maybe not even then."

"You give me a half-hour with them, sir, and by the time I'm done, they'll own up to driving the nails into Christ at Calvary. But one thing's sure. That poor old bugger won't be telling us what happened."

"No, he won't, Jack, and that's a fact."

"And it looks like they come on the poor old fella when he was taking a leak."

"Yes, I noticed that." The old man's pants were unbuttoned, pulled wide open. The display of tired old flesh made the scene all the more pathetic, not a scrap of dignity left.

Stride went back to the body for another look. Corrigan's assessment of the possible series of events might well be accurate. He looked up towards Duckworth at the narrow winding steps, imagining two frightened young men racing down them in near-darkness. The old man hears them coming, turns to take a look, and one of them – maybe both – collides with him. If he was the worse for drink – and there was no disputing Corrigan's observation about the smell of alcohol, delicately nuanced with the odour of stale urine – he wouldn't have been able to get out of their way in time. The alternate version, that they might have thrown the old man down the steps, was also a possibility. Fear and anger could join hands quickly enough. Stride hoped that wasn't the case here. A manslaughter charge, if that's what it turned out to be, was grief enough.

But he also didn't rule out the possibility that the man was already dead when the two youths ran into the laneway. Although it was obvious he hadn't been dead very long, time of death estimates were notoriously difficult. The only really accurate assessment occurred when someone actually witnessed a killing and noted the time.

Stride stood up and looked at his watch, wishing the coroner would arrive soon.

And then he arrived. Dr. Thomas Butcher walked slowly up the steps from Water Street. Stride thought Butcher looked very tired, and although he wasn't quite out of breath when he reached Stride and the others, he was near enough. He stood for a moment looking down at the dead man, not speaking, breathing slowly and evenly.

Butcher nodded while Stride gave him a capsule of the situation, then stepped close to the dead man, kneeling on the concrete step beside him. He took a few minutes to make his examination, touching the face and neck with his right hand, flexing the arms, then testing the resistance of the leg muscles. He took the cap from the man's head and examined the skull, shaking his own head in reaction to what he saw. Then, he stood up and backed away.

"You're right, Eric. He hasn't been dead for very long. Sometime within the last hour, I think. And Constable Corrigan might well have it right, that the two fugitives simply ran into the old fellow in the laneway and sent him tumbling down the steps." He looked at Stride. "Have you found the bottle he was drinking from?"

"Not yet, Dr. Butcher," Noseworthy said. "But we haven't done a thorough search yet."

Butcher went back to the body. "He's had a severe battering. There appears to be at least one serious head injury under the cap, but there are a number of others also, including one in the throat area. I won't know the precise cause of death until I've done the post. The old fellow was also not in a good state of health." He looked at Stride again. "You've noticed the lesions on his face?"

Stride nodded. "Some kind of skin infection?"

"Possibly. But they could indicate something more serious. It's also possible that he might have died of something other than his obvious injuries. He might have had a heart attack or a stroke. Perhaps a combination of the two. That wouldn't be unusual. He's old, he looks poorly nourished, and he's probably had more to drink than is good for him. We might discover that drinking too much was a long term problem with him."

"When can you do the post, Thomas?"

"I'll do it this afternoon. I have two minor surgeries scheduled at the Grace first thing this morning. But then I have rounds, and the usual mound of administrative bumph. After I'm done there, I'll take myself to the General and do the autopsy. You can meet me there. I imagine you'll be busy enough in the interim, chasing down our late friend here, as well as the two fugitives. Shall we say two, two-thirty?"

Stride nodded and looked at Phelan. Harry didn't like autopsies any more than he liked unpleasant crime scenes, but he shrugged a tired agreement.

Butcher was looking at the body again and shaking his head.

"Violent deaths are always disturbing, but the killing of an elderly person is especially offensive." He smiled. "But perhaps that's because I'm closing in on that category myself." He took out his silver cigarette case, opened it, and took out a cigarette. His breathing had returned more or less to normal.

Butcher stood smoking while Stride searched through the man's clothing for identification. He found a leather purse with a metal snap-closure in the left-hand trouser pocket.

"If this is his purse, our victim's name is Samuel Rossiter and he's seventy-one years old." He looked at Butcher. "Not quite as old as we thought."

"Still too bloody old to be hanging around a laneway at this time of night," Phelan said.

"There's six dollars here, all ones," Stride said. "And a few coins." The man was shabbily dressed. One of his shoes was worn through at the sole, and the heels were almost as bad, but they had been quality shoes when they were new. "There's no home address." Stride stood up and gave the purse to Noseworthy. "Does the name Rossiter mean anything to anyone?"

"It's a common enough name," Butcher said. "In fact, one of my patients is named Rossiter."

"I suppose it's too much to hope that this fellow might be a relative?"

Butcher shook his head. "There's no Samuel in the family as far as I know."

"We might end up having to do it the hard way, sir." He pinched the end off his cigarette and dropped the butt in his pocket. "Finding out who he was and where he lived."

"We might get lucky and find an address for him," Stride said. But it was a long shot. From his appearance, it was likely he lived in a rented room or a boarding house, so a telephone listing wasn't likely. It was even possible that Rossiter had no fixed address in St. John's. He might have been indigent, the six dollars in his purse notwithstanding, sleeping any place he could find cover.

Stride continued his search through the man's clothing. He took out his own handkerchief and removed a metal flask from the man's inside jacket pocket. He stood up and held the flask under the beam of Noseworthy's flashlight.

"Is that silver?" Butcher asked.

"It looks like it might be. Silver or pewter, one of the two. And it looks to be very good quality, even if it has seen better days." He held the flask up and shook it. "It's about half full." He turned the flask under the beam of light. "This is interesting. It's monogrammed, but the initials are *LWH*."

"Stolen, probably," Phelan said. "Or he picked it up second-hand."

"Or his name isn't really Samuel Rossiter," Noseworthy said. "He might be Lawrence William Harvey."

Stride looked at Noseworthy. "Who is Lawrence William Harvey?"

Noseworthy grinned. "It's a joke, sir. I just made it up."

"There's a special room in hell for people who make jokes at two in the morning," Phelan said.

"There's an infinity of rooms in hell, Harry. We'll both find that out when our time comes."

Noseworthy took the flask, slid it into an evidence envelope, and gave Stride back his handkerchief.

There was the sound now of people approaching from Duckworth Street.

"That will probably be the crew to take the body to the General," Butcher said.

Two large men appeared, toting a stretcher, picking their way down the steps in the near-dark. A red blanket fell off the stretcher onto the ground while they were dropping the wheeled legs into place and one of the stretcher bearers muttered a curse as he bent to pick it up. He spread out the blanket, ready to enfold the body. The others stood back and watched as the attendants moved the body away from the wall, picked him up, and placed him on the stretcher. The process didn't appear to take much effort. The old man, frail enough in life, seemed shrunken and diminished in death. He couldn't have weighed very much at all.

t h R e e

They spent more than an hour searching the laneway, collecting material. There was a lot of it, and it would take Noseworthy some time to determine if any of it was evidence. But they had found a bottle containing a small quantity of home-brewed liquor. After Noseworthy had done the fingerprints, they would know if the bottle was the one that Rossiter was drinking from. When they were done for the night, the upper and lower entrances to the laneway were roped off and a uniformed constable was stationed at each end. There would be a second, more thorough search of the area as soon as it was light.

Stride and Phelan went to the lockup under the Court House to question the young man Corrigan had arrested. They could have waited until later that morning, but they wanted to have at him right away. As Harry liked to put it, "the fresher the kill, the better the meal."

And David Lawlor, when he was led in to the interview room, definitely looked something like fresh kill. Stride faced the young man from across the interview table. The booking sheet said he was seventeen, although he looked younger than that. Phelan sat to one side, just on the margin of Lawlor's field of vision. That would keep Lawlor off balance. They didn't allow a prisoner to be comfortable during an interview. Not that it seemed very likely that balance or comfort would be an issue here. Lawlor looked terrified. Stride intended to keep him that way.

He went through the routine questions about age, address – Lawlor lived with his parents and two brothers on Merrymeeting Road – and occupation – he had finished high school in June and he was working part-time at his uncle's butcher shop while he looked for a permanent job.

"What do you think you'd like to do?" Stride asked. The question seemed to knock Lawlor a little further off balance, surprising him. "As a job," he added. "Anything in mind, yet?"

"The army, maybe. I was thinking I might join the army."

"That might be a good choice. There isn't a war on just now, and you might learn a skill. You might even learn some discipline." He waited for a response, but Lawlor only continued to look frightened and confused. "Are they recruiting just now?"

"What?"

"The army. Are they actively recruiting people?"

"I don't know. I haven't really looked into it."

"You'll probably find that the flow is in the opposite direction. A lot of men are taking off the uniform, moving back into civilian life." Stride continued to stare at Lawlor, cold-faced, not smiling. "And the army might not be impressed with this evening's escapade."

Lawlor shifted position in his chair. "I suppose so."

"You suppose so?" No response. "Tell us about the tire. Whose idea was that?"

Lawlor looked towards Phelan but found no relief there. Harry only stared at him, without expression.

"We just found it. It was lying on the street. I guess someone put it out for the ashman."

"Yes? Where was that?"

"Bond Street."

"Bond Street?"

"Yeah, on Bond Street. A little ways from Cathedral."

"And you thought it would be fun to roll it down the hill."

"I guess so."

"You guess so. You decided that by yourself? You were the one who decided?"

"No." Lawlor shifted position again. "It wasn't me."

"Who was it, then? Who made the decision?"

Lawlor started to speak, but then stopped. He sat back and stared at the table.

Stride waited. A minute crawled by.

"You had two companions tonight. What are their names?"

"I can't tell you their names. That would be squealing. I can't do that."

"I'm sure that's an admirable gesture, Mr. Lawlor." Stride leaned across the table, bringing his face closer to Lawlor's. "But your loyalty is misplaced."

Lawlor sat suddenly upright and looked around him, as if he expected to find his loyalty lying somewhere on the floor beside his chair. Then, he slumped again.

"It wouldn't be right," he said.

"So, you're willing to take responsibility for the damages?"

"I guess so."

"That's very generous of you. The car was badly damaged. It will probably cost a lot of money to fix. Do you have any idea how much car repairs cost?"

Lawlor shook his head.

"Mr. Lawlor, you are seventeen years old. You're a minor. You have a part-time summer job with your uncle that probably doesn't pay very much. If you don't have the money to pay for the damages to the car, your parents will have to pay. How do you think your father will like that?"

"My father?" Lawlor cast a nervous glance over his shoulder. Now he really was frightened.

"Yes, your father. The man who's married to your mother, Mr. Lawlor. If you cannot pay for the damages, he will have to. I imagine he might be just a little annoyed with you. Especially since you've apparently decided that he'll have to pay the full shot by himself. What do you think about that?"

Lawlor didn't answer. He was starting to sweat now, his forehead glistening under the overhead light. Stride repeated the question, with emphasis.

Lawlor nodded and a drop of sweat fell onto the table in front of him. He stared at it as though it were an omen, a small damp summation of his evening's disaster.

"We will be speaking with your father, Mr. Lawlor. Within the hour, I expect. It won't surprise me if he's here already, waiting for a chance to speak to you. That will probably be an interesting confrontation." He paused again allowing the young man to think about all that had happened, at least the part he knew about, and to speculate on what might happen after his father received the news. Lawlor was very quiet. He seemed to have fallen into a reverie. Stride pulled him back. "Unfortunately, Mr. Lawlor, there's a lot more to come. The damage to the car, and that's serious enough, is less than the half of it. Much less than half."

Lawlor looked up at Stride, then at Phelan, and then back at Stride again. He was truly perplexed now; his mind reeled as he tried to understand what this large policeman might be talking about. He knew about the tire and the damage to the car. Standing with his two friends on Duckworth Street looking at the damage, his stomach did a twist and then a turn; excitement and fear mixed with bitter regret.

When they started rolling the tire down the hill, David Lawlor watched it with something like amazement. The tire was moving fast, and it gathered speed even as he watched. It was at that moment that he felt the first hard bite of fear in his stomach. Then, he saw, for the first time, the car parked on Duckworth, and his fear grew with a speed about equal to that of the rolling tire. Drawing on his well of newfound fear, his mind embraced the possibility that there might be a car, maybe more than one car, moving along Duckworth. Dark and frightening possibilities leapt in his mind: cars colliding, people injured, maybe killed. But those images were wiped away by the sound of the tire thudding into the parked vehicle. The worst had not happened after all. And then, they ran down the hill, and for an instant he was almost joyful with the relief. But the broken glass on the street, crunching under his sneakers, made him think of his father's car. It was a treasured 1935 Buick that the old man had saved for years to buy, that he lovingly washed and polished every Saturday afternoon in the back yard when the weather was good, spring, summer and fall.

While he was busy thinking about that, the cop suddenly grabbed him from behind, coming out of nowhere to wrap a thick forearm around his neck, lifting him off the ground, cutting off his air supply, almost strangling him.

The evening had started off as fun, just fun. Phil had bought a bottle of bootleg from a guy on the South Side. After that, they came back across the river and walked up to Thompson's Field in the west end, where they sat in the shadow of a large rock, drinking, getting slightly drunk, smoking cigarettes, telling stories and lies, laughing a lot, even saying they wished they could somehow get laid, although only Phil had ever managed to actually do that, and only once.

They finished the booze and smashed the empty bottle against the rock, then walked back downtown and just wandered around, all three of them still a bit drunk. Later, when the alcohol was wearing off and the evening's joy was sliding into a kind of tired, sullen restlessness, they had started behaving badly. Nothing big; just small things, knocking over ashcans, throwing rocks at street signs, chasing cats, pissing on doorsteps, and pulling flowers from their beds. And then Phil found the tire in front of a house on Bond Street with a green front door. They all agreed it would be fun to set it rolling down Cathedral, a street so steep it seemed almost vertical.

Now, his evening, like the tire, had rolled all the way downhill, and the impact at the bottom was much worse, much more damaged than the buckled car door and fragmented window glass. His father was going to know about it, might even now be outside, waiting for him, impatient, angry, pulling on a cigarette in his agitation.

And now, if he could believe this large cop with the dark hair and darker expression, something else had happened, something even worse than the tire hitting the car. He couldn't imagine what that might be about. No one had yet told David Lawlor about the body of the old man found in Scanlon's Lane.

Then, Stride did tell him. He took his time telling Lawlor all about it. He included every detail: the lifeless eyes, the bloody mouth, the various injuries, the cuts on his head. Even the denture lying on the step next to the dead left hand. He left nothing out. He even embellished it with speculation on the possible internal injuries, the old man's poor state of health, his obvious poverty, his mean and unhappy life, now ended brutally.

Stride could see that Lawlor was taking all of it in. So he sat back and waited. He could also see that Lawlor was playing a game with himself, the game that people usually played when they were faced with a situation that was just too awful to deal with, that didn't fit into any slot in their experience or in their system of beliefs. Let's pretend, he could almost hear Lawlor thinking, let's pretend that this cop is making it all up and if I hold myself together long enough, if I play his game, he'll suddenly smile and say that he wasn't serious, that it didn't happen, that nothing happened, and that I can go home now.

Stride continued to stare at him, unblinking. Waiting.

It took another minute.

Then, David Lawlor put his head in his hands and started to cry, and once he had started, the tears flowed and his body shook with great engulfing sobs, howls of deepest misery.

The interview was all but over. In a minute, five at most, Stride and Phelan would have the names of Lawlor's two friends, their home addresses, telephone numbers, the names of their parents, and their fathers' occupations. If they wanted it, they could also have their birthdates and the names of any girlfriends they might have had. The spigot was about to turn full open.

It was after four when Stride finally got back to his flat on Circular Road. The first thing he did was to put the kettle on to make a pot of tea. While it was coming to a slow boil, he took a shower. He had the shower installed earlier that summer, in late June. Stride didn't like baths, never had. Showers were faster, and he didn't end up sitting in a puddle of tepid, soap-scummed water. He could never comprehend the great enjoyment that some people claimed they got from baths. He had always thought there was something perverse about baths, a residual longing for the comfort of the womb, maybe. He ran the water as hot as he could stand it, steaming the tiredness out of mind and body both. Then, to finish, he turned off the hot water and stood for as long as he could bear it in the ice-cold stream, sucking in air in short, quick breaths.

He towelled his hair dry as he poured the boiling water into the teapot. He drank his tea and smoked a cigarette sitting in the kitchen in his bathrobe, newly awake for the second time that morning. He had thought of trying for an hour's sleep before heading out again, but he knew it would be futile. He slept badly, even under favourable circumstances. And now that his blood was up, a phrase he inherited from his mother, he only wanted to get on with it. It was going on for five, and there was a broad hint of dawn on the horizon. From his window on the third floor of his house, he could almost make out the profile of the cliffs that bracketed the Narrows, the harbour's entrance.

He ran the particulars of the case through his mind. As Tom Butcher put it, the violent death of an old man was distasteful. Even if the actual cause of death proved to be a stroke or a heart attack, his injuries, the tumble down the steps, had almost certainly brought it on. An old man was dead, and three young men, boys really, were about to have their own lives truncated, their futures compromised.

About Rossiter himself, they still knew almost nothing. Stride thought about the six well-worn dollar bills, possibly all the money the man had in the world, if his tattered clothing was any guide.

The monogrammed flask was a puzzle, though. When they'd convened briefly at Fort Townshend, Noseworthy informed them that it was indeed silver. The flask was an interesting anomaly for an apparently impoverished man. Even more surprising was the fact that it contained not bootleg liquor, but good Scotch whisky, and a single malt at that. Harry was probably right, the man had likely stolen the flask, and the single malt just happened to be in it at the time. He made a note in his book – it was too early in the day for mental notes to be of any use – to check with Bernard Crotty in records to see if anyone had reported a theft.

Stride finished the last of his tea and thought about another cigarette, but decided against it. He pulled the curtain back from the kitchen window again and watched the sky brighten further off to the east, the gathering of the new day. He willed his mind to go blank and concentrated on a patch of cloud that looked something like Ireland. He continued to watch as it dissolved into nothingness. Then, he let the curtain drop back into place and thought about breakfast.

He pulled open the fridge door. A note, written in a small, neat hand on an index card, was propped against a bottle of orange marmalade. Her marmalade, her note. That was in character. He took out the bottle of marmalade and placed it on the table. He read the note, smiling, enjoying the small thrill that flowed through him, an echo of last night's pleasures. The note said that she might not be able to see him tonight, but she would try. She would ring him later on. He folded the card and put it in the pocket of his bathrobe. Then, he went back to the fridge and foraged for the rest of his breakfast.

four

Alex Greene wasn't thinking about breakfast. That would take a while yet.
The morning light, concentrated in a bright ribbon lying across his face, had
wakened him from a not very deep sleep. He had neglected to pull the blind
down last night before he tumbled into bed. He covered his eyes with his
hand and peeked between his fingers at the window. Then, he plucked
his watch off the bedside table and saw that it was just going on for six-thirty.
He thought about pulling down the blind and trying for another hour or two
of sleep, but he thought it was probably too late for that. He was awake
now, and would have to make the best of it. He lay still for a while longer, not
thinking about anything in particular, looking up at the ceiling of his
bedroom. He didn't feel quite as bad as he thought he might, considering how
much he must have drunk last night. Somewhere outside he heard the sound
of cartwheels on gravel, and the clinking of milk bottles, background noises of
a routine morning. He closed his eyes for a moment.

When he looked at his watch again it was just past eight-thirty. He had
slept for two more hours, and felt much better than he had. He reconsidered
his faltering belief in miracles.

From downstairs he could hear more sounds of morning; water running
through the pipes and into the kitchen sink, the low murmur of the radio on
the end of the counter nearest the icebox. That would be Bride Pollard, his
Aunt Bridget's maid and companion. He doubted if Bridget would be up and

about. Not quite yet. Although she had always been an early morning person, over the past year her tempo had changed, she had slowed. There was something going on, Alex thought, but Bride had not said what the problem was, or even if there was one. Bridget had not said anything either. Alex suspected a minor heart attack or a small stroke. Both ran in the family, these small late-life assaults, softening up the target for the main event, somewhere not too far down the road. It was the way Aunt Helena had gone, and Bridget was eighty-two now, three years older than Helena had been when she had died.

Next came the sound of the heavy, copper kettle rumbling to a boil. Alex was suddenly hungry. It occurred to him that he might have forgotten to eat dinner last night. He closed his eyes again, trying to knit together the frayed threads of the evening. It wasn't an easy task. He had drunk a lot – yet again, and much too much – and that had started very early in the evening. At least that much he was certain about. But thinking about it made his head hurt and his eyes water. He gave it up for a bad job and threw back the covers, but took his time sitting up. He sat on the edge of the bed for a little while until the dizziness went away. And now he wanted a drink. He was hungry still, but he also wanted a drink, something to settle him down, to chase the shivers into full retreat. He decided against it, partly because Bride would know, but mostly because he really wanted to be able to resist, to grasp that last straw, to hold on.

He went to the mirror and took a long look at his reflection inside the walnut frame. His face looked even longer and thinner than usual. He wondered if he had lost more weight, but decided to lay the blame on last night. A wash and a shave were definitely in order, though, that was clear. It wasn't that Bride Pollard hadn't ever seen him on the morning after one of his 'evenings,' as she tactfully called them, fortified by a dram of therapeutic whisky and walking too carefully. He just didn't want her to see him that way this morning.

When Alex stepped into the kitchen, the air was softly fragranced with the smell of yeast and flour. Bride was filling the last of four bread pans with freshly made loaves, ready for the oven, their crests shining with melted butter. Two of the loaves were white, two of them brown. It was her standard batch. For Alex's money, Bride Pollard made the finest bread in all the civilised world.

The floor at the doorway creaked under his step and she half-turned to look at him.

"I thought perhaps I heard you come in last night, but I wasn't sure. It was late and I was only half awake." She turned down the volume on the radio.

"It was late. I'm sorry if I woke you."

"You didn't wake me, Alex. Even on a good night, I'm awake a half-dozen times, and it's been that way most of my life. But it doesn't seem to have done me much harm, now does it?"

"Not so much that it shows, Bride."

Bride Pollard was a big woman, tall, large-boned, and lean, as she always had been. At least she'd looked that way for all of the time Alex had known her, and that encompassed most of his life. Now, in her early seventies, she had put on a little weight, although not much. A little fuller around the hips, probably, but a bit smaller in the chest. The effect made her look somehow younger and more vigorous than ever. And vigour was something she had always had in quantity. She was wiping her hands on a cup-towel.

"Will you be wanting some breakfast today, Alex?" She raised an eyebrow.

Breakfast for Alex Greene was a sometime thing. More often than not, he was unable to face food early in the morning. Bride knew that better than anyone.

"As a matter of fact, yes, I do. I'm starving." He sat at the table and crossed his legs. He patted his pockets, looking for a cigarette. He didn't find one. "I don't think I remembered to eat supper last night."

"Not for the first time, I'm sure. Tell me what you would like and I'll get to it as soon as the bread's in the oven." She pulled open the oven door and a wave of heat flowed across the kitchen. "We have just about everything. Including some very nice bacon that Norman brought yesterday."

"Norman." Alex repeated the name.

"Yes. He came by yesterday afternoon with the meat and the eggs. And a nice hen that will find itself in the stew pot later today."

"I thought Norman came on Wednesdays."

"He does, usually, but he's early this week." She slid the last of the four bread pans into the oven and closed the door. The kitchen was noticeably warmer now, pleasant and homey, and it helped to keep Alex's shivers at bay. "He said he had to go down the shore for a few days. A cousin of his passed away. I think it was quite unexpected, he was only a young man, not even fifty yet. But you never know, do you?"

No, you don't, Alex thought, but he didn't say anything.

"He also brought us a nice leg of mutton. He says it's hardly mutton at all, really, almost a lamb. And I will say it does look very nice. I'm going to roast it for dinner tonight. The stew I'll keep for another time. You're more than welcome to join us, Alex. I know Herself would like that. It's been a little while since you had dinner with us here."

"That sheep didn't have a name, did it?"

She smiled at his question. It was a joke between them. When he was a small boy, he had once refused to partake of the Christmas turkey because they had fattened it in a pen out back, and he had named it, "Jeremiah." He would talk to it while it strutted around its pen shaking its wattles and pecking at the handfuls of grain he sprinkled on the straw-covered snow.

"You know I can't eat it if it's been personalised."

"It had no Christian name at all, Alex, so far as I know. It was a total heathen all of its life, and never knew the difference. So you can eat it in good faith."

"Well, that's alright, then. I think I will come."

"Good. Herself will be pleased." Bride straightened up and went to the icebox and levered the door open. "Will it be bacon and eggs, then?" She looked at him, still bent-over in front of the icebox. "And I've got some nice fat mushrooms."

"Norman brought those too? Did he pick them in the wild?"

Bride laughed. "I know what you're thinking. You wrote a story once about a family that almost died from eating wild mushrooms."

"One of them did die. The youngest child, one of the daughters. She was only six."

"So she did, poor thing, and not a nice way to go." Bride took out a flat of brown eggs, a bowl of mushrooms, and a package of bacon. She pushed the door shut with her knee. "But you've nothing to worry about. Norman grows his own mushrooms. He's quite the expert at it, so he tells me." She took a heavy iron pan from a hook on the wall and set about the preparation of breakfast. While she arranged the strips of bacon in the pan, she nodded in the direction of the breadbox. "You can make yourself useful and slice the bread, if you want toast. Cut four slices and I'll have two for myself, and join you at table."

He got up, made his way to the counter, and took a loaf of brown bread from the box. Bride slid a long knife across the counter towards him.

A plummy male voice flowed from the small radio by the icebox. It was the morning newscast. Alex reached over and turned up the volume. The first item was about the referendum campaigns, the ongoing debates between the various factions, for and against Confederation with Canada.

"Same bloody old stuff, every day," Bride said. And she really did look annoyed. "Politicians, they gives me the hives. In the end it's themselves they're really concerned about, not the country."

"Except maybe one or two," Alex said. "They're not all rogues."

"I suppose not," Bride said. "Alright, I will grant you that. There's some of them that's alright." She teased the bacon strips with a long fork, moving them about the pan. "Were you downtown last night?"

"Yes, I was. Why?"

"There was a man killed," she said. "In Scanlon's Lane. They found him last night, or early this morning. An old man, they said. They didn't give out a name, though. I suppose they have to notify the next of kin first."

"Yes, they do," Alex said. He cut another slice of bread, looking at the radio, listening. "It was in Scanlon's Lane?"

"Yes it was. Were you down there last night?"

Alex concentrated on slicing the bread evenly, drawing the knife slowly and carefully through the loaf.

"I probably was, or somewhere near there. At some point."

"It's all a bit fuzzy, I expect." She was smiling at him; her good humour a contrast to the news itself. "One of those nights?"

"Yes, it was one of those nights."

"Someday you'll have to slow down, Alex."

"Yes, I expect I will, Bride." He took a plate from the cupboard and placed four thick slices of bread on it and slid it along the counter, so she could put them in the toaster.

"You could write a story about it. About the old man. It's just the sort of thing the *Sunday Herald* likes to run. Destruction, death, and damnation to greet us every Sunday morning."

"Yes," he said. "It's our stock in trade. We have a saying for that in the business, Bride. Blood sells."

"Well, there you are, then, made to order. You can write the story. And they did say that he was badly beaten, so there's probably blood enough for everyone. That much they did say. But first, you'll eat your breakfast like the good boy you really want to be. And after that, you can take yourself off to Fort Townshend and see what's what."

"Yes, I suppose I will do that. And you're right about breakfast. Although I'm not so confident as you are about the 'good boy' part."

"Well, we'll just pretend that you're a good boy. Herself and me has had lots of practice." She placed the bacon on a plate and slid the bread into the toaster. "Two eggs?" Alex nodded, so she cracked the shells against the edge of the pan and dropped them into the hot bacon fat.

"Did they say who was in charge of the case?"

"Yes, they said his name is Stride. Inspector Stride." She looked at him. "You know him, don't you? I believe you told me that once."

Alex nodded again. He patted his pockets, looking again for a cigarette. Then he saw Bride's package on the table, propped up between the salt and pepper shakers. He took one out and lit it, coughing as he inhaled.

"Yes," he said. "I do know him. I've known him for a while."

"I thought so," Bride said.

Alex sat down at the table and crossed his legs again. He pulled on his cigarette, staring at the floor, trying to slow his mind down to a walk, waiting for Bride Pollard to serve him his breakfast. Then he looked up. The voice on the radio was speaking now about the old man who had been killed.

f I v e

By eleven-thirty that morning, Eric Stride and Harry Phelan were trudging down Holdsworth Street towards yet another tavern in their quest for information about Samuel Rossiter. Before starting out, they had contacted their standard sources. They had found a number of Rossiters, but none of them knew an old man named Samuel. So, as Harry had suggested, they were doing it the hard way: the creative application of sweat and shoe leather, working their way through the various taverns within walking distance of Scanlon's Lane, following the logic that if Rossiter had been drinking about the time he was killed, his last evening might have started in one of the pubs in the area.

There were a lot of taverns in St. John's. There always had been. It was a seaport, after all, and a major locus for convoy operations in the last war. The Admiralty on Holdsworth was their sixth stop. It was already another hot day – August could be like that, even in this far corner of the North Atlantic – and by now they were both feeling tired and out of sorts. Frustration sitting on top of weariness.

At the Admiralty, at least, Stride had the advantage of knowing the owner. Years earlier, during Prohibition, Stride and Hector Gullage had been friends and business partners, running contraband from St. Pierre to the eastern seaboard of the United States. After the operation closed down with the end of Prohibition, they had more or less gone their separate ways: Gullage into the legal side of the alcohol trade, and Stride into the Constabulary. They had stayed close for a while, but after they settled into a pattern of different daily routines, they had gradually seen less of each other. They were still friends, though, Gullage and Stride. That hadn't changed.

Stride tried to recall when he had last spoken to Hector Gullage. It might have been as much as a year ago, on a similarly hot summer day. He delivered himself a mild remonstration and a vague pledge to stay in closer touch in future.

Phelan knocked at the door of the tavern. The Admiralty wasn't a private club, but it did have restricted access. If someone didn't meet Hector Gullage's standards – they were not exacting – they weren't granted entry. Anyone who misbehaved was also summarily ejected. Gullage's establishment, Gullage's rules. It had taken the clientele only a little while to understand that. So, the Admiralty had become one of the quieter pubs in the city. It was a favourite of off-duty policemen because it was unlikely they would have to deal with any unpleasantness while enjoying a beer there.

A small panel in the door slid open and then shut again. A moment later the door opened.

"It's Inspector Stride and Sergeant Phelan, is it?"

"Yes, it is, Johnny," Stride said.

Johnny Blake sat on a stool just inside the door. He had worked for Hector Gullage for as long as Stride could remember. Blake was an old man, not very big, and made smaller by the fact that he was missing his right foot. A wooden peg substituted, the rubber-cushioned tip extending just beyond the pant-leg. A cane leaned against the wall behind him.

"If you're looking for Mr. Gullage, Inspector, I think you'll find him in the storeroom behind the bar."

"Thanks, Johnny. You're keeping well?"

"Very well, indeed, sir, all things considered. And it's grand weather, isn't it?"

In the storeroom, Hector Gullage held up a finger to indicate that he would be with them in a moment. Gullage and his staff were busy preparing for the day's business. Gullage was placing empties from the night before into a box, the bottles rattling against the wooden partitions. When he was done, he hoisted the box on top of two others, wiped his hands on the legs of his trousers, and came over to where Stride and Phelan were standing.

"I don't suppose I can interest either of you gents in a beer this early in the day?" He smiled when they declined. "I guessed it wasn't a social call. We can talk here or go to the office. Your choice."

"The office," Stride said.

Gullage led the way around the far side of the bar and pushed open the door of his office. It was a modest room, not large, with pictures of prizefighters and oarsmen decorating the walls. In his day, Hector Gullage had been a boxer, a talented middleweight with a right cross that was much admired in local boxing circles, as it was still in his current occupation. He rowed in the Regatta on Quidi Vidi Lake every August, and he stayed in shape by training in his own racing scull on a pond a few miles north of St. John's where he had a cabin.

Hector Gullage didn't look a lot older now than he had in the early thirties, when he and Stride were running liquor into the States. He had a bit less hair now, but his weight was unchanged, and his face was remarkably unlined. Gullage said that was because he didn't smoke, except for five cigars each year; at Christmas, New Year's, Easter, his birthday, and one after the final race of the Regatta. He enjoyed his drink, though, which was Demerara rum, the same as Stride's. He took a bottle from the bottom drawer of his desk and waggled it.

"A small glass, in memory of old times? I know it's early, but we can pretend it's an occasion."

Stride looked at Phelan and nodded. A shot of rum might improve both their moods, sagging now from too little sleep and the frustration of finding nothing after more than two hours of inquiries. Gullage took three glasses from a shelf and poured an ounce of rum into each.

"It's over-proof, fifty-seven percent," Gullage said. He gave each of them a glass, then held out the bottle for Stride to read the label. "I've got four bottles left, Eric. Just four bottles out of – how many? – hat we shipped out of British Guiana to St. Pierre, and from there to the States."

"I'm almost embarrassed to think about it," Stride said. He sipped the dark rum and closed his eyes, enjoying both the taste and the feeling. As Gullage had suggested, it brought back memories, most of them good, one or two not so good. He was thinking now about the night his boat was raided and about Gullage with a slug in his leg, pulling himself across the deck to the wheel-house, trailing a smear of blood behind him. Stride, knocked down by a bullet in his shoulder, was able to slide a pistol across the deck to Gullage, a Webley .44. It had probably saved both their lives. Well, no probably about it.

"It was quite the night, wasn't it?" Stride looked up when Gullage spoke. Phelan was looking back and forth between them, guessing at what they might be talking about. Stride had only recently told Harry some of the basics of his pre-Constabulary history. He was doling it out in bits and pieces, in casual conversation. "You had that faraway look, Eric. I do it myself sometimes. Then Mildred gives me a clip across the ear and brings me back to the here-and-now. But I like to hold on to the memories. In the end, memories is what we have, isn't it?" Gullage tossed his drink back, pushed the cork into the bottle and returned it to the drawer. "So, what can I do you for today, gentlemen?"

"A man was killed last night," Stride said. "An old man that Jack Corrigan came across in Scanlon's Lane."

"So I've heard. Herb Motty rang me ten, fifteen minutes ago. Word travels fast in the trade when a stiff's involved. He didn't tell me very much, though, and I kept it to myself. He thought I should hear it directly from the man with the badge."

"The dead man's name is Samuel Rossiter. At least according to the identification he was carrying. Harry has a photograph for you to look at."

Noseworthy had taken additional pictures at the General Hospital after the body had been taken there. He had produced a half-dozen copies of the least offensive photograph. Gullage took his time looking at it, rubbing his chin thoughtfully. Then he handed it back to Phelan.

"His name's Sam Rossiter, alright, and I do know him," Gullage said. "Not very well, but he is something of a regular. He's been coming in, now and again, for the past year."

"Just for the past year? Not before that?"

"No. It was just about a year ago he first came in, give or take a month."

"Was he in here last night?"

Gullage nodded. "He came in late in the evening. I don't recall exactly what time, but I know the crowd was starting to thin out when I first saw him. Sam was always quiet, kept to himself for the most part. So he might have been here longer than I thought. If it's important, I can ask the boys if they have a better fix on the time. Johnny Blake might be able to tell you. He was on the door last night, like he is most nights."

"We're more interested in when Rossiter left, Gully. And who he might have been here with."

"Well, to answer the first part, he stayed until we closed. That would be eleven."

"And the second part?"

"Like I said, he mostly kept to himself. But I know he was talking to Walter Keough for part of the time he was here. You know Walter?"

"I know who he is," Phelan said. "If it's the same Walter Keough who used to work at Mugford's lumberyard."

"That's Walter."

"They were friends, Rossiter and Keough?"

"They might have been, I don't really know. I'd see them having a beer together from time to time. They were of an age, and they were both of them alone in the world as far as I could tell." Gullage sat forward in his chair. "But if they were friends, I'd have to say they were something of an odd couple."

"Yes?" Stride had his notebook open. He wrote down Gullage's comment.

Gullage looked at Phelan. "If you know Walter Keough, Harry, then you probably know he's had a hard life. No education to speak of, and I'm not sure he can read or write. He worked manual labour all of his life, long hours and little pay, usually. He told me once — well, more than once, because people will talk to the man behind the bar — that he started working when he was twelve, and fifty years later he was still working and he still didn't have a decent pot to piss in. He was married once, but his wife and three children perished in a house fire here in St. John's one winter night when Walter was working down north. And to make it even worse, if that's possible, it happened on Boxing Day. It was the Christmas candles on the tree set it off. Walter's been mostly alone since then, and that goes back maybe forty years. Some say he went a bit strange after the fire, and that's probably true. And if that doesn't define a hard life, I'll have to do some serious study and see if I can find out what does."

"It will do until something really awful comes along," Stride said. "But why does that make Keough and Rossiter an odd couple especially?"

"Well, the only thing Rossiter and Keough seemed to have in common was the fact they were both poor and alone and they both liked to drink. Whenever they had enough coin between them to fill a glass, that is. At least, as far as I could tell, that was it. But I think Rossiter came from a different background. Like I say, I didn't know him well, and he didn't say very much on the odd occasion when we did have a chat. And sometimes, to be honest, he made no sense at all. But there was the odd time he did say enough to give me the idea that he might have been an educated man. He seemed well spoken, if you know what I mean."

"Interesting," Stride said. "Do you know anything about him? Where he was from?"

Gullage shook his head. "He never told me where he was from, but if guesses can trade for silver, I'd say he was a local, a St. John's boy originally. But don't take that to church with you any given Sunday, I don't know it for a fact. I think I can tell you where he lives, though. Or lived. Do you know the Burridges on Gower Street? Jimmy Burridge and his mother, Ethel?"

"Jimmy Burridge? A little fat man with about three chins too many?" Phelan said.

"That describes Jimmy well enough."

"Yes, we know the place." Phelan looked at Stride. "We were there last Christmas, sir, maybe a week before Christmas? One of their boarders got into a fracas on New Gower Street and we arrested him for disturbing the peace."

"And for punching out one of our men," Stride said. "I remember the occasion. His name was Howell."

"Caleb Howell," Phelan said. "He collected a fine and a month at the lakeside." The accepted shorthand for His Majesty's Penitentiary on the south side of Quidi Vidi Lake.

"When Rossiter first came in here, he told me he was boarding at the Burridges, Eric. Maybe he was still living there."

"We'll find out. Would you happen to know where Keough lives, Gully?"

"You're thinking Walter might have had something to do with Sam's death?"

Stride shook his head. "We don't know that he did. Or that he didn't, for that matter. But if Keough was with Rossiter late last night, he might know something about what happened."

"Assuming he was sober enough at the time to have anything to remember."

"There is that."

"Yes. But to answer your question, I'm not sure where Keough drops his socks. I've been told he moves around some."

"He didn't live at the Burridges?"

"I don't think he could afford even that, Eric. And Jimmy's place is a peg or two below the Taj Mahal."

"He's not in the Poor House, is he?" The Poor House on Sudbury Street in the west end was the abode of last resort for the impoverished in St. John's, a stark and forbidding structure, inside and out. Stride thought it looked like a way station on the highroad to hell.

"Not as far as I know, he isn't. But he did spend some time there years ago. He was in very bad shape at the time, he told me. He'd broken a leg working on the docks, and while he was laid up he had no place else to go. Same leg he broke in a mine accident down north, one time, so it took a long time to heal. He said he'd never go back there, and I can't say as I blame him for that."

"We think Rossiter was probably drunk on homebrew last night. There was a bottle nearby that still had some of the stuff in it. We don't have a reading on the prints yet, but if it turns out that the bottle was Rossiter's, it might help if we knew where he got the stuff."

Gullage smiled. "Well, he didn't get it from your obedient servant, Eric. I only deal with the legal stuff these days. Not that I don't get offers from time to time. You'd be surprised how much stuff, including quality product, moves through this town on a moonless night. And also where a fair bit of it comes to rest."

Stride shook his head. "No, I wouldn't, Gully. Not for a minute."

"No, I don't suppose you would. Well, you know the midnight merchants as well as I do, Eric, probably better."

Stride smiled and made another note in his book and thought for a moment. He stood up then, and took his hat from the coat rack.

"Thanks for all that, Gully. We'll have a chat with the Burridges. If you happen to see Walter Keough anytime soon, you'll let us know?"

"I will do that." Gullage opened the office door. "About Keough. I just had a thought. Ask Johnny Blake on the way out. Johnny has known Keough for a long time, and he just might be able to tell you where he's living now."

Gullage walked them to the tavern door. Johnny Blake pushed the door open for them, but let it fall shut again when Gullage told him that Stride wanted to ask him a couple of questions. Blake sat on his stool and waited.

"Walter Keough? Yes, I've known Walter for a good while."

"Do you happen to know where he's living now?"

"As a matter of fact, I do, sir. Walter was telling me just last week that he's bunking at Danny Mugford's property on Blackmarsh Road."

"The lumberyard? Isn't Mugford shutting it down, and moving his business to a new place on Torbay Road?"

"Yes, sir, he is. But there's still quite a lot of stuff there on Blackmarsh, Walter told me. Mr. Mugford lets him stay there and Walter kind of keeps on eye on the place for him." Blake smiled. "When he's sober, that is. There's a shed at the back of the property. That's where Walter hangs his hat just now. At least, that's where he was last week, and I haven't heard he's moved."

"I guess that makes sense, if he worked for Mugford once. It sounds a bit grim though, Johnny."

"Well it's no great hell, I suppose, but Walter's had to make do with worse over the years."

"I suppose that's true enough," Stride said. "Thank you for that, Johnny."

"Walter's not in any trouble is he? About last night?"

"No, he's not in any trouble. We just need to ask him a few questions."

Blake pushed the door open again. Stride and Phelan walked up Holdsworth Street towards Stride's MG. Halfway there, Stride stopped for a moment and looked back at Gullage's tavern. Then he turned again and caught up with Phelan.

It was still sunny and hot outside.

S I X

The Burridge house was one in a row of four on Gower Street; a two-story building painted bright red with green window frames. Another house in the row had the same colour scheme, and the other two were green with red window frames. It was a quiet neighbourhood, decent enough, yearning towards what passed locally for middle-class. The rows of houses, two and three stories tall, were punctuated by the occasional laneway.

Phelan looked at the four houses in turn. "It's a bit early in the year, sir, but it looks something like a giant Christmas card. Do you think?"

"Yes, it does," Stride said. "There must have been a sale on red and green paint."

"Or a couple of pots fell off the back of somebody's truck."

"That's the other possibility."

They stood on the sidewalk for a minute longer, looking up and down the street. Stride had parked the MG a few doors away. The street was quiet, only a few pedestrians walking about. Two small children furiously pedalled their tricycles up and down the sidewalk on the opposite side. Three doors down, on the same side, two housewives sat on the front steps of a house, smoking cigarettes and talking, glancing occasionally in their direction. The women noticed Stride's car when he had parked. He imagined they already had guessed his and Phelan's profession. Policemen tended to stand out, a blessing and a curse in about equal measure. Harry's wife, Kitty, said it was the hats, the double-soled shoes, and the imperious manner.

Stride gave the two women a final look, walked up the two steps to the Burridge house, and pushed the black button on the door frame. He could hear the faint sound of the bell from deep inside the house. The window in the front door was covered with a thin white curtain but he could see through it to the interior. A tall, angular woman with heavy facial features and tangled grey-white hair appeared in a doorway at the end of the hall. She stared at the front door for a moment, then leaned around the door frame and spoke to someone.

A moment later, a short, fat man appeared, pushed past the woman and waddled down the hallway. If anything, Stride thought, Jimmy Burridge was even heavier now than when they last saw him eight months ago. Although Burridge and his mother were strikingly different in size and appearance, there was enough similarity between them, Stride thought, to stamp them as mother and son, or at least close relations.

Burridge pulled the curtain to one side and peered at Stride through the window. His face had an almost childlike aspect, with small dark eyes buried within mounds of fat, like raisins in a bread pudding. There was a moment of apparent indecision before Burridge's face rearranged itself into something like a smile and he pulled the door open.

"It's Inspector Stride, isn't it." He looked around Stride to stare at Phelan, the smile still in place. "And Sergeant Phelan, too."

"Yes, it is, Mr. Burridge. If it's convenient, we'd like to ask you and your mother a few questions about one of your boarders."

Stride looked past Burridge towards the old woman. Ethel Burridge had moved several paces down the hall now, her hands clasped in front of her chest. A visit from the police usually meant bad news. It was possible her obvious unease came from her already having noticed that Samuel Rossiter hadn't slept in his bed last night, assuming that Rossiter was still boarding here. She answered the unspoken question.

"Has something happened to Mr. Rossiter? He didn't come home last night. He hasn't been very well lately and I was worried about him." She looked at her son. "We both were. Jimmy and me both."

"I'm afraid we do have some bad news for you, Mrs. Burridge. We have a man at the General Hospital who was carrying identification saying that his name is Samuel Rossiter. He was an elderly man, and I'm sorry to have to tell you that he's dead. Sergeant Phelan has a photograph." Stride looked from mother to son and back again. "Perhaps Mr. Burridge could have a look at it."

Phelan took the photograph from his pocket and gave it to Jimmy Burridge. Burridge looked at face in the picture. His soft features sagged under the weight of recognition.

"It's Mr. Rossiter, Mummy. Yes, it is. No doubt about it."

The old woman turned away suddenly, towards the door at the end of the hallway, walked a halting step. Then, just as abruptly turned back and snatched the photograph from her son's hand. She looked at it for only a moment before nodding her head and giving it back to Phelan. She turned away again and went into the room at the end of the hall, closing the door behind her.

"She's upset, Inspector, that's what it is. She's upset. You see, she had a soft spot for our Mr. Rossiter. Ever since he moved in here, she's had a soft spot for him. And I have to say he was a decent sort of fella. Very quiet, never caused no problems for us. Never a problem." He looked at Stride and shook his head. "And he always paid his board on time. Never a day late, no."

"How long did he live here, Mr. Burridge?"

"How long?" Burridge stroked several of his chins in rapid succession, the flesh wobbling under his small hand. "It's been a year, a year and a bit, maybe. I do remember it was a fine, warm day when he first arrived. But I would have to look at the books to tell you the exact date, sir." He looked towards the closed door at the bottom of the hall. "The books are in there. I can get them for you if you like."

As if that were a cue, the door opened and Ethel Burridge stepped from the room.

"I'm sorry," she said. "I was afraid I was going to cry." And her eyes, reddened and damp, indicated that she had done just that.

Fair enough, Stride thought. If Rossiter had lived here for a year, he might almost be part of the family by now. Ethel Burridge looked to be only a year or two shy of Samuel Rossiter's seventy-one. They might have become friends over the time of his residence, and maybe something more. It wasn't unheard of. There was no sign of a Mr. Burridge, now or the last time he and Harry had been at the house. There was, however, a clutch of rings on Ethel Burridge's wedding finger. Stride counted four of them. They had been there for a long time, embedded now in the flesh of her finger. Burridge ushered them into the front room and gestured towards the collection of chairs.

Ethel Burridge trailed after them but declined to sit, standing between the doorway and an upright piano. The lid of the piano was open. The white keys were yellowing, some of the edges were chipped, and one of the black keys was missing. Stride found himself wondering how that might have happened. He looked away from the piano and pulled his attention back to the investigation. Burridge was speaking now, in response to a question from Harry.

"As far as I know, Mr. Rossiter was from St. John's originally. I think he lived somewhere else for a long while, though." He glanced at his mother. "He didn't tell us a lot about himself, did he, Mummy? He wasn't what you would call a talkative fella."

Ethel Burridge picked up the thread. "He was born in St. John's, he did tell me that, and he lived here for a good part of his life. But he did say that he lived other places. He also lived abroad for a time. He told me that too."

"Abroad? Outside Newfoundland, you mean?"

"Yes, I think so."

"He didn't say where that was? When he lived abroad?"

Mother and son looked at each other. Jimmy Burridge spoke.

"No, sir, he didn't say. Like I said, he wasn't a talkative fella. He kept to himself."

"How did he die?" Ethel Burridge's question was crisp. She was looking at Stride. "You didn't say how he come to be dead, sir."

"There was an accident," Stride said. "He was in Scanlon's Lane last night. We're not sure yet just what happened. It's possible he fell down the steps." He didn't mention the autopsy scheduled for later that afternoon. He was afraid that might set Ethel Burridge off again, and he didn't want to see her upset. But he was wrong about her.

"I suppose now you has to do a post mortem to find out what happened to the poor man," she said. She moved to the piano bench now and sat down, her feet together and her hands clasped on her knees. "Mr. Burridge died in an accident years ago, and that's what they had to do to him, to find out what it was that happened. I had to give them permission to cut him open. I didn't like it, but they said I didn't have no choice. But, Mr. Rossiter don't have no family here in St. John's that we knows about."

"You're certain of that?"

"None that he ever told us about," she said. "And I don't think he was ever married, neither. He never mentioned that he had any children, did he, Jimmy?"

"No, he didn't. I think he was always alone. For most of his life, I mean. He didn't say that, not in so many words, but that's what I got from the little bit he did say." Burridge looked at his mother for a moment, then back at Stride. "He was a bit funny in the head, you know."

"You shouldn't say that, Jimmy. He was an old man. And he wasn't well."

"What do you mean 'funny in the head', Mr. Burridge?" Hector Gullage had said something similar about Rossiter.

"Sometimes the things he said didn't make any sense." Burridge glanced at his mother again. "It's true, Mummy. You know it is. You even said that yourself a couple of times."

This time, the old woman didn't comment. She focused her attention on the window that looked out onto the street.

Stride looked at Phelan and made a note in his book.

"Mr. Rossiter not having any family in St. John's poses a small problem for us, Mrs. Burridge. We need someone to make a formal identification of the body. You and your son knew him as well as anyone, probably better than most." He looked at Jimmy Burridge now. "You'd be doing us a favour, Mr. Burridge, if you would make the identification. We can arrange transportation for you."

Burridge didn't look happy about the prospect, but his only response was a resigned shrug of the shoulders.

Stride looked at his watch. It was close to noon. The autopsy would be done around two. It would be better to have the identification made before Butcher went to work on Rossiter. Butcher had mentioned the possibility of a stroke as the actual cause of death, and that would involve opening the skull. He would arrange for transportation for Burridge before they left.

"You mentioned that Mr. Rossiter hadn't been well. Had he seen a doctor?"

Ethel Burridge shook her head.

"I told him he should, and I give him the name of our doctor. But I don't think he ever went."

Stride directed his next question to both Burridges. "When did you last see Mr. Rossiter? Yesterday sometime?"

"He had his breakfast here yesterday morning," Ethel Burridge said.

"Just like he done every other day for the last year. After that, he went back to his room. I think he was probably reading for the rest of the morning. Mr. Rossiter liked to read. He has books, a lot of books." She said that with a kind of pride, as if to say that a man who liked to read, and read books, not just the daily paper, had a special quality. And Samuel Rossiter, the reader of books, had chosen to live in her house.

"And after that?"

"After that he went out. I think that was about two o'clock. He had a bowl of soup and a cup of tea and then he went out."

The old woman bowed her head as the realisation settled in that that was the last time she had seen Samuel Rossiter, and that she would not see him again.

"And you didn't see him again after that?"

Ethel Burridge shook her head.

"Do you know the name, 'Walter Keough?' Either of you? We've been told he was a friend of Rossiter's."

Mother and son looked at each other. Then, Ethel Burridge nodded and looked at Stride.

"He did mention Mr. Keough to me once or twice. I think they was friends. I don't think Mr. Keough is very well off, poor man."

"Did you know where he lives? Mr. Keough?"

"I believe he lives at the lumberyard."

"Mugford's lumberyard? On Blackmarsh Road?"

"I believes that's the place. It didn't sound very nice when Mr. Rossiter told me about it. I think it's only a shack someplace on the property." Ethel Burridge looked at Stride and Phelan in turn, hesitating. "Did Mr. Keough have something to do with Mr. Rossiter getting killed?"

"We don't know that he did, Mrs. Burridge. We were told they might have been together last night. If they were, then Mr. Keough might be able to assist us with our investigation." Stride stood up and slipped his notebook into a jacket pocket. "You've been a big help to us, Mrs. Burridge. We appreciate it." He turned to Jimmy Burridge. "We'd like to have a look at Mr. Rossiter's room now. Can you show us the way, please?"

Burridge levered himself out of the armchair he was sitting in and started towards the stairs.

Ethel Burridge remained sitting on the piano bench. Her face was turned towards the window that looked out onto Gower Street, but Stride didn't think she was focusing on anything.

Samuel Rossiter's room was at the rear of the house. The single window in the room afforded a view of the backs of the houses on Bond Street to the north. Jimmy Burridge stood by the open door while Stride and Phelan walked around the room. At this point, they were just looking around, getting a feel for the place. Burridge watched for a moment, then stepped into the hall.

"I'll be downstairs if you need me, Inspector. Just give a shout if you want anything."

"Thank you, Mr. Burridge. By the way, this room will have to remain closed and off-limits until we've completed our investigation into Mr. Rossiter's death. No one is to come in here after we leave, not until we tell you otherwise."

"I don't understand," Burridge said. He stepped back into the room. "You said Mr. Rossiter's death was an accident."

"As far as we know it was. But until we're certain of that, this room, and all of Mr. Rossiter's possessions, have to be left as they are." He stepped closer to Burridge, looking down at him. His best official posture. "You do understand that? No one is to enter this room until you hear from us."

Burridge responded with a vigorous nodding of the head. He turned away and started down the stairs, looking back only once. Stride watched him go and then pushed the door shut. When he turned around, Phelan was standing beside the bookcase.

"Mrs. Burridge said Rossiter had books, and so he does." He took one off the shelf. "Leather covers, too. Very nice."

Stride picked up another book. *A Tale of Two Cities.* The cover of this one was also made of fine leather, red in colour. Dark stains on the leather showed that the book had been handled a lot. Stride opened the book. Inside the front cover there was a dedication: *Presented to Samuel Rossiter for Proficiency in English, Christmas 1892. Methodist College, St. John's, Nfld. Presented by Edward Royce, MA (Oxon.), Headmaster.*

Phelan opened the cover of the book he was holding, J.G. Edgar's Heroes of England.

"It's almost identical, sir. Except this one's dated 1886. Six years earlier."

"That adds up. Rossiter would have been sixteen years old in 1892, and only ten in 1886. Edgar's book was written for young boys."

"The ones who still believe there really are heroes in this world."

"I'm worried that you might be turning into a cynic, Harry."

"I think it's the company I keep, sir."

Stride laughed. "No offence taken."

"I'll just have to try harder, then."

"You do that." Stride put the book back on the shelf. "Gully was right about Rossiter being an educated man. And there's also a suggestion of privilege here. He went to a very good school." He picked up several more books, all of them leather-bound, most of them classics of English literature. And all of them awarded as prizes from the Methodist College.

Stride slid the last book back into its place on the shelf and again looked around at the spare little room that had been Samuel Rossiter's last home.

"He appears to have come a long way down, Harry, from his prize-winning days at the Methodist College."

"I'd say so. I wonder what happened?"

"We might have a better idea when we've gone through all of this. You start with the closet and I'll do the dresser."

But thirty minutes later, after they had gone through all of Rossiter's belongings, they had no better idea what might have carried him down from a privileged education in one of the best schools in St. John's, to a shabby boarding house on Gower Street. What they found only confirmed his current state in life. It told them nothing of his background. The clothes in the closet and in the dresser drawers matched the items Rossiter had been wearing when Corrigan found him in the laneway. They were old and well-worn, although two of the jackets bore labels from a tailor in St. John's.

"These were made by Chafe," Stride said.

"Chafe made the suit I wore to my first communion." Phelan looked at the label and gave the jacket back to Stride. "Rossiter bought these second-hand, I suppose?"

"Maybe." Stride placed the jackets back on their hangers and hung them in the closet again. "But there might be more to our Mr. Rossiter than we'd originally thought."

"Or the Burridges did."

"Yes, them too."

Stride closed the closet door and walked to the window. He pulled the curtain back and looked out. Rossiter's diminished situation, the small room with its drab furnishings, bothered him. That Rossiter's life had been a relatively long one and had ended so violently only added to his sour feeling. He stood at the window for another minute, watching a woman on her back step hanging wet clothes on a double clothesline that ran between the porch and a pole on the far side of the small garden. She was a day late, Stride thought. Monday was the traditional laundry day. Suddenly aware that someone was watching her, the woman looked up at Stride standing in the window. He dropped the curtain back in place.

"Do you think we'll have reason to come back here, sir? For another go-round, I mean?"

Phelan was sitting on the side of the bed now, holding an unlit cigarette in one hand and his lighter in the other.

"I can't imagine that we will, Harry, but you never know. Better safe than sorry."

"I'll do the usual, then."

He put the cigarette back in the package and set about the precautions they always took when they wanted to know if someone had come into a place after they had left it. He inserted small pieces of black cotton under the dresser drawers and turned two of the six swing handles on the drawers upwards. Then, he placed several more pieces of cotton under the spines of the books on the shelves. While Phelan was doing that, Stride opened the closet and arranged the articles of clothing, grouping the hangers in a systematic way. If they had to come back to the room for another search, they would know if anyone had been there.

Caleb Howell watched as Stride and Phelan walked down Gower Street towards Stride's MG. He had been standing by his window, smoking and watching the activity on the street when they had arrived. Not that there was much to see, apart from the two kids on their trikes and the two women sitting on the front step talking. Howell had been getting ready to go out. He had a part-time job with Len Stick, who owned a trucking company, hauling goods all over the city and around the Avalon Peninsula. Stick liked to say that if there was a road, he had the truck to match it. Well, that was a bit of a laugh. Some of the local roads, especially outside the city, were not much more than scars on the landscape, challenge enough for a tank or a half-track.

But Howell knew trucks. In Europe during the war, he had driven on roads that weren't roads at all, except in the imaginations of army cartographers, miles away from the fighting, imaginations fuelled by wishful thinking. And after the peace, too, such peace as it was when Howell had been there. So driving Len Stick's trucks in and around St. John's and on the rough tracks between the few outports that were connected, some of them retired army vehicles like the ones he drove in the war, wasn't a great challenge for Caleb Howell. And Howell couldn't only drive the trucks; he could strip them down and put them back together again, blindfolded at midnight if he had to, and under fire besides. It was the sort of thing he'd had to do as the allied armies moved from Normandy's beaches across France and into Germany. If anyone asked, wanted proof of that, he had the medals to show for it, along with a couple of commendations. Which, mated to a handful of dollar bills, would buy him a jug of something nice.

It had taken a toll, though, all of that, and it had aged him. He still slept badly, waking often in the middle of the night with the whistling of shells and sounds of explosions, the snap and crackle of small arms fire. And sometimes the other sounds, nominally human, men screaming and crying, in fear and pain. But that wasn't the worst of it. The worst of all was the horses. It seemed crazy, unreal, that there were horses in a modern war, but there they were, carthorses and riding horses both, recruited from the countryside into the army, pulling the trucks and some of the big guns that had gotten stuck in the spring mud. And once, only one time, and for that he thanked the God he didn't believe in, they had come under a barrage from German eighty-eights, many of the shells set for near-ground air bursts, chunks of hot ragged steel tearing down on them, man and beast both, ripping bodies apart, shredding flesh from bone, shooting ropes of intestines through the air like party streamers at a celebration in hell. Until that day, Howell had not known that horses could scream.

So he didn't sleep well. But at least he was still more or less in one piece. And the alcohol helped. He had worked his way through a seemingly infinite variety of concoctions over the last several years, but since coming to St. John's, he had settled on rum. It was appropriate, a part of his heritage, although he laughed at the very notion of heritage, even as he acknowledged that everyone had one, for good or ill. And his own was complicated enough.

He needed a drink, now, or persuaded himself that he did. Policemen had that effect on him. He poured a quantity of dark rum into the same glass that he had used the night before, took an exploratory sip and lit a cigarette. He was still looking down at the street, watching Stride and Phelan as they stood by the sports car. He remembered them from the night he had been arrested. It was a stupid mistake on his part, but human enough. Christmas having its usual effect on him, a painful longing for something lost, and a brute anger that it wasn't there any longer, and might never be again. He remembered the two men well enough, but he didn't remember the car. Well, it was winter, wasn't it, and who would drive a sports car in the winter? But the moment he saw it, he knew it was an MG. He had seen them in England when he and a few million other guys were there, waiting for the invasion to start. He had driven an MG, more than one in fact, and a few other sports cars besides. Any chance he had. He liked cars, all kinds and sizes of cars. More than people, if it came to a choice.

He sipped his rum and smoked his cigarette, and watched the two detectives. After a minute of talking, they got into the little car. The taller one, Stride his name was — Howell remembered that from his Christmas adventure — fired up the engine and they moved down the street and out of sight. He felt better then. He had heard them come, heard them talking to little, fat Jimmy and his old lady, and knew they had come about Rossiter. He thought about that for a few moments before tossing back the rest of his rum. Then, he pushed the cork tight into the bottle, and put it back in the drawer of his night table.

s e v e n

Stride had long ago learned to deal with autopsies, just as he had learned, as a young boy growing up on the island's south coast, to accept that death and life walked daily in tandem. To a degree that now seemed remarkable, even exotic, his family had lived to a large extent off the land and the sea. His father was skilled in the arts of survival – he was a hunter, a trapper, and a small-boat fisherman. Much of what the family consumed, and some of what they wore, came directly from nature. So the sight of Samuel Rossiter split open from navel to chin, his organs removed, weighed, sectioned, and catalogued, was nothing special for Stride. Man's innate kinship with his fellow mammals, the hare, seal, caribou, and moose that routinely graced their dinner table, was only too obvious. For Stride, the autopsy was all just a part, even if a newly sanctioned and refined part, of the eternal process of life and death.

They had reached the General Hospital shortly after two. Samuel Rossiter was already lying face-up on the autopsy table, naked and pale under the overhead light. An identification tag on the big toe of his left foot gave the scene a bizarre comic aspect, as though the old man might have been a macabre gift that no one had thought worthy of the time and effort it took to wrap.

Butcher was washing his hands at the sink, his back turned to them, but he heard them enter the autopsy room. He glanced briefly over his shoulder, then took his time drying his hands. When he was done, he dropped the towel into a linen basket, turned around, and leaned against the sink. Stride knew from Butcher's expression, without his saying a word, that their day was about to become a lot more complicated.

"His death wasn't an accident, it was murder." Butcher took in Stride's silent response. "It surprised me too. At worst, I had expected to find that Rossiter had died of a stroke or a heart attack, brought on by the unfortunate altercation with the two boys. But in fact, death was probably from suffocation. The larynx and trachea have been crushed."

"Strangulation?"

"No. From a very severe blow to the throat. Perhaps from a kick, carefully directed, I'm not sure. Mind you, we might also find evidence of a coronary accident of some kind in response to the blow to the throat, but that remains to be seen, and its relevance will be academic."

"There's no doubt about this?" It was the routine question. Stride already knew there wasn't any. Tom Butcher was not given to loose opinions.

Butcher only shook his head in response to the expected question. He led them to the table where Rossiter lay.

"I've already done the preliminaries: the weighing, the measuring and the photographing. When I found the injury to the larynx and trachea, I did X-rays of the throat region. They only confirm my initial assessment. Then I noticed this."

He beckoned to Stride and Phelan to move closer to the table. He indicated a small scar on the upper part of Rossiter's left arm.

"I had guessed this might have been caused by a bullet, so I did an X-ray of the area. It essentially confirms what I thought, that it probably was a bullet wound. There's some damage near the proximal end of the humerus that is consistent with a projectile, almost certainly a bullet. I've seen enough to know. But it happened a long time ago."

"How long?" Stride asked.

"I can't say. It's not a recent injury, but that's as far as I'll go with it. But do notice this." Butcher ran his index finger from the scar on the upper arm across to the chest area. "Nine or so inches to the right, and the bullet would have struck the heart."

"An attempt to kill him, maybe?"

"Perhaps. But it could just as easily have been an accidental shooting."

Butcher stepped back from the table and leaned against the adjoining one. He was looking at Rossiter now, taking in the whole of the man. "He's very thin, as you can see. Have you found out anything else about him? Where he lived, what kind of a life he's been leading?"

"He lived in a boarding house on Gower Street. The place isn't grand, but it's reasonably good, and his landlady appeared to have a liking for him. So I imagine he was well enough fed and looked after."

"Then his appearance is probably not due to malnutrition. Well, let me modify that. He may have been getting enough to eat, but if he was seriously ill, as I suspect, the nutrients might not have been getting through, if I can put it that way. The drinking wouldn't have helped. The lesions on his face suggest a serious illness. I took a chest X-ray, and it indicates an abnormality of the right lung."

"Tuberculosis?"

"I don't think so. It might be cancer, but I won't know until I open him up." He picked up a scalpel and looked at Phelan. "Are you comfortable with this, Harry?"

Phelan shook his head. "No, I'm not, but I will manage." He stepped back a pace and rested the heels of his hands on the edge of the table behind him.

"Good man. But if you think you're going to faint, go sideways. Better for all of us that way."

Butcher started the procedure. He went into his sometime role of lecturer, the interpreter and dispenser of treasured, almost holy information. Butcher had never married, had no family in Newfoundland, and his life was almost entirely concerned with his medical skills and his scientific curiosity, his talents in the theatre of life and death. He liked what he did and when the opportunity presented itself, as it did now, he went into a kind of theatrical mode, but always with an understanding that he was dealing with a human being, or something that had once been human, someone who had lived and breathed, felt fear and pain, and had probably formulated thoughts about all of it.

"This is more or less what I suspected," Butcher said after he had laid Rossiter open, exposing the internal organs. "There's an advanced carcinoma of the lung, and it appears to have spread to the liver, although it's possible that's an unrelated cancer. There's considerable evidence of cirrhosis here, also. It's serious enough, but it wouldn't have mattered. I was going to say 'in the long run', but a long run wasn't in the cards for Mr. Rossiter. The cancer was going to kill him long before his drinking would have."

"How much time do you think he had left?"

Butcher shook his head slowly. "It's difficult to say. In someone as old as Rossiter, a cancer will typically advance more slowly and less aggressively than in someone young. In a young man with tumours like these, I would have said that he'd have been dead within a month, possibly in a matter of weeks. But Rossiter might have lived for several months longer, perhaps as many as six. On the other hand, he wasn't very strong. So you could say it's six of one, a half-dozen of the other."

"Would he have known about this, do you think? How ill he was?"

"That's a good question. And I expect he would have known, unless he was a master of self-deception. Some people are. And he might have been one of them."

"His landlady told us he hadn't been well lately. But she didn't know if he had ever seen a doctor here in St. John's."

"Perhaps someone will come forward when Rossiter's death becomes public knowledge. I will put the question to some of my colleagues and see what comes back. I'll let you know, of course. Doctors enjoy chattering as much as anyone. More, probably, because we have such interesting things to chatter about." Butcher shifted his attentions to Rossiter's head. "I've also X-rayed the skull. There's a fracture on the left side. It's quite serious, and it might have led to his death, over a period of time. I won't know that until I've done the craniotomy. I'm going to do that in a few minutes. But I'll make a few additional observations first.

"There are a number of head injuries, possibly consistent with his having fallen down the concrete steps in the lane. Bruises, cuts, and scrapes – all of them painful, but none of them likely to have had fatal consequences. I'm interested in the injury surrounding the skull fracture. Like the injury to the throat, this suggests a deliberate blow, and a very solid one. He might have been kicked there too, but that's more of a guess than anything. But the impact is severe and it's concentrated. I don't believe a fall would have done it. I have seen injuries like this before, back in my army days. Soldiers are trained to inflict damage with whatever comes to hand. Or foot. Unhappily, they sometimes used their skills against each other, particularly when there was drinking involved."

"There seems to be a lot of damage here," Stride said.

"Yes, there is. Perhaps it started out as an argument, trivial at first, but then went rapidly downhill from there. The severe head and throat injuries followed on from the more minor ones. However it all started, whether as a minor argument that escalated or something else, his death ultimately was deliberate."

"He was an old man," Phelan said. "I'm trying to imagine what motivates someone to kill someone as old as Rossiter."

"Well, that is the question that will keep you both very busy for a while, I think. I'll get on with it now."

Butcher cradled Rossiter's head in his gloved hands and picked up a scalpel. He looked at Phelan again. When Harry indicated he was ready, Butcher deftly made a cut through the scalp in the mastoid region behind the left ear, then extended the cut across the top of the head to the identical spot behind the right ear. He peeled the scalp forward and pulled it down over the front of Rossiter's face, exposing the skull. The effect was not unlike a stocking cap yanked downwards in a schoolboy's prank. It seemed to Stride such a remarkably ordinary thing to do.

Butcher picked up the saw and set about opening the skull. The steel blade cut through the glistening canopy of bone and Butcher removed the front quadrant of Rossiter's skull. When the craniotomy was complete, he made a superficial examination, and then removed the brain itself.

When the autopsy was over they went back to Butcher's office. Butcher lit a cigarette, then offered the silver case to Stride and Phelan. Stride took one, but Phelan shook his head. He still looked a little pale, Stride thought, but it was notable that Harry had made it all the way through the procedure, and on the whole he looked alright. Stride would pass the information on to Noseworthy, at the appropriate time. One of the morgue attendants had made a pot of tea and Harry had laced his with a large tot of rum from a bottle that Butcher produced from his desk drawer.

Stride had already called Fort Townshend to inform his District Inspector, Jack McCowan, that they weren't dealing with an accidental death any longer, that it was a murder investigation now.

"I'll get to work on the report as soon as you leave, Eric. I'll have it ready first thing tomorrow morning, even later this evening if I feel inspired. But you already have the gist of it. The cause of death was suffocation from the throat injury. He suffered neither stroke nor heart attack, but the head injuries were severe enough that he might eventually have succumbed to them. I can't really say. But it's academic now. Rossiter was murdered and whatever embroidery I choose to add to the report, that's the nub of it." He looked at Stride and Phelan in turn. "I would judge it's unlikely the two boys had anything to do with it."

"Yes, it is. I can't imagine they had motive, and anyway they wouldn't have had the time to do all this."

"I would guess he was probably dead when the boys came into the laneway. I know he hadn't been dead very long when I examined him last night, less than an hour, I think. You can't quote me on that, but I'll find a suitable phrasing to indicate his time of death for the report."

"I did wonder if he might have been dead when the boys ran down the steps. But at the time, it looked like they were probably responsible."

Butcher smiled. "A bird in the hand?"

"Something like that, yes. I admit it. Open-and-shut cases have a powerful attraction. But I'm relieved that they probably weren't involved."

"I understand. So I take it you don't have them yet? The two who got away?"

"We didn't up to an hour ago. I think it's likely they saw Rossiter's body when they ran down the lane, so I think they're running scared, afraid that we'll think they were responsible."

"That's probably the case." Butcher drew on his cigarette. "But, you know, they might also have seen the killer. Rossiter hadn't been dead very long, and the man who killed him might still have been there, or not far away."

"Or he might have been there, and they didn't see him. There are a couple of places he might have hidden."

"That's true enough," Phelan said. "But if they did see him, and he knows they did, they're probably running from him as well as from us. In which case, it might come down to a question of who catches up with them first."

"Where does this leave you, Eric?"

"Apart from looking for the two boys who escaped down the laneway? We have the name of a man who might have been with Rossiter last night. His name is Walter Keough. They left the Admiralty together around eleven, possibly going on from there to do some serious drinking. It's something they did from time to time."

"Is he a suspect?"

"He might be. But he's about Rossiter's age, and they were friends, apparently."

"Well, friends do fall out, especially where drink is involved. And old men do commit murder. And sometimes they have more reason than the young. It would be very sad, though. You say you have his name. But do you have him?"

"Not yet, no. But we have a lead on where he might live. Ethel Burridge, the landlady at Rossiter's boarding house, told us Keough might be living on the Mugford property on Blackmarsh Road."

"Ethel Burridge? She would be the mother of the fleshy lad who was here earlier to identify the body?"

"Fleshy is a good word for him. Yes, that's Burridge. And he did make the identification?"

"Yes, he did. I can report that he didn't enjoy it very much. He had to sit down for a few minutes afterwards, until his colour came back. And he already has entirely too much colour for someone his age. It's not impossible I will see him here again, ere long."

"Perhaps you should have offered him a cup of your famous tea." Phelan swallowed the last mouthful, and placed the mug on Butcher's desk. "I can vouch for it."

"We serve that only on very special occasions, Harry, and only to a select clientele."

e i G h t

Mugford's lumberyard was near the intersection of Topsail Road and Blackmarsh. In the middle of the yard, two men were loading lumber onto a flatbed truck – two young men, lean and fit, stripped to the waist, sweating under the afternoon sun. The larger and older of the two stopped working when he saw the MG pull up. His partner noticed and followed his lead. He pulled off his gloves and started digging into his trouser pocket for a kerchief to wipe his face. The two men watched as the MG approached. Stride pulled to a stop, turned off the motor, and set the handbrake. The older of the two watched as Stride and Phelan got out. He wiped his hands on the legs of his dungarees, took out a pouch of tobacco and a book of papers, and began to roll a cigarette.

Stride looked around the property. The shed that Blake had talked about was at the far end, near a stand of scrubby spruce and alder. He thought the place had probably been there longer than the lumberyard. It was too far away from the road and the entrance to be of much use as a guardhouse.

The young man was more interested in the MG than in Stride or Phelan.

"My name is Stride and I'm with the Constabulary."

"I thought you were probably a policeman. You look like you might be." He looked at Phelan. "So does your friend."

"And so he is. We always dress to suit the occasion." Stride pointed to the back of the property. "We're looking for a man who might be living here, in that shed, so we've been told."

"Keough, you mean? Old Walter?"

"That would be him, yes."

"I haven't seen him yet today. And we've been here on and off, morning and afternoon both."

"Back and forth, you mean? Between here and the new place on Torbay Road?"

"That's right. Mugford's moving all the wood from here to the new place. Most of the stuff went last week. We're cleaning up the odds and ends. This is our fourth trip today, and we still haven't set eyes on Walter." He looked at his partner, who nodded. "He's usually out and about by now, though. Maybe he's sleeping one off, if you know what I mean. But he might have come out while we were at the new place." He looked at the MG again, then at Stride. "What year is she? The car?"

"It's a 1938 model. I bought it just before the war."

"You don't see many like that around here."

"No, you don't. As far as I know, there's only one other in the city." He gestured to Harry. "We'll take a look in the shed, if that's alright."

The young man looked at the shed, then back at Stride.

"Walter's not in any trouble, is he?"

"We hope not, but we need to speak with him for a few minutes. There are some questions we'd like to ask him."

The young man nodded and turned his attention back to the car. He finished rolling his cigarette and lit it. Then he gave the tobacco and papers to his mate.

Stride followed Phelan to the shed. He knocked on the door and waited. When there was no reply, he knocked again, louder this time. There was movement inside and the door opened. A tired old face looked at them. The eyes were rimed and bloodshot. It looked like the man had a classic hangover. Stride wondered how much worse he might have looked if they had come earlier this morning.

"Walter Keough?"

The old man blinked several times and ran his hand through his thin grey hair. It almost looked as though he was confused by the question, not certain who he was. He half-turned away, as though the question was too much for him, then turned back. He started to speak, coughed, then cleared his throat and tried again.

"Yes, I'm Walter Keough. Who is it wants to know?"

Stride produced his badge. Keough stared at it. He rubbed his eyes and looked at it again. He touched it with one fingertip, respectfully, as though it were a religious icon.

"You're the police?" He backed up a step. "I haven't done nothing."

"It's alright, Mr. Keough. We just need to ask you a few questions about last night?"

"Last night?"

"Yes." Stride looked again at the tired expression, the bloodshot eyes, the general air of confusion. "Do you remember where you were last night?"

"Last night?" Keough furrowed his brow, struggling with the effort. "I went out last night."

"Where did you go? Do you remember?"

Keough concentrated again, breathing hard now, his breath stale and unpleasant. Stride moved his head back and to the side.

"I was at Gullage's. That's where I was. The Admiralty, on Holdsworth Street." His eyes were brighter now, pleased with himself, it seemed.

"Did you see Samuel Rossiter last night?"

"Sam? Sam sent you here?"

"No. No, he didn't, Mr. Keough. Were you with him last night?"

"With Sam? Yes, I believe I was. I believe Sam was at the Admiralty. Yes, he was." Now, he was confused again. He half-turned and started back into the shed, then he changed his mind yet again, and walked outside, squinting in the bright afternoon light. He sat on a wooden box by the wall of the shed, tilted his head back, and closed his eyes. "It's going to be a hot day. Yes, it is."

"It already is a hot day, Mr. Keough. Do you know what time it is?"

"What time is it?" He shook his head. He was smiling, apparently enjoying a private joke. "No, I don't know. I don't have a watch, haven't had one in years." He laughed then and slapped his knee. "I sold it. I sold my watch and I bought a bottle of whisky with the money. It was a good watch. And it was good whisky, too. Irish. Irish whisky is the best. That's what my old dad always said." He looked at Stride again. "I'm Irish, you see, and I should know. My grandfather, he come over from Ireland in..." he puckered his brow. "Sometime in the last century. I should be able to remember exactly when, but I can't." He shook his head, a look of great sadness on his face, as though he had lost something. He looked around him, taking in his surroundings, almost as though he was seeing them for the first time. "Where's Sam? Did you say Sam was here?"

Stride looked at Harry and shook his head.

"You want me to take over, sir? Maybe the Irish connection will turn the tide in our favour."

"Go ahead, Harry. Good luck."

"It's what we're famous for." He knelt down in front of Keough. "Walter."

The old man looked at him closely, trying for recognition. "Do I know you? You do look familiar."

"My name is Harry Phelan. I'm Walter Phelan's son. You see, Mr. Keough, you and my father have the same name. Walter."

"Well, now, so we do. And how is your father, Mr. Phelan? I hope he's well."

"He's very well, Mr. Keough. And I'll tell him you were asking after him."

"You do that, now. Yes, you do that."

"I will. Now, Mr. Keough. I want to ask you a question about last night."

"Last night? You want to ask me about last night?"

"Yes, sir. You were at the Admiralty last night. Hector Gullage's place on Holdsworth."

"The Admiralty." His eyes brightened again with recognition. "Yes, I was. Were you there, too?"

"No, sir, I wasn't. But you were." He put his hand on Keough's knee. "Now, tell me. When you were at the Admiralty last night, did you see your friend Sam? Sam Rossiter?"

"Yes, Sam's a friend of mine. A nice fella, Sam. Yes, he is. You know Sam, do you?"

"No. I don't, Mr. Keough. I haven't had the pleasure."

"Sam's a nice fella. Yes, he is."

"I'm sure he is. Did you see him last night, Mr. Keough? At the Admiralty?"

"Sam was at the Admiralty last night. Yes, he was. I saw him there."

"That's grand, Mr. Keough. Now, I want you to think about last night."

"Yes, I was at the Admiralty last night. Sam was there, he can tell you."

He looked past Phelan, towards the entrance from Blackmarsh. Phelan turned and looked too. In the middle of the lot, the two men were busy loading lumber onto the flatbed again. Keough looked at Phelan. "I don't see him. Where's Sam? Didn't he come along with you?"

"No, Mr. Keough, he didn't. That's what we want to ask you about. Last night, when you and Sam were together at the Admiralty." Phelan gripped the man's knee tightly, pulling his attention closer. "Where did you go after you and Sam left Gullage's place? You had a bottle. You and Sam had a bottle."

Keough was nodding his head now as the memory began to take shape, filtering through the fog of age and confusion. "Yes, we did. Willy Fitzgerald give me a bottle, yesterday night, yes he did. Good old Granny Fitz. And Sam and me, we went off and we had a few. Yes, sir, we did. We had a few."

"Do you remember where you went? You and Sam?"

Walter Keough took in a long slow breath. He closed his eyes, rocking slowly back and forth on the box.

"Scanlon's Lane. That's where we went. Down Scanlon's Lane and sat on the steps and we had a few. Yes, we did." He smiled at the memory, then looked at Phelan with hope in his eyes. "I need a smoke so bad I could almost cry. Can you give me a smoke, boy? You'd be doing an old man an awful good favour."

Harry took out his package and his lighter.

Keough pulled on the cigarette Phelan gave him and looked at the sky, blowing a stream of smoke upwards. Then he coughed twice and drew on the cigarette again.

"Scanlon's Lane," Phelan said. "You and Sam had a drink there last night. From the bottle Fitzgerald gave you."

"Yes, we did. And it was pretty good stuff too." Keough looked at the cigarette. "That's a good smoke, boy. I likes to roll my own, that's what I usually does. But I likes a tailor-made now and then."

"Scanlon's Lane," Harry said again. "Did you and Sam leave together? After you had your drink?"

Keough shook his head. "No. I left Sam there by himself. I had to get on home, you see, and this fella he come along and he said he'd drive me back here. He lives out this way. It's a long walk to here from downtown. So, seeing as how I had the chance of a drive, I left Sam down in Scanlon's Lane and come on back home."

"You left Sam there?"

"Yes, I did. In Scanlon's Lane. I left the bottle with him, too." Keough laughed. "There wasn't very bloody much left in it, though, I can tell you that. Sam and me, we knows what to do with a bottle. From a long time back. Yes, my son, we do."

"Who was the man who drove you home, Walter? Can you give us his name?"

"The fella drove me home?" He scratched his head. "You know, I don't remember his name." He laughed again. "Bloody names. They come and they go, but mostly they go. I can't remember his name just now, and that's a fact."

"Try hard, Walter. It's important that we know his name."

Keough shook his head again. "It's no good. I can try from now until Christ himself comes back wearing overshoes and I still won't remember. But if you want to know the fella's name, just go and ask him."

"Ask him?"

"Sure, ask him." He pointed with the cigarette towards the flatbed truck. "That's him down there. The big fella, by the truck. That's him. He'll tell you his name. Just go and ask him."

Phelan looked at Stride and stood up.

"It's a process, sir. But we're just about there, I think." He turned back to Keough. "You stay here, Walter, and we'll be back after we talk to your friend."

"Clifford Morris." The young man watched as Stride wrote down his name. "People call me Cliff. I guess Walter couldn't remember my name?"

"No, he couldn't."

"On a bad day he has trouble remembering his own. Is there a problem?"

"I hope not," Stride said. "We were talking to him about last night. He says you drove him home. Is that true?"

"Yes, I did." Morris was guarded now. "Did something happen? There must have been something, or you wouldn't be here asking questions."

"Yes, something did happen. We're making inquiries about Samuel Rossiter. Do you know him?"

"I know who he is. Why? Did something happen to him?"

"Yes, something did. Rossiter is dead. One of our men found his body late last night in Scanlon's Lane."

"Shit. Sam's dead? Walter's going to be upset. He doesn't have many friends. What happened to him? I mean, how did he die?"

Stride hesitated. Telling Morris that Rossiter was dead had been a shock for him. Now he had to tell him it was murder. There wasn't any soft and nice way to do that, so Stride simply told him the basics.

"Jesus." Morris tilted his head back and looked up at the sky. Then back at Stride. "Who the hell would want to murder an old man like Sam Rossiter?"

"At the moment we have no idea. We're just getting started here."

"Christ." Morris turned away and looked towards Blackmarsh Road. "Well, I can tell you that Walter Keough didn't have anything to do with it. Sam was fine when I picked him up last night. When I picked up Walter, I mean."

"In the lane?"

"Yes."

"What time was that?"

"Just past twelve. Midnight."

"And Rossiter was alright then?"

"He seemed alright to me. I think he was pretty well hammered. Well, I know he was hammered, pissed to the gills. So was Walter, for that matter. But apart from that, Rossiter was alright."

"You spoke to him?"

"Yes. We chatted for a minute and then I bundled Walter out of there." He laughed. "Actually, he didn't want to leave, they were having a good time. They wanted me to sit down and have a drink with them. But I had a pretty good idea about the kind of stuff they were drinking. I would have thought twice before washing my socks with it."

Stride made another note in his book. "I have to ask you this, so don't take it the wrong way. How did you know Keough would be in Scanlon's Lane?"

Morris shook his head and smiled. "I've picked him up there before. I try and look out for Walter when I can. He has a drinking problem. Well, shit, a blind man could see that. Walter used to work for Mr. Mugford, a long time ago. Mugford asked me to look out for him, if I happened to be in the neighbourhood. So when I'm downtown, I'll sometimes stop by Scanlon's Lane to see if Walter's there. Sometimes he is. It's where he goes to drink, when he's got a bottle."

"Like last night."

"Like last night." Morris turned away again, looking up at the sky this time. Then back to Stride. "Walter's not going to get in trouble about Sam, is he? You do believe me, that Sam was okay when I took Walter out of there?"

Stride nodded.

"They both drank too much, way too much, and that's a fact, but it's not a crime to get drunk."

"No, it isn't. And, no, Keough won't get into any trouble about drinking with Rossiter. We will need you to make a statement about it, though."

"Statement? What kind of statement?"

"Pretty much what you just told me. You found Keough and Rossiter in the laneway late last night, you drove Keough home. And Rossiter was okay when you left him."

"I guess I can manage that. I suppose I'll have to go down to Fort Townshend?"

"Yes. Later today would be good. If that's convenient."

"Later today will be okay. I'll stop by after I'm finished for the day. Will you be there?"

"I might be. But if I'm not, just speak to the desk constable. He'll know that you're coming in and he'll walk you through it."

"Did you tell Walter that Sam's dead? He should be told."

"No, we haven't told him yet. We'll do that now."

"I'll tell him for you, if you like. I know Walter well enough to give him bad news. At least I think I do." Morris stuck the toe of his boot in the ground, then kicked at a small scrap of wood that was lying nearby. "Well, that's not quite the truth. I've never told anyone that a friend of his has been murdered."

The second man had been listening to the conversation. He came over and placed his hand on Morris' shoulder.

"You wants me to come along with you, Cliff?"

"Thanks, Gus. But it might be that three of us will be too much of a crowd for the old man."

"You're probably right. But I'll be right here, b'y, if you needs any help."

Stride looked back at Walter Keough. He was sitting on his wooden box by the side of the shed. His eyes seemed to be closed, and he appeared to be enjoying the sunlight and the warmth of the afternoon.

"I'm tempted to let you do the deed," Stride said. "But it's part of our job."

"Not much fun for you, I guess."

"You're right about that, Mr. Morris. Sometimes it's not much fun."

"I'll come along with you, though, if that's alright. It won't hurt to have me there. A familiar face."

"No, it won't hurt. And we appreciate your help."

Walter Keough was still sitting with his head tilted back when the three men got back to the shed. Harry took the lead again. He knelt down and touched Keough lightly on the knee. The old man's eyes opened and he looked at Phelan for a few seconds. Then, his face creased in a smile of recognition.

"Walter Phelan's boy. That's who you are. I was a little confused earlier on. A wee bit too much of the gargle last night, I think. That's what it was. A drink or two too many." He closed his eyes again and then he laughed. "I expect Sam is in pretty bad shape this morning too. Yes, I expect he is."

Phelan hesitated for a moment, then decided he might as well just say it, get it out there. He almost wished he had a flask of good whisky, like the one Rossiter was carrying in his inside pocket last night. It might help.

"Mr. Keough." Harry gripped the old man's knee and got his attention back. "I have some bad news for you about Sam."

He waited to see if Keough had taken in the words, sensed his meaning, perhaps. It looked as though he had. The old man turned his head until he was looking at Phelan directly. He wasn't smiling now.

"Bad news," he said. He looked at Morris, then at Stride, then back at Phelan again. "Something bad happened to Sam? Is that what you're going to tell me?"

"I'm afraid so, Mr. Keough. Sam is dead. One of our men found him last night in Scanlon's Lane. It must have happened after you left with Mr. Morris."

Keough placed his hands on his knees and leaned forward. His left hand came down on Phelan's and he quickly pulled it back, as though he found the contact offensive. He looked at each of the three men in turn and his face clouded over. "Dirty buggers," he said.

He stood up, stumbled a little, and then walked into the shed and closed the door behind him.

nine

Billy Dickson was on the desk at Fort Townshend. He told Stride that District Inspector McCowan wanted to see him as soon as he came in. Well, that was no surprise. Stride looked at his watch. It was almost five. Dickson also gave him a note and a telephone message from Tom Butcher. He unfolded it and read it through.

"Anything important, sir?" Phelan said.

"Butcher's done an examination of Rossiter's brain. Apparently, Rossiter had suffered a stroke, probably fairly recently, within the last year or two. It's not a huge surprise, he says. Rossiter was an old man, and old people have strokes." He laughed. "For that matter, he says, young people do too."

"Why does that bring me so little comfort?"

"I can't imagine. He's going to do some more work on it. He'll consult with Nigel Roberts."

"The neurologist."

"Yes. He wants an expert opinion on the effects the stroke might have had on Rossiter. It might explain the odd behaviour and speech that almost everyone has told us about."

"When will he get back to us on that?"

Stride shook his head. "He doesn't say. Anyway, I'm off to see the Field Marshal."

"You might be in with McCowan for a while, sir. Anything you want me to do in the meantime?"

"Go and see Bern Crotty in records. He must have finished looking for Rossiters in the files by now. Maybe he found something. There's also the Vital Statistics office. We have an approximate year of birth for Rossiter. That's a start. I forget the name of the fellow we've talked to there. An odd-looking man with hedges for eyebrows."

Phelan smiled. "Staples, sir. Rodney Staples."

"Right, Staples. Give him a call and get him started. If it's not too late in the day."

"They work until six at Vital Statistics, sir, like most other mortals."

"I'm pleased to hear it. Tell Staples one of us will go see him tomorrow morning and we'll expect him to have the information by then. Apologise for not calling him earlier so he could have more lead time. But give him the firm finger, just the same. Nicely, though."

"I'll tell him we've been very busy."

"Yes, do that." He started towards McCowan's office, then turned back. "I almost forgot."

"Sir?"

"The flask Rossiter was carrying. It may have been stolen, as you suggested. Ask Crotty if he has anything on it. He's probably checked it out by now."

"Lawrence William Harvey's flask?"

"Clever fellow."

"You know, Kitty says the same thing sometimes."

"With more and better reason, I hope. Off with you."

Stride looked at Dickson's note again. He placed the folded note in his pocket and went on down the corridor to McCowan's office.

Jack McCowan was standing in front of his desk, leaning against the edge. That was usually a signal that their meeting would be short, which would be nice. It had already been a long day. But this time it only meant that McCowan was agitated. Murder had that effect on him.

"Bring me up to speed on Rossiter," McCowan said. "I take it Butcher has no doubts about his conclusions?"

Stride shook his head. "None whatever, sir. The blow to the throat, and several of the others to the head, were almost certainly intentional." He recounted the particulars, not leaving out any details. McCowan frowned, walked around his desk, and sat down. He clasped his hands on his blotter and leaned forward.

"Well, give me the rest of it. What do we know about Rossiter, and will any of it help us?"

Stride filled McCowan in. It didn't take long.

"What's your feeling about Keough? Anything there?"

"I don't think so, sir. My judgement is that he was taken completely by surprise when Harry told him that Rossiter was dead. He was also very upset." He smiled. "Keough even seemed to think we were responsible in some way. He called us a name."

"Did he, now?"

"Yes, he said we were dirty buggers. Those were his exact words."

McCowan smiled. "A case of dunning the messenger, I suppose. Better than shooting him, at any rate. Consider yourself to have gotten off lightly." He spread his hands on his desk blotter and stared at his fingers. After a moment he looked up again. "It wasn't robbery – what besides a few dollars did Rossiter have to steal, after all? – and we don't know enough about the man to hazard a guess at some other motive. Irritating. Any thoughts you want to share with me?"

"Not many, sir. When we find out more about Rossiter, I might be able to generate a few." He paused and thought about Butcher's comment. "It might turn out to be something truly banal. It's possible that after Morris took Keough away, someone else came into the laneway simply by happenstance. If he'd been drinking too, and was as drunk as Rossiter apparently was, they might have gotten into an argument over the bottle."

"And then one stupid thing led to another, and Rossiter ended up dead." McCowan nodded his head and sat back in his chair. "Yes, some murders are like that. As you say, banal. Those are the worst to deal with because there's no real motive attached, and if that's what happened, we might never find out who did it." He picked up a notepad and scanned it. "Noseworthy was in earlier and gave me the nub of what he's found so far."

"I haven't had a chance to speak with him yet."

"I suppose not. Anyway, he's found Rossiter's fingerprints on the bottle you collected. That's not a surprise, but it's good to have it confirmed. Also, he's found another set of prints that are at least marginally interesting. They're from our former colleague, the unlamented Willy Fitzgerald. Granny Fitz, as he likes to call himself now. Do you think Fitzgerald might have been drinking with Rossiter last night, or did he only supply the bottle?"

"Keough told us Fitzgerald had supplied the bottle the day before. It was one of the few coherent things he had to say."

"Noseworthy found a number of other prints on the bottle, none of which he was able to identify. Which isn't surprising. Fitzgerald's bottles make the rounds, and God knows if he washes them in between times. Some of the prints will prove to be Keough's." McCowan glanced at his notepad again. "What do you think of the possibility that one of the two young ruffians might have killed Rossiter? The ones who ran down the laneway to get away from Corrigan?"

"I think it's unlikely, sir."

"I'm inclined to agree with you." McCowan smiled. "They were, after all, running away from Jack Corrigan. If an angry Jack Corrigan was hot on my heels, Jesus Christ himself, reborn and resplendent, could not persuade me to dawdle." Then he was serious again. "You probably know that they're still at large."

"I assumed as much. We at least have their names and addresses, and we should have photographs of them by now." Stride read from his notebook. "Philip Rowe and Gordon MacLeod. Like Lawlor, they're seventeen years old. They were all in the same class at school. They finished up this past spring."

"Yes, we do have the photographs. Noseworthy showed them to me. The parents were very obliging. Not that they had any choice in the matter." McCowan looked at his watch. "Well, it's late, and I imagine you're tired enough. I'll just keep you another minute, Eric. I have another meeting starting just about now. It's a bit late in the day, but it can't be helped. The Chief and I are meeting with Major Stamp, the head of the Rangers."

The Newfoundland Ranger Force was a paramilitary organisation, established in 1935 to deal with law enforcement in areas of the island not covered by the Constabulary. It also dealt with a variety of other government matters, including the enforcement of game laws and, in some parts of the island, smuggling, especially of liquor. Stride could have made a signal contribution to that part of the Rangers' activity, but he hadn't been asked. Most of Newfoundland, and Labrador as well, came under their jurisdiction. The Constabulary was left with the responsibility for St. John's and the rest of the Avalon Peninsula, as well as the major population centres of Corner Brook on the west coast, and Grand Falls in the interior.

There were ten Ranger detachments initially, including the headquarters located at Whitbourne on the Avalon, about forty miles west of St. John's. By 1947, the number of detachments had grown. McCowan thought that the term detachment was more than a bit grandiose. In many of them, there was only a single Ranger, and he was often responsible for a very large territory.

"Is it something we should know about, sir? Your meeting with Stamp?" He already knew there was more to come.

"Yes and no," McCowan said. "It's not something that will affect us directly. In fact I didn't expect the meeting today. It was originally set for next week, but Tom Stamp rang me this morning from Whitbourne. He was coming to town on other business, so he thought he might as well take the opportunity to have a chat with me and the Chief at the same time. The word is that if the referendum next year goes in favour of Confederation with Canada, instead of a return to national government – as well it might – the Rangers will be disbanded and the serving members will be given the option of joining the RCMP. The Royal Canadian Mounted Police."

"Harry calls them the pony soldiers. Custer's northern cousins."

McCowan smiled. "I've heard them called worse. I'm old enough that I still sometimes think of them as the Northwest Mounted Police. Well, we'll all be learning new words and phrases soon enough, if that little bugger Smallwood and the crowd in Ottawa and Whitehall have their collective way. It's not a pressing matter, not yet, but it's something we might have to deal with, so we've started talking about it. It's what bureaucracies like to do." He looked at Stride. "I just wanted to mention it now. Like a bad meal, it will come up again. There will likely be another meeting later on, and if there is perhaps you'll attend with me. But I know you'll be busy for a while, until this Rossiter business is put to bed."

"I'll make a note of it, sir."

"Good. If you have the time, think about things you might want to speak to Stamp about. Like myself, he's ex-military, but he's a lot more of a martinet than I ever was, or would want to be." He caught Stride's fleeting smile but let it go. "He learned that in the trenches on the Western Front in the Great War. He puts a lot of stock in it and that's fair enough. It's one of the things that kept him alive over there for the better part of four years." McCowan stood up. The meeting was almost over. "This old fellow you mentioned, Keough. I imagine he's at a bit of a loss? It's hard losing a friend at his age. Hard enough losing a friend at any age, comes to that." McCowan looked wistful. "Some of mine are starting to drop away. It's an itch that cannot be scratched effectively."

"He did seem to take it very hard, sir."

"Yes, I dare say." He laughed. "But he did manage to call you and Harry a rude name. I like that. The man has spirit. And good for him."

Harry was waiting for Stride in their office.

"Crotty's done a quick search on Rossiter, sir, but nothing has jumped out at him. He'll spend some more time on it tomorrow and let us know."

"Tomorrow sounds fine to me. Just about now, I'm ready to call it a day." And a night, for that matter. He leaned against his desk and took out his notebook and went over his notes again. After a minute he looked at Harry. "Burridge said that Rossiter was always on time with his board money. Never a day late is the phrase he used, if my notes have it right."

"Yes, he did say that."

"That's interesting. I'm assuming he always paid cash, but I didn't think to ask."

"One demerit point for you, sir."

"And for you, too, faithful friend. At the time it didn't seem too important. But Rossiter must have had some sort of income. Probably not a lot, but enough to pay for his lodging. If we could find out where his income came from, we would know more about him. Just about double our knowledge, in fact."

"He wasn't carrying much cash on him when he was killed. Just those six tired-looking one-dollar bills."

"Which suggests one of two things. He either had some money squirreled away in his room at the Burridges, which I doubt, or he had a bank account." Stride was silent for a moment. "You know, we didn't do as thorough a search as we might have."

"No, we didn't. One more demerit point for each of us."

"I'll take that little secret with me to my grave."

"Me, too, sir. Mind you, the Burridges might have objected to us ripping down the wallpaper and tearing up the floorboards."

"Breeding will out every time."

"A bank account is a possibility, isn't it?"

"Yes, it is. Phone Burridge and put the question to him. Carefully, though. If we put an idea in his head that whispers money, he might go looking for the book himself. While you're doing that, I need to answer nature's call."

When Stride got back to the office, Phelan was just hanging up the phone.

"Burridge says Rossiter always paid his board by cash." Then a small triumphant smile. "Except for one time last winter when he was laid up with a bad cold. That time he asked Burridge to cash a cheque for him at the Newfoundland Savings Bank."

"Well, that's a start. Tomorrow we'll have a chat with the manager. What's his name? Butters?"

"George Butters."

"Right." Stride thought for a moment. "There has to be a bankbook. We'll do another search of his room. It has to be in there someplace."

"You don't think he might have given it to the Burridges to hold for him?"

"I can't imagine he would have, can you?" Phelan shook his head. "I think he might have placed some trust in Mrs. Burridge, she seemed genuinely fond of him. As for her son, though…" Stride left the thought to finish itself. He put his notebook away and stood up and started for the door. Then he turned back. "Are you fond of horses, Harry?"

"Sir?"

"Major Stamp is in town. McCowan and the Chief are meeting with him as we speak. One of the things they're talking about is what might happen with the local policing trade if we all wake up one fine morning next summer and find ourselves Canadians, decked out in maple leaves."

"I will always prefer pitcher plants. Is it the RCMP thing, again?"

"Yes. McCowan didn't say so, but I think the sharp end is wondering if any of our lot might want to change sides, like the Rangers, and join up with the Mounties. Do you fancy yourself back in uniform, Harry? Prancing around in a scarlet coat and a boy scout hat on ceremonial occasions?"

"And tall leather boots? Kitty might like that part. And I'll admit it appeals to the romantic in me." Phelan shook his head then. "But to answer your question directly, I don't much like horses. I don't trust any animal that weighs ten times as much as I do and has a brain the size of a walnut."

"I take it that's a 'no?'"

"Yes, sir. That is a 'no.'"

"I'm with you on that one. My MG has all the horsepower I want to sit on in this lifetime."

Kevin Noseworthy was also about to call it a day. And that was unusual because Noseworthy routinely arrived early and stayed late. But he'd been up very early too. When Stride found him, he was sitting back in his chair looking tired, blowing smoke rings towards the ceiling.

"Don't get up, Kevin. This is only a semi-official visit. I'm just on my way home." Stride leaned against the table and lit a cigarette. "We could all do with a good night's sleep. I suppose you know this has turned into a major crime investigation."

"I heard that," Noseworthy said. "McCowan briefed me on that earlier. But I imagine you know a lot more now."

"Yes, we do." While Stride summarised the autopsy results, Noseworthy closed his eyes, nodding occasionally. When Stride was done, Noseworthy had his puckish smile in place. "You're telling me Harry stayed conscious through the whole thing?"

"Yes, he did. You would have been proud of him."

"Absolutely, sir. And I'll mention that at an appropriate time. McCowan told you about the fingerprints?"

"The Field Marshal filled me in."

"There are a few prints that I haven't identified yet."

"So I heard. Some of those will belong to Walter Keough. He's a friend of Rossiter's. They were together last night, and they took turns on the bottle. We interviewed Keough this afternoon. Well, to the extent that we could. He's about Rossiter's age and he's run enough alcohol through his system for two lifetimes. Keough's currently bunking in a shed on the Mugford property on Blackmarsh Road."

"The lumberyard?"

"That's the place, yes."

"A threadbare sort of life." Noseworthy stubbed his cigarette in an ashtray and swung his legs down from the table. "Rossiter's drinking companion? You said his name is Walter Keough?"

"Yes, why?"

"That name rings a bell. I was going through some old files with Bern Crotty last week at the same time as I was updating my own system. It's just possible we had occasion to fingerprint your Mr. Keough in the last year, year and a half. Let me check."

Noseworthy stood up and went to one of his filing cabinets. It took him a minute to find what he was looking for.

"Here he is. Walter James Keough, August 28, 1946. From the information we got from him, he would be seventy-two years old now. So, you're right, Keough and Rossiter were of an age."

"What was he arrested for?"

"Theft. Nothing major, though. He stole – or tried to steal – some clothing from Rosenberg's department store on Water Street. He wasn't very artful about it, though. A sales clerk spotted him stuffing the goods down his pants and one of our lads collared him on the way out. He was booked and fingerprinted, and spent the night as a guest of the state. He came up before Mr. Justice Curnew the next morning. In the end, though, it was mostly a bit of judicial theatre."

"Rosenberg didn't press charges?"

"To his credit, he didn't. Keough, poor old bugger, had no money to pay a fine, and sending him to jail for a stretch would have been a case of overkill at his age. Mind you, it might have been an improvement over Mugford's shed. He was released after receiving a firm talking to from Curnew."

"Punishment enough. I've been witness to some of Curnew's lectures. I've even had one or two directed at me. A week in jail might have been preferable."

"So I've heard. Anyway, Keough went on his wobbly way, and that, until now, was the end of his story. Give me a minute and I'll see if we have a match for the prints."

Noseworthy placed the fingerprint cards side by side and made the comparison. He took his time, using a magnifying glass to check details. After a few minutes, he sat back and looked at Stride.

"Well, some of these are Keough's. No doubt about that. But there's at least a half-dozen more that aren't his."

"So, there was a third person involved."

"A fourth, if you count Granny Fitz."

"It could have been almost anyone, I suppose. Two old men drinking in a laneway. Someone they knew might have wandered by and been offered a drink. Or for that matter someone they didn't know." Stride thought for a moment. "But someone else did come by. A fellow who knows Keough came by and drove him back to the lumberyard. He said he wouldn't take a drink from the bottle, but he might have handled it."

"That's all it takes. We can ask him for his prints and I can do a check."

"Tomorrow, probably. Or maybe even later today. I asked him to come by and make a statement about last night."

There was a polite tap at the door then. It was Billy Dickson.

"Excuse me, Inspector Stride, but there's a gentleman at the desk who's asking for you. He said you asked him to come by and make a statement on the Rossiter case?"

"And his name is Clifford Morris?"

"Yes, sir, it is."

Stride looked at Noseworthy and raised his hands in a triumphant gesture.

"Well, there you have it, Kevin. Only ask and it shall be granted unto you. Bring Mr. Morris along, Billy. As it happens, we were just talking about him."

Clifford Morris had no objection to having his fingerprints taken. Quite the opposite. He found the process intriguing.

"I didn't touch the bottle, Inspector. I had my hands full trying to get Walter away from there. He wasn't all that willing to come along." Morris turned his attention back to Noseworthy's manipulation of his fingers, rolling them carefully on the inkpad, then transferring the images to the fingerprint card. "I've often wondered how this worked. It must be a hell of a job going through a pile of fingerprints. I suppose there's a system of some kind? Something that makes it work?"

"There is. You're interested in this?"

"Yes, I am."

"Alright, then. A short lecture while I compare your prints with the ones I took from the bottle." Noseworthy did the last print and gave Morris a cloth and a flask of solvent to clean his hands. He waved the card back and forth to dry the ink. Then he set the cards side by side, as he had done with Keough's prints. Again, he took his time. "This part of it is relatively simple, you understand. I have your prints and I have unknown prints to compare them with. All I have to do is match them up. Even that takes a lot of getting used to, but after a while you know what to look for, the important points for comparison."

"It's not always that simple, though, is it? How does it work if you have a set of unknowns and then you have to find a match in your collection?"

"Ah, now that's when you have to have a certified genius on staff, like yours truly." He looked to see if Stride was paying attention. "I'm kidding, of course. It's all very methodical. The primary classification system is essentially numerical, based on a number assigned to a specific digit and the whorls on the print. After that it gets more complicated. There are secondary and sub-secondary classifications."

Noseworthy put in just enough detail to impress Morris — and Stride too — but kept it simple enough that it was easily understood.

It had been years since Stride had really thought about the specifics of fingerprinting, and the most recent developments had only loosely registered in his mind. He knew they were there, he even knew where to find the information, but he also knew that Noseworthy had all the specifics at his fingertips. Assigning Noseworthy to do the work had made the system more efficient, to everyone's advantage. But it had also distanced Stride and Phelan from the technical aspects of the work. Still, running an investigation was their primary responsibility, and that was complicated enough. He accepted that he wasn't expected to be an expert on everything. But even as he formulated the thought, he knew it was a wounded rationalisation.

"Interesting," Morris said when Noseworthy was done. He finished wiping his hands, dropped the cloth on the table, and looked over Noseworthy's shoulder. "So, am I in there? On the bottle?"

Noseworthy took another minute, then placed the magnifying glass on the table.

"No. These are not your prints."

"I would have been pretty bloody surprised if they had been. I knew I didn't touch that bottle." He looked at Stride. "But you know, I was still worried that somehow my prints might be there."

"That's a common enough reaction," Stride said. "Was there anyone else in the laneway last night when you collected Mr. Keough? Or nearby?"

"No, sir. There was just Walter and Sam. And Sam was all alone when we left. I asked him if he wanted a drive home, but he said he wanted to sit under the stars for a while longer."

"Under the stars? He said that?"

"Yeah, he actually did say that. He was pretty drunk. I figured he'd probably fall asleep on the steps and wake up with nothing more serious than a stiff neck and a sore tailbone. I guessed he'd done that a hundred times before. It was a warm night. I didn't think he would come to any harm." Morris buried his hands in his pockets and walked to the window to look out. "Well, I was wrong, wasn't I? I guess I should have insisted he come along with us. Taken him home."

"It's not your fault, Mr. Morris. He probably had done it before, and often enough. But if it's any consolation, Sam Rossiter was a very sick man. He didn't have a lot of time left."

"Really? I didn't know that." He turned away from the window and looked at Stride. "It doesn't help all that much, though. But what can you do?"

"Nothing," Stride said.

"Well, if that's all, I guess I'll get on with making that statement." Morris took a sheet of paper from his pocket and gave it to Stride. "I wrote something down before I came over here. Will that do?"

Stride read through the two paragraphs and nodded. "Come along with me. We'll go through it together and then we'll find someone to type it up for your signature."

"And that's all there is to it?"

"Yes," Stride said. "That's all there is."

t e n

Jimmy Burridge stepped to the side to allow Stride to enter the house on Gower Street. The little man had a cloth napkin tucked into the collar of his shirt, but there was a smear of gravy on one of his chins. It was obvious to Stride that he had interrupted Burridge's supper. It occurred to him that someone should probably conspire to interrupt the man's meals on a regular basis.

It was past six when Stride had finally left Fort Townshend. Although it had been a long day and he hadn't eaten much since breakfast, he wasn't very hungry. He sat in his car in front of headquarters for a few minutes and smoked a cigarette, enjoying a few moments of solitude. Then he remembered the note he'd found on the bottle of orange marmalade in his fridge, and that reminded him he would probably be alone this evening. The knowledge made his flat less attractive than it might have been. He decided he would follow up the tentative lead on Rossiter's bank account by revisiting the Burridges' boarding house.

"I need to have another look at Rossiter's room, Mr. Burridge." Stride treated Burridge to one if his best official stares. "I'm assuming that neither you nor your mother has been in there since we left?"

"Oh, no, sir. We haven't gone near the room since you and Sergeant Phelan were here this morning." Burridge smoothed the napkin that covered his shirtfront. His smile lacked sincerity, and he was perspiring now, a bead of sweat dangling from the edge of one eyebrow. Burridge wiped it away and looked towards the second floor.

Stride began his search of Rossiter's room at the bookcase. All of the pieces of cotton that Harry had placed there, in and under the books, were lying on the dusty carpet. The handles on the dresser drawers were all back in place, none of them turned upwards the way Harry had arranged them. It was the same story with the clothes in the closet. The door had been opened and shut again, and all the articles of clothing had been taken from their hangers and a few items had been replaced carelessly. It was pretty much what he had expected. He would have been more surprised if the Burridges hadn't gone through Rossiter's room after he and Phelan had left that morning. Not that the intrusion necessarily meant very much.

An old man, with no family that the Burridges knew about, had died. Anything that someone like Rossiter might have left behind was potentially fair game for the owners of a boarding house. The Burridges lived on or close to the margin. A few dollars here or there would make a difference. It was basic Darwinism, the survival of the most wily.

Stride took his time going through the drawers and the closet and Rossiter's various possessions. Although it was obvious everything had been searched, and things moved about, nothing appeared to have been taken. The books were all still there on the shelving. Some of them had been moved, and their spines were evenly aligned now, where Harry had carefully left them staggered. He imagined Jimmy Burridge riffling through each book, hoping perhaps that something of value might drop out from between the pages. What Burridge probably didn't realise was that the books themselves were the most valuable items in the room. Not only were they of good quality and well cared for, they were old, so they also had some historical value. People who liked books would pay good money for leather-bound English classics. Jack McCowan was one of those people. Stride was another.

But after going through the books, the dresser drawers, and the clothing in the closet he still had not found a bankbook. There was nothing under the mattress or the box spring, or in the pillows. Next, he eased the dresser away from the wall, moving it carefully so as to make as little sound as possible. There was nothing on the back of the dresser. He slid the thing back into place. Then he took out the drawers and looked on their backs and bottoms. He found the bankbook taped to the bottom of the last drawer. He sat on the bed and opened the book, slowly turning the pages and scanning the columns of figures.

Samuel Rossiter, an apparently impoverished man, living in a boarding house of marginal quality, a man who had drunk himself stupid on bootleg liquor before being murdered in Scanlon's Lane, had more than twelve thousand dollars in an account at the Newfoundland Savings Bank on Duckworth Street.

In a society where forty dollars a week was a decent wage, twelve thousand dollars was a small fortune.

Stride lit a cigarette and sat on the bed. He looked through the bankbook a second time, then put it in his pocket and took a final look around the little room. He wondered if there were any more surprises to be found here, but he didn't think so. Apart from ripping the faded wallpaper from the walls and tearing up the floorboards, as Harry had suggested, there wasn't anything else he could do to search the place more thoroughly. He was already satisfied that the bankbook was all there was to find. The rest of Rossiter's possessions, including the books, would now be removed to the storeroom at Fort Townshend, where it would all be itemised, and examined yet again.

Stride tried to imagine what Jimmy Burridge's reaction might have been if he had found the bankbook first. Burridge would have been surprised, certainly, and probably excited. But consternation tipping into fury would have followed almost at once. All that money just sitting there in the bank, the property of an old man who appeared to have no family to leave it to, and no way for Burridge to reach it. It would have enraged him. But Rossiter's money was as remote now to Jimmy Burridge as was personal salvation.

The image of the little man's almost certain frustration caused Stride to smile. He put it down to the fact that he was tired after another long day. He didn't like to think of himself as harbouring a mean streak under his cultured façade. But he knew that was a fragile conceit.

eLeven

When Stride opened the door of his flat, Dianne Borg was standing by the kitchen window looking southeast towards the harbour. Now she leaned against the door frame, her arms crossed over her chest.

"You're home late, but it doesn't look as though you've eaten yet," she said. "Unless you ate out. Did you?"

"No, I didn't." Stride dropped his keys into the small brass bowl on the table by the door. "I found your note this morning."

"Of course you did," she said. "You were meant to."

She moved close to him, touching the lapel of his jacket with her left hand.

"I didn't think you were coming tonight."

"I didn't think so either. But here I am. You are pleased?"

"Yes," he said. "I am pleased."

And he was. He had been thinking about her as he drove home, trying not to anticipate her being with him this evening because he knew he would be disappointed if she wasn't, if she couldn't make it. But now she was here with him. He touched her cheek and then pulled her closer to him, breathing in her scent, his lips brushing hers, moving away, then moving back again. She responded in kind, and they played hide and seek with each other, with their lips, with their feelings, probing and teasing, layering sensation upon small sensation. Dianne called it their mating dance, a gradual circling, moving closer with each pass, each lifting the other onto a higher plane of desire.

Afterwards, they lay together, sharing a cigarette, not speaking, each for the moment spent, comfortable in the silence that followed from the directed frenzy of their lovemaking.

Stride took a last draw from the cigarette and reached across her for the ashtray. She took the cigarette from him, drew on it, then stubbed it out. She placed her hand on his chest then, tugging at the hair, producing a sensation just short of real pain. Her lips followed her fingers, teasing, probing, all the time moving her body closer until she had raised herself over him, smiling, pinning him to the bed, her hands locked in his, capturing his response, enveloping him, slowly setting the rhythm in motion once again.

Much later, they lay together still, drowsy with pleasure, fully sated. It took a while before the world started to slide back into their consciousness.

"I read the article in the evening paper," she said at last. "Will you be busy for a while, or is this one of your lesser cases?"

"We will be very busy. What the newspaper didn't say was that he was murdered. It wasn't an accident."

"He was murdered?" Dianne raised herself on one elbow. "The article in the paper said that he had died after a fall down the steps in the laneway."

"That's all they knew when the article was written. There will be a more complete account in tomorrow's papers. For that matter, it might be on the radio by now. But I don't know, I haven't been listening."

"Do you think it was the two boys who did it, that they murdered the old man? The ones who've run away?"

"No, we don't think so. But we need to question them first, before we let them completely off the hook. I'm keeping an open mind at this point."

"Your famous open mind."

"Yes, my famous open mind." He liked it when she mocked him. She seemed to have known from the beginning just how far she could go without riling him.

"Can you tell me about it?"

"The case? Well, just now there isn't a whole lot to tell. The old man…"

"What's his name? The paper didn't say."

"His name's Samuel Rossiter. The papers will have that too, in tomorrow's editions."

"So his family has been notified?"

"As far as we know he hasn't any family in St. John's. It's possible he hadn't lived here for a while, but we're still looking at that."

"How did it happen?"

"Well, Rossiter was drinking with a friend in Scanlon's Lane, late last night..."

"Probably while we were making love."

"Probably while we were making love. Sometime around midnight his drinking partner went home. A friend, a young man who's a sort of Good Samaritan, picked him up and drove him to the shed on Blackmarsh Road where he lives. And sometime after that, Samuel Rossiter was killed."

"It wasn't a fall like the newspaper said?"

"No. He may have been injured in a fall, but he was also severely beaten. One of the blows he took crushed his windpipe. It might have been intentional. His death was from suffocation."

"Dear God." Dianne closed her eyes for a moment. "That doesn't sound like something a boy would do."

"No, it doesn't. That's one reason we think they weren't involved. But like I say, we're just getting started."

Stride rolled over and reached for another cigarette. He was fully awake now and the other hunger was starting to bite at him. He held out the package of cigarettes for her.

"I'll share yours." She took his cigarette from him. "Can you tell me more about Mr. Samuel Rossiter?"

"There isn't much more to tell. Not yet."

"Alright. You can tell me about the autopsy, then, if you feel like it. You know, I've always wanted to see an autopsy."

"Why am I not surprised? Why do you want to see an autopsy?"

"I don't know. It's just something I've always wanted to do. Well, not always, of course. But for years and years. I'm a curious sort of person. Things like that interest me."

"Yes, you are a curious sort of person."

"But you don't mind, do you? Not really?"

Stride shook his head and touched her hair. She was curious. And different. That was part of the attraction.

"No, I don't mind, but I won't tell you about the autopsy. Anyway, autopsies are not easy to describe. And they take a lot of getting used to."

"Was Harry there? You told me he doesn't like autopsies."

"He doesn't. But he managed this one very well."

"Good for him."

"Yes, very good for him," Stride said.

He drew on the cigarette, then gave it to her again. She took a puff and exhaled the smoke into the hair on his chest. It looked like a small brushfire.

"I'll bet you're starving."

"I'm getting there. But I'm almost too comfortable to move."

"Good. I wanted you to say something like that."

"Yes?"

"Yes."

Dianne moved closer to him, resting her head on his chest. He pulled her closer and stroked her hair, combing it with his fingers. She had told him she liked it when he did that.

She hadn't said how late she could stay. He had been surprised, and pleased, to find her in his flat when he got home. He was relaxed now, almost beyond measure, all of the tension of the day drained out of him.

"I really will need to eat soon," he said.

She smiled at him and drew on the cigarette again.

"I imagine you do," she said. "I ate earlier, before I came over. I had called but you weren't in, so I had something, and I'm not really very hungry. Well, even if I was, I can't stay too much longer."

"No?"

She shook her head, looked wistful for an instant, but quickly recaptured the good humour that seemed to define her. That was another part of the attraction, a pleasing contrast to his own shifting moods.

"When I wrote you that note this morning, I really didn't think I would be able to come. I wanted to, but I didn't think it was likely."

"But here you are."

"Yes, here I am. And we're both happy, right?" He nodded. But she wasn't looking at him now. She stroked his arm with her fingertips. "When I left here this morning, I thought Marty would be back late this afternoon. That was the original plan. But he rang me from Stephenville, from Harmon Field, to say that he had another meeting and wouldn't get in until late tonight. Around midnight, he said."

"I see." It was all he could think to say.

"It might be a while before we can see each other again. Like this, I mean."

"I know." The words came out with greater emphasis than he had intended.

"I don't like it either, Eric. But it's the way it is." She was looking at him now. "Do you sometimes wish we hadn't started this?"

"Do you?"

She laughed. "You're such a policeman. As often as not you answer a question with a question." Then she was serious again. "Yes, sometimes I wish we hadn't started this. It's hard, and sometimes it's too hard, when we can't be together, when we have to be apart. Do you feel that?"

"Yes. Of course I feel that sometimes, that it's too hard. And, yes, sometimes I wish we hadn't started it."

"But that doesn't mean that you want it to stop, does it?"

"No," he said. "That doesn't mean I want it to stop."

Why did she have to be married? It wasn't the first thought he'd had after he met her, but it was the thought that came back to him again and again, pinballing around inside his head until sometimes his brain ached.

They had met two months ago, in June, at a soiree at Hercules Parsons' studio. Parsons had invited a group of friends and admirers to view his latest canvases. When Stride was last at the studio, there were eleven new paintings in all, but on that evening there were twelve, an even dozen.

"I dislike odd numbers," Parsons said when he saw that Stride was counting them.

"So you did a twelfth, just to even things out."

Parsons laughed and held up his hands. "I confess. There were three in progress when you were here that afternoon. The day I did the sketches for you of the unfortunate Ambrose White. At the time I had thought I wouldn't finish them before my trip to New York. But then the inevitable happened. The unfinished canvases began to woo me in the night when I was sleeping. The time of least resistance. Sleep can be tyranny of the very worst kind. All manner of suggestions can wriggle into the undefended mind and create absolute havoc. But I think you already know that, my dear."

"Too well."

"Indeed. Anyway, I began to find myself up and at it in the wee hours, labouring away at the twelfth. But it became a labour of love in the end, as it usually does, and I'm really quite pleased with it." He looked inquiringly at Stride. "Do you know which one it is? Think carefully, now, my dear. This is a test of your devotion to my craft and my art."

Stride looked at each of the twelve paintings in turn, taking his time. But he was doing this for Parsons' benefit. He already knew which one was the twelfth.

"It's the one in the centre, with the upturned dory."

"Very good, Eric. I am pleased with you."

Even if he hadn't remembered the original eleven, he would have picked this one anyway. There was something different about it, an element lacking in the others. There appeared to be a skull, almost, but not quite concealed by the tall grasses growing on the shore. Parsons didn't often include animate objects in his paintings, unless it was a commissioned portrait. He preferred to stay with structures, and he somehow managed to imbue them with a sense of their makers, displaying the touch, but not the hand. It was something he did very well. The skull, if that's what it was, was indistinct, but a presence nonetheless. Its nature also wasn't clear. Stride couldn't tell if it might be human or animal.

"Is that a skull, in the grass there? To the left of the boat?"

"You know, it might be. I'm not entirely certain myself."

"A ghost in the night?"

"You know, that might be it. I had a sense of something when whatever-it-was wrenched me from my sleep." Parsons was studying his own work now, almost as though he was seeing it for the first time. "I'm not really sure what I was trying to do there. The something I sensed was indistinct, and I pursued it as far as I could. And that," he gestured grandly, "is what came of it. The question, of course, is what will become of it." Suddenly he slapped Stride on the shoulder and laughed again. "I do go on, do I not? And it's mostly a lot of self-absorbed twaddle. Lord knows you are familiar enough with that. But come with me, dear boy. I want you to meet someone."

The someone was Dianne Borg. Stride had seen her when he came into the studio, a slender woman with short blonde hair and a confident, even determined, expression, but one that was flecked with humour. Stride guessed she was in her late twenties. She was sitting with a man who appeared to be in his middle fifties, a man of middle height, middle weight, middle-everything, Stride thought. He was smoking a cigarette in a deliberate, almost theatrical way, alternately taking puffs, exhaling carefully to the side, away from her, and then pushing his glasses back against the bridge of his nose with the middle finger of his free hand. It was a practised gesture, a social affect, and Stride thought it was very irritating. He had met the man before, he was sure of that, but he couldn't remember his name. He thought he probably worked for the government in some dull grey capacity, just beyond the public view.

Dianne had noticed Stride also. He could see that. Most of the people in the studio were paired, or coupled. Most of them, he knew, were married. Technically, at the time, Stride himself was coupled – a term that made him twitch – but Margaret Nichol was not with him this night. Things had been going not well between them for some time, a natural drift that had gathered momentum and more than a trace of menace, during and after the Taylor case in the spring. Although Margaret liked Hercules Parsons, and he her, she had declined to attend this particular evening, a decision they each gave too much weight. It didn't have to mean anything, but it did, and they both knew it, and it quickly grew in size and gravity in the weeks that followed.

Then, one evening not long after that, after a dinner at his flat, she told him that she had applied for a position at a music school in Bristol and had been accepted. It had been a surprise, a shock in fact. But there was also relief, even if he didn't say it. He really didn't need to. She knew him well enough to know that if he wasn't actually chafing in the relationship, he was growing edgy, shaving small thin strips from their intimacy, and sending unspoken messages that he could never articulate.

His immediate response to Margaret's news that night was to say that there was a symmetry to it, that after all, Bristol was where it had all started. It took her a moment to assess the comment, and then to realise that he was making an absurd reference to the island's history, Bristol being the port John Cabot had sailed from, to Newfoundland, exactly four-and-a-half centuries earlier on his voyage of discovery. And having deciphered it, she had laughed, they both had. But then the laughter faded.

Herc's fondness for Margaret, and his often-expressed opinion that Margaret was good for Stride, didn't stop him from loosing his inner Puck on this night. This was a quality of his that was sometimes charming, occasionally irritating, and once in a while destructive, although usually to Parsons himself. Stride wasn't sure which descriptive was appropriate for this evening, but he was pleased to meet Dianne Borg anyway. The poseur with the strategic cigarette and the sliding eyeglasses pretended not to be annoyed when Parsons introduced Stride to Dianne, although he clearly was. He lit a second cigarette from the not-quite-fully-smoked end of the first and wandered away to join a group on the far side of the room, where he was greeted with politeness of the diluted kind.

After the introductions, Parsons, alluring after his fashion in a colourful caftan that too often revealed the fact that he was wearing no underwear, scampered off to stir the social pot elsewhere.

Stride and Dianne Borg moved in the direction of the kitchen to replenish their wineglasses, and to distance themselves from the rattle of conversation. He had already noticed the wedding ring and wondered vaguely what Parsons was up to, if anything.

"I take it you and Herc are friends," she said.

"Yes, we are. And you?"

"Sort of friends. But I got to know him when I signed up for some art classes."

"With Herc? I wasn't aware that he gave classes."

"Well, he doesn't as a rule. And that begs a story, doesn't it? I first met him in New York City, if you can believe it. A year ago. I suppose, if you're friends, you know that he lives there about half the year."

"Yes, of course."

"Well, I was there, visiting, on a sort of holiday." She paused, twisting the gold band around her finger, looking past him. "My husband and I were there on a sort of holiday. In New York. The art scene was just picking up steam again after the war, and Hercules Parsons was having a show. It seemed so bizarre that an artist from Newfoundland was having a show in New York City then, even if it was only a small one. Well, of course we went. What else could we do, after all? It seemed providential somehow. Anyway, that's how I met him."

Stride smiled and looked back towards the main room.

"He isn't here," she said. "He's out of town just now." When Stride looked back at her, she was smiling. "That was a little embarrassing, wasn't it?"

"My looking for your husband, or your reluctant explanation?"

"Both, I think."

"Yes, I suppose it was. You're from here, aren't you? From St. John's?"

"In spite of the name, you mean?"

"In spite of the name."

"Yes, I am. St. John's born and ill-bred."

"It doesn't show," he said. "The ill-bred part."

"I was fishing for a compliment."

"I know you were. But I think there's a moratorium on that just now. Fishing for compliments."

"Proper thing, too. The stock could become dangerously depleted. But to answer your non-question, my husband's an American. Captain Martin Borg, United States Army. Marty's from Wisconsin, originally, actually a little place almost on the border between Wisconsin and Minnesota. There are a lot of Swedes in those parts."

"Yes, I know."

"We met when he was stationed at Fort Pepperell, of course."

"I assumed so. So you did grow up in St. John's?"

"Yes. We lived not very far from here in fact. My father works for the Hurdles. Hurdle and Company Limited, on Water Street."

"He keeps good company, so to speak."

"He always thought so. And now it's my turn to be curious. How do you know Hercules Parsons?"

"We met a long time ago, back in the thirties, before the war. Not long after I joined the Constabulary."

"You're a policeman?"

"Yes."

"I was about to repeat your line, that it doesn't show. But actually it does. You have the sharp, inquiring look."

"And I didn't even have to go fishing."

"No, you didn't. And it was meant as a compliment. Truly." She touched his arm. "You do believe me?"

"Yes, I do believe you." He affected a theatrical bow. "And thank you."

"So it's more than ten years now? That you've known him?"

"I suppose it has been that long. There was a break-in at his flat one night. I was on duty and his place was on my beat."

"You were in uniform then?"

"Yes, I was. Everyone starts in uniform and works his way up the ranks. Why do you ask?"

Dianne Borg gave him an appraising look.

"I was wondering if that was the attraction. The uniform?" Her eyes were bright as she took in the flicker of surprise. "Well, I know that Hercules is attracted to young men in uniform. Were you one of them?"

"You know, I think that probably was the case."

It was her turn to look surprised, but only for a moment.

"I expect you looked quite alright in your uniform."

"Uniforms do have their attraction."

She laughed. "I will concede that one. Touché."

"I just got lucky. In my case, though, it was entirely one-sided. We really are just good friends."

"I assumed so. And you don't mind? A lot of men do, you know."

"Yes, most men do." He looked into the larger room. For no reason that was immediately clear, Parsons was effecting some kind of a dance with a pillow, the caftan swirling around his thighs, while a semicircle of people looked on with amused approval. "No, I don't mind. Herc made a polite overture, and offered me a drink. I politely declined the overture, but told him I'd come back for the drink sometime when I wasn't on duty. We've been friends ever since." He offered her a cigarette and she took one. She reached into her purse for her lighter. "So you're here alone tonight?"

"Not exactly. I came with a girlfriend, but she's already taken off with a nice young man who claimed to be a poet. I imagine they're off in his car some-place, frantically rhyming couplets."

"Very probably."

"She wasn't really interested in the paintings, but when I told her there might be exotic people here, and that the drinks were probably free, well, she came along in a flash."

"Art is important."

"I've always thought so. And it doesn't hurt if the drinks are on the house."

"It's said that alcohol sharpens the senses."

"It certainly does for me. Right up to the moment I fall flat on my face and people point and stare."

"I do know that feeling."

"Do you? Or are you just being nice again?"

"A bit of both. But I have fallen on my face more than a few times."

"Lately?"

He looked at her, wondering about the question, the earlier momentary evasion about her husband, and the sense that something was happening between them.

"Perhaps," he said. "I'm not sure."

"Is that why you're here alone?"

"Maybe." He looked into the larger room again. Parsons' frantic dance had ended. "Yes, that is why I'm here alone."

She started to say something but turned away and reached for a bottle of wine. She filled both their glasses. And the thought came to him, unbidden, that she knew something about him. It was possible. More than possible, in fact. Hercules Parsons wasn't a gossip, but he liked to chatter, so it amounted to the same thing in the end. The way he described it was that he thought out loud, especially when he was working. And he had worked with Dianne Borg as her teacher, probably thinking out loud, his mind skipping across a range of subjects, like a flat stone on still water, expertly tossed. There wasn't any malice in him, not really, but he had an irresistible penchant for drama, or comedy-drama – it was the way he lived his life. He thrived on emotional chaos, it seemed to fuel his creative drive, and he often was unable to imagine that others did not live the same way, or if they didn't, would not happily embrace the opportunity. It was possible, probable even that he hadn't thought anything through, but that he had sensed the possibilities inherent in a meeting between Stride and Dianne Borg.

And that raised the complementary question. Parsons knew that Stride and Margaret Nichol were stumbling in their relationship. Perhaps he also knew that Dianne and Martin Borg were in a similar situation, and he was acting on that knowledge in his bizarre way.

Stride sipped his wine and let the thoughts and conjectures run through his mind. Dianne Borg was sipping her wine, not looking at him now. Their conversation had flagged for the moment. They had said too much, and at the same time not enough. He didn't know where to go with this now. He already knew he was attracted to her, wanted to say more, or at least did not want their conversation to end, forcing him wander off to try and make conversation with someone else, like the unfortunate man with the migratory spectacles. As it turned out, he didn't have to. She made the decision for him, for them, with the kind of determination that he was too often incapable of, and which he found, and would continue to find, irresistible.

"He isn't out of town." She was looking directly at him now. "My husband. He's just not here."

"Does that happen a lot?"

"Lately, yes."

"I see."

"Yes," she said. "I think you probably do."

And that was how it had started.

twelve

Alex Greene helped Bride Pollard clear up after dinner. He washed and she dried, the old routine they had established years before. Alex didn't like drying dishes, but washing brought him an odd satisfaction. He liked seeing the grimy cups, glasses, plates, and utensils come clean under his touch. He believed this peculiar pleasure probably had something to do with his lifestyle. If he often could not care properly for himself and just as often felt bad about it, he could at least occasionally absolve himself by doing mundane tasks like this.

Alex's Aunt Bridget sat at the kitchen table alternating between sips of hot tea and cold, dry sherry while they worked at the sink. It was pleasant in the kitchen, homey. The lamb – and Norman was right, it was closer to lamb than mutton – had been superb. Bride's cooking was on par with her bread-making, and she did lamb especially well, prepping it with a marinade of her own creation, then roasting it slowly under a low heat, basting frequently to keep the meat moist and flavourful.

"Will you stay the night, Alex, or are you going back to your flat?"

He turned and looked at his aunt but didn't answer right away. He wasn't sure what he was going to do, hadn't really thought it through. More correctly, he had been avoiding thinking about it. Now he had to, but he decided he would waffle as much as he could, although she had only asked where he would spend the night. He slept at his flat most evenings, but stayed at the house at least once a week, sleeping in his old room at the back. The house on Battery Road held mostly good memories for him and it was more comfortable than his flat on Duckworth Street, where the sounds of the city invaded until late into the night. Here, far away from the main part of St. John's, and close to the ocean, the house was secluded and quiet. Often, when he lay awake in his bed, he could hear the sound of the sea, the water caressing the rock faces that defined the harbour.

But he did have to go out this evening, at least for a while. That was already decided. He sneaked a glance at the clock on the wall. He still had some thirty minutes, so he needn't hurry. He finished the last pieces of cutlery and dropped them in the dish drainer for Bride to attend to. Then he took a cup-towel from the handle of the oven door and dried his hands. He sat at the table across from Bridget and picked up the sherry bottle. The glass was damp with condensation and the label puckered at the margins. Bridget liked her sherry cold and kept the bottle in the fridge. Alex poured some of the sherry into a glass. He needed a drink, but he didn't feel comfortable just now getting himself something stronger. The sherry would have to do. He sipped it slowly, fighting the impulse to toss it all back at once.

He looked at his aunt, and felt the sadness creep over him again. There was something wrong with her, seriously wrong, he was sure of that. He looked away from her, towards the sink. Bride was finishing the last of the dishes, sliding the cutlery into their places in the drawer. She caught his look of worry and shook her head. That small admonitory movement told him more than he wanted to know. He pushed away his concerns and focused all of his attention on Bridget. She was looking weary, but not unhappy. With her glass of cold Spanish sherry and her cup of tea she looked very comfortable in fact. Although she had the same distant look in her eye that he had seen more and more often lately. He called it her summing-up look, and while it was not unexpected it was inevitably, almost unbearably, sad.

"I was looking through some of the old albums this afternoon," she said. "Some of them go back a long way, Alex, to when you were just a baby."

"Oh, dear," he said. "I wasn't such a pretty baby, was I?"

"No, you were not, poor dear, but it doesn't matter if babies are pretty. They only have to be healthy. That's enough to ask for."

Bride came over to the table. She was carrying the teapot. "There's still another cup in the pot, Bridget, if you would like it."

"I'll have it then. Unless you want it, Bride."

Bride shook her head and poured the tea into Bridget's cup.

"I'm really feeling very good, just now," she said. "The dinner was lovely and I do like a glass of sherry with my tea. I could say I am feeling quite sufficed. That's what papa used to say after a good dinner. Sufficiently sufficed, he would say. Poor papa." She drifted away for a moment, her features softening in the embrace of memory. Then she was back again. "One of the albums I was looking at was from your time at Haleybury, Alex."

"Good old Haleybury," he said. He picked up his glass and took another taste.

"You didn't say that at the beginning, did you? It wasn't good old Haleybury, then. But it was a shock for you, I know, going off to a school in a strange town, in another country even. At the time you hadn't even been off the island yet, and suddenly there you were in New Hampshire all on your own. But you did alright, didn't you?"

"It was an enlarging experience, as Aunt Helena liked to say."

Bridget laughed. "She did say that, didn't she? I had forgotten." And then she looked sad again for a moment. She drank some of the fresh, hot tea. It lifted her spirits again. "That man at Haleybury, the one you didn't like, what was his name? The one who claimed to be an Englishman, but wasn't?"

"Pendleton," Alex said. "James Pendleton. At least he claimed that was his name. Some of us used to say that his real name was Bill Smith and he was from Podunk, Idaho. We liked to say that he had renamed himself James Pendleton and affected an accent, which, if it wasn't exactly British, at least wasn't obviously American. Odd how some Americans like to be thought of as Brits. I've run into that more than once over the years. In their starred and striped hearts, I believe a lot of them hold a secret nostalgia for the royal connection."

James Pendleton had been a mystery to the boys and young men at Haleybury School. Pendleton was just shy, in Alex's opinion, of being a comic figure, a cardboard cut-out. He told each new class he taught that he had been a member of the Guards, but it was never made clear just who the Guards were. No one dared ask, and Pendleton never offered. The inference was, of course, that he had belonged to some sort of gallant outfit that served the British Crown, possibly the Royal Horse Guards, the Blues. Alex thought Pendleton was a charlatan, a native-born American, perhaps even a Canadian, who affected a British accent and postured in a fine family background that was entirely of his own invention.

But there were always rumours at Haleybury about teachers that no one liked, or that the students were especially afraid of. Almost anything was possible in the enclosed and autocratic environment of Haleybury School. The place had, Alex always thought, an incestuous atmosphere, something like that which must have existed in the palaces of ancient Egypt where brothers mated with sisters to maintain and purify the regal line, only to end up with a declining string of fragile rulers, deformed imbeciles some of them, who finally vanished into the vast Saharan dust.

Pendleton was no imbecile though. Mean and nasty, certainly, but almost as sharp as the blade he claimed to have carried in the service of his supposed monarch. The Beau James, as he was sometimes called, had taken a particular dislike to Alex Greene over the several years of their acquaintance. Alex thought that it had less to do with his coming from a place in the lower world, Newfoundland, than Pendleton's concern that Alex might have known enough real Englishmen well enough to enable him to penetrate the fraud Pendleton was perpetrating. That never stopped him from giving Alex a dressing-down whenever he had the opportunity, but he was always careful not to go too far.

Over the years it became something like a fencing match. Pendleton employed just enough calculated aggression to ensure that Greene was off balance and under some duress, but never so much that Alex might lodge a complaint with the board of directors who ultimately ran the school. A formal complaint would necessarily be pressed forward by attorneys on both sides, to Pendleton's disadvantage and possible undoing. By dint of his being at Haleybury, it was a certainty that Greene had financial resources that someone like Pendleton could only dream about. And Alex knew that. He had learned a thing or two over the years.

Fascism with a feather's touch was how he described Pendleton's attitude towards him. But there was a power balance here, and Alex had learned to respond to Pendleton's feints with fairly graceful moves of his own. So he was always deferential and polite.

Their difficult relationship had come to a kind of head towards the end of Alex's tenure at Haleybury. The caretaker at the school had been accused by one of the students, an especially unpleasant and spoiled young shit named

Kennady, the third generation of his line to attend Haleybury, of stealing money from a locker. Alex, like most of the students, knew that it wasn't true, that Kennady had made it up for reasons best known to himself. But as it was his last year at the school, Alex didn't care that his blowing the whistle on Kennady, telling the truth about the fraud, would estrange him from at least part of the student body, and would also cause him some difficulty with the teaching staff. Honesty and democratic principles were taught at Haleybury, of course, and they were deemed alright in their place, but they didn't extend to taking the side of a caretaker, one of the semi-articulate low-born, to the disadvantage of the son of one of the school's wealthy patrons.

In the wake of Greene's intervention, Alex had been summoned to James Pendleton's study yet one more time.

"You're very much an outsider, here, Greene. You're only the second boy the school has ever accepted from Newfoundland," – he mispronounced the name NewFOUNDland, the way most Americans did – "and I have sometimes wondered if you've properly understood the privilege you were granted by being accepted here? And I am wondering that again now."

"I understand that, sir. And I am very pleased to be a student here. I know for a fact that it will give me a leg up on life."

Greene's response, carefully worded, was ambiguous enough to cause Pendleton to start just a little. Getting a leg up was a popular Haleybury euphemism among the boys for taking a piss. Greene was certain Pendleton knew that, but it was also a phrase that had no currency between students and faculty. There were rules about that sort of thing.

"Yes," Pendleton said, a little off balance now. "But you know it wasn't good form to have pointed the finger at Kennady. His family is well thought of, and they are one of the most generous patrons of Haleybury. But we'll keep it quiet, of course. There will be no paper record of this sorry affair."

"I was concerned for the caretaker, sir. As I knew for a fact that he hadn't taken the money, I couldn't really stand by and see him punished wrongly. A gentleman could not do that."

"Your concern for the working class is noted, Greene. Some might actually consider it admirable. But we have our own ways of dealing with these things, without embarrassing a young man from a good family." Pendleton paused for effect, walked over to the window, and stood there for a few moments, looking out. Then he turned back to face Greene. "The caretaker, of course, will have to be moved along. We've found a position for him at the hospital in Seaward. Same sort of duties, similar pay. You understand, of course, that there was no possibility of his staying on here as a constant reminder of a student's unfortunate indiscretion."

Pendleton looked at Greene, as if challenging him to reply, to protest even. Alex knew it wasn't worth his while. It was the system. For a caretaker, or anyone else in a low social position, there literally was no way out of this sort of situation. Alex knew that before he pointed the finger at Kennady. He knew the caretaker would be moved along, as Pendleton discreetly put it. But he also knew that there would be no police involvement, and that the school would be obliged to find the man another job, or at least not set up barriers to his finding one on his own.

"I wonder what might have happened to that Pendleton person," Bridget said. "A man like that, living a pretence. It isn't much to go on, in the final analysis, is it? I suppose he was too young for the First War and too old for the last one, so he probably didn't have an opportunity to prove himself in the real world."

"I don't think so, Auntie, no. I'm not sure he would have wanted to. Pendleton wasn't the sort to put himself in any real danger."

"Well, he didn't mind having an altercation with you. That thing about the caretaker."

"It wasn't really an altercation, Auntie. Pendleton gave me a lecture about behaving in a manner suitable to my station. Something like that. I didn't pay a lot of attention, although I pretended to."

"Well, we thought you did well, Alex. It was strange, though, wasn't it, about the caretaker, the poor man having been a Newfoundlander like yourself? And you taking his side against the lot of them?"

"I suppose you could say it was strange, but I've found there are Newfoundlanders all over the place, in the States and Canada both."

Bride Pollard laughed. "Next to codfish, people are our best export. I don't know how many young women have married Americans, even Canadians, and moved away to live. I tell anyone who mentions it that it's our secret agenda, that we're moving out to take over the world."

"Somebody should," Alex said. "The world needs taking over."

"I'm trying to think of his name," Bridget said.

"Whose name, Auntie?"

"The caretaker. That poor man who lost his job at Haleybury. I know you told me his name at the time."

Alex picked up his glass of sherry and stared into the pale, straw-coloured liquid.

"Howell," he said. "His name was Wesley Howell."

"Oh, yes, of course. And you did tell me that Mr. Howell had a little boy? A son?"

"Yes, he did, Auntie. He did have a son."

"I thought so." She looked triumphant. "You see, I can still remember a few things."

"Yes," Alex said. "Of course you can."

He picked up his glass again, and this time he drank off the rest of his sherry.

thiRteEn

Clara Jones pulled the heavy drapes across the front windows. She stepped back and looked at them, then leaned forward and tucked one leading edge under the other. Now the world outside was completely excluded. She walked back to the kitchen, took off her apron, and hung it on a hook near the back door. Then she opened the door to allow the cooler night air to flow into the kitchen, still warm from the cooking of dinner.

The evening paper lay on the counter, folded so that the front-page article describing the death of the old man in Scanlon's Lane was on display. She glanced at it again, running her eye down the column. She lingered on the paragraph that suggested the death was an unfortunate accident, that the man was knocked down the steps by two boys running away from a policeman after an act of vandalism. The article concluded with a homily about the decline of standards and values among the young, especially regrettable so soon after the great sacrifices of their elders that had brought a glorious conclusion to the recent world war against the forces of international evil.

Elizabeth Cooke came into the kitchen. She glanced at the paper but didn't pick it up. Like Clara, she had already read the article.

"I would like a drink," she said. "Don't spare the whisky, and easy on the soda."

"Yes, alright. I'll have one too."

Clara went to the liquor cabinet and came back with a bottle of Scotch. It bore the label, Cragganmore, a single malt from a small distillery in Speyside. The whisky had been the favourite of Elizabeth's father. He liked his Scotch with a small amount of water – just a drop to bring out the flavour he liked to say. But Elizabeth, and Clara too, had always preferred it with a splash of soda. Clara poured generous quantities into two heavy crystal glasses, part of a set that had been in Elizabeth's family for more than a century. She added soda from a siphon-bottle and gave one of the glasses to Elizabeth. Clara picked up her own glass and cradled it in her hands.

"Poor Sam," she said.

"Yes, poor Sam. But what's done, is done."

But then she laughed. Clara looked at her, and she laughed too.

"I know what you're laughing at. You're thinking about Jimmy Burridge having to make the identification at the General, aren't you?"

"Yes, I am. It's not the sort of thing he would enjoy at all, poor little man. I can see him standing there, all atremble, looking down at Sam's body lying on a table. Poor man. He must have been terribly uncomfortable ."

"I won't lose any sleep worrying about James Burridge's comfort," Clara said. "Or his discomfort."

"And I won't either."

"How do you feel about it, Liza? Sam being killed like that, alone and frightened in a laneway?"

"I don't know exactly how I feel about it. It might take a while to get used to it. But he is dead, and that can't be changed. And it's not as though we were really close any longer. After all, until he came back here last summer, we hadn't seen him in years." She looked at Clara. "I can't even remember now, how many years it was. Can you?"

Clara closed her eyes for a moment, thinking. "It must have been three or four years, at least. I think it was four years, on one of those quick visits he made to St. John's."

"Yes, I think you're right."

"There will be an investigation, of course, and I think we have to accept that the police eventually will find their way here. Even if it takes them a while to make the connection."

"I know," Elizabeth said. "I don't think we can count on their charging the two boys with his death." She looked towards the counter where the newspaper still lay, folded open to the article. "Hubert didn't phone?"

"No, he didn't. And I was here all day. Do you think he will?"

"Hubert will do what he will do. I won't be surprised if he calls later on. Or just as likely, if he shows up here unannounced."

"You could call him."

"I could. But I think I'll wait. If the two boys really are charged, then we might not hear anything more about it."

"And that might be the end of it. *Requiescat in pace.*"

"We can hope." She was silent again, thinking. "You know I half expected Sam would come and see us again. Although I'm just as happy he didn't."

"Much happier."

"Yes, alright, much happier. He had changed so much. Not just that he was older, but he wasn't the same person we knew in the old days. Not even the same person from four years ago. He rambled so much. Some of what he said made no sense to me at all. It was obvious he wasn't well, even if he didn't say so. And he was so shabby. Sam used to be fastidious about his appearance, a bit of a dandy even. It was so sad to see him looking the way he did. I felt ashamed for him."

"But more uncomfortable than ashamed."

"Yes, you're right. I won't pretend. He did make me uncomfortable. If his mind really was wandering, there's no telling what he might have said, or done."

"And he'd been drinking. That was plain enough."

"I thought that, too, but I wasn't really sure. I wondered if it was something else. That he really was very ill and it affected him somehow, made it seem as though he'd been drinking."

"He had been drinking, Liza. I didn't tell you this at the time, but he helped himself to the Cragganmore when he thought I wasn't looking. You were in the study, and I was in the kitchen making tea. He took a flask out of his pocket and he filled it. I watched him. I didn't say anything. I just let him do it."

"You didn't tell me that. Oh, dear. Sam Rossiter stealing whisky. And he had a flask?"

"Yes. It looked like one your father owned. The silver flask he sometimes carried with him when he travelled?"

"I remember that flask. Mummy gave it to him for his birthday. I was just a little girl then." She picked up her drink, but put it down at once, as though the thought of her father's flask and Sam Rossiter stealing whisky from them had taken away some of the joy of it. She was silent for a moment. "Well, I suppose I don't mind. If it brought him some pleasure at the time, I don't mind, not really." She picked up her glass again and drank what was left. "I think I would like another drink, Clara."

"In a little while," Clara said. "Wait a little while."

"Yes, alright. I will wait."

They sat together quietly, not speaking. The air in the kitchen was cooler now.

fourteen

Harry had told Stride he thought George Butters looked something like a pouter pigeon, and had the mannerisms that matched. As usual, Harry had it just about spot-on.

Butters was not very tall, but his erect stance seemed to lift him a good three inches off the floor. He wore a three-piece suit with a four-button vest that gave a sleekness to his torso that otherwise would not have been there. He moved gracefully from behind his desk, seeming almost to glide across the floor. He shook hands with Stride, and raised a delicate right hand to point the way to a chair set in front of his desk. He seated himself behind his desk and smiled. His manner was slightly imperious, his chin raised high, reminding Stride of actors who played the butler in American films, imagining they were capturing the essence of upper-class British society. It took Stride a moment to understand that the raised chin was effected to enhance Butters' profile, while at the same time camouflaging an opulent second chin. He imagined the man practising in front of a full-length mirror, rehearsing carefully, striving to get it just right.

There was a single file on the green desk blotter. There was a photograph of a woman and two children, strategically angled for the visitor to observe. One of the children, a boy of about ten, looked alarmingly like his father in miniature, an embryonic banker almost certainly.

Butters pulled open a desk drawer and took out the morning newspaper, folded so that an article, circled darkly, was on display. He placed it on the side of his desk, glanced at it briefly, then rested his soft hands on top of the unopened file. There was a large ring on the fifth finger of his right hand, a gold ring with a reddish insignia of some kind. Stride focused his gaze and saw that it was the Masonic crest. He was surprised Harry had not mentioned that.

"You were inquiring about one of our depositors. A Mr. Samuel Rossiter. Who is, unhappily, now deceased."

"Yes, he is." Stride said.

Butters glanced at the newspaper again.

"An unfortunate accident, so the paper tells me?"

"The article you have is out of date, Mr. Butters. It must have been put together before they received the latest information from Fort Townshend."

"Yes?" For the first time, the bank manager's structured poise faltered, if only slightly.

"Mr. Rossiter's death was not accidental. He was murdered."

The news had the effect Stride hoped it would. Butters sat back in his chair, his poise falling completely away. His second chin, so carefully tended until now, lost its competition with gravity and sagged over his collar. Part of his necktie vanished under the drape of soft pink flesh.

"Dear God," he said. He looked at Stride from across his desk, blinking rapidly. It took him a few moments to regain some control. "Murder." The word did not sit comfortably on his palate.

"Yes, I'm afraid so," Stride said.

"Was it the two boys, do you think? There were two boys mentioned in the article. Are they the ones who did it?"

"The case is still under investigation, Mr. Butters. I can't say more than that right now."

"No, I suppose not." He shook his head slowly back and forth and wedged a finger under his collar. He put the newspaper back in the drawer and slid it shut. "What an awful business. Mr. Rossiter was an old man."

"Yes, it is awful," Stride said. Butters tried on a smile. Stride waited a moment longer, then held up the bankbook he had found in Rossiter's room. "Mr. Rossiter had an account here at the bank. According to this deposit book, the account stood at just over twelve thousand dollars two weeks ago. That's a lot of money. A very great deal of money, considering Mr. Rossiter's general appearance, and his place of residence."

"Yes, indeed it is." Butters reached across the desk. "May I see that, please?" Stride gave him the book and Butters took a minute to go through it, page by careful page. "Yes, it is a very substantial amount of money. You've probably seen from the bankbook that the account was opened just over a year ago. And I note that it has not been updated recently."

"No? Is there more or less money in the account now than the book indicates?"

"More," Butters said. "Not a lot more. Just several hundred dollars."

"If the book hasn't been updated, am I correct in assuming that Mr. Rossiter didn't make the most recent deposit himself?"

Butters hesitated for only a moment. Then he nodded. "That is correct. In fact, Mr. Rossiter didn't make any deposits to this account." He hesitated again. "This is a tricky business, you understand, Inspector Stride. Banking information is confidential."

"I'm aware of that. If it will make you more comfortable, sir, I will obtain a warrant empowering you to release the information."

"Yes. I would like to have such a warrant on file. Just in case. Although it's not likely that anyone will make an issue of it."

"But you would like to have the paper."

"Yes, please. I would appreciate that. For our records, you understand. In the meantime, though, I don't mind giving you what information I have. It is a murder investigation after all, and I don't want to delay you on a formality."

"I will have the warrant delivered to you later today."

"Thank you."

"Let's go back to the start," Stride said. "Rossiter appears to have been living in St. John's for about a year. It would also appear from this account book that the account was opened at that time."

"Yes, it was. Until then, Mr. Rossiter did not have an account with this bank. And I have checked our records. This is his first account with us. And the records, I can tell you, go back for decades, extending even to the period before the bank crash of 1894."

"So the money in his account was transferred here from another bank?"

"No, not exactly. The money was deposited by a law firm here in the city."

"A law firm?"

"Yes. The firm owned by Mr. Lawrence Jeffrey. I imagine you know him?"

"I know the name, but I've not had occasion to deal with the firm. They don't handle criminal cases."

"No, you're quite right about that, they don't do criminal law. Jeffrey's father handled criminal cases, but that was years ago. Before your time, I expect."

"Yes, it was. Can you tell me where Mr. Rossiter's money came from, originally? Before it was deposited here?"

Butters shook his head. "I can't tell you that. And not because I don't want to. The fact is, I don't know. It may have come from another bank in the city, or from somewhere else entirely. You would have to ask the lawyers about that. All of my involvement with Mr. Rossiter was through Mr. Jeffrey's firm. Very much at arm's length, as the saying goes. Mr. Jeffrey is an accommodating man, very pleasant, but you will almost certainly need a warrant, or a court order, to obtain that information from him. I would say that it is a certainty. At his end of things, there are other people involved. You will understand that he would have to be very circumspect. And I would appreciate it if you did not contact Mr. Jeffrey using the information I have given you, until you have the necessary warrant. You do understand that he might not be happy that I have been as candid with you as I have been."

"Yes, I understand that," Stride said. "I will respect your wishes on that." He made a note in his book. "You said 'deposits.' Were there regular deposits to the account? Was Rossiter receiving a pension of some sort?"

"It was a regular income and the deposits were made monthly, but I don't know if it was a pension or not. In fact, I'm afraid I don't know where the money originated. We received a deposit each month from the lawyers. It was five hundred dollars, deposited twelve times a year on the first day of each month. But as to where it came from originally, I have no idea."

"So it might have come from an annuity, or from investments managed by Mr. Jeffrey's firm."

"Either of those is a possibility." Butters hesitated for a moment. "You understand that I have to be careful what I say, especially in a situation like this. A homicide." Butters coughed then, as though the word had pinched his throat. "Pardon me. This is a very unusual situation, I'm sure you will agree. Absolutely unique to my experience, and I have been in the banking business for almost twenty years. Mr. Jeffrey's firm is well-established. His grandfather started the firm some eighty years ago and his father carried on, as the present Mr. Jeffrey has also. I'm not aware, though, that they are active in financial matters. It's not really what they do. There are some firms who are, of course." Now that the discussion had moved beyond the walls of the Savings Bank, Butters was more at ease. "You will want to have a talk with Mr. Jeffrey himself. He should be able to help you. But as I suggested, you will probably need a court order to have the information released." Butters held up his hand in a cautionary gesture. "That's assuming he has the information."

"You're suggesting that he also might not know where the money comes from? That he's only the middleman?"

"That is entirely possible. More than possible, I would say. As I said, I have been in this business for almost twenty years now, Inspector Stride, and I have seen more variations on financial matters than I can easily enumerate. I should probably write a book." He managed a conspiratorial smile. "I imagine, though, more than one has already been written. Where money is involved, people can be very creative. But in your experience and line of work, you probably know quite a lot about that."

"Yes." Stride attempted to read something more into Butters' expression, but found nothing there. "What happens now that Mr. Rossiter is deceased? I assume the monthly deposits will end?"

"Yes, they will." Butters opened the file, put on his glasses, and scanned the top page. "In the event of Mr. Rossiter's demise, and the receipt of said information by Mr. Jeffrey's firm, the monthly deposits will cease, and the balance of the account, if any, will be returned to said firm." Butters took off his glasses. "That isn't exactly word-for-word, but that is the essence of it."

"Do you know if Mr. Rossiter had a will?"

"No, I don't know. The bank's only business with Mr. Rossiter involved this account."

"No safe deposit box?"

Butters shook his head. "No. Just the account."

"In a sense, then, it would seem that Mr. Rossiter was living on a sort of allowance from somewhere."

Butters lifted his hands and then dropped them back on the desk. "I don't know. But it would seem that was more or less what it was. If it was a pension of some sort, I would have assumed that the deposits would have come directly from the source, not through a third party."

Stride nodded and made another note.

"Did you know Mr. Rossiter well, Mr. Butters?"

"No, I did not. I only met him twice. I don't think we traded more than a few words on either occasion. He wasn't a talkative man. In fact, he said almost nothing on either occasion. I can't say I knew him at all, really." He hesitated. "He seemed...how can I put this?"

"Poor?"

"Well, that certainly. But I was going to say addled, or confused. And he also seemed unwell. In fact, I wondered if he might be very ill. My wife's father died last year, from cancer. Mr. Rossiter had the same sort of look. And, not to be unkind, there was an odour about him. I thought it was my imagination at first, a prejudice perhaps, but my own doctor has told me that there can indeed be an odour with certain types of cancer. The body dying from within."

Butters looked ill at ease again, as though he regretted having spoken so frankly, delved into an area of personal intimacy.

"In fact, Mr. Rossiter did have cancer," Stride said. "He probably didn't have very long to live."

"That was what was found at the autopsy?"

"Yes."

The news seemed to make Butters even more uneasy, as though his speculation was somehow complicit in Rossiter's illness. He stared at his desk blotter for a few moments. Then he managed a smile and changed the subject.

"I believe he lived on Gower Street? In a boarding house?"

"Yes, he did. It was a boarding house."

"As you have suggested, that is very odd. The man had a very decent income. And money in the bank, as they say." He managed another smile. "I would have thought he could have afforded something considerably better than a boarding house on Gower Street. But I suppose he was comfortable where he was, or he wouldn't have stayed there."

"I believe he was comfortable enough. It seemed he had a good relationship with the lady of the house. I believe she cared about him." It was not quite the truth, a soft embellishment, but it could do no harm. Butters had been courteous and accommodating. It didn't hurt to respond in kind, even if he stretched the facts a little.

Butters was silent again, looking towards the drawer that held the folded newspaper. His features softened further and his head slumped forward allowing his chin once more to assume its natural expansive shape.

"I was just thinking how awful it must be to be alone in the world, without family, perhaps without friends." He looked at Stride. "Did he have any friends? Mr. Rossiter?"

Again, Stride did his best. "He had at least one friend that we know of. And they spent his last evening together, Rossiter's last evening. From all accounts they had a pleasant time."

"The evening he died, you mean?"

"Yes."

"Well, that is something, isn't it?"

f i f t e e n

There were some that said that Mr. Justice Robin McGinn was, at heart, something of a fishing admiral. It wasn't true, but McGinn was never heard objecting to the characterisation. People who knew him well believed he halfway enjoyed the reputation, false though it was.

Fishing admirals were the first judges in Newfoundland. It was truly a primitive judiciary, a rough and ready institution established long ago, at a time when the island was seen as a convenient mother ship for fishing fleets from England's West Country, as well as from elsewhere in Europe. It was also a time when permanent settlement of the island was not only forbidden, but actively discouraged, sometimes with brutal dedication. The restriction on settlement had nothing to do with concern for the welfare of the prospective settlers, faced with the demands of a rough land beset by a sometimes harsh climate, and a sometimes hostile indigenous people. It most certainly had nothing to do with any concern for those indigenous populations, the "Red Indians," as the Beothuk were called. As a postscript of this unconcern, when permanent settlement finally did come, the Beothuk were eventually consigned to extinction, victims of superior firepower and European diseases.

The early prohibition of settlement in Newfoundland had everything to do with the commercial exploitation of the fishery, roped to a fear that permanent communities might, at some point, compete with the visiting fleets for jurisdiction over the great ocean resource, the apparently inexhaustible schools of codfish. The English West Country merchants, draped in wealth and privilege from the annual bounty from the *New Founde Lande*, liked things the way they were, and they bent every effort towards keeping them that way. They were quite aware of what had transpired in America, in the New England colonies, when permanent settlements were established there. Such settlement in Newfoundland might even lead to local government, and that – God forbid! – might even give rise to a form of democratic rule, an outcome deemed inimical to continued commercial largesse.

The fishing admiral did not achieve his status because of any training in the law, or sensitivity to the human need for justice. In fact, he was not even an admiral. In some cases he might not even have been able to master the written word. The fishing admiral was simply the captain of the first fishing vessel to reach a particular harbour at the start of the year's fishing season. That alone conferred upon him an almost absolute authority over those who came later, and who, therefore, fell under his jurisdiction.

But he was first of all a captain, and his job was to catch and process fish in a quantity and quality that would keep the money flowing into the accounts of his ship's owner. He was more than likely to be a hard man – a soft man had little chance of becoming a ship's captain, after all – a man unafraid to use the lash, or worse, to maintain something like order in his zone of jurisdiction.

Mr. Justice Robin McGinn was not a soft-looking man. He was tall and ruggedly made, with a ruddy complexion and the thick hands of the labourer he had been in his youth, when he worked in the fishery and in mining. McGinn was now in late, middle age, a little north of sixty, and he had spent almost thirty years toiling in what he called, "the legal landscape." He was exceptionally well-read, and just as well-spoken. His voice was deep and resonant, and could fill any courtroom, but he also knew the strategic value and power of silence. As often as not, early in his career as a lawyer, he won his arguments, legal and otherwise, by saying as little as possible, his soft, blue eyes fixed on the disputant, the hint of a knowing smile on his lips. All of that had the effect of inspiring an opponent, lawyer or layman, to overfill the silence with a cascade of words, so many words that contradictions were almost inevitable, and these conspired to dilute the substance of the counter-argument.

Justice McGinn's law clerk ushered Stride into the judge's chambers. McGinn was seated at his desk, writing on a pad of yellow paper, his back turned to the door. The clerk indicated a chair where Stride was to sit. McGinn acknowledged his arrival with a small nod of the head but he continued writing for several minutes more. Then he sat back in his chair and read through the page of neat script, all the while tapping his chin with the middle finger of his left hand. Finally, he pushed the pad to one side and swivelled his chair around ninety degrees so that he was facing his visitor.

"You've caught me at an appropriate time, Inspector Stride. I'm writing an opinion on the wisdom, usefulness, and morality of capital punishment. Hanging, to speak its name. A cruel business, hanging. Do you think so?"

"Yes, sir. I think hanging is indeed a cruel business."

"Indeed? Not all policemen think that way, nor all members of the public. Most of them, of course, the public and police alike, have no direct experience with the practice. I have, and so, I think, do you. I believe you were a witness at the hanging, four years ago, of the unfortunate Herbert Spratt?"

"Yes, sir, I was."

"I thought so." McGinn looked thoughtful and tapped his chin again. "The word unfortunate has been often used to describe the particular occasion and the circumstances, but that descriptive doesn't begin to capture the misery of the affair. No single word could. I'm not sure a thousand would suffice. You may be aware of the fact that I opposed Spratt's execution, and I was not alone. But I was a part of the unhappy minority on that occasion. Happily — and I use the word with due care — because of the wretched outcome, and the general revulsion that flowed from it, there may never be another such punishment meted out in this country. How do you feel about that, Inspector, the possibility that there may be no more executions here on this island? As a policeman, do you feel that hanging has a deterrent effect?"

"On the whole, no."

"I'm inclined to agree with you, although with some reservations. The obvious one being that a murderer hanged will not murder again. There is a small but certain comfort in that, especially with some of the more heinous criminals who have taken the life of another person." McGinn smiled. "Judges are known for their reservations, or we are supposed to be. Without reservations, and their discomfiting effects, we might not be inspired to think beyond the obvious and the reflexive, and justice might be diminished, if not actually placed in peril. I will argue that more good grows from discomfort than from pleasure, and most certainly from pleasure's sometime companion, sloth." McGinn looked at Stride over the top of his glasses. "Feel free to disagree with me. This is not a formal test."

"I have no disagreement with anything you've said so far, sir."

McGinn continued to regard Stride, but did not offer an immediate reply. He picked up the yellow legal pad, studied it for a moment, then put it down again.

"The unfortunate Spratt presented us with an exemplary opportunity for the exercise of judgement, using the broader definition. That he was of unsound mind, at least to a degree, was without question. You will recall that he was a naval rating in the war, with a good record in His Majesty's Service. He was discharged for medical reasons, but then he discovered that his betrothed had been unfaithful to him during his absence at sea, an absence occasioned by military service in a time, and location, of great peril. Even worse, the young woman was pregnant with another man's child. Spratt's grief and his anger — acknowledging that we are unsure which emotion came first — inspired him to bludgeon her to death with a flatiron. A brutal act, and a crime by any definition. As testament to his deranged state, he then ran into the street and confessed the crime to anyone who cared to listen, and to more than one who did not. Spratt's guilt, narrowly defined, was without question, and the jury found him so. But they also recommended mercy. Based, as the foreman stated, on Mr. Spratt's 'youth and indifferent health and good service record.' I am able to quote exactly from the transcript because I have only just been writing those very words. Nonetheless, he was sentenced to hang and as we both know too well, Mr. Stride, he was hanged on the eighth of May 1943, from a scaffold in the northeast corner of His Majesty's Penitentiary on the lakeside."

McGinn fell silent then and picked up the writing pad again. He swivelled his chair around and wrote something in the margin of the topmost page. Then he faced Stride.

"And now, I am given to understand by my able clerk, Mr. O'Neill, that the Constabulary has another murder to deal with. Although I also understand that it was first thought to have been an unfortunate accident, caused by two young men racing down a laneway in the dark, colliding with the victim, the late Mr. Samuel Rossiter."

"Yes, sir, that was the original thought. The constable at the scene could only work with the evidence he had at hand. It wasn't until the autopsy was performed that it became clear that Mr. Rossiter's death was due to a series of blows, one of which crushed his trachea and larynx."

"In my experience, that sort of directed violence often suggests a degree of prior involvement of the killer with the victim, and possibly some degree of premeditation."

"That has been my experience as well, sir." Stride's mind went back to the Taylor case from earlier that spring.

"So I have been given to understand." McGinn smiled. "I am familiar with your most recent homicide investigation, and the personal toll that it levied on you. Such an experience can only inspire care and caution in a thoughtful man."

"That is indeed the case."

"In the present circumstances, is there a possibility that there might have been a degree of — and how shall I put this? — a degree of the unintentional in Mr. Rossiter's death? He was an old man, quite ill I understand, and therefore fragile."

"I suppose that is a possibility, sir. Rossiter's assailant might not have meant to kill him."

"So, a verdict of manslaughter, perhaps." McGinn closed his eyes for a moment. "I believe it was Tom Butcher who conducted the post mortem?"

"Yes, it was. I have a copy of the autopsy report for you."

McGinn held out his hand for the document. He quickly scanned the contents, then closed the file and placed it on his desk.

"I will read it through more carefully later, but I have learned to place much faith in Tom's conclusions. And the two young men? Are they your prime suspects?"

"They are suspects, of course, but I won't give them the designation of prime until we've had the opportunity to question them."

"Carefully put, Mr. Stride. They will at the very least be important witnesses. When you are able to find them."

"Yes, sir."

"But as of this moment, they are still at large?"

"They were as of thirty minutes ago, yes."

"I see. No doubt they will be found, sooner than later. Two young men, not much more than boys really, without much in the way of financial or material resources, cannot remain at large for very long. The unusually clement weather notwithstanding."

"That is our expectation."

"And now you would like to have a warrant from me to open up Mr. Rossiter's financial situation, which would permit you to ask Mr. Jeffrey for that information. And you also need a second warrant for Mr. Butters at the bank."

"Yes."

"All of which may bring a third party under the umbra of your investigation."

"I am aware of that possibility, sir."

"Yes. That is rarely, if ever, an enviable position for someone who might have no connection with the seminal event."

"That is understood. But we believe that the information will assist the investigation."

"Believe or hope?"

"A bit of both."

"With hope leading belief by the hand." McGinn's middle finger became active again, rhythmically tapping his chin. "I believe in giving the Constabulary as much assistance and leeway as is possible and practical, with the understanding that I am not supporting a fishing expedition. Our national preoccupation notwithstanding." He smiled. "This isn't one, is it?"

"No, sir. If the two youths are not responsible for Mr. Rossiter's death, and if, as seems likely, robbery was not the motive for the attack, additional information on Rossiter himself could assist us a great deal."

"I see no flaw in your reasoning, Mr. Stride. But it's also possible that Mr. Rossiter's financial affairs will prove to have nothing to do with the case. In which circumstance, I will rely on you to handle the information with due care."

"That's also understood, sir."

McGinn looked at Stride for a long moment, then nodded.

"I take it you have only limited information at the moment on the late Mr. Rossiter."

"Yes." Stride told McGinn what they knew about Samuel Rossiter.

"An apparently poor man living in very modest circumstances, who also has a large bank account. That is indeed very interesting. And almost reason enough on its own to justify warrants to learn more about the man."

"That is my feeling, sir."

"Quite so. Your speculations about Mr. Rossiter's attendance at the Methodist College also have merit," McGinn said. "And it also speaks to a degree of privilege, and a more complicated background than would initially have been suspected." McGinn took off his glasses now and dropped them on his desk. "My own schooling, as you may have heard, was much less grand than the late Mr. Rossiter's. I grew up in a small outport on White Bay. We had a school, but I can tell you it was no Methodist College. We had one lone teacher, and he taught all the grades. He did what he could, but much of what I know about most things I had to garner on my own. Don't get me wrong. I don't resent that. I subscribe to the belief that self-education is often superior to the sort of rote-learning practices that currently infest our educational system." He looked at Stride. "Not everyone agrees with that point of view, of course."

It wasn't a question exactly, but Stride knew a comment was expected.

"I've always thought that my real education began after I left school," he said.

"You would have made a good lawyer, Mr. Stride. You take great care with words."

McGinn leaned back in his chair. He wasn't done yet. Stride had more or less expected this. McGinn's reputation as a pontificator was well known.

"I will pass this along for what it's worth. An aside, really, but your knowing it will do no harm. I met Mr. Edward Royce one time. The headmaster at the Methodist College when Mr. Rossiter was in attendance there. He had recently retired from his position and was planning to return to England to live out his final years. Our meeting was a little unusual. Royce was touring schools in various parts of the island on behalf of the government of the day, and he visited our community. I was twelve at the time, very young for the making of judgements, but my youth permitted me a young boy's natural instinct for fear, which often becomes lost in later years as we develop the skill of rationalisation. Rationalisation being defined as judgement in bondage. I thought Royce was an awful man. Although he was very soft-spoken — it was said that he had lost a lung to tuberculosis — I could see the sadist leering at me from behind the veil of good manners. Years later, speaking with some of his former students, I had my suspicions confirmed. He was all that I suspected him of being." He smiled again. "I do ramble. It is one of the perquisites of my situation and I indulge it as often as I can. You shall have your warrants. You may think of them as partially a reward for your patience, Mr. Stride. And I will rely on your using them with care."

McGinn swivelled his chair around again, took two sheets of paper from a folder, spent a few moments looking at them, then signed both with a flourish. He turned again and gave the papers to Stride.

"Thank you, sir. I appreciate your doing this."

Stride stood up and the two men shook hands. McGinn walked him to the door. He paused with his hand on the knob.

"Are you interested in names, Inspector?"

"Sir?"

"Yes, it must seem an odd question in the circumstances. But family names are one of my hobbies, something of an avocation, in fact. Rossiter, like many surnames, comes originally from the name of a community. In this case, it might have come from Rochester, which is a town in the county of Kent, in England. The other possibility, and I personally like this one very much better, is a place called Wroxeter, which is in Shropshire. It is the site of an old Roman city, a fortress in fact, variously known as Uriconium or Viroconium. There has been considerable digging in the place, the uncovering of the foundations of buildings, artefacts, that kind of thing. It's the sort of place I would enjoy visiting someday." McGinn looked wistful for a moment. "Had I not opted for a career in the law, I think my choice would have been for archaeology, which deals with the departed instead of the extant, and is therefore almost always less troublesome. In which context, a good friend of mine is Dr. Parsons, an amateur archaeologist like myself. You know him, I believe. He has mentioned to me that you are acquainted with his son, Hercules, the painter."

"Yes, I am. He is a friend of mine."

"A talented fellow, young Parsons. So, once more, we see that it's a smaller world than we are often wont to think."

"Yes."

"You know, I've been trying to persuade some of the people at the College to pursue the history of the family names on this island as an academic project, and I might even be having some success. If a country is defined by its people, it follows that people are defined to a large extent by their family histories. It will be a while yet before anything happens with it, of course. We shall have to wait for the political dust to settle, and see whose fingers grip the strings of the public purse. That in itself is a somewhat frightening prospect."

"I think so," Stride said. "But, about your interest in family names, sir. Do you have any information on the Rossiter families in Newfoundland?"

"Apart from what I've just told you about the possible origin of the name, I'm not sure. I will have a look in my files, which I keep at home. If I find something that would seem to be of relevance, I will contact you."

McGinn pulled the door open and shook hands with Stride.

After Stride left, McGinn stood at the window of his chambers which looked out on Duckworth Street. Presently, Stride came out onto the sidewalk. McGinn watched him walk east on Duckworth until he disappeared from view. Then he went back to the paper he had been working on. He read the first pages through again and made a few jottings in the margin, but after only a few minutes, he gave up the effort and put the document back in its folder. He picked up his hat and his cane, went to the door, and spoke to his clerk.

"I will be going out for a little while, Peter. I need to stretch my legs, as well as my mind. My next appointment is at two this afternoon?"

"At two-thirty, sir."

"Yes, of course, two-thirty. I will be back before then."

"You do have your luncheon engagement, sir. At one."

"Yes, I have not forgotten."

"If you think you'll be busy, sir, I could call Sir Hubert and cancel."

McGinn shook his head. "No, that won't be necessary. I will meet him at the restaurant as scheduled. If his secretary calls in the meantime, as she no doubt will, you will duly inform her of that."

s i x t e e n

Harry Phelan was waiting for Stride in a teashop on Duckworth Street, a few minutes walk from the Court House. It was a popular gathering place for lawyers, policemen, and court functionaries. Here, the variable shades of guilt and innocence were sketched in, punishments debated, the noisy tumult of fractured lives muted over cups of hot tea and scones dripping with butter and jam.

Harry had been here for at least a few minutes by the time Stride arrived. A plate and a butter knife sat beside a large teapot and Harry was sitting back in his chair smoking a cigarette. He looked pleased with himself, Stride thought. He slid onto a chair across the table from Phelan and took out his own cigarettes. He lifted the lid of Harry's teapot and looked inside, then signalled to the waitress.

"You've had some success, Harry?"

"Yes, I have, sir. Mr. Staples has come through for us one more time."

"And a little faster than usual."

"I think it's a slack time for Staples, these dog days of August. The death rate is down, although he says the birth rate's up a bit. He mentioned that specifically. He suggested that people like to snuggle a little closer in the cold winter months."

"A civil servant with a sense of humour. What next, I wonder?"

"I'm almost afraid to think." Phelan opened his notebook. "Our man's full name is Samuel Kent Rossiter. He was born in 1876. His father was Daniel Kent Rossiter, and his mother's name was Sarah. Her middle name is listed as Hibbs, but Staples thinks that was probably her maiden name."

"They were from St. John's?"

"Yes. Staples dug a little further, but he didn't find any other children in the family. The mother died in 1878, but her husband lived to a decent age. He was seventy-two when he passed over in 1910."

"No record of a marriage for Sam, I suppose?"

"No, sir. No marriage record. But Staples pointed out that that didn't mean he'd never married. The records aren't complete. And, anyway, he might have gotten married someplace outside St. John's. Outside Newfoundland for that matter."

The waitress arrived then, carrying a tray with Stride's tea. He lifted the lid and stirred the leaves in the pot, then poured milk into his cup and added the tea after that. He took an exploratory sip and put in a drop more milk. He told Harry what he had learned at the bank and showed him the order that would allow them to ask Lawrence Jeffrey for Rossiter's financial records.

"So McGinn came through for us. I've always thought he had more imagination than the average judge."

"Some of them have no imagination at all," Stride said. "Axles without wheels. We had a decent chat, as a matter of fact. Did you know he had an interest in family names and their history?"

"McGinn's an onomatologist?" Phelan laughed when Stride stared at him. "Kit was doing a crossword the other night. The word came up."

"You had me worried there for a moment, Harry."

"I frighten myself sometimes, sir. I take it we're off to see Lawrence Jeffrey next?"

"As soon as I finish my tea, we are."

"I could help you along with that." Phelan slid his cup closer and reached for the pot.

"I was concerned you might not offer."

"No worries there, sir. I have a kind and generous nature. Everybody says so."

Lawrence Jeffrey had been expecting someone from the Constabulary to call. He had read about the death of Samuel Rossiter in the morning paper. The relevant file was on his desk when Stride and Phelan were ushered into his office. He had also had his secretary type up a short statement summarising the discussions that had led to the financial arrangements that provided Rossiter with an income.

Lawrence Jeffrey didn't look the part of a successful attorney ruling a family enterprise of long standing. He was small and wiry with prominent features, sharply chiselled, surmounted by a gleaming pate that was hedged by an unruly tangle of greying hair much in need of a disciplined trimming. A crook pipe was clasped in the left side of his mouth, the bowl dangling over his chin. Faint wisps of aromatic smoke wreathed his head, and the lapels of his Harris-tweed jacket were frosted with tobacco ash. He gazed at Stride and Phelan with dark brown eyes that suggested a Welsh heritage, although his family had originally come from Ulster. Stride thought Jeffrey was in his late forties or early fifties.

"No question that it was an unusual situation, Inspector Stride. But unusual situations are a principal reason that lawyers were invented. We are here to regularise the bizarre and the unusual, so that the world will continue to spin comfortably on its axis. Without us, chaos would ensue and there would, God forbid, be even more conflict than there is already. Of course, that's a thoroughly biased view, and there are not a few who would argue the opposing case. But the embracing of bias is one of our other great predilections."

Stride had heard that Lawrence Jeffrey liked to think of himself as something of a philosopher. He was also a published poet. Perhaps that explained it.

"It's our understanding that Mr. Rossiter had not lived in St. John's for a while," Stride said.

"That is indeed the case." Jeffrey placed his pipe in an ashtray on the front of his desk. He lifted the sheet of paper containing the summary statement an inch off his desk blotter. "It's all in here. Well, not all, of course, but all that I know about it, or needed to know in order to handle the file. Do you know where Mr. Rossiter was living before he came back to St. John's?"

"No, we don't. We're hoping that you will be able to tell us."

"And so I shall." A dramatic pause. "Samuel Rossiter had been living in Bermuda for a long time. A very long time, in fact."

"Bermuda?"

"It is a surprise, isn't it? Although not as great a mystery when you consider that the history of the two colonies goes back a very long way. There are more connections between this place and Bermuda than the average Newfoundlander might think."

"You say he was living there for a long time. Do you know how long?"

"Not precisely, no. But decades, certainly. And it was anticipated that he would remain there to live out his days. Or so I was given to understand. I'm not sure why he came back to Newfoundland, to St. John's. It seemed an odd choice to me. I think if I had the option of spinning out my declining years in Bermuda, I would be loathe to turn my back on the place and settle here. Individual choices never cease to amaze me."

"Rossiter's return to Newfoundland came as a surprise, then? To his benefactor, I mean."

"I don't know if surprise captures all of the flavour of it, Inspector, but surprise would be a part of it, I'm sure."

"Can you enlarge on that, Mr. Jeffrey?"

"Not very much, no. I'm only a functionary in this situation. I generated the bits of paper that helped guide the way to Mr. Rossiter's current solvency, something like the trail of breadcrumbs that were supposed to guide Hansel and Gretel to safety from the dark and dangerous forest. Legal paper, of course, is more durable than bits of bread. And more expensive." Jeffrey smiled. Phelan gave Stride a furtive sideways look. Jeffrey caught the motion, and the smile faded. He opened the file that lay in front of him. "Well, enough of fairy tales and breadcrumbs. We move on to the meat of the occasion. You wish to know who was providing funds to Mr. Rossiter, a reasonable question in the unhappy circumstances. His benefactor, to use your term, Inspector Stride, is Mrs. Reginald Cooke." He peered at them over the top of the file. "Are you acquainted with the lady? Either of you?"

Stride shook his head. He looked at Harry, who responded to Stride's look with a silent shrug of the shoulders.

"Well, I'm not really surprised." Jeffrey had recaptured his good humour now, and he was smiling again. "Mrs. Cooke has led a quiet life. She's been a client of this firm for more than thirty years. In recent years, I have personally looked after her legal requirements."

"She is a widow? Mrs. Cooke?"

"Yes, she is. Her husband passed on quite a long time ago. It has to be some thirty years now." He consulted the file. "Well, I had it almost exactly right. He died thirty-one years ago, in 1916."

"He was killed in the Great War?" Mention of the date automatically brought forward the memory of the opening of the Somme offensive, on the first day of July 1916, where the Newfoundland Regiment paid a terrible price for the strategic blundering of their British commanders.

"No, Mr. Cooke was not in the Great War. However, he was indeed a war veteran, but from an earlier conflict. The Boer War. He was an officer, in fact, a Major, I think. He was quite some years older than his wife."

"He was English?"

"Yes. They met in London not long before the Great War, in 1913, I believe it was. They married a year later. They left England not long after that, and moved here to St. John's. By that time, of course, the war was on."

"I assume Mr. Cooke must have left his widow quite well off, if she was able to offer Mr. Rossiter a comfortable income."

"Yes, Mrs. Cooke is well off, there's no doubt about that. But her husband had little if anything to do with it. In fact, I'm not sure he had much besides his uniform and good breeding to recommend him for marriage. I hope that doesn't come across as an unkind sentiment, it wasn't meant to. But Elizabeth Cooke's money was, and is, her own." Jeffrey looked at them again, half-smiling, prolonging the moment. "Before she was married, Mrs. Cooke was Elizabeth Hurdle. You're familiar with the name, of course."

"She's related to Sir Hubert Hurdle?"

"The president of Hurdle and Company Limited. Yes, she is one of those Hurdles. She is Sir Hubert's sister."

Jeffrey enjoyed their reaction of surprise. He picked up his pipe, tapped the dottle into the ashtray, and began refilling the bowl from a leather pouch.

"I'll ask the obvious question," Stride said. "Why would someone like Elizabeth Cooke provide an income for Samuel Rossiter? What is the connection between them?"

Jeffrey finished packing tobacco into his pipe before he replied.

"You will have to ask her yourself, Inspector. She never told me why she chose to be Mr. Rossiter's benefactor." He smiled briefly. "Benefactress, I suppose."

"Did you ask her?"

"No, I didn't. I did not need the information to facilitate setting up the account here in St. John's, or to arrange for the transfer of funds."

"From Bermuda?"

"Yes. Mr. Rossiter's original account was with the Commerce Bank of Bermuda. When he decided to move back to St. John's — that was just over a year ago — I made the necessary arrangements to transfer the monies in the Bermuda account to the Newfoundland Savings Bank. It was a simple enough transaction."

"But before that, the money from Mrs. Cooke went in the opposite direction, from St. John's to Bermuda. To Hamilton, I assume."

"Yes, the Commerce Bank is in the capital, Hamilton. It's one of the smaller banking institutions on the island, dealing mostly with offshore accounts and financial transactions. I believe that sort of activity is quite a going concern in that part of the world. The rules appear to be, shall we say, a little more flexible than in some other places."

"How long has Mrs. Cooke been supporting Mr. Rossiter?"

"For quite a long time, in fact." Jeffrey struck a match and applied the flame to the bowl of his pipe. He did not reply until he had it going nicely. "You see, the original arrangement was set up by my father, some thirty-odd years ago. In 1913, in fact. A year before the last war."

"It started in 1913? Samuel Rossiter was only a young man then, not yet forty years old. And Mrs. Cooke was even younger. And she wasn't married then."

"All of that is correct, yes. At the time, Elizabeth Hurdle had only just reached the age of majority. Which included the freedom to do whatever she wanted with her money. Her father, Sir Leonard Hurdle, had left her very well off."

"And you don't know what it's all about? This arrangement with Rossiter?"

Jeffrey shook his head. "No, I don't. It's possible that Mrs. Cooke told my father more than she told me. I don't know. I never discussed the matter with him. In fact, I didn't know about the arrangement until after my father died. That was when I inherited the business, and it became necessary for me, as head of the firm, to familiarise myself with our clients." Jeffrey put on a thoughtful expression, pulling on his pipe and looking past Stride and Phelan towards the window that gave him a view of Signal Hill. "My father and I weren't as close as some people assume we were. This being a family firm of long standing, I mean. Also, I didn't always work here. Anyway, when the original arrangements were made I was only a boy." He smiled. "With much more important matters to think about than such mundane things as making a living."

"But you do know Mrs. Cooke personally?"

"Yes, I do. Not well, but I handle various legal matters for her. And I see her occasionally, several times each year."

"Did you know Samuel Rossiter?"

Jeffrey shook his head. "No, I never met him. I took my instructions from Mrs. Cooke, and all of my subsequent dealings with the Rossiter file had to do with the Commerce Bank of Bermuda, and with Mr. Butters at the Savings Bank. As I said, the transactions were not complicated. I handled the file personally because Mrs. Cooke asked me to. But once the arrangements were made, that ended my direct involvement. My clerk took care of the monthly deposits after that."

"So, Mrs. Cooke had no objection to Rossiter coming back to St. John's."

"She wasn't aware of the fact until it was a *fait accompli*, and I think she may not have been entirely happy about it."

"But not unhappy enough to cut off his income."

"No. Whatever their arrangement was, Mr. Rossiter's coming back to St. John's was not sufficient reason for her to terminate the arrangement."

"Were you aware of Mr. Rossiter's situation here in St. John's? Did you know that he was living in a manner that suggested he was in circumstances not far removed from poverty?"

"No, I didn't know that. Although I have noted from the newspaper account that he lived in a boarding house on Gower Street."

"Was Mrs. Cooke aware of Rossiter's situation."

Jeffrey shrugged. "Again, you will have to ask her about that, Inspector. I simply don't know. I would suggest that you contact her. She lives on Winter Avenue. She is listed in the phone book, under her late husband's name."

"She lives alone?"

"Yes." Then Jeffrey shook his head. "No, not alone. She has a housekeeper, or companion. I think her name is Clara. Yes, it is. Clara Jones. She has been with Mrs. Cooke since before Mr. Cooke passed on."

"Was Sir Hubert Hurdle involved in this in any way? Was he even aware of the arrangement?" It was the obvious next question, and Stride thought he knew the answer already. But the question appeared to take Jeffrey by surprise. Once again he looked past Stride and Phelan towards the window before replying.

"I'm not aware that he knew anything about it, no. Until you mentioned his name, I really hadn't given Sir Hubert more than a passing thought in connection with the matter. Sir Hubert isn't one of our clients. And in point of fact, I don't know who handles his legal affairs."

"And Elizabeth Hurdle never mentioned her brother in any of the discussions she had with you about Mr. Rossiter?"

"No, she didn't. Not that our discussions about Rossiter were substantial. In fact, I wouldn't even call them discussions. The Rossiter file wasn't complicated, as I have said, apart from the odd fact that it existed at all. It was a simple transfer of funds, from one bank account to another. But to enlarge on the point, I can't imagine Sir Hubert will be best pleased about any of this. The connection between Rossiter and his sister, I mean. He's a prominent man, and the stain of murder can spread wide." He looked across the desk to see if the comment had registered with either of them.

Phelan picked up the thread.

"There's a body of opinion that says Sir Hubert Hurdle has at least one eye canted in the direction of Government House." Phelan glanced at Stride before going on. "If the vote goes in favour of Confederation, they'll be looking for a Lieutenant Governor to replace Governor MacDonald. I've heard it said that Hurdle is interested, never mind that up to this point he's been listed among those most opposed to Confederation."

"As almost all of his kind are," Jeffrey said. "The merchants, I mean. I will add that I've heard that rumour too. It is interesting, isn't it?"

"Yes, it is," Stride said. "Can you tell me if Elizabeth Cooke is a director of Hurdle and Company Limited?"

"There's no harm in telling you that she is. It's public knowledge. The list of company officers is published in their annual report. I'm not sure to what extent she's involved in the operation of the company, or even if she has any active role at all." He paused. "I don't know why you would need that sort of information, but if you do need it, you will have to ask Mrs. Cooke." A smile. "Or Sir Hubert himself, of course."

Stride and Phelan walked along Duckworth Street after leaving Jeffrey's office. Harry was adding to the notes in his book as he walked, glancing up now and then so as to avoid bumping into a pedestrian or impaling himself on one of the iron pegs on the telephone poles that lined the street.

"Curiouser and curiouser," Phelan closed the notebook and stuffed it into a pocket. "Are we going to pay Sir Hubert a visit, sir?"

"I'm open to almost any suggestion right now, Harry. Except maybe that one."

Stride had been playing juggler-balls with the bits and pieces of information they had received from Jeffrey and George Butters. He was also thinking about last night, when Dianne Borg had mentioned that her father worked for the Hurdles. Dianne herself worked for the Newfoundland Mercantile Association, which was the best source of information on businesses in Newfoundland, and particularly in St. John's. The association's office was only a block away from where he and Harry were standing.

"Asking Sir Hubert Hurdle for some intimate family information isn't high on my list of ambitions just at the moment either, sir. Especially as I haven't been to confession in almost two weeks."

"A not-unwise consideration in the circumstances. How much do you know about Hurdle and his family, Harry?"

"Not a whole hell of a lot. My Old Man works for the company from time to time, servicing their marine engines, and he's met Sir Hubert a couple of times. He says he's decent enough, not that they've ever talked about anything much, or hoisted a glass together. He's a bit grand, my Old Man says, with a velvety accent that he picked up in England at university. Oxford, I think he said it was. Or maybe it was Cambridge, I forget."

"I think it was Cambridge. I met Hurdle once. More British than the Brits was what I thought."

"My old man might have said something along those lines. And he thought Hurdle looked the part. On the whole, though, my Old Man thought he was a decent enough fella, and he always made certain his office settled the accounts in short order. Not like some."

"I think we'll take the indirect route, Harry. I want to know a lot more about the Hurdles before either of us goes to see one of them."

"Do you think one of them might have had something to do with Rossiter's death?"

Stride turned the question back to him. "Do you?"

Phelan laughed. "It would be a hell of a lot of fun, wouldn't it, if we could show that one of them did? The shit would hit the fan in quantity."

"To coin a phrase."

"Coining phrases is one thing we Irish do well, sir."

"And the other?"

"I'll have to think about that."

"The downside of all the fun-time being that we had better get it right first time out. We wouldn't get a second shot at it."

"Not walking a beat in Upper Gullies, we wouldn't. So, where next? The Mercantile Association?"

"I think so. Bertie Prim can probably tell us a thing or two."

"He probably can, sir. But can you think of something else you'd like me to do while you talk to him? He's not my favourite human, and that dog of his doesn't help."

"Fair enough," Stride said. They were standing across the street from the Mercantile Association now. "From what Jeffrey told us, it seems the association between Rossiter and Elizabeth Hurdle goes back a very long time, to before the last war. I'm wondering if there's anything in our records that might make mention of a Rossiter or a Hurdle back around that time. I know that Bern's been working to cross-index the old files, but I don't know how far he's gotten with it. What do you think, Harry? It's a pretty vague reference, but it might be worth a shot."

"If I get to miss spending an hour with Bertie Prim, it's definitely worth it, sir."

"Every cloud has it's silver lining."

"I'll see you back at the Fort later on?"

Stride nodded and turned to cross over Duckworth, pausing at the curb to allow a horse-drawn delivery cart to pass.

seventeen

The Newfoundland Mercantile Association was housed in a two-story structure in Spartan grey, and two slender *faux*-Corinthian columns flanked the entrance. The two front windows on the ground floor, one on each side of a heavy black door with an ornate brass knocker, stared almost menacingly at the street. The dark green blinds were pulled halfway down the panes, giving the façade a heavy-lidded aspect, vaguely threatening, as though something unpleasant was lurking inside, waiting patiently for suitable prey to step across the threshold.

The Association had stood on this same spot for just over half a century, constructed on the foundation of a similar building that had been destroyed in the 1892 fire that had levelled much of the old city. The organisation had started out as the Chamber of Commerce, and the original building had been erected on a site that had once hosted a tavern. Some people thought that was more than appropriate. A frighteningly large amount of the early commerce of St. John's had to do with oak barrels, jerboas, jugs, bottles, and flasks: an almost infinite variety of liquor containers. A writer from an earlier time had once opined there was almost as much liquid in the various premises along Duckworth and Water Streets as there was in the harbour itself.

Bertie Prim's office was on the second floor at the rear of the building, and Stride took his time walking up the stairs, thinking of questions he might ask about the Hurdles. When he reached the landing he looked around, wondering if Dianne Borg might happen by. The clandestine nature of their relationship annoyed and excited him in about equal amounts. But they had a rule about meeting in public. They would act as strangers, or at most as casual acquaintances. He knew that her office was at the far end of the building, well removed from Prim's. He would have liked to be able to just walk in and say hello, to chat for a minute before moving along to deal with the business he had come for. But caution trumped desire. There was no choice. He went directly to Prim's office.

Bertie Prim was a very large man. His desk chair had been custom-built to accommodate his bulk, but even then he overflowed it, substantial portions of his hindquarters spilling over the sides and back. His daunting appearance notwithstanding, it was generally agreed that Prim was very good at his job. He probably knew more about businesses and businessmen in Newfoundland than any other single individual.

Prim had only one other obvious passion in his life. And that was a spoiled-rotten, little Pekingese named Snuffle. In fact, there had been a succession of Snuffles in Prim's life. Stride had heard that the current one was number seven. If the average life span of a small dog is about fourteen years, seven Snuffles for a man in his early fifties could be said to have been at least four too many. No one would argue against the proposition that Bertie Prim's Snuffles were privileged little beasts, as in fact they were. But there was unanimous agreement also that every one of them was doomed to a premature departure from this earth once they tumbled, however joyously, into the lush ambit that was Bertie Prim's life, a glorious neverland of caloric excess. Prim ate almost continuously, an efficient process of nibbling, chewing and swallowing. He couldn't imagine that the object of his affections would not share his obsession with food.

When Stride arrived at the doorway to Bertie Prim's office, Prim was sitting at his desk. He smiled a welcome and leaned back in the chair, spraddle-legged. The current Snuffle was perched on one massive thigh. Prim rubbed the back of her ear and poked small bits of food into her flat, moist face with his free hand. Aware that someone had encroached upon her domain, the Pekingese turned her head and gave Stride a sullen glance. But after a tense moment, the little animal decided he posed no competition for the bits of food, and she refocused her attentions on her master's ministrations.

"This is a pleasant surprise, Eric. What brings you into this hallowed precinct of sainted commerce?" He raised one soft hand before Stride had a chance to respond. "I will guess information, my stock in trade. Come in, have a seat, make yourself comfortable, but please do not smoke. Snuffle doesn't like tobacco smoke, do you, Snuffle dear?"

He picked up the Pekingese and held her in front of his face, his lips moving soundlessly in some sort of visual chant that the dog seemed to understand. Snuffle wagged her tail and made damp snuffling sounds. After a moment, Prim placed her gently in a wicker basket on the floor beside his desk and patted her head.

Stride pulled up a chair and sat down. He took a final glance down the corridor and then pushed the door closed.

"I do need some information, Bertie. On the Hurdles."

"On the Hurdles? Sir Hubert and his lot? Are the Hurdles in some sort of trouble with the law?"

Stride shook his head. "No, they're not in any trouble that I know of. I just need some general information about them and their company."

"Hurdle and Company Limited. Well, you have come to the source, dear boy. We have masses of information on file about the Hurdles and their business activities, which you probably know are extensive, and have been since the founding father, Cornelius Hurdle landed on our shores more than a century ago. You say you want general information, so I take it you will want broad strokes, at least to start. A question, though. Is it the company you are interested in primarily, or is it the family itself?"

"Both," Stride said.

"I see. Well, our files also have a good deal of personal information on the family, birth and death dates, marriages, children, that sort of thing."

"Would the Hurdles approve of that?"

"Approve? Dear boy, they provided much of the information themselves. They have a vested interest in our getting the facts right when people such as yourself come to call. From their perspective, of course."

"I suppose so."

"No supposing about it. You may think of it as the careful management of personal information, predicated on their view that the family is the company, and vice versa." Prim clasped his hands over his great middle and stretched his legs out in front of him, one foot crossed over the other. He regarded Stride for several moments. "Is this part of an investigation, Eric? You say the Hurdles are not in any trouble, and I cannot quickly imagine that they are, or

I think I would have heard something about it already. But I also cannot imagine that this is a casual expedition."

"It is related to an investigation, but I want the information only as background."

"And the attendant phrase, unspoken, is *at this point.*" Prim looked directly at Stride for a moment longer, then his gaze moved to the morning newspaper that was folded on the side of his desk. "Would that be a reasonably accurate thing to say?"

"It would be close enough."

"Ah. Well, we'll say no more about that, shall we?" A comfortable smile. "At this point."

"You mentioned the name Cornelius Hurdle as the founder of the company. I have heard of him."

"I imagine you have, and I also imagine that what you heard was both inaccurate and embellished. Being dead for a long time, the sharp edges have been rubbed off and he has attained a place in the folklore of our island. Humans have an inborn romantic bent, it's what separates us from the rest of the animals and makes us more interesting than our mostly furry cousins. As well as infinitely more dangerous. Which is alright, really. Were it otherwise, life would be dull and boring. You do agree?"

"I do."

"Good. To continue, then. Cornelius Hurdle, and therefore the Hurdle family, do have a considerable history. But all I can give you on short notice, and in a reasonable time-frame, is a synopsis."

Prim glanced at the clock on the wall over his desk.

"Am I interrupting something?"

"No, dear boy, not at all. I have a meeting not too much later on, but we do have a few minutes to play."

"A synopsis will do for the present." Stride took out his notebook and uncapped his pen.

"Alrighty, then." Prim folded his soft hands across his middle again and half-closed his eyes. "The Hurdle family, and their involvement in commerce, goes back a very long way, in Newfoundland and elsewhere. They are well established here, of course, and have been for more than a century. But, to go back to something like the beginning, to the early years of the last century, the 1800s, one finds Hurdles resident in Bermuda. Those Hurdles, some of them at least, including I think our lot, came originally from the south of England. Devonshire, to be specific. As a matter of fact, if you were to consult a suitably detailed map of southern England you would find a place there called Hurdlecombe. There is also, I believe, a lake of the same name."

"You say our Hurdles started out in Bermuda?" The name had caught his attention.

"On this side of the pond, yes. There is, coincidentally, a strong historical connection between Bermuda and Newfoundland, both being early colonies of the Empire." Prim opened his eyes and looked at Stride. "As an amusing aside, did you know that one of our Bermuda connections can be seen at Government House where the union boffin, the Welshman MacDonald, currently holds court? The Bermuda residence, you see, was designed to be surrounded by a moat, one assumes to prevent the wildlife of a near-tropical locale from invading the premises. Or perhaps it was the restless natives they were worried about, no doubt with reason.

"Newfoundland, for all its many hazards, was to have had a more traditional structure, sans moat. But the architect's plans, legend has it, were accidentally switched. If you visit the granite pile near Bannerman Park, you will see that there is indeed a moat around our Government House. And not a viper or any other dangerous beast in sight. If one discounts, that is, the lurking presence of one Joseph Smallwood and his Bolshie Confederate cabal, scheming away in the shadows of Devon Row."

Prim was silent for a moment, waiting for Stride to offer a comment. When none was forthcoming, he sighed and let his eyelids droop again.

"So, to continue. The Bermuda Mercantile Company is the place our tale begins, and as I have suggested, the man to look at is Cornelius Hurdle." Prim raised a cautionary finger. "Or Hurdell. The name is spelled both ways on various documents. Cornelius started the branch of the family business that we're concerned with in the early 1800s. Some say it was 1809, other sources list 1811 or 1812. Cornelius was well placed, geographically and otherwise, to pursue an international business career. He was already well-off when he left England and moved to Bermuda. You see, his aunt, his father's half-sister, Harriett, familiarly known as Hattie, married into a Dutch mercantile family that was also, as one would expect, prominent in shipping circles. Hence, one assumes, the given name Cornelius. Hattie and her husband owned estates in both England and Holland. An interesting margin note here. The Dutch branch of the family at one time had an interest in the slave trade. Well, of course they did, and it was a substantial one, even if they don't like to talk about it any longer. The Dutch ever were pragmatic in their business pursuits.

"But I digress. As I said, Cornelius was already well situated when he arrived in Bermuda, and his business progressed rapidly. The Bermuda Mercantile Company was headquartered in Hamilton, and I've been told the foundation of the original building still exists. The firm eventually had branches in many places: Jamaica, Barbados, New York, Boston, Halifax, and Quebec, among others."

"And he left Bermuda for Newfoundland?"

"Yes, he did. Interesting, isn't it? It appears Cornelius made his first visit here in the early 1820s. Our bracing climate notwithstanding, he immediately saw the possibilities for commercial advantage, in part because then, as now, the country was essentially run by the merchant class, backed up by the military." Prim opened his eyes wide again and looked at Stride. "You know, of course, that we didn't achieve even a semblance of democratic government in Newfoundland until 1855. Which means that Cornelius Hurdle and his lot had the better part of thirty years to establish themselves without the botheration of popular opinion and the ballot box."

"Did you say Cornelius Hurdle moved from Bermuda to Newfoundland in the early 1820s?"

"No. That was when he first visited Newfoundland. He continued on in Bermuda until the Bermuda Mercantile Company went out of existence."

"Went out of existence? You said the company was a success."

"I did, and indeed it was. But the company did come to an end in 1828. The various branches, those that survived — and some did not — were taken over by local management and given other names."

"I'm guessing that the company's end wasn't entirely an honourable one."

"Indeed you are perceptive, Eric. I put that down to your suspicious nature. Yes, the company's end was both shrouded and clouded, and there are conflicting views about what happened, but I doubt the matter will ever be settled. In my own opinion, and it is shared by others, it was to Cornelius Hurdle's advantage to have an end to the company. The business game then, you understand, was played by even looser rules than exist today, and that is saying something. Cornelius Hurdle wasn't the only shareholder in the company, but he was by far the largest. A persistent rumour has it that Cornelius looted the company's assets and transferred them to St. John's, but that can never be proven. The evidence, you see, is long gone. The ship carrying the company's records foundered off Nantucket on its way north and west to St. John's."

"Sabotage?"

"Such was suggested, but that can never be proven either. But it is a matter of record that the ship carrying the records was one of the oldest in the company's line, and said to be destined for break up."

"And the crew? The ship didn't sail on its own."

"Of course it didn't. There was — dare I use the term? — a skeleton crew on board, and only two of them survived the tragedy, the captain and his mate. They managed to save themselves in the ship's single lifeboat." Prim made a noise, halfway between a snuffle and a grunt. "There was an inquiry later on. It brought down the expected judgement. Misadventure, perils of the sea, God's will. Probably the last. When in duress, we like to blame the Almighty for awful happenings, if we can. Such a very human thing to do."

"And the captain and his mate?"

Prim looked at Stride and half-smiled.

"The captain retired from the sea after his misadventure and settled into the life of a gentleman farmer on a modest but comfortable estate in Massachusetts. The mate, poor fellow, met with a second unfortunate accident, even before the inquiry was convened. A firearm he was cleaning discharged, accidentally it was said, removing most of the back of his head, and not a minor portion of the front. It was suggested that he had consumed a quantity of whisky that evening. No one brought forward contrary evidence, at least none that was ever recorded."

"And the case was closed."

"Yes, it was," Prim said. "Nailed tight shut, like the unfortunate mate's burial box. To continue. After the company re-established itself in St. John's as Hurdle and Company Limited, the enterprise thrived as before. Probably even better than before, smaller, more tight knit, and greatly profitable. It remained a family company, of course, with Cornelius at the helm until he passed on in 1870. It might, or might not, be worth noting that Cornelius Hurdle married quite late in life. He was in his fifties when his son Leonard was born." Prim giggled and his belly came to roiling life with the effort.

"That's not to say Cornelius wasn't active in his youth. There were the usual stories of a goodly number of half-breed, but unacknowledged, Hurdle offspring in Bermuda."

"Another reason for his move to Newfoundland?"

"Oh, I doubt that. A man like Cornelius Hurdle wouldn't have given a damn. Such interracial activity was common enough among the men of his class. I imagine it was almost a rite of passage, even a statement to the world that the lords of colonial business were, in their tolerant generosity, conferring improvement on the local stock. You might even say it was the New World's tawdry version of the infamous *droit de siegneur*. It's said that things are better now. It might even be halfway true." Prim adopted a fleeting expression of mild distaste. "Cornelius' son, Leonard Hurdle, later Sir Leonard, became principal shareholder and president of the Company after his father passed on. They say he was a good man, Leonard, very different from his father. He died in 1912, of typhus. An awful affliction. There was an epidemic in St. John's that year, apparently. I believe his widow still lives, though. Leonard's son Hubert, the current president, took over the company. He was quite young at the time, only twenty-four. Rumour has it that he and his father did not get along. Grating friction among the well-to-do is not unheard of. It even brings a modicum of cheer to lesser beings like ourselves."

Stride looked up from his note-taking.

"I'm assuming that bit of information was not given you by the family."

"No, of course not. Good old fashioned rumour and gossip, although from a reliable source."

"Sir Hubert seems to have done well since his father died."

"The company has, certainly. Whether Sir Hubert is entirely responsible is a point of some debate, although he does appear to have the right stuff. Education at a private school and at several universities, both in the States and in England."

Prim fell silent then and looked distractedly through his window. Stride wondered if the recitation had drained him of his energy. He was about to ask another question when there was a knock at the office door and a moment later it was pushed open. Stride turned to see Dianne Borg standing there.

"Ah. Dianne. Is it that time already?"

"It will be in five minutes, Bertie."

"Ah," he said again. He looked at Stride. "This gentleman is Inspector Eric Stride, Dianne. But perhaps you've already met?"

"Yes, we have met." She looked at Stride. "We met at an art show, some little while ago."

"At the studio of the young and gifted Hercules Agamemnon Parsons. Yes, I remember you telling me about that. The art show, I mean. I don't believe you mentioned Inspector Stride, though."

"I probably didn't, Bertie." She turned to Stride again. "Is something up?"

"Eric was asking me about the Hurdles. I have responded with a short dissertation on their interesting history."

Dianne reached across Prim's desk and picked up the newspaper. It was folded open at the article on Samuel Rossiter. She held it up so that Stride and Prim could see it.

"Did the Hurdles have something to do with this?"

"Not that we're aware of," Stride said. "I only needed some information as general background."

Down at floor level, the Pekingese had emerged from her basket beside the desk and was snuffling at Prim's dangling hand, looking for something more to eat. Stride took the distraction to catch Dianne's eye. She caught the motion and nodded.

"It would be quite exciting if there were," she said. "An involvement of the Hurdles, I mean. Something to distract us from the current heat wave. Things to chat about over tea."

"My dear Dianne," Prim said, "I have never known a time when we lacked something to talk about on our tea breaks."

"You're probably right about that, Bertie."

"Of course I am."

"Of course you are, dear man." She looked at Stride again. "I'm sorry to have to disturb your meeting, Inspector, but we need Bertie for an hour of earnest discussion. But when we're done with him, you can have what's left over, and welcome to it." She looked then at the basket under Prim's desk. The Pekingese had clambered back inside, and under Dianne's cool and steady gaze seemed almost to shrink away, burrowing into the folds of her blanket. "And don't bring your dog with you, Bertie dear. If you do, I may be inspired to revise my supper menu."

"Dear, dear, dear," Prim said. "Pay no attention, Eric. Mrs. Borg's bark is much worse than her bite."

"You have no personal experience of my bite, Bertie. Take good care you keep it that way." She patted him on the head and he responded with a giggle that set his vast assemblage of flesh aquiver. Dianne stepped back into the corridor. "Two minutes, Bertie. Don't be late. And don't forget what I said about the dog."

She directed a half-smile towards Stride, and then she was gone. He watched her as she walked down the corridor and entered a room at the far end. When he turned back, Prim was regarding him closely. But if he had something on his mind about him and Dianne, he did not voice it.

"I am afraid we will have to continue at a later time, Eric."

"One more question before you go. The Hurdle family seems to have a dodgy background, if what you told me about Cornelius is correct."

"I can assure you that everything I told you was factually correct. I may have fiddled with the nuances and the punctuation, just for the pleasure of the exercise, but nothing was made up."

"And the present generation? Have they distanced themselves from their romantic heritage?"

"I imagine you're using the word romantic in its broadest sense. I will respond by saying that most large and successful family businesses, here and elsewhere in what we like to call the civilised world, have a plenitude of skeletons rattling about. As to the present tribe of Hurdles, I imagine you might find the odd leg or arm bone on the premises, if you looked hard enough. But I will withhold further comment at this point."

"But you might have more to say later."

"I will direct my thoughts to the Hurdle family, and see if I come up with anything you might be interested in. And I know we will be in touch. But for now, less interesting duty calls. Mrs. Borg commands and I must perforce respond."

Prim heaved his bulk out of his chair and took a file folder from a drawer in his desk. "I imagine I'll be unavailable for the rest of the day. When Dianne says an hour, it means all of that, and often much more." He looked at the Pekingese in her basket, shook his head and sighed.

"I appreciate your taking the time, Bertie. If you find anything that might interest me, give me a call and I'll come back and see you again."

"It's always a pleasure to see you, Eric." He paused in the doorway. "She's been a very useful addition to our little group, Dianne. A very bright lady. I do hope she doesn't do something awful, like follow her American husband back to the fruited plains of Wisconsin, or wherever it is he hails from. It would be a great loss."

"I would be inclined to agree with you, Bertie." Too late, he tried to bite his tongue.

"Yes, I thought you might." Prim treated Stride to another smile and patted him on the arm, then raised his hand in a farewell gesture and trudged down the corridor towards the room Dianne had entered.

Stride was wondering now if Prim might have heard something about him and Dianne. As careful as they had been, there was always the possibility that someone had seen her entering or leaving his house on Circular Road. St. John's was at heart a small town, and people liked to gossip. It was a popular recreation hugely enhanced by the fact that the telephone system was still run by operators sitting at switchboards. A new dial system was still a year in the future. So there were ways, and there were ways. An inspector of police carrying on an affair with the wife of an American army officer was the sort of giggle that would make the rounds, better than a night out at the Nickel Theatre. Stride thought about all of that as he watched Prim ease himself through the doorway of the meeting room at the end of the corridor.

Inside the room, Dianne Borg was talking with a man much older than she was, grey-haired and slight to the point of frail. Stride recognised him as one of the directors of Hurdle and Company Limited. Dianne glanced at Prim as he came into the room, then looked past him down the corridor at Stride. She was careful not to smile this time, but she held his gaze for a moment. Even from that distance he could feel her warmth. Then an unseen hand pushed the door closed.

eiGhteEn

When Stride came out of the building that housed the Mercantile Association, he saw Alex Greene leaning against a telephone pole near the spot on Duckworth Street where the MG was parked. He was holding a pipe in his right hand and was poking at the interior with the blade of a pocket knife. When he caught sight of Stride, he stood upright, stepped away from the pole, closed the knife, and dropped it into his pocket along with the pipe.

"If I guessed that you were just inside there consulting with Pekingese Man, would I be far off the mark, Eric?"

"No, you would be right on it. Can I ask how you happen to know that?"

"You can ask. But if I answer truthfully you might think less of my investigational skills than you do already."

"I don't think that's likely."

"An uncomfortably ambiguous response. I ran into Harry about a half-hour ago. He was hot-footing it back to Fort Townshend, and he mentioned that you were having a chat with Bertie Prim."

"And so I was." Stride took Greene's place by the telephone pole and lit a cigarette. That inspired Greene to take out his pipe and start working on it again. "Are you about to ask me some questions about the Rossiter case?"

"Yes, I am, but in a tit-for-tat sort of way. I suppose you're aware that the news is out now that Rossiter's death wasn't an accident, that he was murdered."

"I imagined it was. You said tit-for tat, Alex. Do you know something about the Rossiter case that you think I should know?"

"I'm almost certain I know one thing you don't."

"Which is?"

"That your colleagues have taken into custody the two young men you were looking for."

"Have they? Where did they find them? Or did they have the good sense to come in voluntarily?"

"Your tone of voice suggests that you might not consider them to be the primest of suspects in Rossiter's death. That true?"

"Yes, that is true. But it's not for attribution. Agreed?"

"Agreed. The two of them were found huddled in a leftover American gun emplacement on the Outer Battery Road. The one near Chain Rock. They were tired and hungry, and more or less scared shitless. Rumour has it they also didn't smell very good. A local resident saw one of them taking a surreptitious pee early this morning. After a period of careful thought and struggle with her inner self, she did the proper thing and called in the cavalry. It has been duly recorded that the tykes surrendered without a fight."

"That would be the first intelligent thing they've done in the last several days," Stride said.

"I imagine you and Harry will be having an earnest chat with them fairly soon?"

"In due course. But I don't mind letting them stew in their own juices for a little while longer, and serve them right. Are they at Fort Townshend or at the Court House?"

"The Court House." Greene looked down the street. "Easy walking distance from here. Will you be available for an interview when you've questioned them?"

"I might be. It all depends on what if anything they have to add to the investigation. If, as I suspect, they had nothing to do with Rossiter's death, I'll only make a statement that they hadn't, and that the investigation is continuing. There isn't much of a story in that." Stride dropped his cigarette onto the sidewalk and stepped on it. "Do you have something else about the case that you want to tell me?"

"Maybe. I don't know if this is useful or not, but Sam Rossiter used to work in the mining industry, down north."

"Down north covers a fair piece of real estate."

"Do you know of a place called Chapel Bight?"

"Notre Dame Bay, near Tilt Cove?"

"That's the spot. Sam Rossiter worked there for a time."

"It must have been a long time ago. He's lived in Bermuda for more than thirty years."

"Yes, it was a long time back. Before the Great War, in fact."

"How do you know this, Alex? Did you know Rossiter personally?"

"No, I didn't. Although I have been to Bermuda a couple of times over the years. But that's neither here nor there."

"I don't suppose you ran into Sam Rossiter while you were there?"

"If I did, I don't recall it." Greene drew on his pipe and then he laughed. "Mind you, there's been more than a few nights I have a bit of trouble recollecting."

"Something of an occupational hazard, isn't it?"

"That's as true as sunshine and moonlight. Or was that moonshine and sunlight? I forget. No, I just did a bit of nosing around when the news came out about Rossiter being killed. It's my job to know what's happening in the old town, after all."

"Aided and abetted by your standard sources."

"The usual suspects, who must remain unnamed. Anyway, after you and Harry repaired to Fort Townshend from Blackmarsh Road yesterday afternoon, I took the opportunity to have a chat with Walter Keough at his residence. His valet was off for the day, and Sir Walter himself answered my knock."

"Tell me about that. Harry and I had almost zero success talking with Keough. We were lost in a fog of mutual incomprehension."

"That's a nice term, Eric. You should consider a newspaper career yourself someday."

"I'll give it all due consideration. Tell me about your chat with Keough. He was feeling less than friendly towards us when he abruptly concluded our interview. He even called us a rude name."

"Walter knows a lot of rude words, and he doesn't mind sharing them around. The trick is to know how to talk his language."

"And you would know how to do that."

"Of course I would. It's called the dialect of the gargle, and Walter and I are about equally fluent. Practice does make perfect. It also didn't hurt that

I had a flask of Eire's finest in my hip pocket. After a couple of libations, Walter Keough can become downright articulate. Anyway, it was in Chapel Bight that he first met Sam Rossiter. Keough was working underground, chunking out copper ore with a pickaxe, and Rossiter was busy in the office upstairs, playing piddly sticks with the company accounts."

"You're saying that Rossiter was cooking the company books?"

"Every company's books are cooked to some degree, Eric. It's all in the technique. In the end it comes down to a matter of palatability and presentation. He who employs the most accomplished chef gets to set the menu, and ends up ruling the world of business. And, by extension, all the rest of us."

"What year was that? When Rossiter and Keough were in Chapel Bight? You said it was before the First World War?"

"Walter was a bit vague about dates. There's only so much a flask of Irish whisky can accomplish in one afternoon. But I know it was before the Great War, in 1911. I had to look that part up. Anyway, I gathered the two of them discovered a mutual devotion to matters spiritual, so to speak, and a kind of friendship developed. Then, decades later, they were able to rekindle it."

"For as long as it lasted," Stride said.

"Just over a year, "Greene said. "Not a very long time."

"No, it isn't a very long time," Stride said.

Greene's story had tied up one small loose end, more or less explaining how Sam Rossiter and Walter Keough, polar opposites on the surface of it, came to be drinking partners in their old age.

"I imagine you have to be moving along, now that you have fresh bodies to interrogate," Greene said. He made a small production of looking at his watch.

"Soon, yes."

"Was any of that a help to you?"

"It doesn't hurt, and I appreciate it." Stride had the sense that Greene had more to say. "What was the name of the company they both worked for? In Chapel Bight?"

Greene took his time. He looked into the bowl of his pipe, then tapped the ash out against the telephone pole.

"An outfit called Centaur Minerals," he said finally. "The name has a kind of grand ring to it, doesn't it? Evocations of Greek mythology, and an age of intellectual opulence now sadly diminished."

"On the other hand, the centaurs could be said to have been the finest collection of horses' asses the world has ever seen."

"Now, there's cynicism writ large."

"Size does matter, Alex. Tell me. Who are – or were – Centaur Minerals? I've never heard of them."

"Which is fitting enough. They were around for only a short while, a common enough thing for mining companies, here as well as elsewhere. Those companies came and went like the coastal fogs. But the Chapel Bight find – copper, mainly – was for real, and a lot of money was made out of it. A little of it even trickled down to the lads below the subsoil, although it's been argued it was not nearly as much as it should have been. Nothing new there, either. Anyway, not long after the Chapel Bight operation was started up, Centaur Minerals was formally absorbed into a much larger entity."

"And the larger entity? Who was that? A local company, or a come-from-away?"

"Oh, it was a local outfit, alright. It was Hurdle and Company Limited. Sir Leonard was at the helm in those days, of course."

Greene had taken him by surprise with the information, which might well have been his intention in the first place, maybe the reason for the apparently impromptu meeting on Duckworth Street. Stride knew he should not have been surprised. The Notre Dame Bay region where Chapel Bight and Tilt Cove were located was one of the richest mineral areas in Newfoundland. Mining operations moved in and out, shafts were sunk, worked or abandoned, a few companies striking it rich, many others only being struck. It would have been surprising if the Hurdles hadn't been there, along with all the others.

Now Greene was looking at his watch again.

"I hope that's been of some help to you, Eric. But just now, I have to scarper. A fellow I knew once upon a long time ago has recently resurfaced, and he's offered to buy me a drink."

"Not something you'd be inclined to turn down."

"Certainly not. Friendship is important. You will let me know if you plan to release some information after you've done a nose-to-nose with the two underage unfortunates?"

"I'll do that, Alex."

"That's grand. You can leave a message for me at the paper. I call in every so often." He laughed. "When I can remember the number."

And then he was off. Stride watched Greene move on down Duckworth Street with his peculiar loping stride. He was wondering now if Greene also knew — somehow — that Sam Rossiter had been receiving money from Sir Hubert Hurdle's sister for more than three decades. He half-suspected he did. Greene was a journalist, and a good one. He had as many contacts in and around St. John's, and elsewhere, as anyone who'd ever worked the game. Stride thought about that as he walked along Duckworth towards the Court House.

nineteen

Chesley Bavidge made a note in the logbook when Stride came up to his desk in the Court House. Bavidge had been pulling duty at the lock-up for almost a year now. He was the largest man on the Force, over six-four and weighing in at a good two-twenty. Even the most unruly prisoner went quiet and docile with Bavidge standing close. His was a large and useful talent.

Stride looked at his watch. It was just after three now and he wanted to get the interviews over with. The two young men might have something useful to tell them. But he wanted Harry with him for that.

"What's your take on them, Ches?"

"Our new clients? A pair of very unhappy and frightened young lads is my opinion, sir."

"Do you think they're the sort who would be likely to murder an old man in a laneway?"

"I wouldn't bet any part of my pension on it. But if I've learned one thing in my fourteen years in this business, it's that appearances don't always count for a hell of a lot. I imagine you'll want to wait for Sergeant Phelan before you have a go at them?" Bavidge looked at the clock on the desk beside the logbook. "He should be here in a few minutes, sir. I tracked him down at Fort Townshend after they brought the boys in and had them settled. He was doing some work with Bern Crotty. He said he'd be along soon."

"A few minutes he said?"

"Yes, sir. He said he'd get Hynes to drive him here. I should also tell you that Alex Greene was here when they brought the two boys in."

"As a matter of fact, I did know that, Ches. He was the one told me they were here."

"Greene keeps his hand in. He's been in and out of here two or three times today, already." Bavidge looked past Stride. "Here's Sergeant Phelan, now."

"We'll take MacLeod, first, Ches, then Rowe after that."

"Give me five minutes, sir. I'll bring him along."

"You have that pleased-with-yourself look again, Harry. Did you and Bern find something useful?'

"We might have, sir. One interesting file. Crotty came across an old one a couple of weeks ago, and he remembered it when I asked for anything to do with Hurdles or Rossiters."

"How old, exactly?"

"It was a missing persons file from 1912. Elizabeth Hurdle went missing for a time that summer." Phelan opened his notebook. "She disappeared on July 18, which was a Thursday. That same day, her father, Sir Leonard Hurdle, sent his man to inform the Constabulary that his daughter was missing. That's when the file was opened."

"Nineteen-twelve. I came across that same date earlier today, when I was talking to Prim. Leonard Hurdle died that year. How old would his daughter have been then?"

"Elizabeth Hurdle would have been twenty in 1912. Not much more than a girl, really."

"What was it all about, Harry? Her disappearance?"

"Well, it doesn't seem to have been all that dramatic, sir." Phelan looked at his notes again. "She was missing for eight days altogether, from July 18 until Friday, July 26."

"Where did they eventually find her?"

"She wasn't found, exactly. The file says she came back home under her own steam. And it appears she was alright. According to the report, she was in good health."

"That's all there is? There's no explanation for the disappearance?"

Phelan shook his head. "No, sir. There's nothing in the file to say what it was all about. It seems to have been something of a squall in a saucepan, a false alarm, maybe. But there's no way to tell. Not without asking Elizabeth Cooke about it. Or Sir Hubert."

"We would need a good reason to ask either of them questions about an incident from thirty-six years ago, and I can't think of one offhand. I suppose the officer involved is out of the picture now?"

"They're both walking beats on high, sir."

"There were two officers involved?"

"Yes, sir. The first one assigned to the case was Donald Ash. He was a Detective Constable at the time."

"I remember Ash. He died two years ago. We went to his funeral."

"Yes, sir. I was in the honour party."

"Who was the second officer?"

"That was District Inspector McCarthy. He took over the case from Ash and he wrote up the report."

"The one they called Seamus McCarthy?"

"That's the one. His real name was Sidney. Seamus was a nickname, Crotty told me, him being of good Irish stock and all."

"That's a little unusual, his involvement in a case like that. McCarthy's position was about the same as McCowan's is now. Supervisory for the most part."

"The Hurdles might have asked that someone senior be assigned to the case, sir. It wouldn't have been unusual. Sir Leonard Hurdle swung a lot of weight at the time. At least as much as Sir Hubert does now."

"You have that right. Like you say, it seems not to have been much of a case. She wouldn't have been the first young woman to wander off for a few days."

"It doesn't seem like much, does it?" Phelan said. "My romantic nature whispers in my ear that the whole episode might have involved a dalliance of some sort."

Stride laughed. "A dalliance? Is that your word of the week?"

"Last week's," Phelan said. "This week's word is 'onomatologist.' Remember?"

"I can't imagine how I could have forgotten that. But if Elizabeth Hurdle went missing because of some romantic adventure, it probably wasn't with Reginald Cooke. He didn't come along until a year later."

"Well, we don't know that for sure, do we, sir? Jeffrey says they met in England, in 1913, just before the war. But what does he know, really? They might have met earlier than that. "

"You're right. Maybe they met here in St. John's that first time, and then when she was twenty-one, she went off to England to finish whatever it was they started."

"And in the end it finished him off. Didn't Jeffrey say he passed away not long after they were married?"

"It was in 1916. I remember the date because I wondered if he had bought it at the Somme, on July 1." They were in the interview room now. Stride lit a cigarette and sat on the side of the table. "Still, I'd like to know what it was about. Maybe it was only a dalliance, Harry, just as you say, but it looks like a loose end, and I don't like loose ends."

"We seem to be collecting a few. It was around that time, or a couple of years later, that Rossiter went off to Bermuda, with a monthly stipend from Elizabeth Hurdle."

"Yes, it was around that time." Stride went over to the door and peered down the corridor. There was still no sign of Bavidge and the prisoner, MacLeod. "We have all these bits and pieces of information, and we don't know what they might mean. It's irritating. Who was it said that the worst kind of fate was to be nibbled to death by butterflies?"

"I didn't know anyone said that. But, you know, it doesn't sound all that awful, being nibbled into extinction by pretty little things with fluttery wings. In fact, it sounds pretty damned enticing to me."

"You know, it doesn't sound all that bad. And here's another happy nibble for you. Rossiter and Keough both worked for the Hurdles back before the First War. That's when they met originally. The Hurdle Company owned the copper mine at Chapel Bight."

"On Notre Dame Bay."

"Yes. Rossiter worked in the office, while Keough toiled away underground. Alex Greene gave me that information this morning."

"I ran into him on my way up to Fort Townshend. We chatted for a minute. Did he say how he knew that? About Rossiter and Keough?"

"Apparently he managed a more successful interview with Keough than we did. Aided and abetted by a flask of Irish whisky."

"Technique can be all-important," Phelan said. He nodded towards the doorway. "Enter Constable Chesley Bavidge, accompanied by shit-baked young man with pale complexion."

And so he was. Gordon MacLeod stopped at the entrance to the interview room and looked at Stride and Phelan in turn. He had heard what Phelan had said, and it had done nothing for his spirit. He looked away from the two detectives, taking in the sparse appointments of the interview room. Stride thought he might have been looking for truncheons and thumbscrews. MacLeod was a bit taller than David Lawlor, and he looked older, although the booking sheet said they were the same age. He also had the look of an athlete, solidly constructed and with a compactness of movement that suggested he would do well on a soccer pitch or a baseball diamond. No doubt he wished that was where he was, instead of being lodged in the bowels of the Court House, surrounded by large men with cold expressions.

Bavidge steered MacLeod to the designated chair, told him to sit, and then loomed over him.

"If he gives you any trouble, Inspector, just give a shout, and I'll come running." Bavidge gave Gordon MacLeod a final look and left the room, closing the door behind him.

Phelan took his seat in the flanking chair and Stride sat across from MacLeod, duplicating the arrangement they had had with Lawlor. Stride uncapped his pen and opened his notebook, taking his time. He looked at his watch and wrote down the exact time, speaking it aloud while he did so. It was three-forty-one. Taking note of the time reminded him again that he was hungry. He wondered vaguely if MacLeod might be also.

"I'll dispense with the preliminaries, Mr. MacLeod. We'll go directly to what happened on Monday night." Stride recited the events described by Lawlor, which led to the tire rolling down Cathedral Street and colliding with the parked car, Corrigan's sudden appearance and apprehension of Lawlor, and MacLeod and Rowe escaping down Scanlon's Lane. He paused and waited for MacLeod to make a comment, but he only stared at the table in front of him without speaking. "You agree with the sequence of events as I have described them?"

"Yes, sir." Two words only. MacLeod continued to stare at the tabletop. After a moment he glanced to his left at Phelan.

Stride made a note in his book.

"Do you want to add anything to that?"

MacLeod shook his head. "No, sir."

"You're satisfied that the events, as described, are correct?"

"Yes, sir."

"After Constable Corrigan appeared on the scene, you and your friend, Philip Rowe, ran into Scanlon's Lane?"

"Yes, sir."

"You ran down the steps."

"Yes, sir."

"It's tricky, isn't it? The steps are steep and winding, it was dark. There wasn't much illumination."

MacLeod nodded but didn't reply. Stride could see that he was retracing his and Rowe's movements of Monday night, bringing it all back. He managed to maintain a calm expression but there was a movement behind the eyes, a subtle progression of emotions, a building towards the moment.

"And then?" Stride stared at him, pen poised over the white, blue-lined page of his notebook. "What then?"

MacLeod stole another glance in Phelan's direction. Harry was making notes. He turned back to Stride.

"There was someone in the lane, lying on the steps. I didn't see him at first. It was pretty dark in there." He hesitated. "I almost tripped over him. Phil saw him before I did, and he caught hold of me."

Stride waited for MacLeod to continue, but he went silent, looking inside himself, revisiting the memory.

"Tell me exactly what you saw."

"Just the old man, lying there," MacLeod said. "I thought at first he might be asleep, but then I could see he wasn't."

"How did you know he wasn't asleep? You said it was dark in the laneway."

"There was a bit of light, from a bulb up on the side of a building. But I knew he wasn't asleep from the way he was lying. No one would sleep like that."

"Like what?"

"He was all crumpled up. So I thought he must be hurt or something. I went over to him, to see if he needed help." He looked straight at Stride, as if trying to judge the effect his words had had, perhaps hoping for a show of sympathy. Stride didn't change his expression.

"You went over to him?"

"Yes, sir. And when I got closer, I could see he was hurt really bad."

"What did you see?"

"I could see there was blood on his head. His hair was all tangled and matted with it. There was blood on his mouth, too."

Stride looked across the room at Phelan. Harry had paused in his note-taking and he was looking back at Stride. MacLeod, catching the change in their attitudes, glanced back and forth between them.

"Go over that again," Stride said.

MacLeod was nervous now, unsettled.

"What?" The one word was all he could manage.

"What you just told us. Start from when you first saw the body lying on the steps."

MacLeod went through it again, how he almost tripped over the body, how he sensed the man wasn't sleeping but instead, might be injured, and how he went to see if he could help. The blood on the old man's head, the matted hair, the blood on his mouth. This time he also included the denture on the step by Rossiter's left hand.

"Alright, take a breather." Stride wrote in his notebook, taking his time. Then he looked at MacLeod again. "You saw that the man was bleeding from the head and the mouth. Did you touch him?"

"Touch him?"

"Yes. Did you touch the old man?"

MacLeod shook his head vigorously. "No, I didn't touch him."

"You're sure about that?"

"Yes." MacLeod sat more upright in his chair. "I never touched him. I didn't get a chance. Phil grabbed hold of me again and said we had to get out of there."

"Yes?"

"And we did. We took off down the steps and out onto Water Street."

"And you didn't touch the body. You didn't touch him at all?"

"You keep asking me that."

"Yes, I do. I want you to be sure about this." Stride leaned forward, and the movement caused MacLeod to sit even straighter in his chair. "You are certain you didn't touch him?"

"No, I didn't."

"Did your friend Rowe touch him?"

"No, he didn't touch him, either. He didn't even get as close to him as I did. He was behind me, pulling me away from there, and on down the steps."

Stride sat back, looking steadily at Gordon MacLeod. The young man was sweating now, holding onto the seat of the chair with both hands.

"And after that. After Rowe took hold of you again, and you ran on down the steps to Water Street. Then what?"

"We went east on Water Street, and then out onto Battery Road."

"To the gun emplacement."

"Yes."

"And you stayed there for the better part of two days. Until the police came and arrested you."

"Yes, sir. We went out a couple of times, I mean one or the other of us went out to buy some food at a corner store. But we spent most of our time there, hiding. There, or on the hills nearby, down by the water sometimes."

"Almost two days in a concrete gun emplacement on the Outer Battery Road. Not much fun, I guess."

"No, sir." A pause. "We didn't know what else to do."

"No," Stride said, "I suppose you didn't. You could have saved yourselves and everyone else a lot of trouble if you'd just come on in, given yourselves up."

"I guess so."

Stride could see that the boy was tired now, deflated. Whatever small store of courage he had carried into the interview room had been used up. He seemed close to tears. Stride hoped it wouldn't come to that. Not again.

He looked at Harry to see if he had anything he wanted to add. Phelan shook his head, but continued making notes.

"Is the old man alright?" MacLeod asked suddenly.

The question took Stride only halfway by surprise. When they had found Rossiter's body, he had given instructions to everyone involved in the investigation that when the boys were found, they were to be told nothing about the old man's fate. It was the standard precaution. The less a suspect knew about events and developments surrounding a crime, the less chance he had to make up stories, to send the investigator down a garden path, to cover his tracks. And for once, the message had gotten through, the instruction heeded by everyone. It was apparent, also, that the boys hadn't seen a newspaper on any of their trips to a store to purchase food.

But Stride wasn't ready to tell MacLeod the facts about Sam Rossiter, not yet. They wanted to question Rowe first, and after that they might want to interrogate MacLeod a second time, if the two accounts differed in any substantial way. It seemed almost cruel, keeping MacLeod in the dark, because

Stride had a sense that the boy actually cared about the old man, was concerned about him. He picked his words carefully.

"He's at the General Hospital," Stride said. "He is being looked after."

Gordon MacLeod looked at Stride, as if he hoped he would say more, go into more detail about Rossiter's condition, offer him more tangible comfort. But Stride didn't add anything to what he had already said.

"There had to have been someone else in the laneway when MacLeod and Rowe ran down those steps," Phelan said. "When we got to the scene, Rossiter's cap was on his head. We know Corrigan didn't touch the body, so the cap must have been on his head when Corrigan found him." Harry went to his notes from Monday night. "That's what he said at the time, when he described the appearance of the body when he found it. The cap was definitely on his head. Rossiter's killer must have been there when the two boys came through."

They were still sitting in the interview room, fleshing out their notes, editing and rewriting while the information was still fresh. The interviews were completed now. Philip Rowe had confirmed all of the essentials of what Gordon MacLeod had told them. Stride read through the last of his notes and screwed the cap back on his pen.

"There's a couple of places in that laneway he could have hidden when he heard MacLeod and Rowe coming down the steps," Stride said. "And the light there wasn't very good. After they left, whoever was there must have put the old man's cap back on his head."

"Why the hell would he do that? He'd killed Rossiter, beaten him to death, Rowe and MacLeod come running through, and then he takes the time to put his cap back on his head? And with Corrigan charging down the steps after the two boys? It makes no sense."

Stride shook his head.

"No, that's not quite right, Harry. Corrigan didn't go into the lane until a few minutes after the boys did. First, he took care of Lawlor. He knew that he couldn't catch MacLeod and Rowe unless one of them had fallen on the steps and hurt himself. That delay gave Rossiter's killer some extra time. Just enough, obviously. And anyway, he didn't know that Corrigan was anywhere near the laneway. He only knew that the boys had been running down the steps, and were frightened when they saw the body."

Phelan nodded. "You're right. He would only have seen MacLeod and Rowe. He couldn't have known there was a policeman close by. And when Corrigan came into the laneway with his flashlight, that would have given him enough warning to get out of there. Jack said he took his time coming down the steps."

"Or he went back into his hiding place. It's possible he didn't leave the laneway until after Corrigan went to the Court House."

"Corrigan would shit a rib if he thought the killer was right there all the time, maybe only a few feet away from him."

"I expect he would." Stride laughed. "It sounds improbable, doesn't it? But, you know, it's a variation on hiding in plain view. Corrigan assumed, reasonably enough, that the two boys were responsible for Rossiter's death, and he also knew they were long gone. He wasn't too concerned about that because he had Lawlor handcuffed to a telephone pole on Duckworth Street. In Jack's situation, I think I would have reacted in exactly the same way. I wouldn't have looked for a third party. I wouldn't even have thought about someone else."

Phelan was nodding his head. "You see what you expect to see. But that doesn't explain why he put the old man's cap back on."

"No, it doesn't. That part is really strange. I wonder what the hell it was all about?"

Phelan sat forward in his chair, leaning his elbows on his knees. He looked at the floor for a minute and then raised his head.

"Maybe he was in shock?"

"The man who killed Rossiter."

"Yes, sir. Maybe he hadn't meant to kill him. Like Butcher said, maybe Rossiter was killed as the result of an argument. The guy loses his temper and attacks Rossiter, hits him three or four times, and then Rossiter is dead, or nearly. And when the fellow sees what he's done, he goes into shock. I know that sort of thing can happen. And people will do strange things when they're in shock."

"Maybe." Stride walked into the corridor and stood there looking up and down the length of it. He was thinking now about the night he and Gullage had fought off the raiding party on his boat, the disorientation that followed with the pain from the bullet in his shoulder that had knocked him down. When he saw Gullage crawling towards him, trailing blood along the deck, his first thought was about washing it away before it made a permanent stain on the planking. It had taken him precious moments to pull his attention back through his pain and shock to the real peril they were in. Now he placed himself in Scanlon's Lane, taking his memory of that night with him, and he looked down at the crumpled body of an old man he had just killed, at the bloody tangle of hair, and at the cap lying on the step there beside him. He saw himself bend down and pick up the cap, dust it off, and place it on the man's head, taking care not to get blood on his hands.

He went back into the interview room.

"That just might be the answer, Harry. Putting Rossiter's cap back on his head might have seemed like a really important thing for our man to do."

By the time they left the Court House, it was almost five, not late really, not yet quitting time, but they were both tired, buckling a little now under the accumulated weight of the day. So, instead of going back to Fort Townshend, Stride drove Harry to his house on Victoria Street, just below Queen's Road. The sun was still bright, but the wind seemed to be picking up some, and it was a little cooler than it had been. A new weather system might be moving in, Stride thought, cooler weather in the offing, maybe. But there was still no real sign of rain despite the rolling clouds that topped the Southside Hills, moving east out over the Atlantic.

The Phelan house was on the east side of Victoria and the front was blanketed in bright sunlight. Kitty Phelan was sitting on the doorstep smoking a cigarette. A mug sat on the step beside her.

Kitty and Harry Phelan gave credence to the claim that opposites attract. Harry looked every inch and ounce a policeman, close to six feet tall and not far off two hundred pounds. Kitty was small and slender, with thick, dark hair, stylishly cut. Her skin was deeply tanned, testimony to a lot of time spent outdoors.

The Phelans had no children as of yet. Stride didn't know if they were trying for a family or not, but he had always assumed they were. It was what married couples did. But Harry hadn't said anything about a family, and Stride hadn't asked. He wondered sometimes if Harry and Kit might buck the trend, and simply continue to enjoy each other's company, unencumbered by children, the weight of a family. But he also knew that that line of thought said more about himself, and his own predilections, than it did about the Phelans.

Stride and Kitty had been friends since the first day they met six years ago.

There had been an immediate rapport between them — and Kitty had always called Stride by his first name, a contrast to Harry's routine formality — the sort of quick friendship that didn't happen often for Stride. That had been during the war, when the Phelans had been married less than a year.

Stride and Phelan were already friends, an odd thing on the face of it, because they seemed to have very different personalities. Harry was a St. John's boy, easygoing and popular with the other members of the Force. Stride was not. In common parlance he was a bayman from the island's south coast. And while he was respected for his intelligence and his abilities, he wasn't generally liked. His relative affluence, highlighted by the MG he drove, and the house he lived in, only complicated the situation.

Harry was in uniform then, walking a beat, and Stride was a Detective Sergeant, lusting openly after a promotion to Inspector. Stride already knew Harry was going to be in plainclothes, it was only a matter of time. And he was looking ahead to a time when they might be partners.

"A successful day?" Kitty looked up at them, shielding her eyes from the sun with her left hand. Cigarette smoke curled over the top of her head.

"An interesting day," Harry said.

"Interesting, was it? That's a word that covers a multitude of sins. I take it you haven't made as much progress as you would like?"

"Progress comes in a variety of forms," Stride said. "We know both more and less than we did this morning. We're deep in the wheat-and-chaff stage just now."

"Well, tomorrow, as they say, is another day. I guess you'll just have to hope for the best."

She picked her mug up from the doorstep and drank a toast to their prospects.

"And just now, my dear, I frankly do not give a damn." Harry took the mug and sniffed at the contents. He raised his eyebrows, then drank some of it. "But this might help."

"Go easy on that, my darling man. I don't want you to topple off the step and hurt yourself. I might have some use for you later on." She smiled at Stride. "Has the dear man been working too hard, Eric?"

"He'll tell you he has been, and I wouldn't dream of arguing the point."

"Then I will be very gentle with him this evening."

"Please do. I'll need him again tomorrow."

"I will fix him up proper, and he'll be as good as new come morning.

I know that's not saying a lot, but I'll do the best I can with the materials at hand."

"Now you understand why I've been urging you to get married, sir. It's an experience no man should miss out on."

"I will take that in the spirit in which it is rendered." Stride laughed and looked at Kitty. "Who was it that said revenge is a dish best eaten cold?"

She smiled up at him.

"Almost certainly a married woman, Eric."

He took his time driving home, wishing that the wind that was blowing through his hair would take away some of the tension and tiredness of the day. He drove east, more or less in the direction of his house, and then turned north along Portugal Cove Road. As soon as he was outside the city proper, and an opportunity presented itself, with no traffic or people in sight, he punched the accelerator and the MG leaped forward, the engine howling. When the needle on the speedometer touched eighty he throttled back and downshifted, and the car quickly slowed.

He continued driving north for another mile or so until a panel truck with a single horse in the back passed him going in the opposite direction. Stride turned the MG around and followed behind. The horse was an old one, swaybacked with age and hard labour, and with a tired look in its eyes. Stride thought the animal was probably on its last excursion, on a trip to a slaughterhouse he knew was located on a side road about a half mile away. He wasn't sure where the horse would go from there. He had never really thought about it before, even though the city had a large population of horses. A lot of the city's commerce still depended on horse-drawn vehicles of various kinds. All those horses had to go somewhere at the end of their days.

As Stride pulled close to the truck, the horse turned its head and looked at him with a vacant expression in large eyes that were too weary even to hold fear. Under the animal's near-lifeless gaze, the exhilaration he had enjoyed only minutes before fell away. He throttled back until he had dropped far behind the truck. He maintained the interval until it had turned right onto a side road and disappeared around a turn. A cloud of brown dust hung in the warm air to mark its passing.

The telephone was ringing when he let himself into his flat. It stopped just as he reached it. His first thought was that it might have been Dianne who had called, even though simple logic told him that was unlikely. He knew he would not see her this evening, not with her husband back in town, but the wish was there anyway. He stood in the kitchen and stared at the phone, hoping it would ring again, hoping it would be her. But a knuckle of anxiety was pressing against the back of his head now, a familiar, unwelcome sensation that had first started up not long after he and Dianne had begun their affair, when the first frantic passions had begun to wane.

He stared at the silent phone for long moments, then abandoned his ridiculous vigil, went to the bedroom and took off his tie and shirt. The air of the room was warm on his skin and he saw that he had forgotten to open the window before he went out that morning. He went to open it now, but quickly stepped back when he saw two of his tenants sitting in the backyard. Then he moved forward again to look out, staying just far enough away from the glass that he could not be seen from outside.

The couple was sitting on white-painted wooden lawn chairs under the largest of the three oak trees. They were young, in their early twenties. They had moved in a year ago, married only recently. The husband was not long back from war service in the navy, happy to be alive and not damaged in any obvious way. They were sharing a glass of something cold in the warmth of the late summer afternoon. Stride imagined they were exchanging stories about their day, perhaps planning something for the evening ahead. While he continued to watch, the young woman leaned towards her husband and placed her head on his shoulder as they linked hands. With her free hand she stroked his arm.

He watched them for a few moments longer. He went into the living room and stood there looking at the painting he had bought from Herc Parsons, thinking about the night he and Dianne had met, and all that had happened since. Not for the first time he was alternately wishing that she could be here with him now, and regretting having started the affair in the first place. He took a bottle of rum from the liquor cabinet and poured a large quantity into a glass, not bothering to add water as he usually did. He sipped it quickly and deliberately. Still looking at the painting, his mind danced the idiot's manic gavotte of emotional pluses and minuses, staying with it long enough for a heavy pain to build behind his eyes. He looked into his glass and saw that it was almost empty, so he topped it up. He stood for a minute longer in the room, still sipping rum, not looking at anything now. Then he went down the hall to the bathroom and turned on the shower.

t w e n t y

Stride was awake before the sun came up. The sky in the east was slate-grey and indecisive, and cool air drifted into the bedroom through the open window. He wondered if the heat wave might be over.

He lay for a while in the semi-light, listening to the faint and reassuring sounds of morning. He felt good, and he had slept more soundly than usual, two unexpected dividends from last night's calculated foolishness. An excess of rum, especially when laced with self-pity, usually had him awake and wandering around his flat in the early morning hours.

He wasn't hungry, though, but he would soon want coffee, or strong tea. He wasn't sure which. He swung his legs over the side of the bed and sat there, looking through the window, thinking about it. A house sparrow was sitting on the ledge. Man and bird looked at each other for a few seconds before the bird took flight. He decided on coffee.

While the percolator grumbled on the stove, he showered, turning up the heat until the water pounding down on his head and over his back was almost too hot to bear. He stayed there for long minutes flexing his back and shoulder muscles.

He drank his coffee sitting at the kitchen table watching the morning develop. He took his time going over his notes on the case, and when he had finished, he went over them again. He wondered if the connection between Rossiter and the Hurdle family was coincidence, or if it had some relevance to

Rossiter's death. But Butcher might have been right, that Rossiter's death was only a tragic accident, two drunken men fighting in a laneway. That possibility was only increased by the fact that Rossiter had a brain injury that made him intermittently irrational. And that brought Stride back to McCowan's suggestion that the absence of motive and premeditation meant they might never find the killer.

He put the notebook away, fetched the morning paper from the front step and perused the headlines as he walked back upstairs. He was hungry now, so he toasted a slice of bread and had it with a tablespoon of Dianne's orange marmalade. That brought their relationship back into his mind. He allowed himself to think about it for a few minutes, once more weighing the positives and negatives, but the scales would not balance. He felt his sad and sour mood from last night starting to come back. He gave it up, poured a fresh cup of coffee and went to the bedroom to dress.

When Stride left the house at seven-thirty, the cloud cover had melted away and it looked like it would be another fine, hot day. The wind, a near-constant in St. John's, was blowing hard now and the top branches of the tall trees along Circular Road were dancing against the blue of the sky. He backed the MG out of the garage and drove west on Circular, heading for Fort Townshend, but when he reached the intersection with Rennie's Mill, he changed his mind and decided to pick Harry up at his house on Victoria Street. He needed company.

He parked the MG across from Phelan's house, facing down the hill, the wheels turned in against the curb. He looked at the house and checked his watch again. It was still very early, so he decided to wait until there was some activity behind the curtains in the front room. He smoked one cigarette and was about to light a second when Kitty Phelan pulled the curtains back from the front window. She waved when she saw the MG. A moment later the front door opened and she stood on the step, watching as he crossed the street.

"You're in time for breakfast, Eric, if you're in the mood. Harry's still upstairs muttering to himself about the state of the world, but he'll get over it."

"I am in the mood, as it happens. I haven't really eaten yet this morning." With the mention of breakfast he was suddenly very hungry.

Kitty stepped back into the hallway and headed for the kitchen. Stride followed after her. Upstairs he could hear water running into a sink and the sound of a safety razor being rinsed.

"Harry's like his father, he likes a big breakfast. I used to make do with just tea and toast, but he's made a convert out of me. He's the one who gains weight, though. God's judgement, I call it. Today his worship has asked for sausages and eggs. Will that do?"

"That will do better than well. Can I help?"

"You can be in charge of the toast." She pointed to the breadbox on the counter and took a bread knife from a drawer. She placed a frying pan on the stove and opened the icebox. She glanced at him as she moved back and forth between icebox and stove. "We don't see you this early as a rule. Is something up? Something other than the case, I mean?"

"Yes and no." He concentrated on slicing the bread, cutting thick slices, waiting to see if she challenged his reply. He thought she would – probably hoped she would. But she took her time, arranging three rows of small sausages in the pan. She punctured each one with a fork, to let the fat bubble out. When he didn't add anything, she turned and looked at him.

"Yes and no doesn't quite do it, Eric. Is something going on with you, something more personal than the late Sam Rossiter?"

"Maybe." He placed a slice of bread in each side of the toaster. He thought he saw her smile.

"Wait until I have the sausages almost done before you fire up the toaster." She took six eggs from the cardboard container and placed them in a bowl and handed it to him. "Anyway, I've just decided it's scrambled eggs this morning, and you're in charge of that too. There's a whisk there in the second drawer." She leaned against the stove. "So, does *maybe* have a name?"

"Yes," Stride said. "Yes, she does."

"But you're not about to shout it out loud."

"No. I can't do that."

"That's alright with me, Eric. But the question is, is it alright with you?"

"Sometimes I pretend it is, but on the whole, probably not."

"If I guessed she's married, would I be a long way off the mark?"

He had known the question was coming. Maybe that was what he wanted in the first place.

"Funny you should ask that," he said.

"It's right bloody hilarious, but I don't quite hear the sound of laughter. We can play *twenty questions*, if you like, but I can probably do away with nineteen of them."

"Probably."

"Well, you're not writing an original script here, old son, it's all been done before. Not that that brilliant insight helps you very much, does it?" she gave him another look. "Or her."

"No, it doesn't."

"How serious is it, then? Is she thinking of leaving her husband?"

"She might be. We haven't really talked about that."

"But the subject has come up."

"A few times."

"This is like pulling wisdom teeth. Are there children involved?"

"No. No children."

"Well, that's one silver lining in your overcast."

She went back to the sausages, moved them around the pan, then moved the pan to another part of the stove, off the direct heat. "You don't want advice from me, do you?"

He shook his head. "No, not really."

"I didn't think so. I imagine you'll muddle through on your own, the way most people do, for better or for worse." She laughed. "Bad choice of phrase, that."

"I guess so." He looked at her. "Do you resent my telling you about it?"

"A little, yes. But it's alright. And I can understand that you need to talk. You're not that much different from the regular herd. In a way, it's flattering that you chose me to talk to." She pointed at the counter where four plates were stacked. "Pass me one of those, will you? The sausages are almost done. Now you can start taking out your frustrations on those eggs."

That much he could do. He began whisking the eggs, gradually increasing the rhythm, watching the mixture grow in volume. He moved over to the stove. Kitty had transferred the sausages to a plate and had drained the fat from the pan, wiped it, and dropped in a square of butter. They stood side by side watching as it melted, bubbles forming around the perimeter. She canted the pan from side to side to spread the butter around, then placed it on the burner.

"Are you in love with her?"

"I don't know. Sometimes I think I am."

"And sometimes not. It's so hard to tell at first, isn't it?" She jabbed him with the handle of the fork. "All that frantic activity and heavy breathing? But you might figure it out eventually. Rumour has it you're all grown up."

"Appearances to the contrary."

"Let's say it requires a careful sifting of the available evidence."

"Evidence? I refuse to talk about evidence and other criminal matters until I've eaten my breakfast." They hadn't heard Harry come downstairs. If he was surprised to find Stride standing in his kitchen, he didn't show it. And if he had heard any other part of their conversation, he didn't let on. He was carrying the morning paper.

"No more talk about evidence, then. Anything exciting in the paper, love?"

"I'm looking even as we speak," Harry said.

"He always goes to the sports section first, Eric. An overgrown boy is what I married, and time has not improved him much. But I'm working on it."

"And she's a tireless worker, sir." Harry looked up from the paper. "Is it scrambled eggs we're having this morning?"

"Yes, it is. And your boss is doing the honours."

"I warn you, sir. Kitty's very particular about her scrambled eggs. She likes them light and fluffy."

"Like the general run of your conversation, dear heart. How did the Dodgers make out yesterday?"

"They won, six to four over the Braves. Branca went the distance and Furillo doubled in two runs in the eighth."

"Well, that's to the general good."

Harry folded the paper and put it on the table. "Anything for me to do?"

"You can make the tea, love. The kettle's on the boil."

Stride attended to the eggs, at the same time watching and listening as Harry and Kitty moved through their morning routine, working around him, accommodating his unexpected arrival. He felt like an intruder, someone who didn't belong, someone who also had carried his own tensions and foibles into their home. He could feel his sour mood returning. Kitty Phelan read his change in attitude. She moved close beside him and prodded him with her elbow.

"Light and fluffy is the way I like my eggs, old son. Pay attention, now."

Stride climbed the stairs to the second floor of the Newfoundland Mercantile Association building on Thursday morning, but when he got there, he didn't find Bertie Prim in his office. His first thought was that Prim might be in another meeting, but that probability diminished when he saw that the Pekingese wasn't in her basket under Prim's desk. It was more likely, then, that dog and master both were out of the building. Bertie Prim and his Snuffle were all but inseparable.

He went along the corridor and looked into the first office he came to. A man in early middle age, his bald head set atop a gaunt frame, sat at a desk in his shirtsleeves. He was reading the business section of one of the local papers. Wire-framed glasses sat on the end of a long nose. Stride wasn't sure if he was looking through or over them to read. The man glanced up to see Stride standing in his doorway.

"You have the look of a man who might be lost," he said. His voice was unusually deep. He sounded as though he was talking from the bottom of a rain barrel. Interesting that such resonance could come from a frame so slight and so apparently fragile.

"Not lost, exactly," Stride said. "Just not found."

"Looking for someone?"

"Yes. Bertie Prim left a message at Fort Townshend for me."

"You're from the Constabulary, then. Didn't I see you here talking to Prim yesterday?"

"Yes, you did."

"Well, you won't find Bertie, I'm afraid. He was here until about an hour ago, but then that dog of his started breathing strangely, worse than usual, even. Bertie was worried it might be having a heart attack or something. Which wouldn't be a great surprise, considering the way he siphons food into the poor beast. Anyway, he skedaddled out of here all in a sweat, anxiety writ very large. I expect he's probably at the vet's now, or at home mourning his loss. Either way, I don't think we'll see him again today. Prim is very much involved with his dog, poor fellow. Maybe you know about that."

Stride nodded. "Perhaps you can tell me where I might find Mrs. Borg, then? Bertie said I should see her if he wasn't in." It wasn't true, but this man, whoever he was, couldn't know that.

"Mrs. Borg?" He took off the glasses and dropped them on the desk. "I saw her earlier. She's either in her office," he gestured to the right with his thumb. "Or she's in the library." A double gesture in the same direction. "If you don't find her in the one or the other, then I'm afraid you're on your own. Unless, of course, I can help you? My name's Chamberlain, by the way. Willis Chamberlain."

He stood halfway erect and leaned forward to shake Stride's hand.

"My name's Eric Stride and I'm pleased to meet you, Mr. Chamberlain. But it's Mrs. Borg I want to see."

"I can't say as I blame you. If I carried twenty fewer years on my person, I would probably feel much the same way." He sat back in his chair, crossed his long thin legs, picked up a pencil, and held it between his two hands like a tiny swagger stick. "I will guess you're here about the Rossiter case?"

"Yes. Bertie has been assisting me with some information."

"Information is what Prim is all about. Well, that and obnoxious little dogs with wet faces. So, are you making progress in your investigation?"

"Some."

"But no arrests yet?"

"Not yet, no. The investigation is continuing."

"You know, we say the same sort of thing here when we find ourselves walking around in circles of decreasing magnitude. Our line is that the matter is under active consideration." He tossed the pencil onto his desk. "Where would we be without our clichés, I wonder?"

"Striving to invent some, I expect."

"Yes, I think so. But perhaps things will start looking up for you once you've seen Mrs. Borg."

And with that, Chamberlain smiled again and went back to his newspaper.

Dianne Borg wasn't in her office, but Stride found her in the library two doors farther along. She was hovering over a table and perusing a large book that looked like an old company ledger. She looked up when he tapped on the doorjamb.

"Hello. I've been expecting you. I'm afraid Bertie's gone for the day, though. Canine problems."

"So I was told by a tall, thin fellow with a well-honed sense of humour." Stride nodded his head in the direction of the office he had just left. He stepped into the room.

"Willis Chamberlain. He does have his moments. Bertie did leave you some material, though, and he asked me to give it to you. It's in my office."

She closed the ledger and led the way. Her office was even smaller than the one Stride and Phelan shared at Fort Townshend. She caught his look.

"It's not very large, is it? But if we take turns breathing, we should be alright."

"Well, it is cosy," Stride said. Now that he was standing close to her again, most of his turmoil from last night and earlier this morning was slipping away.

"You're very diplomatic." She moved closer to him, sensing the residue of tension in him. "Are you alright? Did you sleep badly again?"

"Not as well as I would have liked." Not telling the truth grated on him, but this was neither the time nor the place.

Dianne looked into his eyes for a moment and touched the back of his hand with her fingertips. She moved a little distance away from him and changed the subject.

"I'm reliably informed that this office was a closet not so long ago. But it's a start." She turned around, picked up an envelope, and gave it to him. "The information Bertie was able to find is in here. Just after he had it all assembled for you, his sweet little Snuffle started having her heart attack, or whatever it was, and he was on his frantic way."

Stride opened the envelope and took out three pages of material. He scanned it quickly.

"You've read this, I suppose?"

"Yes. In fact, I was the one who found most of it, although Bertie told me where to look. Except for a few bits, for which he dug into his prodigious memory. Some of what he found has to do with mining ventures the Hurdles were involved in."

"I see that. Notre Dame Bay and Chapel Bight are mentioned here. That ties in with some other information I've gotten recently."

"So this might be useful to you. Do you know much about the mining industry here on the island?"

"I don't actually know a lot about mining anyplace. Although my father did work for a time at a mine in Rencontre East."

"Rencontre East? That would have been quite a long time ago."

"Yes, it was in 1915. And if you've heard of the mine, you probably know the place is on the south coast, not far from where we lived in Bay d'Espoir. A company had hopes of establishing a molybdenum mine there. My father was part of the crew digging out ore for export to the States."

"But I don't think that ever happened, did it?"

"No, it didn't. We were at war in 1915, but the Americans weren't. The government classed molybdenum as a strategic mineral, and it couldn't be exported to a neutral country. It's used as a substitute for tungsten in steel products. So, the twenty tons of ore they dug out stayed where it was."

"I take it your dad didn't do any more mining after that?"

"No, that was his one and only shot at it. My father was an outdoorsman. Working in a hole in the ground didn't suit him at all. He told me he needed to feel the sun on his face."

"Like father, like son?"

"To a degree, yes. But he really has lived that way, for almost his whole life. I didn't. I did other things."

"Yes, I know you did." She glanced towards the open doorway, and seeing no one she stepped close to him again and kissed him quickly on the mouth. Her action seemed to surprise her as much as it did Stride. "I wish we could be alone, together. Right now. I miss you."

"I miss you," he said. And it was true, he did.

She touched a finger to her lips and then to Stride's.

"I want to do something about that. I just don't know when. Or how." She stepped away. "I guess we had better get back to the business at hand."

"Yes, we had." He sat on the corner of her desk.

"Alright. I'm assuming you know that the whole region around Notre Dame Bay where Chapel Bight is located is a prime mining area in Newfoundland. There are almost as many mines in that one area as there are on the entire island. I've been told the geology in the region is particularly interesting, for any number of reasons. Do you know Grace DeJohn, by the way? She's the one who helped us on this."

"The geologist? Yes, I've met her a few times. She's associated with the College."

"She did mention that she knew you. She keeps hoping the College will be able to afford a full-time geologist sometime soon. In the meantime, she has to do other things to earn her beef and brandy, but they're all of them in some way related to geology. A woman in what is generally considered a man's field."

"You would know something about that."

"Damn right, I do. So, if you know Grace, you probably know she's from Pennsylvania originally."

"Yes, I knew that. She's been here for almost ten years now, since just before the war. I know she did some of the background work on soil and rock formations at Gander and Torbay, and in Labrador too, when the military was looking to build all those airstrips."

"And she became fatally attached to this place, like so many come-from-aways do. I have a high opinion of Grace. There isn't much about geology and mining in this country that she isn't familiar with."

"I found out yesterday that the Hurdles were involved in a copper mine at Chapel Bight. It was a long time ago, but it might be relevant to our investigation. The Hurdles owned a company there called Centaur Minerals."

"Well, you have been busy. Bertie knew something about that too, of course. So did Grace."

"Alex Greene told me that Centaur Minerals was taken over very early on in the game by Hurdle and Company Limited. Before the First War."

"Alex Greene told you that? That is interesting."

"That Alex Greene knew about it?"

"Yes, that, too. But I'll come back to that in a minute. You already know that it was Sir Leonard Hurdle who ran the company then. Sir Hubert's father?"

"Yes, Bertie told me. He also said that Hubert took over the company when Sir Leonard died."

"Yes, he did. Sir Leonard was an interesting man."

"Rich men often are. But interesting in some special way?"

"I think so, yes. They say he was dictatorial, which is not unusual for someone who ran a large and successful family company. The man who owns the company usually calls all the shots, for good or ill. The clever dictators survive and grow, like the Hurdles, and the not-so-clever ones go ass-over-teakettle. But Sir Leonard also had the reputation of having a strong social conscience. Which is not exactly in keeping with the established cliché for a captain of industry, but he made a ton of money anyway. He had interests in a lot of areas, but the mining part of his company was not trivial by any means. The interesting thing about all this is that Centaur Minerals was a company only on paper. It never really existed in actual fact. It was created by Leonard Hurdle specifically to engineer a takeover of the mining lease at Chapel Bight."

"Centaur was owned by the Hurdles from the beginning?"

"Yes, it was. Right from the start."

"I don't understand," Stride said. "Why bother with a paper company?"

"You're not alone in your wonderment. No one seems to know why he formed a paper company. Maybe he did it just to confuse his competitors. But, remember, we're talking about very wealthy people here, in a very competitive industry. Mark Twain famously described a mine as a hole in the ground with a liar on top, and he knew whereof he spoke. Mining has had as many rogues in its history as any activity, and probably more than most. And here in Newfoundland, mining and politics go hand in glove."

Stride smiled. "It's not a state secret."

"One of our esteemed Prime Ministers, Charles Fox Bennett – and it's been said he was more than aptly named – was up to his chin whiskers in dodgy mining ventures. He even had special legislation enacted to backdrop some of his schemes. But there were legitimate mining operators, too. One of the best was Randolph Mills. Do you know anything about him?"

"Randolph Mills." Stride shook his head. "Not really, but the name rings a bell."

"Mills was mostly active back in the last century, but he was still at it in the early years of this one. He made most of his money in copper, but there was also lead and zinc, along with the odd bit of gold and silver. What most people don't know is that there's usually some quantity of the precious metals in copper ores. It can be quite substantial."

"Mills wasn't born here, was he?"

"No. He came from the west of England originally. Cornwall. That's where he got his start in the mining trade, as an engineering apprentice. But he made his money in Newfoundland. It was said that he had the knack of sniffing out promising ore bodies, a sort of Midas touch for the baser metals."

"And Mills had something to do with Centaur Minerals?"

"This part will appeal to your lawman's sensibilities. Mills had a number of leases on Notre Dame Bay around that time. We're talking about the period around 1910, roughly. He had one property in particular that was especially promising and he was planning to develop it."

"The original Tilt Cove mine was in that area, but it was mostly played out before then, wasn't it? By the end of the last century?"

"Yes, it was. But there were still some good ore bodies around. Mills' last best prospect was at Chapel Bight. He was just about ready to start operations, and then one bright morning he found that his claim to the mining lease was being challenged."

"By Centaur."

"Yes. It came almost totally out of the blue. Centaur was located in London. Randolph Mills had never heard of the company, but the lawyer who represented them was a local fellow from St. John's. Wilfred Jeffrey."

"That would have been Lawrence Jeffrey's father?"

"Yes. Mills counter-challenged their claim, but it was too little and too late. He had been euchred. When the litigious dust had settled, Centaur owned the lease."

"And Centaur turned out to be the Hurdle Company."

"Sir Leonard Hurdle was known to create companies to match the occasion. In fairness, though, Randolph had made an important mistake when he filed his original claim. It was a simple surveying error, a couple of critical numbers recorded incorrectly. And that gave Hurdle an opening to challenge his ownership and take over the lease. There was also talk at the time about undue influence being applied to the judge at the hearing."

"Well, there's nothing novel about that, either."

"Only too true. Hurdle won his case, and it's said he went on to make a lot of money out of the Chapel Bight lode."

"And what about Mills?"

"He nursed his wounds and retired from the field not long after that. He was also getting on in years. He sold his various mining interests and consolidated his assets in stocks and other securities. Mills was a very wealthy man when he died. There were two daughters, Helena and Bridget. Helena was the older of the two, and she turned out to be something of a financial wizard. She managed Randolph's money after he retired and made the family wealthier than he had ever imagined they could be."

"Helena Mills."

"Did I just hear a penny drop?"

"Alex Greene," Stride said.

"Helena Mills was Alex Greene's aunt. She died a few years ago, but her sister Bridget is still alive. She lives in that big house on Battery Road, at the intersection with Cabot Avenue."

"I know the house you mean. It's the one on the corner, almost hidden behind some tall trees."

"That's the one. Alex didn't mention that his great-uncle was involved in the Chapel Bight business, did he?"

"No, he did not."

"Why do you suppose he didn't?"

"I don't know," Stride said. "I'll have to ask him about that."

twenty-one

The building that housed the *Sunday Herald* was on Duckworth Street, only a few blocks from the Mercantile Association. Stride didn't really expect to find Alex Greene at the office this early in the day, but it was worth a try. He took his time walking there, smoking a cigarette and thinking about Greene.

Stride had met Alex Greene in the thirties, during Prohibition. Greene was already a working journalist and he was interested in doing a story on the booze trade between the French island of St. Pierre and the American mainland. Greene had done his homework well enough that he managed an informal interview with Stride's partner, Jean-Louis Marchand, a French national who was living on St. Pierre at the time. When Marchand broached the project, Stride had done a bit of homework of his own. He had asked around.

One of the things he learned was that Alex Greene didn't need to work as a journalist, or at anything else, if he didn't feel like it. His family had money, apparently, quite a lot of money. It was also said that Greene had gone to a private boys' school somewhere on the mainland, or in the States. That wasn't unusual for the sons of wealthy families in St. John's. A private-school education conferred a certain imprimatur, useful in later life. And sometimes even carried with it a superior cache of learning, although not always.

The Depression and a world war had passed since that first meeting and Stride had lost track of Alex Greene for a time. Later, he learned that Greene had spent almost a decade in the States, reporting and writing for a number of newspapers and for radio too. His springboard to the larger enterprise, Stride was amused to learn, had been the series of articles he had fashioned out of his one trip between the French islands and the Eastern Seaboard.

There had been much to write about, even though that particular trip was relatively uneventful. The near-disaster on his trip with Gullage came later. But the articles Greene wrote succeeded in placing him in front of a Congressional Committee in Washington to answer questions about the trade in illegal alcohol. Greene told the legislators all that he knew, and more besides, making some of it up as he went along. It was what journalists often did. Respecting his promise to Marchand and Stride, though, he gave no names, and the congressmen accepted his plea of journalistic privilege.

Although they heard nothing they didn't already know about bootlegging, the honourable legislators furrowed their brows and nodded their collective heads as the hearing droned on. Coffee and doughnuts were served after the formal proceedings ended. A committee report appeared in due course. It made for easy reading, and it was comfortably innocuous. The segment of the public that paid attention to such things was comforted to know that their elected representatives were attending to the matter.

Greene emerged from the occasion with a reputation as an investigative journalist. The Niagara of illegal booze flowed on, fortunes were made and lost, and anyone who wanted to drink could. Almost everyone was happy.

After the invasion of Poland in September 1939, Greene went to London. He spent most of the war in Europe, working as a correspondent for a number of news services. He never seemed to stay with any one organisation for very long, but he certainly got around. To England and France, and even to Eastern Europe and the Balkans. Someone said that he had also gone to Palestine, by way of Italy, the year after the war ended. With all of that in his portfolio, it seemed he was on his way to a satisfying career in journalism, experienced and comfortable on the international stage.

But not long after the rumoured trip to Palestine, Greene was back in St. John's, and for a time, he was not working at all. Stride ran into him twice after his return. The first time was late on a Friday night, when Greene was very drunk, half asleep in a tavern. They hadn't talked much on that occasion. The next time Stride ran into Greene, he appeared to be sober, emerging from the Gosling Library on Duckworth Street carrying a leather briefcase filled with books.

Then, a month after that, there was a piece in the *Sunday Herald* with Alex Greene's name attached. The *Herald* was a weekly tabloid, the brainchild of a St. John's entrepreneur, that had soared to bestseller status on a stream of back-alley stories that the daily papers usually didn't bother to print. And if suitably grim news wasn't available in any given week, it was popularly believed that the *Herald* would invent some. Another popular view was that the *Herald* was a useful source of wrapping material in a city whose economy included a brisk trade in fresh fish. Stride rarely missed an issue.

Greene's article described an accident on the Ruby Line in the Goulds, a rural area west of St. John's. Late on a Saturday night, a rented sedan with four American servicemen had run over a sheep that had wandered away from a flock on a small farm. The farmer had had to shoot the injured animal, and then he suggested he might do the same to the four Americans. A crowd gathered. Some of them offered encouragement to the farmer. A local clergyman intervened and a sum of money eventually changed hands. The Americans went on their way, the sheep became the main course at the farmer's Sunday dinner, and Alex Greene had his first story in the *Herald*.

It had to be a comedown from Greene's days in Europe, Stride thought, where he had covered the recent war, as well as aspects of the complicated peace. Stride wondered if this latest oeuvre was only a hobby with Greene, something to do to pass the time until a better opportunity came along. He also wondered if something might have happened to Greene over the past year, something that had spun him backwards, inside himself, making him into a kind of displaced person, a faint echo of the countless thousands he must have seen on his journeys across the war-ravaged European continent.

Whatever it was that brought Greene back to St. John's and kept him here, a reporting job at the *Sunday Herald* seemed an odd choice for an educated man who had done better and more challenging things, one who had money besides. But eccentricity and money have an easy companionship, all the more so when alcohol is a part of the blend.

On this Thursday afternoon, the *Herald* office wasn't a beehive of activity, but the paper wasn't put to bed until Saturday. By Friday, there would be the weekly rise to the crescendo of activity that would culminate with Saturday's frenzy.

"Alex Greene?" A young man wearing a short-sleeved open-necked shirt and a detached look ran his eye over Stride's suit and tie and drew a conclusion that seemed to hold no appeal for him. Stride thought he looked vaguely familiar. He wondered if maybe they had met professionally at some point. The young man might have been thinking the same thing because he turned away after a few moments, presenting Stride with only a quarter profile.

"Has he been in, today?"

"Greene?"

"Yes, Greene. The one whose first name is Alex. Has he been in today?"

"I don't think so. Mornings aren't Greene's best time as a rule. And it's still only Thursday. He's usually here on a Friday, though, usually in the afternoon."

He had turned back far enough now that Stride had a half profile to look at. He was more certain than before that he recognised him. He had a good memory for faces, although names were often a problem. That was where Harry came in especially handy. He had almost as many names in his storage locker as there were in the phonebook, more probably, because not everyone in St. John's had a telephone.

Now the young man turned to face Stride. Maybe he had decided that Stride wasn't the enemy after all, or he didn't care any longer. But his lack of enthusiasm about Stride's inquiry was becoming annoying. Stride thought about pulling out his badge, but that would make him look like an officious prick, and for once, he wasn't in the mood.

"If you should see Alex today, tell him I was here looking for him. The name is Stride. I'd like him to call me when he has a chance. He'll know who I am and where to reach me."

"I guess he will." The young man stepped closer. "You're with the Constabulary, right? So I guess this probably has something to do with the Rossiter murder?"

"Yes, it has."

"Okay, then. I'll make sure he gets the message." He turned away and then turned back again. "I was pretty sure I recognised you. We did a story on your car last year. You're the guy who owns the MG, right?"

"I am that guy," Stride said. "I don't remember you from that occasion, though."

"I was a face in the crowd. It wasn't a large crowd, but it was large enough that I wasn't noticed."

"Your face is familiar, though."

"Well, it should be. You arrested me once. My name's Hobbs. Derek Hobbs."

"Did I?" The name was vaguely familiar. "I don't remember that. Enlighten me."

"It was two years ago, so you probably don't remember. Anyway, it was no big deal, just a drunk and disorderly charge. I got into a scrap with a couple of hillbillies from the American base at Pepperell. They seemed to have the idea they were among God's chosen, sent here on a sacred mission to enlighten the savages. Some of them are like that. It took me a few minutes to straighten them out on the matter. I thought they were better off for the experience, but they didn't think so. That's when you got involved, and I ended up spending a night in jail."

"I think I remember the occasion. But I've had more than one case like that."

"I imagine you have. And you've arrested a lot of people, but I've been arrested only that one time. So I guess I have an advantage on you."

"I guess you do." Stride tried to remember if he had that big a chip on his shoulder when he was that young. He concluded that he probably did. "You will give Alex Greene my message?"

"Sure. If he happens to come in today, I'll make sure he gets it. But if you don't hear from him, drop by later this afternoon. He sometimes comes in late on Thursday, as often as not sweating one off and trying to get a story going." He laughed then. "Talk about drunk and disorderly. You should arrest Alex Greene sometime."

"That idea has some merit," Stride said, as he turned to leave, but more to himself than to Derek Hobbs.

He stood on the sidewalk outside the *Herald* building and thought about what he would do next. The Gordian Knot that was the Rossiter case was starting to unravel. But as sometimes happens, the loose ends that were popping out were as perplexing as the intact original. It was becoming a question of which string to pull first. He would have to think about that some more.

He was surprised that Greene's family had been involved with the Hurdles through Randolph Mills losing his claim to the copper mine at Chapel Bight. And that Sam Rossiter had worked at the mine in the employ of the

Hurdle Company. Playing piddly sticks with the accounts was the way Alex Greene had put it. That might mean something, or it might mean nothing at all. Greene had a penchant for clever phrases, and using a boy's schoolyard game as a metaphor was the sort of thing that would appeal to him. But it now seemed likely that the Rossiter case meant more to Greene than just a couple of stories in the *Sunday Herald*.

And there was Elizabeth Hurdle – Elizabeth Cooke – who had been paying Rossiter some kind of a pension for more than thirty years. What that might have been about, Stride had no idea. One thing was certain, though. Rossiter's life, and therefore his death, had become both complicated and interesting.

He looked east and west on Duckworth, thinking about what he would do now. Nothing leaped to mind. When in doubt, it was a useful dodge to light another cigarette and attempt to appear thoughtful. So he did that, watching the traffic move up and down the street. It was still warm, but the sun had retreated behind a skein of clouds now, again suggesting there might be rain in the offing, perhaps even an end to the heat wave. But that was as much wishful thinking as anything. He pushed his hat back on his head and leaned against the front of the *Herald* building.

After a moment or two, he realised he wasn't very far from one of the buildings that housed Hurdle and Company Limited. The main building was on Water Street, backing on the harbour. The lane next to it that ran down to the wharf at the water's edge was called Hurdle's Cove. Stride didn't know which Hurdle – Cornelius, or Sir Leonard – the lane might have been named for. He thought Harry might know.

The building on Duckworth housed that part of the Hurdle company that dealt with imported liquors and wines, and a variety of food products, some of them coming from England, but most from Canada and the States. Looking at the building now, he remembered that Jean-Louis Marchand had done some business with the company, drawing on his established connections with the wine industry in France. He tucked that bit of information into his store of mental notes.

A black sedan pulled up across the street in front of the Hurdle building. The uniformed driver stepped out and opened the back door on the sidewalk side, then stood in the at-ease position, waiting. A minute later a tall man, grey-haired, with a trim moustache under a prominent nose, came out of the building. Sir Hubert Hurdle was a familiar figure in St. John's. His picture was often in the paper, attending a social event, standing with a group of fellow businessmen, meeting with government functionaries. Hurdle looked more English than the English. Harry's father had that part right. Everything about Hurdle spoke softly of Cambridge and Savile Row, even from a distance. It wasn't just the quality of the clothing, but also the movements and gestures. Stride thought Sir Hubert would make a fine Lieutenant Governor, on appearance alone, if the political situation evolved as some thought it might.

Stride glanced down at his own suit, tailor-made in St. John's and of quality material, but suddenly looking less than fine. He also noticed that his shoes needed polishing. He buffed the toes against the backs of his rouser legs.

The driver attended to the door of the sedan and when Hurdle was settled inside, he pushed it shut. He went around to the driver's side and got in. The car pulled away from the curb, going east on Duckworth. As they came abreast of the spot where Stride was standing, Hurdle looked through the window, and for just a moment the two men stared directly at each other. There was a flicker of recognition in Hurdle's expression.

Stride hadn't thought that Hurdle would remember him from the one time they met, but it was obvious he had. It was two years ago, just after the end of the war, at a function that involved senior officers of the Constabulary and the Fire Department. Stride was there because Jack McCowan had been indisposed that evening. He shook hands with Hurdle while they exchanged a few perfunctory words.

But it was Hurdle's second reaction that had Stride's attention now, a sudden stiffness in the man's posture, a quick averting of his gaze. Then, the sedan moved on past. Stride watched it turn onto Cavendish Square, and he continued to watch it until it had disappeared from view.

twenty-two

"I spent another hour with Rodney Staples, sir. You know, he's not a bad sort of fellow when you get to know him a little better. Let's just say it takes a certain type to do the kind of job he does."

"I'm sure it does. You found something useful?"

"It might be." Phelan consulted his notes. "Elizabeth Hurdle was born in 1893, so that makes her fifty-four now, five years younger than Sir Hubert. This next part is interesting. Her husband, Reginald Cooke, was a lot older than she was. He was sixty-six when he died in 1916."

"That is interesting," Stride said. "Cooke was sixty-six in 1916, and his wife was twenty-three. Forty-three years between them."

"I wonder how that works, what the attraction might be? Mind you, one of Kit's uncles got married for the third time when he was sixty-eight, and his new wife was only in her thirties. He fathered three more children after that, to go with the seven he had by his two previous marriages."

Stride looked at him, shaking his head.

"Just how many uncles does Kitty have, Harry? You seem to be able to pull one forward for just about any occasion."

"You know, I don't really know how many there are, but there's a lot. And good breeding stock, every last one of them." He went back to his notes. "Reginald Cooke – Rex to his friends, apparently – was a Major in the British Army, and he did fight in the Boer War. Jeffrey had that part right."

"It must have been the first Boer War, 1880-1881. I think Cooke would have been a bit long in the tooth for the second one."

"Staples didn't say which war it was. But he did say Major Cooke was seriously wounded in one of the important battles that the British lost."

"Majuba Hill, maybe?"

Phelan looked at his notes.

"Yes, that probably was it. I think I spelled it wrong, though. I have a second m in there."

"Make it your word for next week. After onomatologist, it should be a piece of cake."

"I think so. Anyway, Staples said he remembers seeing Major Cooke walking about town. He walked with a cane, Staples said, and he had a very strict military bearing. The story was, Major Cooke lost a leg in that last battle, but Staples said he cut a very fine figure, cork leg and all. For the few years that he survived after he married Elizabeth Hurdle, that is."

"A very young wife, and only one good leg to work with," Stride said. "Maybe it took a toll."

"Maybe it did." Phelan closed his notebook. "Do you think Mrs. Cooke will be inclined to tell us anything about Rossiter, sir? Her relationship with him, whatever it was, isn't really any of our business. If it isn't directly related to the case, I mean."

"She might toss us out on our collective ear, Harry. But the Hurdles are involved in this somehow, and we need to talk to them."

"From what you told me, Sir Hubert wasn't very happy to see you in his neighbourhood."

"He didn't seem to be, no. But it's Elizabeth Cooke we need to talk to right now."

"An exciting prospect, sir."

"You could put it that way. But if we don't ask the questions, she won't ever give us the answers."

Winter Avenue, like Circular Road where Stride's house was located, was a prestige address, a street of large trees and fine homes. Some of the houses dated back to the Victorian days, when the divisions between the well-to-do and the rest of the population were even greater than they were now in the post-war years.

Winterton was one of the oldest houses in St. John's and it dominated the street. Located in the east end of the city at the intersection of Winter Avenue and King's Bridge Road, Winterton was set among a grove of tall leafy trees, a collection of maple, oak, and horse chestnut, and something Stride thought might have been a kind of elm, at their most lush now in late summer. In the 1800s, Winterton had been an inn, a stopping place for coach passengers on their way to the packet boats that docked at Portugal Cove. Now it was a private residence.

"I've always liked that place," Harry said, looking across the street at Winterton.

"It's probably big enough to house your entire extended family, Harry, uncles and all."

Elizabeth Cooke's house was halfway along the street, a sedate, two-story Victorian structure painted white, with green shutters on the upstairs windows. A white picket fence with two gates separated it from the street. Behind the fence was a low hedge, privet Stride thought, or something similar. One of the gates led to the front door, a majestic affair in dark panelled wood with a polished brass knocker. The second gate led around the east side of the house to a large backyard. From where they were standing across the street, they could see trellises with blue and purple flowers ascendant, and a series of flower beds with an array of brightly coloured blooms. The part of the garden they could see also had three small trees, damson plums probably, gearing up for a harvest of hard, bitter fruit that made good jam when laced with quantities of sugar and pectin.

The house itself was quiet, no sign of life behind the lace curtains that veiled the larger windows on the first floor. The front door was slightly ajar, though, and a large tortoise-shell cat sat on a hemp mat on the broad front step, its attention focused on something in the hedge that backed the picket fence. The animal was so still, so intent, that Stride wondered for a moment if it might be a replica, not a real cat at all. But then it moved, flowing from the step like liquid, one careful paw placed in front of another, and suddenly it flew across the green expanse of yard, tail held high, and vanished into the thicket.

They moved along, turning their attention now to the rear of the house, as more of the garden came into view. A woman was sitting in a wicker chair beside a table of similar structure. A book lay on the table beside a tall glass that was half full. Although the sun wasn't shining just now, she wore a broad-brimmed straw hat, sunglasses, and a sleeveless dress with a bright summer pattern.

"Elizabeth Cooke, maybe?" Stride said.

"The age looks about right, sir."

"Jeffrey said she had a housekeeper."

"Clara Jones. He said she had been with Elizabeth Hurdle since before she married Major Cooke."

While they watched, the woman picked up the book, opened it and took out the bookmark. But only moments later she gave up on reading, reinserted the bookmark, closed the book, and returned it to the table. She looked over her shoulder, and appeared to speak to someone behind her, nearer the house.

"Come on, Harry. I don't want her to see us standing here like a couple of tourists at Government House. It might give her the wrong idea about us."

"What would be the right idea?"

"Ask me a different question. That one's too hard."

Stride had his hand on the brass knocker when he saw there was also an electric doorbell. When he pressed it, it made a very loud and shrill noise that seemed to echo throughout the house. He heard footsteps coming from the rear of the house and moments later, the door was pulled wide open. The cat that had vanished into the privet hedge had reappeared, and took the opportunity to dash into the front hall. Stride watched it gallop up the stairs. It stopped halfway up and sat on the carpeted step. There was something in its mouth, and that something was moving, tiny legs and a tail wriggling in helpless captivity.

He hoped it was not an omen.

The woman who had opened the door was not the same woman they had seen sitting in the backyard. And just now she was paying more attention to the cat than she was to Stride and Phelan. Stride guessed this was Clara Jones, the housekeeper-companion. She was a substantial woman, slightly taller than average height, stocky of build, and had reddish hair that was cut unfashionably short. It was obvious she had spent time in the sun recently. The skin on her forearms and face had a bright glow, the kind of skin that would never tan.

"Does that happen often?" Stride said, looking past the woman at the cat on the stairs.

The woman turned away from the cat and looked at him, and crossed her arms over her chest. "More often than I would like. But that's a cat for you.

Natural-born killers, every last one of them." Her accent placed her origins somewhere outside St. John's. She looked Stride over carefully, running her gaze up and down, then did the same to Phelan. Her expression registered little, but she had seen all she needed to. "You're from the police?"

Stride smiled. "Yes, we are. We would like to speak with Mrs. Cooke, if she's in."

"Yes, she is in. She's out in the backyard. We've been expecting you to call, ever since we heard about Mr. Rossiter. To be honest, we expected you sooner that this." She stepped aside to allow them to enter.

"Your name would be Clara Jones?"

"I see you have done some homework. Well, of course you have, or you wouldn't be here, would you? Yes, Clara Jones would be my name. And what would your names be, if it's alright to ask?"

"Inspector Stride and Sergeant Phelan."

"And quite decent names they are." She turned and strode down the hall towards the kitchen, beckoning them to follow.

Through the window in the kitchen door, Stride could see Elizabeth Cooke in the yard, still sitting in the chair by the table. She had the glass in both hands now, holding it on her lap. "I'll introduce you to Mrs. Cooke, and then I will have to go and find that bloody cat, and whatever it is he's brought into the house this time. Another field mouse, I expect. They seem to be his favourites."

She pulled the door open.

Elizabeth Cooke looked at them through her darkly tinted sunglasses. "The sun has gone away for the moment, and it's even more pleasant now than it was when it was out. I know Clara thinks so. She doesn't tan very well. Wrong kind of skin, you see. Please sit down. Your name is Stride?"

"Eric Stride. We need to ask you some questions about Samuel Rossiter."

"Yes, I thought so. Poor Sam. You can imagine that it was quite a shock to me when I heard he had been killed. To Clara and me both. And now we understand he was murdered." She put on a smile, a well-practised gesture. "Well, I suppose you are the ones who say it was murder, and not just an accident. Have you made any progress with finding the person who did this?"

"We are making some progress, yes."

"And I suppose this visit is part of that, isn't it? The progress, I mean."

"In a way it is."

"You're tracking down anyone who might have known Sam, I suppose. Although it's been such a long time since he lived here in St. John's. Before he moved back last year, I mean. There probably weren't too many people who knew him any more. Does that help you or hinder you, I wonder? That there aren't too many people left of his acquaintance?"

"It all depends on the people," Stride said.

"Yes, I suppose so. But I imagine it's easier for you if there are only a few suspects, instead of hundreds."

She punctuated the comment by taking a sip of her drink. Then she placed the glass on the table.

"Was it a surprise to you? His moving back to St. John's?"

"Yes, it was. He visited St. John's every so often over the years, short visits. It was his home once, after all, but coming back apparently to stay? Yes, that was a surprise." She looked reflective. "He had been away for so long that he was quite out of place here. But I think he might have been out of place anywhere."

"Why do you say that?"

"He had changed a great deal. Even allowing for the fact that he was older, an old man now, the change was very noticeable. Shocking, really. He just wasn't the same person."

"How had he changed?"

"He was older, as I said, it had been four years since his last visit. But he also wasn't very well. He had lost weight and he seemed feeble. I think that's the word I want." She pushed the glass a little further away on the table, and leaned forward slightly as if to impart a confidence, smoothing her dress along her thighs. "And he had also changed...inside."

"Inside?"

She tapped the side of her head. "Inside here. He was a different man. Something must have happened to him. A stroke, possibly. I've known people to change like that after a stroke."

Stride hesitated and looked down the garden, focusing on one of the flower beds for a moment. There probably wasn't any good reason not to tell her about the autopsy. Elizabeth Cooke was as close to family as Rossiter had, it seemed. And it would all be public knowledge in due course.

"In fact, Mr. Rossiter did have a stroke, sometime in the past several years, probably."

Elizabeth Cooke sat back in her chair and reached for her glass.

"You know that from the post mortem, I suppose."

"Yes."

"I don't like the idea of post mortems," she said. "It seems so much like interference, a violation of the individual's privacy. Especially so when the skull is opened, which it must have been. But I know that you don't have any choice, not when someone has met with a violent death, as Sam did."

"No, we don't. It's a requirement when someone has been murdered. Did Mr. Rossiter visit you here? At your home?"

"After he came back last year? Yes, he did, but just the one time. That was something of a surprise also. That he visited only once, I mean. And also that he waited so long after his return. It wasn't until about two weeks ago that he came to see us. It was quite out of the blue."

"Did you know he was back in St. John's before his visit here?"

"Yes. Mutual acquaintances had told us that they had seen him."

"But you hadn't made an effort to see him?"

"No."

"Was there a reason why you didn't?"

"No special reason. We had stayed in touch over the years, Sam and I, but we were not close. On previous occasions when he came to St. John's, he would pay us a visit, out of courtesy more than anything else. When he didn't visit this time, we assumed he had his reasons for not calling on us. We respected that." A small hesitation. "Also, we didn't know where he was staying. We could have found out, I suppose. But we didn't."

"So you don't know if there was a particular reason why he came back to St. John's this time?"

"Something pertinent to your investigation, you mean? To his murder?" She shook her head. "No. To be honest, neither Clara nor I knew why he came back. Or for that matter, why he had waited so long between visits. But as I said, he was very changed, not the same man we had known."

She looked past them now, and Stride heard the door to the kitchen open. Clara Jones took a seat at the table beside Elizabeth Cooke. She had brought a tray bearing a pitcher of something cold, and four glasses.

"It's lemon crystal," she said. "If you would like some?"

She filled three glasses and passed them around. Elizabeth Cooke chose to stay with whatever it was she was drinking when they had arrived. Stride thought it had the look of something more substantial than lemon crystal.

"Just to bring you up to date on where we are, Mrs. Cooke, we have looked into Mr. Rossiter's financial situation." Stride paused for a moment to see if either of the women wanted to make a comment. "We've talked with Mr. Butters at the bank, and to Mr. Jeffrey."

"Oh, dear," Elizabeth Cooke said. "I feel strangely exposed." But then she laughed and Clara Jones laughed with her. "Pay us no mind, Inspector Stride. It's just that it struck me rather funny, the idea of having one's little secrets looked at by the police. Everyone we know says that Clara and I share an odd sense of humour."

Stride saw that Harry was giving the two women one of his guarded and appraising looks. He could guess what was going through his mind.

"Our information is that Mr. Rossiter had been receiving a stipend from you, and for quite some time. Since before the last war, in fact."

"Yes, it's true, he has been. It was a private arrangement, between Mr. Rossiter and me." She looked evenly at Stride, then at Phelan. "I don't believe it's illegal, is it? To give someone a stipend, as you call it?" She looked at her companion. "Isn't that an interesting word, Clara? We never thought of it as a stipend before now, did we?"

"What did you call it, Mrs. Cooke?"

"I never called it anything, it had no name. It was only money. But I suppose if I had given it a word, that word might have been 'allowance.'" She frowned. "But that doesn't sound right, either, does it? An allowance is what one gives a child, or a deficient relative. Sam was a grown man, and not especially deficient. Well, not then. So, no, 'allowance' doesn't seem the right thing to call it. Sam would have been annoyed with that. Do you think so, Clara?"

"Yes, I think he would have been, Liza. Sam had his pride."

"Yes." Her attention was back on Stride again. "I don't really mind your knowing about Mr. Rossiter's allowance, or stipend, or whatever one chooses to call it. It doesn't matter any longer what word we use. Mr. Rossiter is dead. A part of history now."

"What was your history with Mr. Rossiter?"

He had decided to take a chance, but without much faith that it would yield anything. Harry was right. Elizabeth Cooke didn't have to tell them anything about her relationship with Rossiter if she didn't want to. And it already was looking like she wouldn't talk about it. The woman had a strong will, that was obvious. And the other half of her, Clara Jones — and Stride wondered at how easily that thought had come to him — was as strong as she was. He had the sense that he and Harry were outnumbered and outgunned here in this pleasant garden on Winter Avenue.

"My history with Sam Rossiter?"

She hadn't reacted in any overt way. Neither had Clara Jones. The practised smile was there again.

"Mr. Rossiter worked for your father's company at one time. Including at the mine site in Chapel Bight. He didn't work underground, I understand, he had an office job."

He had dropped the name Chapel Bight to see if there would be a reaction.

"I can't imagine what Chapel Bight has to do with all this, but yes, Mr. Rossiter was one of the managers at the mine there. He was there for about a year, I think a little more than a year." She looked at Clara Jones, who nodded in agreement. "He had been working with the company here in St. John's before that, but when the mine was gearing up for production, he was sent up to Chapel Bight."

"And he was there for just over a year?"

"Yes."

"But not long after that, he left the company. In fact, he left Newfoundland and moved to Bermuda. Why did he do that?"

Elizabeth Cooke didn't reply at once. She looked at Clara Jones again, and the two women seemed to exchange some kind of unspoken message.

"Poor Sam," she said after a few moments. There was a touch of sadness in her tone, but whether it was real or feigned, Stride couldn't tell. "Sam Rossiter had a drinking problem. No one knew how serious it was. All we thought at first was that he enjoyed a drink, as most people do, although perhaps a little more than most. It didn't seem to be a problem. But in fact, it turned out that he was an alcoholic, and he was drinking almost constantly. It had been going on for years. And like a lot of alcoholics, he was able to hide it, and also to function reasonably well, even under the influence. But eventually, someone took notice and told my father about it. At about the same time, one of the company auditors found that Mr. Rossiter had been pilfering money from the accounts to pay for his drinking."

"And then he was fired from the Company?" Phelan said.

Elizabeth Cooke looked at him, almost as if she was surprised to find him sitting there.

"In effect, that was what happened, yes. But it was done very diplomatically. My father was from what people now like to call 'the old school.' He asked Mr. Rossiter to resign, with the understanding that would be the end of it. No charges were laid. My father even gave him a letter of recommendation, not a glowing recommendation, but one that would at least not carry a huge stigma. And Mr. Rossiter went on his way."

"All the way to Bermuda."

"Yes. Perhaps you're aware that our company's origins on this side of the Atlantic were located in Bermuda?"

"Yes, we knew that. We also understand the Bermuda operation ended when your grandfather, Cornelius Hurdle, moved the company to Newfoundland."

"That is true." Another cool smile, but reflective also. "I never knew my grandfather other than by reputation, you understand, only anecdotes really. Although there were a lot of those, certainly. He died years before I was born. But to go back to your question, although the Bermuda Mercantile Company ceased to exist, the original building and some of the company activities continued under different ownership. The company that finally emerged some years later was called the South Island Trading Company. It's still in existence, and in fact we do some business with them even now. Mr. Rossiter had a job with them for quite a number of years. Not a senior job, but one that brought him some income, and also gave him a reason to get out of bed in the morning. That was as important for him as it would be for any of us. The pleasant climate didn't do him any great harm, either."

"Did your father arrange that? The job in Bermuda?"

"More or less. And it worked out well enough for all concerned."

"But there was more to your history with Mr. Rossiter than that."

"Yes, of course there was. But our history is just that, ours, and it was personal. And as I have said, my contact with Mr. Rossiter had diminished over the years."

"But you continued to send him money?"

"I wouldn't put it quite that way. Money continued to be sent to him in Bermuda. Mr. Jeffrey looked after it. I was no longer directly involved. It was an arrangement that was made a long time ago. You're not suggesting there is any question of illegality here?"

"No, I'm not suggesting that," Stride said.

"I'm pleased to hear it. My relationship with Sam Rossiter was a personal thing from a very long time ago. And I don't know that the personal aspect is pertinent to your present investigation, Inspector. Possibly, you believe it might be, and it is your privilege to think so. And, I imagine, you are required to speculate in your line of work." She picked up her glass again and looked into it, then placed it back on the table. "I am willing to answer any question that I think might help your investigation, and I'm also willing to give you the benefit of any reasonable doubt in that regard. I would like to see Sam's killer brought to justice, or what passes for justice in this country now. But I don't intend to launch into a dissertation on my history with Mr. Rossiter. For one thing, it would take too long. A lot of things happen over more than three decades."

"And the other thing?"

"It's none of your business. I don't mean to be rude, but really it isn't. Some things are private."

"Alright. Can I ask if your brother knew about your arrangements with Mr. Rossiter? Did he know that Mr. Rossiter was receiving a stipend from you?"

"Hubert?"

"Yes, Sir Hubert."

"He knew that I had maintained some contact with Sam, even after he left Newfoundland, but he wasn't privy to the details. I imagine he knew that there was money involved. But as it was my money, not his or the Company's, the particulars were no more Hubert's business than they are yours."

Stride and Elizabeth Cooke looked evenly at each other for a moment. He had no real argument with anything she had said. She had a right to her privacy. He had thought of asking about her brief disappearance from home in 1912, but now he decided not to. It had no obvious tie to the case or to Rossiter's death. So he went to the standard question, the one that was pulled out on any occasion when the investigative mind was running close on empty.

"Do you know of anyone who might have wanted Mr. Rossiter dead?"

She smiled again, warmer this time. She seemed to understand that the interview was coming to an end.

"I imagine there is probably someone who might want any one of us dead," she said. "At least from time to time." She looked at Clara Jones again, and again they both laughed, their sense of place and comfort secure. "But, seriously, no, I really cannot think of anyone who would have wanted Sam dead. I can think of one or two who might not be shedding many tears over him, but that's another story, isn't it? And it doesn't necessarily mean anything, so I won't mention any names. That would not be appropriate."

He decided to take another chance. The last one hadn't done much good, but neither had it done any great harm, other than to demonstrate, as if demonstration were needed, that Elizabeth Cooke was fully in control of her situation and not at all intimidated by their visit. But the memory of Sir Hubert Hurdle's discomfort was still fresh in his mind.

"Has your brother contacted you or made any comment on Mr. Rossiter's death?"

Her smile told him all that he needed to know about the reply that was coming. It was a kind of declaration of victory. He had not made any guess as to what she might offer in reply, but it was a question he felt he had to ask. Sir Hubert Hurdle's reaction when he had seen Stride standing across the street from his building was still clear in his mind's eye.

"Oh, dear, no. Hubert hasn't said anything at all to me about Sam. But I expect he will say something to me sooner or later."

"Sooner than later," Clara Jones said.

"Yes, I think so." She smiled at her companion. "Perhaps you should have a talk with Hubert, Inspector."

"You think he might have some information that would be useful to our investigation?"

"You never know. And it never hurts to ask, does it?"

Elizabeth Cooke looked at Clara Jones again, and as if on cue, together they looked at Stride. They were both smiling.

Phelan half-sat on the door of the MG and lit a cigarette. He was looking down Winter Avenue, in the opposite direction from Elizabeth Cooke's house. He took out his notebook and began flipping through the pages. He went back to one of the early entries, then compared it to one he had written later.

"You've found something, Harry?"

"Nothing earth-shattering, sir, but it might tie up a loose end. I made a note here from the day Bern Crotty and I were looking through the old records, the time we found the file on Elizabeth Hurdle's disappearance." He looked up from his notebook. "Sir Leonard Hurdle's full name was Leonard Wrixon Hurdle."

"LWH."

"The initials on the silver flask that Rossiter was carrying. The flask probably belonged to Sir Leonard. The question being, did Hurdle give it to Rossiter, or did he steal it?"

"Good question," Stride said. "If it was a gift, it suggests that Rossiter was a lot closer to the Hurdle family, or at least to Sir Leonard, than what you might expect of a mere employee."

"Even if he stole the flask, it still suggests he was pretty close to them."

"Close enough to have access. Yes, it does suggest that. Well, one mystery solved, maybe?"

"A bloody small one."

"You know what they say about the longest journey, Harry."

"They say it's supposed to start with one small step. Maybe the guy who wrote that once walked a beat in the wind and the rain, although I wouldn't bet on it. But we still don't know where Rossiter got the single malt that was in the flask. It couldn't have been there since Sir Leonard's time."

"I don't imagine it was. And I doubt he got it from the Burridges. Definitely not among the single-malt crowd." Stride looked back at the Cooke house. "If Rossiter didn't bring it from Bermuda with him, which isn't really likely, he might have pilfered it that one time he visited Mrs. Cooke."

"They're probably well enough supplied. I think Elizabeth Cooke likes a drink now and again. In the middle of the day, even."

"I think so."

"It didn't seem to affect her all that much, though. Except maybe to make her even feistier than I imagine she is the rest of the time."

"Feisty is a good word for her. Imperial is another. People in her class are accustomed to holding the world at arm's length, including working stiffs like us. Our main consolation is that when someone like Elizabeth Hurdle takes a tumble, she falls a long distance, and the bruising really shows."

"Elizabeth Cooke, sir."

"Elizabeth Cooke. I'm inclined to think the name change was only academic. A matter of convenience."

"I think I agree with you on that. Now that I've seen her and Clara Jones together, I have to believe there was a good reason why she married a man so much older than herself."

"I think so," he said again.

"He really must have felt like the odd man out," Phelan said. "Major Cooke."

"Maybe he was an odd man to begin with, Harry."

"I suppose that might be it. Makes for an interesting family, doesn't it? I suppose we're going to have a chat with Sir Hubert? When do we do that?"

"To borrow a phrase from the two ladies of Winter Avenue, sooner than later." Stride opened the door of the MG and dropped onto the seat. "I'm as sure as I can be that there's something going on with this family. Well, as sure as I can be without having any real evidence to show anyone. Call it a gut feeling."

"Gut feelings have their place, sir."

"Usually better confined to the bathroom, though." He looked at Phelan. "We didn't do spectacularly well back there, did we?"

"Better than the field mouse, though."

Stride laughed and pulled shut the door of the MG.

"You know, I was just thinking about that."

twenty-three

Stride ran into McCowan when he and Phelan returned to Fort Townshend. There was also a message to call Thomas Butcher, but that would have to wait until McCowan had had his say. He beckoned Stride to follow him to his office, closed the door after them, and motioned for Stride to sit down. "I've read your briefing on the Rossiter case." The file was lying open on his desk.

"Is there a problem, sir?"

"With your report? No, not a problem. But it's interesting that Sidney McCarthy's name has come into it. You probably know he was my District Inspector when I joined the Force?"

"Yes, I knew that."

"I never got to know McCarthy all that well, but I thought he was a decent enough fellow, and he had a good record. He was even-handed when it came to discipline and routine, and a chap appreciates that. He came from a modest background, if I can put it that way. His parents had come over from Ireland in the late 1840s, at the tail end of the potato famine. They were lucky in their timing, if nothing else. They missed out on the great fire of 1846, and the city was well along to being rebuilt by the time they arrived. The McCarthy family wasn't exactly destitute, but it's a fact that they didn't have very much. Seamus himself worked damn hard and he pulled himself up through the ranks. He was with the Constabulary for thirty years altogether, and he was still a fairly young man when he retired. He joined up when he was only twenty."

"So, he was only fifty." McCowan was leading up to something, but as usual he was taking his time about it.

"Yes, and on a full pension, too. Not a bad situation, really. Mind you, a full pension wasn't exactly a king's ransom back in the twenties, and it's no great hell now, for that matter." McCowan glanced at the file again. "You've probably guessed it was the incident in 1912 that's caught my attention."

"Elizabeth Hurdle's disappearance."

"Yes. You and Harry interviewed her this afternoon. Did she have anything to say about that?"

"No, sir. I had thought about asking her about it, but it was my judgement that she wouldn't answer any question not directly related to the investigation. When I did ask about her personal relationship with Rossiter, she told me it was none of my business."

"That's in character." McCowan sat back and smiled. "I've never known Elizabeth Hurdle to mince words. She speaks her mind."

"Do you know her well, sir?"

"Elizabeth? No, not very well, but her parents, Leonard and Gertrude, were friends of my parents. Well, perhaps that's a little too strong. They knew each other, and we socialised from time to time. Elizabeth and I are about the same age, a year or two one way or the other. I remember her from parties, church picnics, that sort of thing."

Jack McCowan came from a well-to-do St. John's family, and he was familiar with the kind of privilege that attended the Hurdles and people like them. It didn't surprise Stride that the two families were acquainted. But as a member of the Constabulary, even as a senior officer, McCowan had moved a long distance away from the privileged world in which he had grown up. He could still walk comfortably among the haves, make pleasant conversation, deliver useful comments on the quality of single malts and clarets, and always match the correct piece of cutlery with the course being served. But after his service in the Great War, McCowan had put on a policeman's uniform and walked a beat. His family had been querulous about that, astonished even, wondering if his time on the Western Front might have permanently unhinged him.

When McCowan climbed quickly through the ranks of the Constabulary, his family were at least somewhat relieved. Surely, he would in due course rise to the Chief's office, a position they could live with comfortably. It didn't happen. McCowan had been a District Inspector for years now, and he evinced little interest in moving on. He seemed to have found his niche, comfortable with himself and his place on the Force. Part of that comfort came from a store of family money. That was something McCowan and Stride had in common. But Stride's money was new and tainted and McCowan's was old, far enough removed from the rough and tumble of his family's early history in the St. John's business community to be nominally respectable.

In fact, McCowan had become unhinged by his service in the Great War. As he had recovered from that, he found the war had permanently changed him, for the better, he said. Those who didn't know him well, or who had not worked with him at close range, thought that his carefully cultivated facial adornments – the moustache and mutton chops that had earned him the sobriquet of Field Marshal – were ridiculous anachronisms, the posturing of a man mired in a fading past. In fact, they were just the opposite, a puckish slap at the conventions of an earlier time when class distinctions were deemed essential and all the more delicious to him for the ambiguity.

"Was there a connection between District Inspector McCarthy and the Hurdles, sir? Maybe after he retired?"

McCowan swivelled his chair part way around and looked through the window that gave onto a view of the Narrows and Cabot Tower. When he finally replied he was only half-looking at Stride.

"This part could be tricky, Eric. Even if I didn't know him very well, I had a lot of respect for McCarthy, and I would be unhappy if anything were to compromise his reputation." He pivoted all the way around now. "I suppose you know that Seamus was a nickname? Some men might have bridled, but he actually took some pleasure in it. He wasn't ashamed of his Irish roots, and he also didn't lack a sense of humour. The thing is, you see, I made it to this office despite my family having money and social status. Seamus got here in spite of not having any of that. It's an interesting contrast, and I think about it from time to time. It helps keep me balanced."

"Then I take it there was some connection between McCarthy and the Hurdle family?"

"Yes, there was. As you've noted, McCarthy was only fifty when he retired after thirty years on the Force. A man who stops working at that early an age is a fool. Even more of a fool if he doesn't work much at all. I think it's one reason some of the privileged sons of good families end up as arseholes, useless to themselves and everyone around them. A man needs a vocation." He smiled. "That's a personal view of course."

"McCarthy went to work for the Hurdles?"

"Yes, he did. No one raised an eyebrow at the time. There was no reason to, not that any of us knew about. We shook his hand and wished him well. And we still don't know that there is anything off-colour about it. But now, with this Rossiter case, and the man's history with the Hurdle family, we are perhaps obliged to take a fresh look at things."

"Did the Hurdles ask that McCarthy be assigned to investigate Elizabeth Hurdle's disappearance?"

"There was a request, yes. It was Sir Leonard Hurdle himself who contacted the Chief and asked that a senior officer take charge. I can tell you that Don Ash was more than a bit miffed. He didn't much like being shunted aside. Although Don did have a tendency towards self-importance."

"It seems to have been unnecessary, though. Elizabeth Hurdle came back home on her own."

"Yes, that seems to have been the case. But we enjoy the gift of hindsight. We have to appreciate that when Elizabeth first went missing, no one in the family had any idea what was going on, or where she was. Sir Leonard's first thought was that his daughter might have been kidnapped. Or worse. When a child disappears, more especially a daughter, there is a certain amount of anxiety. It's a natural response. I have no personal experience, of course. And as for asking that a senior officer be assigned, that's one of the perquisites of wealth and power. You're familiar enough with that. And Seamus was a good man for a situation like that. He was both intelligent and thoughtful."

"Which obviously made a favourable impression on Sir Leonard. What sort of job did McCarthy get with the Hurdles? A position with the Company?"

"No, nothing like that. It was less a job than a 'situation,' as such things were once called. Has a Dickensian ring, doesn't it? Perhaps you know that the Hurdle family owned a small hotel in St. John's, Devon Manor. It catered to a very good sort of clientele, and it was quite genteel in its way. Much of the food that was served there was produced at Devon Lea, the farm the family owned. They still own it, in fact, although the hotel was sold years ago, before the war. It's a private home now. Cornelius Hurdle was granted a tract of good land west of St. John's not long after he arrived here from Bermuda. Paid next to nothing for it, of course. It's the way things were done back then."

"And that was the position that McCarthy got? At Devon Lea?"

"Yes. Do you know the place? It's in the Goulds, on Heavy Tree Road."

"I've driven past it any number of times. And I think I did know it belonged to the Hurdle family. The house is set well back from the road, isn't it? And there's a tall fence around the garden in back."

"The Hurdles do like their privacy, and they always have. The original house was much closer to the road, but it was demolished a year before Sir Leonard died and a new one was built. Then, after Sir Leonard died, the new house was enlarged with a couple of new rooms added at the rear. It's quite a grand place, in fact, at least the part of it that Seamus showed me."

"Interesting that McCarthy took a job like that."

"Yes, but the McCarthys were farmers in the old country, one of the thousands who were driven off the land during the famine. You can understand why Seamus was more than happy to live out his retirement as a gentleman farmer." McCowan smiled. "He liked to call it his anteroom to the happy hereafter. The Irish can be stubbornly romantic. I visited him at Devon Lea from time to time. He wasn't a very social fellow, Seamus, a very private man in fact, and like me he never married. He never told me why, never even talked about it. Well, why would he? To the extent that we had a friendship, it was based on my being with the Constabulary. I was his source for information and gossip, and he liked to stay in touch."

"Was it a reward, McCarthy's situation at Devon Lea?"

"I don't know. Seamus never said, and I think he would have been offended if I had asked. But I always wondered if it was a reward of some kind."

"Possibly for his assistance to the family that time Elizabeth ran off?"

"That's the obvious one, isn't it? Although the record doesn't say that he had to do very much."

"This was in the twenties? When McCarthy went to work for the Hurdles?"

"In 1920, if memory serves. Sir Leonard had passed on long since, and Hubert was running the company. But I believe it was Elizabeth who arranged for his position at Devon Lea."

"I've heard there's some question about who really runs Hurdle and Company Limited. Whether it's Sir Hubert, or his sister."

"It has been talked about. There might be something to it, I don't know. I do know for a fact that Elizabeth always seemed the brighter of the two when we were all young together. But don't take the gossip too far. I don't think Hubert is any kind of a fool, although he can sometimes seem to be."

"You said that Elizabeth Hurdle hired McCarthy. Does she own Devon Lea?"

"Yes, the farm belongs to Elizabeth. Sir Leonard left it to her in his will."

"What does she use the farm for now, with the hotel gone?"

"As far as I know, Elizabeth and her companion use it as a sort of retreat. I know they have a stable with riding horses, and the house and property are very well maintained. But I haven't been there in years, not since Seamus passed on."

"I suppose there's still a full-time manager at the farm?"

"Yes, there is. I met the fellow once or twice, not long after he started there, when he was working under Seamus' tutelage." McCowan paused. "Names are a challenge these days. Vickers. Frank Vickers. I think he's one of McGinn's nephews."

"Justice McGinn?"

"Yes. McGinn and the Hurdles go back a long way. Robin articled with a legal firm associated with the Hurdle Company and then went on from there. Interesting coincidence, then, that it was McGinn who signed the warrant for you to look into Rossiter's financial history."

Phoning Thomas Butcher during the day was a catch-as-catch-can proposition, but this time Stride was pleasantly surprised. Butcher picked up on only the second ring.

"You caught me just in time, Eric. I was about to leave for a meeting. I'll start off by apologising for having taken so long getting back to you on the Rossiter thing. Life has been even more hectic than usual."

"It's alright, Thomas. We've been out and about, too. I take it you've had an opportunity to consult with Roberts?"

"Yes, I did, finally. He was unusually busy also, which was another reason I've been delayed. Appropriately, the plaints of the living have been interfering with our concerns for the departed. But we got together finally, and Nigel has confirmed my opinion about Rossiter. He did have a stroke, quite a serious one. It was in a region of the brain that would have had some effects on his behaviour. There would likely have been some dementia, sporadic but noticeable. You understand, though, that we can't be as precise as we would like to be. For all the advances that have been made in neurology, a lot of that coming in the wake of the last war, there still is much that we can only guess at."

"But you're comfortable ascribing Rossiter's odd behaviour to a stroke?"

"I am. Nigel thinks it probably happened sometime in the last two to three years, but you will understand that's a rough estimate. It would help if you knew when was the last time someone saw him in good health."

Stride had to think about that for a moment.

"It was four years ago, the last time he visited St. John's. We interviewed someone today who had seen him then. She said that between then and now he had aged a lot and that he had also changed a great deal. She even suggested that Rossiter might have had a stroke."

"Did she? That is interesting. Who is she by the way? Are you at liberty to say?"

"It's confidential, of course, but you're trustworthy enough, Thomas."

"I feel complimented. Who is she?"

"Elizabeth Cooke. Her maiden name was Hurdle. She's Sir Hubert Hurdle's sister."

"Sir Hubert's sister? Also interesting. She was married to an English fellow, wasn't she? A retired Major from the British Army?"

"You're well ahead of the game. Yes, he was British. His name was Reginald Cooke. And he was a Major. He was in the Boer War, and he was in the battle at Majuba Hill."

"Majuba Hill?" Butcher laughed. "Now you have me digging back into my modest knowledge of British history. But I do know that Majuba Hill was a major victory for the Boers and an embarrassing loss for the British. The British were both outfought and outmanoeuvred. It was a brilliant guerrilla operation on the part of the Boers. Majuba Hill wasn't a huge engagement, but it did have a major impact on the first Boer war."

"We've been told that Cooke was seriously wounded in the battle. He lost a leg."

"Lost a leg, you say?" Butcher was silent for a few moments. "Now, that does ring a bell. Uncanny how things are connected. In fact I know a little something about Major Cooke. His first name was indeed Reginald, Rex to his friends. I never met him, of course. He died before I moved to Newfoundland. About 1916, 1917?"

"In 1916," Stride said. "How do you know so much about him?"

"After-dinner chatter over many glasses of port at regimental reunion dinners, and other such fare. In England for the most part, but there have been a few here, and elsewhere too. Put a gaggle of old army types together at table and keep the port bottle circulating, and you have an information transfer system that's about as efficient as any wire service. You can trust me on that. The old warhorses may not be able to fight any longer, but they can most certainly chatter. And the chatter does range far and wide."

"Interesting that you should have heard so much about Major Cooke. What else did you hear about him?"

"Some. He wasn't famous, exactly."

There was something in Butcher's tone.

"What was he, exactly?"

"Well, you know I don't like to tell tales, Eric, and I do much more listening than talking at the gatherings I mentioned. Mind you, not all of the chatter one hears at such functions can be taken to the bank. In the circumstances, though, with you investigating a murder that might involve the Hurdle family, I will pass this along for what it's worth. The story I heard was that after the war, the one in South Africa I mean, Rex Cooke was asked to resign his commission. It appears he had a liaison with a junior officer from another regiment, someone he met in hospital while he was recuperating from Majuba. They were eventually found out, and they were both asked to resign. Which of course they did, that being the lesser of several evils."

"So much for gallant service under fire."

"Yes. Justice is not yet universal, as though I need to tell you that. And that kind of attitude is arguably worse in the military than elsewhere." There was the sound of a match being struck on the other end of the line. "It makes Cooke's marriage to Elizabeth Hurdle interesting, though."

"I was about to mention that," Stride said. "Cooke was a lot older than she was. There were more than forty years between them."

"I had known there was an age difference, but I didn't know it was that large. Did Mrs. Cooke have anything to say about any of this? I can't imagine she did."

"I didn't ask about her marriage. I had no reason to, even if I was curious. And I'm sure she would have refused to comment. She's been living with a housekeeper-companion for a long time, someone she knew before she married Cooke. A woman named Clara Jones." He groped for a descriptive. "They appear to be very close."

"I'm sure that's true, and good for them," Butcher said. "How does the Hurdle family come into all this, Eric? About Rossiter, I mean. Can you tell me?"

"Rossiter worked for the Hurdle Company a long time ago, but I think there might have been more to it than that."

"In what way?"

"I think he was more than just an employee. He might have been very close to the family. Anyway, he was fired from the Company, or asked to resign. It comes to much the same thing in the end. Elizabeth Cooke told me he was caught with his hand in the till, that he was also an alcoholic." He gave Butcher a summary of what he knew of the relationship between Rossiter and Elizabeth Cooke.

"That is interesting. I take it Sir Hubert wasn't involved in this in any way? The allowance, or whatever it was that Mrs. Cooke was sending to Rossiter?"

"No. She was fairly definite about that. I'm not sure what kind of relationship Elizabeth Cooke has with her brother."

"I might be able to help you out there."

"You know something about them?"

"A little. One of the advantages – if advantage it is – of being a senior doctor as well as the city coroner, is that I get invited to a large number of high-level social events in town. What one does at most of these affairs is sip drinks and chatter a great deal. Some of the conversation is very interesting, so on the whole, it's a pleasant enough burden to shoulder." He laughed again. "I will admit, though, that regimental gatherings are often a great deal more entertaining, in their scabrous way."

"Do you know Sir Hubert Hurdle?"

"I've met him often enough, but it would be an exaggeration to claim that I know him. We do have a kind of natural bond, though. I was born in England, and Sir Hubert very much wishes he had been."

"I sometimes think you have an evil inner twin, Thomas."

"He is my sword and buckler. To get back to your question, I have heard, although not from Hurdle himself of course, that there was friction between brother and sister after the father died, over who would run the company. It is the tradition, of course, that the son takes over, unless he is shown to be a drooling idiot, and even then he might win the day. The rich and powerful arguably are even less egalitarian than the rest of us."

"I think I heard a rumour to that effect."

"I've no doubt of it. To her credit, I believe Mrs. Cooke makes her presence felt on the board of directors of Hurdle and Company Limited, and she isn't shy about expressing her views. I have heard some talk that she's the one who really runs the company, and leaves the politicking and glad-handing to Hubert. I take that with a large grain of salt, and you should also. You have to understand that Hubert Hurdle has enemies in rough proportion to his status in the community. That sort of thing is almost inevitable."

"Caution noted."

"Do you have any idea why Elizabeth Cooke might have been giving support to Rossiter for all these years?"

"Not really, no. She was quite blunt about that. She said it was none of my business."

"That would seem to be in character, from what I know of her. Did you say that her relationship with Rossiter started about the time the father died?"

"It would have been sometime after Sir Leonard died, yes. When Elizabeth came into both her majority and her inheritance."

"I seem to recall that Sir Leonard died rather young."

Stride opened his notebook. It took him a moment to find the page.

"Sorry, Thomas, I needed to look it up. Leonard Hurdle was fifty when he died. So not very old at all. That was in 1912. He died of typhus, apparently. There was an epidemic that year."

"Typhus? Interesting. And a tragic irony. Sir Leonard Hurdle donated a large sum of money to the building of an infectious-diseases wing at the General Hospital. That was just after the turn of the century. Back then it was known as the 'fever wing' of the hospital."

"I didn't know that," Stride said.

"Not many people did. The donation was anonymous. I only found out about it myself a few years ago. By the way, did you know that Sir Leonard's widow is still alive?"

"Sir Leonard's widow? Yes, in fact I did know that."

"Gertrude Hurdle is one of the barely-walking wounded. Perhaps you knew that, too?"

"No, I didn't. What do you mean by 'barely-walking wounded?'"

"It's thought to be fairly high-level gossip, but you know how these things are. Probably more people know about it than one might think."

"Well, I'm not one of them." Butcher's comment had the effect of setting him to wondering again about his own situation. "What is Mrs. Hurdle's story?"

"Lady Hurdle."

"I stand corrected."

"It will do you no great harm. When people mention Leonard Hurdle's widow, and they don't very often, the conversation typically starts with something like 'Poor Gertrude.' She had a drinking problem that started early in their marriage, possibly before that, and it went on for many years. It has culminated in a serious overall health problem, mental as well as physical. She's an invalid now, although she lives at home still. She has a nurse-ompanion who looks after her. Washes and dresses her, reads to her, takes her for walks, that sort of thing."

"It sounds very sad."

"It is sad, there's no doubt about that. But such things do happen, even to the very wealthy. Happily, if that's not an inappropriate word, the Hurdle family can well afford to pay for her care."

"There is that."

"Yes. Possibly some of this will prove helpful to you and Harry?"

"It can't hurt, Thomas." Unless the weight of anecdote contrived to knock them off course.

"Alright, then, I'll leave it at that for now, Eric. I have to get along to my blessed meeting, and I know you have things to do. I'll send you an addendum to the autopsy report on Rossiter. You will have it in a day or two."

Stride hung up the phone. Harry Phelan was standing in the doorway of the office.

"Something?" Stride said.

"Yes, sir. We had a call from the Admiralty."

"From Gullage?"

"No, sir. From one of Gullage's people, Ted Murphy. He says he has something he wants to tell us about Rossiter. I told him we'd be down sometime in the next hour. He said he would be there."

"We're off, then. I'll fill you in along the way on what Butcher had to say."

Johnny Blake was at his usual spot at the door of the Admiralty.

"If you're looking for Mr. Gullage, Inspector, I'm afraid he isn't in just now. He went home to have an early tea with his missus. Mr. Murphy is looking after the place in the meantime."

"It's Ted Murphy we want to see in fact."

Blake pointed to the bar where a small, wiry man with black hair and wire-framed glasses was talking to one of the customers.

Ted Murphy always wore a crisp white shirt with a black bow tie. The sleeves of the shirt were cinched above the elbows with elastic garters. It gave him the slightly exotic look of a riverboat gambler. He lacked only an eye-shade to complete the picture.

Stride and Phelan started across the room towards the bar. Murphy saw them coming and motioned in the direction of Gullage's office. When they were inside, he took a final look around the bar before closing the door.

"I didn't know whether I should call you or not, Inspector. I had to think about it for a while first. I'm still not sure, to be truthful about it."

It was clear enough that Murphy was agitated, but Stride had halfway expected that. Phelan had told him on the way down to Holdsworth Street that Murphy was an excitable sort. Harry had known Ted Murphy for most of his life. They had been at school together, at Holy Cross, contending with the occasional tyranny of the Christian Brothers who ran the place. Harry said Murphy was like a tangle of wire coat hangers plugged into a wall socket when he was worried about something. And he was worried now.

Stride tried his best.

"Anything you have to tell us won't be heard by anyone outside this room, Ted."

"I'm counting on that," Murphy said. He looked at Stride over the top of his glasses. He dissipated some of his tension by rolling a cigarette, his fingers busy, the veins standing out on the backs of his hands. He was silent until he finished the job. Harry leaned forward and gave him a light.

"This is something about Monday night?"

"Yes. Monday night. The night Sam Rossiter went across the river. We were busy as hell on Monday. Hot night, cold beer, you can fill in the rest of it. Late in the evening, maybe a half hour before we closed, I was out back in the storeroom stacking empties. We had a lot because the truck didn't come by that morning like it usually does, so we had all the empty bottles from Friday and Saturday still there to deal with. Hot weather is great for business, and great for the bank account, but hard on the back. You can quote me on that." He drew on the cigarette and looked through the veil of smoke at Stride and Phelan, as though trying to decide whether or not to continue. "Anyway, I took a break around eleven o'clock, just about closing time. It was even hotter in the storeroom than it was outside, so I stepped out for a smoke. I walked around the back of the building to the corner of Water and Holdsworth." Another pause. Murphy took a breath. "There was someone sitting across the street from the Admiralty, on the steps of Connors' warehouse."

"Yes? Who was it?"

Murphy took another nervous pull on his cigarette.

"Caleb Howell."

"Howell? You're sure about that?"

"Yes, sir. I'm sure of it. Howell is one big sonofabitch." Murphy shook his head. "He stands out in a crowd, never mind when he's alone."

"Was he in the Admiralty Monday night?"

"Yes, he was. He was here for a couple of hours. I don't know what time he got here, though, and I don't know what time he left."

"But you're sure it was him sitting there across the street around closing time?"

"Yes, sir. That part I am sure about. I know it doesn't have to mean anything, but I know Howell was in trouble with you people last year, and spent some time at the lakeside. And there's been a couple of times Gully had to ask him to leave here when he got to being testy."

"Anything serious?"

"Not very, no. Gully has a way of dealing with trouble before it really gets going. He keeps a hardwood bat under the bar, and he's not afraid to use it. The word's got around long since. Maybe you know about that."

"Yes, I do know about that," Stride said. "Did he ever have to use it on Howell?"

Murphy shook his head. "Not that I ever heard."

"Was Howell still there, across the street, when Rossiter and Keough left the tavern?"

Murphy shook his head again. "I don't know. He might have been. But by the time they left, I was back in the storeroom. When I was finished in there, the tavern was empty except for the staff."

"What time was that?"

"Ten, fifteen minutes past eleven. I must have just missed the two of them, though, Keough and Rossiter. They stayed a little past closing time, Johnny told me. That reporter fella who works for the *Herald*, he'd bought them a beer each, and Gully let them stay past closing time to finish up. He'll bend the rules, sometimes, Gully will, if it's to someone's benefit and no one gets hurt. He's a decent sort of man that way."

"Yes, he is." Stride said. "You said a reporter bought Rossiter and Keough a beer. Who was that?"

"I think his name is Greene. Alex Greene? A long, tall drink of water." Murphy laughed. "Not that I think he ever touches the stuff himself."

"Is Greene a regular here at the Admiralty?"

"I think he's a regular at half the pubs in St. John's, Inspector. I know he's in here often enough. Why? Does he have something to do with this?"

"Not that we know of. Do you know what time he came in Monday night?"

"No I don't." Murphy shook his head. "But he was here for a while, that much I do know. I know because I learned a long time ago to run an eye over the crowd from time to time, especially when the place is full and there's a lot of beer going down, like it was on Monday."

"Alright. Anything else you want to tell us, Ted?"

"Just that I'd like you to keep my name out of this. Like I say, I don't know that it means anything, Howell being nearby around closing time, but I thought you should know about it."

"You were right to tell us. Every bit of information helps. If we do anything about what you've told us, your name won't come into it. That's a promise. So don't worry about it."

"I appreciate that," Murphy said. "Life's enough of a challenge without someone like Caleb Howell holding a bad opinion of me."

twenty-four

Sir Hubert Hurdle drove himself in his Morris coupe to his sister's house on Winter Avenue. Hurdle usually went about in his Packard sedan, with his driver, but when he wanted to be on his own, to do something in relative anonymity, he preferred to drive himself. The little, brown Morris had anonymity to spare.

He stood on the front step and pushed the doorbell. A minute went by and there was no answer, so he pushed it a second time. The lack of response started his impatience rising again. He was there because Elizabeth had asked him to come, and while he couldn't believe that she wasn't home, he knew that almost anything was possible with Elizabeth and Clara. He was about to push the button a third time when the door opened and his sister was standing there looking at him.

"Hubert. I am sorry. I was in the backyard and I wasn't sure I had really heard the bell until you rang the second time."

"Clara isn't here?" He looked past her, down the hallway towards the kitchen.

"Yes, she is here. She's upstairs, having a bath. At least that's what she was doing fifteen minutes ago. When Clara takes a bath it's usually a long one. I believe Gertrude Ederle swam the Channel in less time than it takes Clara to complete her ablutions." Then, as if on cue, there was the sound from upstairs of more water pouring into the tub. "Well, there you are. She'll be down before too long, I'm sure. She probably heard the doorbell." She started down the hallway. "Can I get you something? For a change, I'm having some lemon crystal. Clara made it earlier today. It's quite pleasant in the hot weather."

"No, thank you."

"I can get you something stronger if you would like."

"No, I don't want anything."

"Everyone wants something, Hubert." She laughed and picked up her glass from the kitchen table.

"Can we get on with this, please?"

"In a little while. We'll wait for Clara to join us. She's involved in all this as much as anyone." She sipped her drink. "We can sit in the garden, if you like. It's very pleasant outside, not as hot as it's been over the past week."

"I don't want to sit in the garden. I think it's better if we talk inside."

"Yes, I suppose it is. Are you sure I can't get you something?"

He stared at her, rattling his car keys in his hand. He put them in his pocket and sat down at the table. He looked at the pitcher of lemon crystal on the counter. Condensation clouded the glass.

"Alright. I will have some. It is lemon crystal, the same stuff Molly used to make for us in the summertime?"

"Yes, it is. It's even from the same company that made it back then, all those years ago. Did you know they've been in business even longer than we have?"

He shook his head. "I didn't know that. I don't even know who makes the stuff. But I do remember we had it only in the summer." He managed a half-smile. "I wonder if I still like it." This small reminder of their shared past, a simple summer drink, was having a calming effect on him. He relaxed a little and sat back in the chair, crossing one leg over the other. "You remember that Mother would say it was a special treat and we couldn't expect to have it all the time?"

"She did say that, didn't she?" Elizabeth dropped two ice cubes into a glass and poured the lemon crystal over them. "Have you seen her, lately? Mummy?"

"No, I haven't. It's been at least two weeks now. And I know I have been remiss. I will go see her tomorrow, or the day after." He picked up the glass. "I've been busy."

"That isn't reason enough, Hubert. We're all of us busy, but I manage to visit her at least three times a week. Clara, too."

"You're right, of course. But I do find my visits with her very trying. And, you know, I'm not sure she can actually recognise me a lot of the time. If at all."

"That's probably true. And it is hard." She sat at the table across from him. She looked towards the ceiling. From upstairs there came the sound of water running through the pipes. "I'm not sure any longer how much she is aware of. But she remembers things from the past. Sometimes she will suddenly start talking about things that happened a long time ago."

"Dear God." Hurdle put a lot into the two words.

"Yes, it is a worry. But Alice Martin is very dependable."

"I hope so."

"I know so. I don't think you need to bother yourself about that."

"You said she sometimes talks about things from a long time ago. What, exactly?"

"Snippets, odd bits and pieces of events. They wouldn't make much sense to anyone who wasn't familiar with our family history. For that matter, I doubt they would mean very much to anyone who wasn't there at the time, even if they did know something about us."

"Give me an example."

"Oh, Lord." Elizabeth sipped her drink and thought about it. "It's almost all of it quite innocuous, Hubert. Last week she was going on about the time you stepped on the wasp's nest at the country house. Do you even remember that? It was, how many years ago? Going on fifty, I think."

Hurdle smiled and shook his head.

"Of course I remember it. How could I forget? The bloody things got inside my swimsuit. Try and imagine that. It was excruciating. I thought I would die. I bloody well wanted to die."

"I don't have to imagine it, Hubert dear. I was there. Molly and I had to hold you still so that Mummy could pull your suit off. You were wriggling like a fish on a hook, and in the end Molly had to sit on your chest." She laughed. "You were spectacularly swollen in your nether regions, Hubert, a sight for the ages. I wanted to get my camera and take pictures, but of course Mummy wouldn't let me do that."

"I remember that part too. It was your first camera and you took pictures of everything. Father used to complain about the money you were wasting."

"Daddy complained about many things. But I learned the trick of only appearing to pay attention."

They were silent then, picking their way through unspoken memories. Then Hurdle spoke.

"You said 'almost.' I take it she also says things that are not innocuous?"

"Yes, sometimes she does. But as I said, they are only fragments of events. I usually know what she's talking about, but almost no one else would. Certainly, Alice would have no idea."

"For instance?"

"One day not long ago she talked about that policeman. McCarthy."

"Inspector McCarthy."

"District Inspector."

Hurdle shrugged. "What did she say about him?"

"Nothing at all revealing. She talked a little about the night he brought me back from Chapel Bight. She remembered that Alfred drove us to the house from the boat, McCarthy and me, in Daddy's new Ford."

"That's all?"

"Well, let me see. She remembered McCarthy and the car, and that Alfred was driving. And that I had been in Chapel Bight. Of course she would mention that. And she remembered the colour of the blanket that I had wrapped around me that night. It was blue. It was cold that night, even if it was almost the end of July. But it was a cool summer that year wasn't it?"

"And that was all? She remembers you coming home that night, and McCarthy and the car. But all the rest of it? She doesn't remember any of that?"

"I don't know if she does or not. After she talked about McCarthy and the blanket for a minute, she drifted off again."

"And Alice was there at the time?"

"Yes, but I don't think she paid much attention. She was doing her cross-stitch and that takes concentration. I don't believe she even heard what Mummy was saying. When I'm there, or Clara, I think Alice takes the opportunity to tune everything out. And one can hardly blame her for doing that."

"That's marginally encouraging."

"Yes, it is. But there are times when I have to wonder if that's all there is, and about what might be going on with her. Inside, I mean. It's less in what she says, more in the way she looks at me, sometimes. As though there really is something she wants to talk about, but she can't quite get it organised well enough to say. It's very sad."

"It's more than sad. 'Sad' doesn't begin to capture it."

"You're right, of course. It doesn't."

Elizabeth's mood had changed now. She stood up and walked to the back door and looked through the window into the yard. Then she turned and looked towards the kitchen door. Hurdle followed her gaze.

"I thought I heard the doorbell." Clara Jones was standing in the doorway. She wore a dark blue dressing gown. Her pale skin glowed from the heat of her bath. "Hello, Hubert. We haven't seen you for a while. But they do say trouble brings people together." Hurdle acknowledged her with a nod of his head, but Clara was looking at Elizabeth now. "Have you been talking about Sam?"

"No, not yet. We were waiting for you to come down." Elizabeth went back to the table and sat down.

"I'm going to make some tea," Clara said. "Will I make a full pot, or just a cup for myself?"

"Just for yourself," Elizabeth said. "We're enjoying your lemon crystal. You know, I might get to like it all over again, turn over a new leaf, give up the Cragganmore altogether."

"Not bloody likely, you won't. The age of miracles is long gone." Clara looked at Elizabeth from where she stood by the stove. "And anyway, I won't let you. I don't like to drink alone."

"Can we talk about Rossiter now? Please? That is why you asked me to come here. You said Rossiter came to see you?"

"Yes, he did come to visit. Just once, though. That was a few weeks ago. And he didn't stay very long. For which we were grateful." Elizabeth glanced at Clara. "He didn't have a lot to say, and a lot of what he did say didn't make much sense. He wasn't the Sam we used to know, Hubert. Apparently he'd had a stroke, sometime in the last year or two."

"How do you know he'd had a stroke?" Hurdle said. "Did he tell you that?"

"No, the police told us. They were here earlier today. An inspector and his sergeant."

"What was his name?"

"Which one? There were two of them."

"The inspector. Was his name Stride?"

"Clever Hubert. Yes, it was Stride. Do you know him?"

"No, I don't know him. But I did meet him once, a year or two ago. And I saw him again today, in fact. This morning."

"He interviewed you?"

"No. I didn't speak to him. I saw him on Duckworth Street. I think he was watching our building."

"Watching the building? Are you certain of that?"

"No, I'm not certain. But he was there, standing across the street from the building when I came out. Did he say anything about that today? When he was here?"

"No, he didn't mention it."

"Well, I don't suppose he would, would he?"

"I don't know what he would or wouldn't say."

"Did he know that you'd seen him standing there?" Clara asked.

The kettle was whistling now, and the noise distracted them for a moment. Clara made her tea and carried the pot over to the table. She sat directly across from Hurdle.

"I suppose he did know." Hurdle said. "We looked right at each other."

"Did you? And were you as agitated then as you are now, Hubert?"

"I probably reacted when I saw him standing there, yes." Hurdle sighed. "And I think he may have seen that."

"Well, I probably would have reacted too." Elizabeth touched his hand. "But what's done is done."

"What did they ask you? Inspector Stride and his man?"

"Questions about Sam, of course. Any number of questions about Sam. But I didn't tell them anything especially revealing. Did I, Clara?"

"No, you didn't."

"I suppose they asked about the money?"

"Yes, of course. They knew about that, though. They had already learned a lot about Sam and about us. I wasn't very surprised. It's what the police do. They ask questions and they get answers. But nothing I told them will cause us any problem."

"You can't really know that."

"I think I can. All I told them was that Sam was dismissed from the Company and after that he went to live in Bermuda. And of course they know I arranged for money to be sent to him."

"They must have asked you about that."

"Yes, they did ask." Elizabeth and Clara exchanged smiles. "I told them it was a personal matter, that it was none of their business."

"And they accepted that?"

"I don't know if they accepted it or not. But they also understood how far they could go in that direction."

Hurdle got up and walked to the door and stood there looking out at the backyard. He turned back to the table.

"They're only just getting started, you know. This isn't over."

"No, of course it isn't over. Not yet."

"Christ! Why didn't the bloody fool stay in Bermuda? If he had, he'd still be alive. And we wouldn't have to deal with all of this now."

"I expect the stroke had a lot to do with it, Hubert. As I told you, he wasn't himself."

Hurdle took his car keys from his pocket. Then he picked up his glass and drank the rest of the lemon crystal.

"Are you leaving? We've hardly talked at all."

"We've done all the talking I can stand for the moment. I need to go away somewhere and think about all this."

Elizabeth stood up and moved close to him. She put her hand on his cheek, turning him so that he was looking at her. He was breathing rapidly now and his colour was high.

"Alright. Take some time and think about it. That's probably a good idea. Work your way through it, one bit at a time. And for just this once keep your bloody temper under control. And don't do anything foolish, Hubert, like tearing off on a trip somewhere. That's the worst thing you could do right now. What we need to do is just carry on as though everything is the same now, as it was a week ago when Sam Rossiter was still alive and sitting in his wretched boarding house on Gower Street, muttering to himself. Or whatever it was he did when he was there alone."

"That's easy to say," Hurdle said.

Elizabeth patted him on the cheek. There was a surprising amount of warmth in her smile.

"Yes, it is, Hubert. It really is very easy to say."

twenty-five

Stride picked Phelan up at his house on Victoria Street and they drove to
Fort Townshend together. They arrived just as Noseworthy was walking
towards the parking lot from the direction of Bonaventure Avenue. Stride
held the station door open until Noseworthy caught up with them, then he
followed them inside. Billy Dickson was at the reception desk.

"Mr. McCowan's been here and gone, Inspector Stride. But he left a
message that he'd like to see you later on this afternoon."

"Something to do with Major Stamp?"

"I know he's with the Major just now, sir, and they're going to be out and
about most of the day. I'm not sure if Stamp wants to see you or not, or if it's
something else. I don't think it's very urgent, whatever it is."

"If you see McCowan again, tell him I'll look for him later in the day."

On the way down to Noseworthy's enclave, Stride filled him in on their
visit to the Admiralty the previous evening. By the time he was finished,
Noseworthy had assembled the collection of fingerprints that he had lifted
from Rossiter's bottle and laid them out on his bench. Then, he took the
card with Caleb Howell's prints from a filing cabinet and prepared to make
the comparison. Before setting to work, though, he took off his jacket and
with great ceremony rolled up his shirtsleeves, smoothing out each turn as
he completed it.

"If it turns out that Howell was involved in this, you gentlemen might have an interesting morning. If I remember correctly, the last time one of our finest made his acquaintance, a couple of teeth went south and they didn't belong to Mr. Howell." He looked at Phelan. "It was Max Woolgar, wasn't it?"

"It was Woolgar and he did lose some teeth."

"I've heard he's not all that happy with his new set. Maybe you should think about taking him with you on this foray, sir. There's a better than even chance Woolgar will be very motivated for the occasion."

"We'll leave him out of it," Stride said. "We need Howell more or less in one piece and able to answer questions. That's assuming he had anything at all to do with this."

"I should have an answer for you in a couple of minutes."

Noseworthy sat down and took his magnifying glass from a drawer. He worked his way through the collection of prints, moving back and forth between the two sets, making comparisons. His estimate of a couple of minutes was well off the mark.

"Problems, Kevin?" More than five minutes had crept by. Stride stepped close behind him and looked over his shoulder.

"Yes, sir. Some of the unknowns aren't as well-defined as I would like. That's the problem when you have an item that's been handled by a lot of people, or for that matter if it's been handled a lot by only a few people. The prints get overlaid by other prints and there's a lot of smudging."

"Is it hopeless?"

"Not altogether." A minute later Noseworthy sat back and swivelled his chair partway around. He held up the sheet with the unknown fingerprints. "I have two prints that might belong to your man Howell. There are just enough points of comparison for me to say *probably* in a quavering tone."

"Enough to go to court with, if it comes to that?"

"Not without an anxious visit to the bogs, sir. Do you want to have a look?"

"No, I don't, Kevin. I'm going to trust your judgement on this."

"I was afraid you'd probably say something like that. Well, my judgement is that these two prints belong to Caleb Howell. In support of that brave conclusion, the prints are larger than average, suggesting that the owner has very large hands. If memory serves, Caleb Howell has mitts on him like fielders' gloves." Noseworthy smiled at Phelan. "I think I'm right about that, Harry."

Phelan did not return the smile.

For the third time in a week, Stride found himself standing in front of the Burridge house on Gower Street. The same two housewives were sitting on the steps of the house across the street and the same two children were pedalling their trikes madly up and down the sidewalk. It gave the occasion a bizarre patina of *déjà vu*, but that conferred no comfort at all.

"Dare we hope that Howell isn't touchy about surprise, early morning visits, sir?"

"I doubt it. But if we'd phoned ahead, he might be long gone by now. Let's find out."

Ethel Burridge answered their ring. She stepped back into the hallway to allow them to enter.

"Is it about Mr. Rossiter, again?" She closed the door behind them. "Jimmy's not here just now. He went out for some groceries. I expects him back in a few minutes, though."

"That's alright, Mrs. Burridge. It's not your son we want to see." Stride looked towards the dining room at the end of the hall, and seeing no one there he looked at the stairs. "Is Caleb Howell in?"

"Mr. Howell?" She followed the direction of Stride's gaze, then looked at the two policemen in turn, cautious now. "I believes he is. I hasn't seen him yet this morning."

"You're not sure if he's in? Was he down for breakfast?"

"Mr. Howell don't usually eat any breakfast, sir."

"But you think he might be in?"

"I didn't hear him come down or see any sign of him. And I had the door to the dining room open all the time." She looked at the stairs again. "Do you want me to go get him for you?"

Stride had anticipated the question. It was a case of Hobson's choice, really. Damned if you did, damned if you didn't. If either of the Burridges went to get Howell, it could produce a tangle of too many people. If Stride and Phelan went on their own, the potential for trouble was probably increased, but at least there would be no extra bodies involved. On balance, Stride liked to keep the innocents out of these situations.

"No, it's better if we go and see him on our own." He was looking up the stairs now. If Howell were suddenly to appear, it wouldn't really solve their problem, but it would at least take away the burden of decision.

Ethel Burridge was twisting a handkerchief around her fingers. Stride thought she probably had a good memory of the last encounter Caleb Howell had with the police.

"Is Mr. Howell in some trouble, sir?"

"We just want to ask him some questions, Mrs. Burridge. Just tell us which room is his."

"His room is on the next floor up, sir. The stairs takes a sharp bend to the left near the top. You keeps to the left when you reaches the landing, then it's the second door on your right, at the front of the house."

"How many boarders do you have, Mrs. Burridge?"

"We've got four all together. Well, three now that Mr. Rossiter is gone. There's one in the room across from Mr. Howell and then two others at the back of the house. One of those was Mr. Rossiter's room."

"The room across from Howell? Is the boarder at home?"

"No, sir. That's Mr. Kelsey. He does the early morning shift at the dairy on Kenmount Road. He's up and gone before five."

"And the other man? The one in the room next to Rossiter's?"

"That's Mr. Rose, sir, and he's gone off to work, too."

"Thank you, Mrs. Burridge. Sergeant Phelan and I will take it from here."

"There's not going to be no trouble, is there?"

"I hope not."

Stride knew it was a hollow assurance. The back of his neck was already prickling, not a good sign, and it was one he had learned to pay attention to. They started up the stairs, Stride in front. They set their feet carefully, testing each step for noise before putting their full weight on it. When they reached Howell's room, they stood outside the door for a minute listening for sounds from within. A narrow band of light showed under the door, contrasting the deep shadows of the hallway.

Stride tapped on the door, waited a half-minute and tapped again, louder this time. There was still no sound from within. He turned the knob and pushed the door open an inch or two, far enough to see a large man sprawled on a single bed on the far side of the room. He wore dark trousers held up by black suspenders, and a rumpled white shirt open at the collar. A pair of boots lay on the floor beside the bed and his feet were clad in heavy wool socks. A black necktie hung over the back of a wooden chair by the side of the bed on top of a suit jacket. Howell's mouth was open wide and his breathing was deep and even.

A brass light fixture with five bulbs hung from the centre of the ceiling. Only two of the bulbs were lit.

Stride looked at Phelan and saw that he was thinking along the same lines as he was. Whatever kind of night Howell had had, he obviously hadn't bothered to make himself ready for sleep, hadn't even managed to turn off the overhead light.

He pushed the door open wider and stepped cautiously into the room. The place was sparsely furnished. There was a dresser at the foot of the bed, close against the back wall. Next to that was a door that probably opened to a closet. Next to the door, an armchair with a tear in the fabric on one of the arms, and behind that a lamp with a patterned shade. A small wooden table stood in front of the curtained window. The curtains were heavy enough that only a hint of the morning light filtered through to compete with the two bulbs overhead.

There were five books, dime novels, on the small table, neatly propped between brass bookends shaped like a vessel in full sail on a roiling sea. On one side of the table was a portfolio, tied shut with a black ribbon. A bottle of dark rum, half full — or half empty — stood on the table beside a small glass. A large metal ashtray lay beside that.

Stride looked at Howell more closely. The man appeared to be in his early forties but Stride knew from the arrest sheet that he was years younger than that, in spite of the greying hair and the coarse complexion. Howell had the ravaged look of a man who had not been kind to himself for a large part of his life. The atmosphere of the room was heavy with stale smoke. Stride counted eleven cigarette butts in the ashtray.

Stride picked up the rum bottle, read the label, and replaced it on the table. Then he noticed a second bottle, empty, in a wastebasket under the table near the back. He picked up the glass and sniffed it. There was a trace of rum in it still.

He stepped close to the bed and placed his hand gently on Howell's shoulder. Howell stirred, grunted, and turned over onto his left side. His breathing went back to its slow and even rhythm. Stride prodded him with a little more force. Howell's right arm lifted and he made a pawing motion at the empty air. Stride poked him again, more forcefully this time, and stepped back a pace. Howell rolled onto his back, blinking and coughing. He clapped a hand over his face, a sharp slapping noise, shielding his eyes from the overhead light. Now it seemed he was trying to rearrange his features, the hand working hard, the movements accompanied by a series of grunting sounds. He seemed lost in a fog of alcohol and sleep.

Phelan thought the man probably didn't know where he was, much less who the two men standing over him might be. He looked at Stride and raised his eyebrows, half-smiling. So he was unprepared when Howell suddenly launched himself off the bed and sent him reeling across the room with a deftly executed shoulder block. Phelan collided with the closet door and the doorknob caught him low on his left side. Pain knifed through his lower back and into the hollow of his stomach. His head swam and tears blocked his vision. He was bent over now, feeling suddenly ill. He grabbed at the top of the dresser to keep from falling. He tried to take a breath but the pain in his back got in the way.

Phelan looked up. Stride and Howell appeared to be dancing a sort of tango, two hands clasped and held high in the air, pointing at the ceiling, the closely paired bodies turning this way and that. Phelan steadied himself and pulled a slow and careful breath through the curtain of pain, fighting back nausea and the taste of bile. He wiped tears from his eyes and took a step forward. It was then that he saw the gun in Howell's right hand.

Stride's left hand was locked onto Howell's right wrist. With his right hand he had twisted Howell's left arm behind his back. The two men slowly pirouetted in their bizarre embrace, faces close together, feet scrabbling for purchase on the worn and dusty carpet. They had moved away from the bed now, their breathing slow and laboured. Howell was almost a head taller than Stride, and he was the younger man, but Stride was in control, choreographing their movements, his face calm, his eyes staring straight into Howell's, moving them gradually closer to the place where Phelan stood. Harry pulled in another long, slow breath, his eye on the gun, and waited for his moment.

One more step, a final half-turn, and Howell was within reach. Harry balled his right fist, took careful aim, and delivered a short sharp punch to the region of Howell's right kidney. The man cried out in pain and shock, and the gun fell from his hand, thumping onto the carpet almost at Phelan's feet.

Harry kicked it across the floor and saw it slide under the table by the window. He was making ready to throw a second punch when Stride suddenly spun Howell around and pitched him across the room where he collided heavily with the door frame. He seemed to dangle there, as if from an invisible tether, staring at the two detectives, his eyes more clearly focused than either of them might have anticipated. Then, decision reached, he slid down the door into a sitting position on the floor. He pulled his knees up under his chin, embraced his legs with his arms, and let his head fall forward.

Stride kept his eyes on Howell and moved quickly across the room. He reached under the table for Howell's pistol. It was a .45 Browning semi-automatic. Howell still sat with his head on his knees. Stride ejected the chambered round and slid the clip out of the butt. He squeezed the bullet into the clip, then put it into his jacket pocket. He sniffed at the muzzle. It didn't seem to have been fired recently. He tucked the gun under his belt

"You alright, Harry? You looked a little peaky there for a moment."

"I ran into that bloody doorknob there." Phelan rubbed his lower back. "But I was happy to return the compliment."

Howell looked up at Phelan briefly, grimaced, and let his head fall forward again onto his knees.

The chair that had stood by the side of the bed had been knocked over. Howell's jacket and tie lay underneath it, partially covering a leather holster and a belt. Stride tossed the jacket and tie onto the bed and picked up the holster.

"Shoulder holster," he said. "What's the sentence in these parts for carrying a concealed weapon, Harry?"

"Thirty years hard labour and surgical removal of both testicles."

Howell looked up sharply and saw that Phelan was grinning at him.

"Fuck you," he said.

"You already tried that, matey." Phelan took a step closer to the man on the floor, again rubbing the bruised area on his back. Howell watched him closely, apprehensive now, staring at Phelan's double-soled brown oxfords. Stride put a restraining hand on Harry's shoulder.

"Anytime you're ready, Mr. Howell, we'd like to ask you a few questions." He tossed the holster onto the bed next to the jacket. He picked up the chair and set it down in front of the table. "You can sit here."

Howell glared at Stride, but he braced himself against the door and worked his way to a standing position.

"Take your time, Mr. Howell. A sudden move might be misinterpreted. You don't want that."

Stride leaned against the edge of the table while Phelan stood by the bed, the two detectives bookending the man on the chair. Howell sat and stared at them without expression. His white shirt was now even more rumpled than before. Dark splotches of sweat showed under the arms and on the back, and a sour odour seeped from him. Stride tapped the toe of his shoe against Howell's foot.

"Tuck your feet around the legs of the chair, Mr. Howell. We want you nicely relaxed." Howell hesitated just long enough for Stride to prod him again, sharply this time. "We'll start with simple questions. Your name is Caleb Howell?"

"Yes." A smoker's voice, harsh and raspy. He coughed twice.

"How long have you lived here?"

"Here?"

"In St. John's."

"A year, I suppose. Maybe a bit less than that." He rubbed his neck and thought about it. "About ten months."

"What was it all about, Mr. Howell?"

"What?"

"That little fracas we just had. Tell us what that was all about."

Howell looked away and shrugged. Seconds passed in silence.

Abruptly, Stride grasped Howell by the hair and turned his head so that the two men were looking at each other. He took the Browning from his belt and pointed it at the centre of Howell's forehead. Howell stiffened and leaned back in the chair, his eyes wide open now. Stride pulled the trigger. The hammer struck harmlessly against the empty chamber, a solid slap of metal on metal. Howell blinked rapidly, his eyes bright, sweat beading his face and forehead.

Stride tucked the pistol back under his belt. The burst of anger had surprised him almost as much as it did Howell and Phelan. Maybe it was the gun, the fact that he had come near to being shot with a weapon that could bring down a caribou. Or maybe it was something else.

"I didn't know who you were," Howell said finally. He was breathing deep and fast now. "I was dead asleep when you came into the room. You startled me. There's been times in my life..." He wiped sweat from his eyes with the back of his left hand. The hand was shaking slightly.

Stride looked into the man's eyes, saw something familiar there. He picked up the bottle of rum, pulled the cork, and poured a quantity into the glass. Howell took the glass and sipped a little of the dark liquid, then tossed back the rest. He closed his eyes.

"Better?"

Howell stared at Stride and then looked away. His breathing had slowed, but he was still sweating. A large bead ran down his left cheek from his hairline and clung tentatively to the edge of his jaw before it dropped onto the sleeve of his shirt.

"Another?" Stride held up the bottle. Howell appeared to consider it, but only shook his head.

"Why the gun?" Stride took the pistol from his belt again and held it up. He turned it back and forth, as if admiring it.

"Just protection. I've carried one for a while."

"Really? We've always thought St. John's was the very model of the peaceable kingdom." Stride tucked the pistol under his belt again. "Why would you need a weapon here?"

Howell shrugged again.

"I just feel better having it on me. I haven't always lived here, you know." He rubbed the back of his head and winced.

"Where have you lived, Mr. Howell?"

"Here and there. All over."

"Start with where you were born."

"I was born in New Hampshire, in a place you never heard of. A town called Seaward."

"I know Seaward," Stride said. "It's on the New Hampshire coast, near the border with Massachusetts." He knew the place from his days running liquor into the eastern seaboard. He'd spent almost a week there once, a holiday from his adventures.

Howell stared at him, surprised.

"And after that?"

"Like I said. Here and there."

"Here and there doesn't do it. Where were you before you moved to St. John's?"

Howell looked around the room. Stride wondered if it was an excuse to delay answering, to allow him to think.

"I was in Chicago for a while," he said finally. "For maybe two months. Then I was in Boston for a while, three, four months. After that Halifax and North Sydney. Then I came here on the ferry. I guess it was November last year."

"That's a complicated itinerary. You're an American citizen. Why did you come to St. John's?"

"I was here during the war. For almost a year."

"With the army? At Fort Pepperell?"

"Yes."

"You must have liked it here."

Howell smiled for the first time. "It reminds me of home. I like to be near the sea." He looked at Stride again. "Anyway, my father was from here. My mother, too."

"Here? St. John's?"

"No, not here. A place called Scat's Arm. It's around the bay, on the east coast."

"Your family moved to Seaward?"

"Yes," Howell said. "A long time ago."

"Alright. And after you left Pepperell? What then?"

"I was in Europe. France and Germany. That was in '44-'45."

"You were part of Overlord?"

"What?" Howell didn't appear to recognise the name.

"Overlord," Stride said. "The D-Day landings."

"No. I went in after that. A few days later when the landing areas were secured. I was with a transport group. Trucks."

"Behind the lines?"

"The lines moved around a lot. Sometimes we were behind them and sometimes we were in shit up to our ears. I paid my fucking dues." Howell was bristling now, growing angry. His hand automatically went to his shirt pocket then, and finding nothing, he looked at his jacket lying on the bed.

Phelan took out his package of cigarettes, looked at Stride, who was shaking his head. He put the package back in his pocket. Howell looked from one to the other, and made a fist with his right hand. He took a deep breath. He was sweating again.

"You know, Mr. Howell, all of this uproar was unnecessary. We only want to ask you some questions about Samuel Rossiter."

"Rossiter? Why?"

"It's straightforward enough. Rossiter is dead. He was murdered. He lived here in this house, just down the hall from you. He spent part of his last night at the Admiralty. You were there that same night." Howell started to speak but Stride raised his hand, silencing him. "And we found your fingerprints on a liquor bottle that Rossiter had with him that night."

"My fingerprints." Howell looked straight ahead, massaging the back of his neck again with his right hand. Stride watched the man's eyes but he couldn't read anything there. Perhaps there was nothing after all, he wasn't sure. What he was fairly sure about was that Howell had been through this kind of thing before, and now he was dipping into his past experiences, measuring his answers, modulating his tone.

"Your very own fingerprints," Phelan said. "You provided us with a complete set the last time you were a guest of the state."

"Eight months ago," Stride said. "I imagine you still recall the occasion? You made the acquaintance of three of our finest that evening."

Howell glanced at Stride and Phelan, but he only shrugged.

"Alright," he said finally. "I was at the Admiralty. And I know Rossiter was there."

"And you saw him after he left?"

"Yes. He was with Walter Keough."

"You know Keough?"

"I know who he is. I've seen him around."

"Did you go to Scanlon's Lane with them? Or did you see them there later?"

"Where?"

"Scanlon's Lane. It runs between Duckworth and Water."

Howell shook his head. "I don't know the names of all the streets in St. John's. Anyway, I didn't go anywhere with them."

"How did your fingerprints get on the bottle?"

"Shit." The word had some feeling in it. "I was outside the tavern when the two old geezers came out. Rossiter recognised me and they came across the street to where I was sitting. He had a bottle in his pocket, Rossiter, and he showed it to me. He was in a good mood, halfway pissed I think. He offered me a drink. I took it."

"And that's how your fingerprints got on the bottle?"

"Yes. Rossiter offered me a drink. He said someone had given it to him or to Walter. It was horrible fucking stuff." Howell tilted his head back and closed his eyes for a moment. "And that's what this is all about? I take a drink from an old man, just to be polite, and I wind up with half the Constabulary down on my head? Jesus fucking Christ."

Stride looked at Phelan. What Howell had said might have been true. Maybe this exercise had all been for nothing. Or maybe Howell was just a very good actor – playing tag with the police was probably not something new to him – acting out a role he had rehearsed more than once. Stride couldn't tell. Maybe it was all just coincidence. But they would take him in anyway. At least they had him clean on a weapons charge.

He looked at Howell for a few moments, then turned to Phelan. "Phone the Fort, Harry, and have the Black Maria sent round. I'll wait here with our friend."

"You're arresting me?"

"Yes, we are." He held up the forty-five and tapped Howell on the shoulder with it. "Unlawful possession of a handgun and assaulting a police officer. Make that two police officers. Stand up, Mr. Howell."

Howell stood up, his body tense. His face was flushed red and his fists were clenched. He looked ready for another fight. Stride didn't know if it was the arrest, or if the anger came from somewhere else, from another time, other circumstances. But they were all locked into the situation now and there was only one way to go.

"I can use the phone downstairs, sir. Are you going to be alright here alone with him?"

Stride took the ammunition clip from his pocket and slid it into the butt of the Browning. He chambered a round and pointed the gun in Howell's direction.

"Do we have an understanding, Mr. Howell?"

Caleb Howell glared at Stride for a moment longer, then he took a step back and held his hands at shoulder level, palms outward.

Phelan left the room and his footsteps came back to them from the carpeted stairs. Stride gestured towards the jacket on the bed. Howell picked it up and checked for his wallet and cigarettes. Then he picked up his necktie, folded it with exaggerated care, and put it into a side pocket of his coat. Stride didn't bother to tell him that he wouldn't be allowed to keep it in jail, that it would be taken away from him, along with his belt and his shoelaces. He believed Howell already knew about things like that.

t w e n t y - s i x

Stride left Harry at the Court House to book Howell, and drove down to the American base at Fort Pepperell. He found Muff Conway sitting behind a stack of files in his office. Conway had a bottle of Coke in one hand, a pencil in the other, and a weary look in his eyes. He wasn't his usual cheerful and ebullient self, not today. He didn't get up when Stride came into his office. Instead, he only rolled his chair back from his desk until it collided with the wall behind him. He raised the bottle of Coke in a tired gesture of welcome and drained it in a single gulp, his Adam's apple bobbing in a neck as thick and hard as a mature spruce. He dropped the empty bottle into a wastebasket where it clattered against a collection of empties. He stood up and waved his hand at the files.

"Paperwork, Eric. Fucking paperwork. Some folks say it's how we really won the war."

"Usually the ones who generate it, Muff."

"You got that right. For every guy on the front line, there's six doing combat with paper, pencil, and stapling gun."

Melville Conway, who had answered to "Muff" for as long as Stride had known him, was a Master Sergeant with the United States Army Air Force. He was a large man with a matching personality, a native Mississippian from a town called Hub Purvis. One of his responsibilities was enforcing what he liked to call, "gentlemanly conduct" among U.S. military personnel when they were on leave in St. John's and elsewhere. It was a heady proposition, given that the principal preoccupations of many of the men in uniform involved getting drunk and getting laid, preferably both at the same time – activities that inflicted a degree of irritation on the local population. Especially the latter one. There were just so many women to go around. Competition with the locals could be fierce.

Conway took two bottles of Coke from a cooler that sat beside a filing cabinet, popped the caps, and gave one of them to Stride. He picked up a file and waggled it over the pile on his desk.

"I'll take it that's the file on Howell?"

Conway nodded.

"Caleb Wesley Howell is your man. He enlisted in the army in March 1942 in his home state of New Hampshire. In Concord, if you want the specifics. Age at the time, twenty-four years."

"He told us he was born in Seaward, on the coast."

"He grew up in Seaward, but he was born in a little place near there, name of Haleybury. It's on the record."

"Haleybury."

"That's what it says here." Conway looked up from the file. "That mean something to you?"

Stride shook his head. "I've heard the name, but I can't quite place it. I was in Seaward once, though, years ago. If Haleybury's near there, maybe that's why it's familiar."

"Your hunch about Howell was right on the mark, Eric."

"He has a record?"

"Yeah, he does. He was arrested, tried, and convicted for a string of break and enters just before the war started in '41." Conway grinned. "Our version of the starting date. He was suspected of armed robbery, too, but they didn't proceed on that one. If the Japs hadn't bombed Pearl, he would have done time, maybe five years, not even counting the armed robbery."

"That's in the record, too?"

"No. That I got by phone from a buddy of mine in D.C. who sits in the tall clover in the Pentagon and worries a lot about his golf handicap. Not that I'm envious, you understand. I like short summers and eight-month winters."

"They build character, Muff. You're a better man for having been here."

"My wife says the same thing." He looked at Stride. "At least she did before she packed her bags and moved back to Mississippi."

"When did that happen?"

"It's a recent development," Conway said. "Six weeks back, but it was something that was gaining traction for a little while. We'll have a beer or three sometime, maybe even a little Jack, and I'll fill you in. But right now it's Caleb Howell you want to hear about."

Stride looked at him, searching without success for something to say. Conway was right. It would have to be another time.

"So Howell had the choice between prison and going into the army."

"That was it. Prison or the military. And it was a lot more common than many of our good citizens would like to think. Something that never made it into any John Wayne movie, far as I know."

"We had our share too," Stride said. "It doesn't quite fit on a recruiting poster, does it?"

"No, it surely do not." He turned a page in the file. "The thing is, though, Howell did okay once he got the uniform on. He did good in basic, and after that he worked real hard, got hisself promoted all the way up to sergeant. And all that in a year and a bit. It's a good record. Better than good. With a bit more luck and the right connections, Howell might've got his face on one of those recruiting posters you mentioned. An inspiration for the nation's wayward youth."

"He shipped out to Pepperell, and that's almost as good. When was that?"

"He arrived here in '43, a year after I did. He was here for six months, then he moved on to England. He was there for six months before his outfit went over to France. That happened a couple days after the invasion."

"He told us he was in a transport group."

"Trucks," Conway said. "Howell was a driver, a mechanic too. And as a sergeant, he would also have had some responsibility for organisation and coordination, making sure stuff got where it was supposed to, and got there when it was needed."

"He gave us the impression that he was caught in the middle of some heavy fighting."

"He was. His outfit was caught in the middle of the Bulge, and a bunch of them was either killed or wounded. It was a blood and guts on the wallpaper kind of scene. Howell took a hit, a shell fragment from an eighty-eight, in the chest. He was out of action for a while, but it wasn't bad enough that he got sent stateside. He went back into it and made it to Germany late in '45, when the official shooting was over. There were only about a million trucks in Germany and Austria about then, hauling stuff and people all over hell's half-acre. And it was indeed hell's half-acre. Between our side's bombers and the Red artillery, it was a fucking wasteland. Still is, lots of places."

They were silent for a minute. Conway's comments made Stride think about Howell's ravaged look, the need for alcohol. Maybe that's where it started, in the Ardennes when he was wounded, or later when he found himself in the middle of Germany's destruction.

"He's come down a long way," Stride said. "I would have guessed he's at least ten years older than this file says he is."

"Some guys do look that way," Conway said. "War can age a man and there's often more than one reason for it."

"Do you remember him personally, Muff?"

"Yeah, I did know him, and I remember he was a man of very few words. He minded his own business and expected others to mind theirs. He was on my boxing team for a little while, though and he was pretty good. Fact is, I thought he had talent. And Lord knows he was big enough. But he dropped out, told me he wasn't a joiner." He smiled at Stride. "I guess you can relate to that?"

"But you say he behaved himself all the while he was here in Pepperell?"

"Yeah, he did. If he hadn't, I would've seen a lot more of him. There's nothing on his file that says he didn't do his job and more than enough that says he did. He wasn't here all that long, Eric and then he was gone across the water."

Conway went through the file, turning pages. He looked up at Stride.

"Something interesting?" Stride said.

"Moderately. You mentioned how old Howell looks now." Conway turned the file around and pushed it across the desk. "Personnel files don't usually have photographs, other than a mug shot. But here's one of Howell and couple of the men in his outfit here at Pepperell. It was probably a public-relations photo, one of the ones we gave to the local papers during the war, to show the good citizens that our guys didn't have horns and tails. Horny and tail-chasing being another story, of course. Someone must have thought the picture made for a homey touch, so they stuck it in here."

Stride looked at the photograph. There were four men standing and leaning against a large truck, all of them smiling. There was snow on the ground and the men were wearing winter gear: two in bulky greatcoats, two in parkas. It took him a moment to identify Howell, he had changed that much.

"This was 1943?"

"I guess so. Or early '44. He was here from July 1943, until February the next year. There might be a date on the back of the picture."

Stride turned the photograph over. The notation read, "1/12/44," which didn't make sense. It took him a moment to remember that the American numerical shorthand for dates reversed the day and the month.

"January 12, 1944. A month before he went to England." Stride pulled the file closer and looked up at Conway. "I suppose I'm not allowed to look through this?"

Conway shook his large head. "Personnel files are strictly confidential. I'd have to get you permission from the base commander and that would be a bitch. Our present commandant goes strictly by the book, not one single inch of wiggle room. Tightest ass I ever met." He stood up and took the file from Stride, closed it, and dropped it in the middle of the desk. "But just now you'll have to excuse me for a bit. Too much Coke. I really have got to take me a leak." He paused by the open door. "Five minutes."

When the door closed, Stride turned the file around and opened it, quickly scanning the pages. In addition to the typed information that was attached to the file, there was a page of notes in Conway's handwriting. He read through that, then went back through the whole thing again. Nothing leapt out at him. It was all routine, or at least what Stride assumed to be routine for the American military, for all bureaucracies, probably. The file wasn't strikingly different from those kept on members of the Constabulary back at Fort Townshend.

He looked at the photograph again, four tall men standing by an army truck, all of them looking cold, but all smiling for the lens. Although the first contingent of American soldiers was mainly from Minnesota, later arrivals came from all over the forty-eight states, north, south, east, and west. The Newfoundland climate was a particular shock to men who had grown up in the south and the southwest, men for whom snow, ice, and freezing rain were climatic novelties, if they had any experience at all of such weather. Some of them had expected to see Eskimos and igloos, and komatiks pulled by sled dogs, when they arrived in St. John's.

He went back to Conway's notes. They filled in the gap between Howell's departure from Pepperell, summarised his time in England, and then they gave a rough sketch of his movements through France and Germany, a journey interrupted in late January 1945 in the Ardennes with the surprise German counter-offensive. That was when a chest wound from a shell fragment had taken Howell away from his unit, sending him to a field hospital behind the American lines in France. But two months later, in March, he was back with a transport unit near the German border. Later, after the surrender in May, Howell was in Germany and Austria both. Stride wrote down the names of the towns and cities, one or two of them vaguely familiar, hoping that Conway's spelling was accurate. It probably was. Conway had a good hand and he wrote carefully, a skill Stride admired, but had never mastered.

He looked through the frosted glass of the office door but could see no sign of Conway yet. The file hadn't yielded anything much, apart from the striking difference between Howell now and the way he looked in 1944, three and a half years earlier. He went back to the photograph, studied Howell's features again, then looked at the three other men. He wondered if they had all gone to England together and from there to the combat zone in France. And because his mind worked that way, the human element up front, he found himself wondering if any of the three had been killed in the war. He looked closely at the faces, moving from one to the other, as though that might establish some kind of contact. He was still looking at the photograph when the door opened and Conway was back in the office, making clucking noises of mock despair.

Then he peered over Stride's shoulder at the photograph. "You find anything that helps?"

"Not really." He gave the file to Conway. "But it doesn't hurt to know something more about Howell."

"Can't imagine it does. A guy goes through what Howell did, it becomes part of him, and it stays." He sat on the edge of the desk. "You question him yet?"

"This morning, in his room when we arrested him," Stride said. "We have him for weapons possession and assault."

"Who'd he assault? You or Harry?"

"Both of us."

"He's a reckless fellow. But you don't look all that bad, my friend."

"I was lucky. Harry has a bad bruise on his lower back, but he'll live to fight another day. It could have been a lot worse. Howell had a pistol, a Browning .45."

"He was packing a Browning? What the hell was that all about?"

"I don't know. He told us he's carried a gun for a long time. You have any ideas?"

"Not really. Might be a holdover from the war, I suppose. Or from before the war. Either way, he looks like someone you might want to be concerned about. What is he doing here, anyway? He's a long way from home."

"Not as far away as you might think. His family is from Newfoundland, originally, a place up the coast called Scat's Arm." It occurred to Stride then that he still didn't know where that was. "He drives a truck for Len Stick's outfit, off and on. Maybe he's just trying to figure out who he is and where he belongs."

"It could be that. It's not all that unusual. I've known more than a few guys who come back from Europe and the Pacific not knowing who the hell they were any longer, assuming they ever did know. Most of them were not much more than children when they went overseas. It's a bigger problem than most people think it is, or want to think it is. It can get awful lonely and quiet when the parade is over and the band goes home."

"You think we should cut Howell some slack when he comes to trial?"

"I won't go that far. But he's been through a lot. It wouldn't be unfair to mention it."

Conway's comment had a certain resonance. Stride was thinking now about McGinn's recounting of the trial and execution of Herbert Spratt. It wasn't the same situation, but there were uncomfortable parallels.

"You're right. I'll keep it in mind."

"Never hurts to rope in all the variables before making a decision. You said Howell is a drinker?"

"Yes, he is. That was obvious when we arrested him. And from other information we have."

"It's something that didn't show up when he was here at Pepperell. I told you about the boxing. The man was better than halfway along to being an athlete. Anyway, keeping track of bottle-babies was one of my jobs, not quite an official duty, but necessary. I got to be pretty good at it."

"So the drinking must have come on later. After his experience in the Ardennes, maybe?"

"Might have been like that," Conway said. "We've both known men who got cosy with the bottle after a real bad experience. Mind you, Howell was posted to Germany and Austria for almost a year after the regulation shooting ended. There was a lot of booze flowing around then, along with a lot of stuff that pretended to be drinkable but really wasn't. Men got lonely and bored, especially after what they'd just been through. Bored and lonely men can do dumb things."

"Maybe that was it." Stride pointed at the file. "The other three men in the picture. Did they ship out with Howell? To England and the war?"

Conway opened the file again and looked at the photograph. His brow puckered as he ran the faces and names through his memory.

"Two of them did. This one," he pointed at the man standing in front of Howell. "He was posted back stateside from here and then he was discharged. Turned out he was borderline diabetic. This one is dead." He pointed to the soldier on Howell's right. "It wasn't combat, it was an accident in England. Skull fracture, I heard it was. He got hit by a bicycle on a country road, if you can believe it." Conway shook his head. "And this one here, the lieutenant, he's dead too."

Stride looked at the picture again. He hadn't noticed there was an officer in the group. Now he could see the bars of rank on his greatcoat. "Combat?"

"Not exactly." Conway shook his head again. "The story I heard was Lieutenant Weldon Pryor got hisself involved in some serious black-market activity."

"I've heard stories about that."

"There's a lot of stories. Pryor bought the farm in some little town in Austria. No one has told me what exactly happened, but black marketeering was said to be the thing that got him killed, and it was not pretty. Someone poured a can of fuel over him, dropped a match, and made him into a jump-about torch."

"He was still alive?"

Conway nodded. "So I was told. But that's between you and me. For the record, and the folks back home, Lieutenant Pryor was in a road accident and the vehicle he was driving caught fire. An unfortunate victim of tragic circumstance."

"Were Pryor and Howell still in the same outfit when this happened?"

"So I was told." Conway gave Stride a cautionary look. "I made a point of trying to keep track of the guys I knew who went off to the shooting war after they left here. Maybe because I felt guilty about being posted here in Newfyjohn for the duration, safe as houses. When I heard Pryor was dead, I did a little more looking. I found out there was a bunch of his guys got interrogated after the body was found. Howell was one of them."

"If they had found anything to link him with Pryor's death, he wouldn't be here. He'd be in a stockade someplace."

"That is a fact. They might have had their suspicions about him, but nothing to back it up. So he got an honourable discharge last year and walked free. Until you nailed him this morning, anyway."

"That case is closed, then."

"Nailed shut as far as I know. The army has a lot more things to worry about than another dead black marketeer, even if he was an officer."

"Hard on Pryor, though."

"You know what they say: 'You play with fire, you might get burned.' There was more truth than poetry in that for Lieutenant Pryor."

Stride picked up the picture again, focusing on Pryor.

"There's something about Pryor, Muff. I thought at first I was imagining it, but he looks different from the others somehow."

Conway smiled. "I wondered if you would notice. No, you're not imagining it. He was different. You familiar with the term 'high yellow?'"

"Yes." Stride looked at the picture again and it was clear now what it was, subtle differences in Pryor's facial bone structure and general appearance, a black man under the pale white skin.

"Thing was, I was the only one here who caught on to it. Maybe the only one anywhere. You know that our military is segregated, just like most places back home, including during the war. The blood supplies was segregated too, even in the fucking war zone."

"Did Pryor know that you knew?"

"He knew, but we never talked about it. Part of the reason for that was the officer-non-com gap. It made him real perplexed, though, me being from Mississippi. He probably thought I would blow the whistle on him, might even organise a Klan meeting, white sheets, torches, be the grand master of the asshole parade. It took him a while to get used to the idea that I didn't care.

In the end, we just pretended there wasn't anything to care about. And then he was off to Europe and that was the last I saw of him. Or heard about him until the word filtered down that he was dead."

Stride looked at the photograph a moment longer, then put it back in the file folder and stood up. He drank the last of his Coke and gave the empty to Conway.

"I'm sorry to hear about Midge," Stride said. "You knew Margaret had moved to England?" He wondered if Conway knew Dianne's husband, maybe knew something about him. It was tempting to ask, but it was the kind of inquiry that could get complicated very quickly. Muff Conway had a better-than-average ability to read between the lines.

"Yeah, I heard about that," Conway said. "Condolences all around, I guess. I was gonna give you a call but I didn't feel much like talking about it right then. And I knew we'd touch base sooner or later."

"And so we have. I'll ring you when things quiet down, Muff and we'll have a drink."

"More than one, if I have any say in the matter."

"That suits me," Stride said. He picked up his hat and glanced at the Howell file one more time. Then he left.

twenty-seven

They finally caught up with Alex Greene at his flat in the east end of the city. Stride had guessed that Greene wouldn't be up and about with the first rays of the sun, and he was right about that. From the weary look that Greene brought with him to the door of his flat, Stride thought he might not have made it to the outside world by early afternoon.

The flat was a surprise, though. Stride had thought that Greene's tosspot reputation would find tangible expression in the appointments of his living quarters, and he had expected something resembling a hovel. What he found himself looking at was a tidy bed-sitter that was also a well-appointed study. There seemed to be both less and more to Alex Greene than met the eye.

Greene stepped aside to let Stride and Phelan enter. The light in the flat was dim, except for a well-lit area by the desk on the far side of the room. Three tall bookcases presented row upon row of books, the spines neatly in line. History books seemed to dominate, many of them dealing with war. A second large category included books on painting and sculpture. That was also a surprise. In all the time Stride had known him, he couldn't remember Greene talking about art or artists of any kind.

Greene went to the desk and turned off the light. He closed a file he had been working on. Then he raised the blinds on the two windows that looked out onto Duckworth Street.

"I can make either tea or coffee, if you like," he said. He looked at his desk again and picked up the pad he had been writing on and placed it on his desk with the top page facing down. "Something I'm working on that's not quite ready for public consumption."

"Will we be able to read it in the *Herald* this Sunday?"

"You read the *Herald*, Eric? You surprise me. I thought better of you than that."

"I have my secret vices."

"Not me. Mine are all laid out there on display, for the world to see and marvel at."

"The world doesn't pay as much attention as you might think, Alex."

"You know, I've sometimes thought that."

"We will take you up on your offer. Coffee's good for me. Harry?"

"Coffee is fine." Phelan was standing in front of one of the bookcases, looking at the titles. "You've read all these, Alex?"

"I could say yes, but it wouldn't be true. I've read about half of them. I like books - they bring me comfort, just by being there. Think of me as a casualty of a superior, private-school education that placed great value on books." He was in the kitchen area now, spooning coffee into the percolator. "For all its faults, Haleybury had some damn fine people on its staff. Along with the usual complement of shits and arseholes. But you always get some of those, I've been told, even in the best schools."

Stride was standing by one of the other bookcases while Greene was speaking, browsing through a volume on French impressionists. At the mention of Haleybury, he slid the book back into place and went over to where Harry was standing. From the kitchen area Greene watched as Phelan's expression changed and the two detectives turned to look at him. He finished preparing the coffee and placed the percolator on the stovetop. He came back into the living area carrying his tobacco and pipe.

"You were at the Admiralty on Monday night, Alex, the same time Rossiter and Keough were there. Why didn't you tell us that?"

Greene shrugged and sat at his desk. He finished tapping the tobacco into the bowl of his pipe.

"I suppose I could say it slipped my mind, but I don't think you'd buy that. My reputation notwithstanding."

"Your famous reputation. And how much of that is manufactured for show?"

"About the same proportion as applies to my collection of books. I discovered a long time ago that if one is careful to lower expectations of oneself, life is usually easier all round. It's the civilian version of the wise soldier's credo. Never volunteer for anything. It's stood me well over the years."

"Let's focus on expectations. You were at the Admiralty Monday night, yes?"

"Yes, I was there. In fact, it was one of several stops I made that evening. It was a warm night. I drank a lot of cold beer. No crime in that, is there?"

"Don't get smart with me, Alex. I am not in the mood. Let me lay it out for you. We may have enough already to bring you in on a charge of obstruction and we might actually find a Crown Attorney to agree with us. This being a murder case, we might even get a conviction. And I don't think your tenuous membership in the fourth estate will work in your favour. Your editor might even enjoy having you in gaol for a time. It would make a good story." Stride made a rectangle with his hands. "*Herald Reporter's Inside View of Prison Life: A Continuing Series.* He smiled at Greene. "I probably don't need to point out that the lakeside has little to recommend it for an extended stay. The regular clientele leave a lot to be desired."

"You make a strong case for active compliance, Eric. Yes, I was at the Admiralty and I did see Walter Keough and Sam Rossiter there. Both of them. They were there when I arrived and they were still there when I left. I even bought them a beer each just as I was leaving. It seemed the decent thing to do for two old men down on their luck and sweating as much as everyone else. I suppose it was my small act of generosity that made me stand out in the crowd?"

"More or less. The crowd wasn't all that large by then. It was almost closing time."

"I suppose that's true." Greene picked up his lighter from the desk. A moment later, his head was wreathed in aromatic smoke. In the kitchen, the coffee pot was rumbling. "I bought Keough and Rossiter a beer, traded a few words with them, and then I left. That really is all there was to it. I've already told you I knew Keough from years ago."

"And Rossiter?"

"I knew his name, but that's about all."

"Where did you go after that?"

"I went east along George Street, heading for home. Then I ran into an old acquaintance I hadn't seen in a long time and we repaired to his hotel and had a few more drinks."

"His name?" Stride opened his notebook.

"His name's Guy Wilton. He's a Brit. He's visiting Newfoundland on holiday."

"How do you know him?"

"I knew him during the war, in London. And other places. He was with the RAF."

"Will he be able to verify that you were together that evening?"

"And will he be able to remember what time I left his hotel? God, I hope so. Otherwise I might find myself on another part of Duckworth Street, being watched over by Chesley Bavidge. I like Ches Bavidge, but not that much."

"No, you wouldn't like it at all. Which hotel is Wilton staying at?"

"He's at the Barrett. He prefers small hotels."

"The Barrett? Not a prestige address. Why there?"

"Possibly because it's cheap. I don't know."

"And what time did you leave there Monday night?"

"Tuesday morning, actually. It was probably sometime around two, or shortly after that. We got to reminiscing about people we knew in the good old days, that happy time when bombs and rockets were dropping all around us and life had a special meaning."

"How long is Wilton staying in St. John's?"

"A few more days, I believe. He told me he's going to Gander to do some salmon fishing. He knows the place from his time in the war, flying transports in and out of the airport."

"So we won't have any problem finding him today?"

"I do hope not. It seems my continued liberty might depend on him."

"That's more or less the case." Stride sat at the table and took out his cigarettes. He took one and slid the package across to Phelan. The coffee had ceased rumbling in its pot. Greene went back into the kitchen. Stride waited until he had poured out three cups and they were all settled again. "How long have you known Caleb Howell?"

The question surprised Greene as much as Stride hoped it would. It took him a moment to gather himself. He looked towards the window, focusing on a pigeon strutting up and down the ledge outside. He drank some coffee. Then he looked at Stride.

"Why do you ask?"

"Howell was at the Admiralty Monday night. He was born in Haleybury, New Hampshire. You went to a private school there, which given your relative ages, would be about the time Howell was a young boy. And now we find you were both at the same pub as Rossiter, the night he was murdered. I'm not a big fan of coincidence, Alex."

"I suppose not. Alright, I have known Caleb Howell for a while."

"A long while?"

"Yes, quite a long time. I take it Caleb's done something to attract your attention again? I know he spent a month at the lakeside last Christmas."

"Yes, he did, and he might be going back there again very soon. We arrested him this morning. One of the charges against him is carrying a handgun. A .45 Browning semi-automatic, if you're interested in the details. He also assaulted two police officers."

"That was you and Harry?"

"Yes, it was. And if we work moderately hard at it, we might get him arraigned on something very serious. He pulled the gun on us and I think he had a notion to use it."

"Christ." Greene sat back and looked at Stride. He took a few moments before speaking again. "So it's possible he might be going away for a long time. That would be unfortunate. Caleb isn't really a bad fellow, you know. He's had a difficult life." Greene looked into the bowl of his pipe, then placed it in the ashtray. "Will it help his cause if I tell you he did well during the war?"

"We already know about that. And it might help his case, depending on the judge and our testimony. We haven't submitted a formal report yet."

"Alright. Do I sense the start of a negotiation here?"

"No. We're only here to ask questions. You met Howell in Haleybury, at that private school you attended?"

"That is where I first met him. He was only a boy then, just as you said. If you've already questioned him, and I assume you have, you probably know that his father was originally from Newfoundland, a place called Scat's Arm."

"Let's pretend we don't know very much and that you're going to enlighten us. Start with Scat's Arm. Where is it? I looked for it on a map and couldn't find it."

"It's not shown on all the maps. It was originally called 'Scot's Arm,' but the name got misspelled somewhere along the way. It's on the northeast coast.

Like I said, it's a very small place. It's a fishing community, or used to be, although some of the men also worked in the various mines in the area."

Stride made a note in his book. He saw that Phelan was looking at him.

"If I guess that Scat's Arm isn't far from Chapel Bight, would I be very wide of the mark?"

"No, you'd be pretty close, in fact. Chapel Bight is on the northern extremity of Notre Dame Bay. Scat's Arm is on the other side of the headland, the north side, near Confusion Bay."

"I like the sound of that," Phelan said. "I think I'll move there after I retire. It will be a useful reminder of my brilliant career in law enforcement."

"It could become a crowded place," Stride said. He went back to Greene. "Go on. What's the story with the family's move to the States? New Hampshire is a long way from Scat's Arm."

"Yes, it is. I'll start with his father. His name was Wesley Howell. His mother's name was Sarah."

"They're both dead?"

"Yes. They both died about the same time, some years back. Before the war or just after it started. I forget. They left Scat's Arm late in 1911, and moved to New Hampshire."

"Caleb was born a long time after that. In 1918."

"Yes, he was born in 1918. Wesley and Sarah kept their Newfoundland citizenship, which makes Caleb one of those very fortunate creatures. He has dual citizenship in both Newfoundland and the States."

"How did you get to know them? Apart from your both being Newfoundlanders, I mean? What was Howell doing in Haleybury?"

"Wesley Howell had a job at the school, one of the people who looked after the place. It wasn't until after I was there for a while that I found out he was a fellow countryman."

"Your paths couldn't have crossed all that often."

"Of course they didn't. We had a broken window in our residence one day, and Howell was the one they sent to repair it. I just happened to be there at the time. As soon as he spoke, I knew he was one of ours. As we were the only two Newfoundlanders in the place, we got to talking from time to time. I even visited them at their home a couple of times."

"In spite of the class difference."

Greene smiled. "I've never been a big fan of class. My great-uncle Randolph Mills, the man who made the family money, liked to call himself a bootstrapper. And he was just that. He started out as an apprentice in the tin mines in Cornwall and worked his way up from there. Randolph had strong views about the class system, and he passed them along to me in what might be called a crude but effective manner. Some say I'm a better man for it."

"It's all in the eye of the beholder," Stride said. "You stayed in touch with the Howell family after you left Haleybury?"

"No, I didn't. There wasn't any reason to. I never expected to see any of them again. But life can be funny, even when nobody laughs. I was in England in the spring of '44, waiting like everyone else for the invasion to begin, and I ran into Caleb in a country pub. It was wildly improbable, but it's the sort of thing that happens sometimes. Anyway, I was a reporter writing stories about the personal side of the war, especially about soldiers far from home. Meeting people in uniform was a big part of my job at the time."

"And Caleb Howell just happened to be one of them."

"Yes. And I ran into him again later on, in Germany, after the surrender. We've stayed more or less in touch since then. Not really close, but we touch base from time to time." Greene started working on his pipe again, glancing up at Stride. "Do you think Caleb was involved in the Rossiter murder?"

"Maybe. What do you think, Alex?"

"You really want my opinion?"

"Yes."

"I can't imagine that he was. I don't know what his motive would be."

"Motive is the obvious question. But motives are funny things. People sometimes get murdered without any motive, no premeditation at all. Sudden anger, an argument flaring into violence. It can happen like that. We know from personal experience that Howell is a violent man. Rossiter was an old man and he was sick. It didn't take a lot to kill him."

"Maybe not. But it does take a bit of effort to crush someone's trachea and larynx, no matter how old he is."

Stride should have known that Greene would have information on the autopsy results. He might even have gotten hold of a copy of the report through his contacts at the hospital. There were ways. Discarded carbon paper was one of them. Greene was known to be resourceful.

"Point taken. And you do know that Howell was at the Admiralty on Monday night?"

"Yes, I saw him there early on. But he left before I did."

"He didn't go home, though. We have a witness who saw him sitting on the warehouse steps across the street from the tavern at closing time."

"What did Howell have to say about that?"

"He admitted it."

"Okay, but it doesn't prove anything. Surely it's in his favour that he acknowledged he was there."

"It might be. But sometimes the best defence is no defence at all. It impresses the naïve and the gullible."

"Sometimes it does."

"You obviously wanted us to take a close look at the Hurdles. Why?"

"I thought it might be relevant to the case. Rossiter and Keough both worked for the Hurdles, and Walter told me he'd heard that Rossiter had a dodgy past and that he had, in a manner of speaking, been exiled to Bermuda years ago."

"Rossiter was that open with Keough?"

"They got drunk together a lot. Drunks and candour are not strangers. I'm something of an expert in the area."

"Did he tell you why that happened? The exile?"

"No, he didn't."

"Do you think he knows the answer?"

"I don't know. But he said Rossiter had been expected to stay in Bermuda until his lights went out, not move back to St. John's. But he came back and when he did it was obvious to anyone who cared to look that he was unbalanced somehow. He might have become a problem for someone."

"That someone being one of the Hurdles."

"It's been suggested that Sir Hubert has an ambition to be a senior officer on our ship of state, someday."

"We've heard that. So you're suggesting that the Hurdles might have had something to do with Rossiter's death? Maybe Sir Hubert himself? It's a very long stretch, Alex."

"I know it is and I'm not suggesting anything. But it is part of a journalist's job to speculate."

"Speculate some more, then. What do you think Rossiter might have known that made him a candidate for a fast and sudden exit?"

"I don't pretend to have an answer for that."

"But you're doing a good deal of pretending, anyway," Phelan said.

"Why didn't you tell us the Mills family had a connection with the Hurdles through the Centaur affair in Chapel Bight?"

Greene sat back and sighed.

"I guess I knew you would find out about that."

"And so we did," Stride said. "It's the sort of thing we're paid to do. Find out things."

"It looks to us like you wanted to settle an old score on behalf of your great uncle Randolph," Phelan said. "You could do that by pointing us in the direction of the Hurdle family. Even if it was bullshit, you knew we might make them uncomfortable. At least for a while."

Greene shrugged. "Alright, maybe that's what I did want, revenge of a sort. A partial settling of an old grudge. It was always a sore point with the family, and it was something I grew up with. The resentment about the Centaur takeover was as much a part of our little household as the overstuffed furniture in the living room. It was always there. Anything that made a Hurdle uncomfortable was thought to be a good thing. That sort of attitude seeps into your bones."

"Some would call that making mischief," Phelan said.

"A judge might even call it interfering with an investigation," Stride said.

"So we're back to that again."

"We never left it. By day's end, you could be sharing digs with your friend Howell at the lockup."

Greene didn't reply to that. He got up and went back to the kitchen area and came back with coffee pot. He refilled the three cups.

"Well, you will do what you will do. But I'm gambling that you're as interested in a possible connection between Rossiter's murder and the Hurdles as I am. Investigations are always more fun when someone at the top might be involved."

"Fun has a variety of definitions," Stride said. "Some of our less principled colleagues find pleasure in putting irritating journalists in jail for a stretch. Tell us some more about Caleb Howell. Does he have a connection with the Hurdle family. Or with Rossiter?"

"If he did, it was probably an indirect one. Wesley Howell told me that he worked sometimes in the mines in the Notre Dame Bay area. A lot of the men in that part of the island did at one time or another around the turn of the century. The big attraction of mining was that you were paid cash for your labour, something the fishery could never guarantee, no matter how hard you worked. And mining, for all its hazards, was probably less dangerous than being out on the North Atlantic in a small boat."

"Did any of those mines belong to the Hurdles? Before the Chapel Bight operation, I mean."

"One or two of the mines that Wesley worked might have belonged to them. He didn't say, and I don't know."

"And Rossiter? Did Wesley Howell know him?"

"Rossiter was also working for the Hurdles in that area for part of that time. Their paths might have crossed. But Caleb wasn't even born then. I don't know that he knows anything about any of this."

"Or that he doesn't. Alright. Let's go back to the reason Wesley and Sarah Howell left Chapel Bight for New Hampshire. It still seems to me like an odd choice and a high risk one, unless he had a job waiting for him in Haleybury. Did he?"

Greene shook his head. "I don't know the answer to that. Maybe he did. He might have had family or friends in the area." He gave Stride a knowing look. "I don't have to tell you there's always been a lot of traffic between Newfoundland and New England."

"No, you don't. And, yes, I have made a few trips there myself."

The three men lapsed into silence. The interview was about over. Stride stood up and stretched, then went to the window, and looked out at the street. The sun was beating down on the concrete sidewalk. He wished he had put the top up on the MG. The leather seats would be as hot as the hobs of hell by now. He went back to the table.

"So, should I prepare myself for a sojourn behind bars?" Greene didn't look too concerned about that. He flicked open his lighter and commenced firing up his pipe again.

"Not today. But you can consider yourself on probation."

"I'm used to it, Eric. It pretty much defines my life to date."

"We will be in touch, Alex. And you will call us if you remember anything else we should know about."

"I have your number."

"And you know we have yours," Stride said.

twenty-eight

Harry Phelan was familiar enough with the Barrett Hotel. Most members of the Constabulary were, for one reason or another. Harry's earliest memory of the place, which was a pretty cheerful one, went back to the start of the war. That was before he had met Kitty Johnston. He hadn't told Kitty about that particular occasion, but there were a few things she hadn't told him, either. Vague and gentle hints of past adventures had flowed between them from time to time, in both directions, but so far they had agreed to leave out the details. It seemed better that way.

Harry had also been at the Barrett on any number of occasions when he was in uniform, and always on official business. The little hotel had been a busy and lively place during the war, the creaking of bedsprings in the rooms upstairs sometimes audible to bystanders in the lobby, anxiously awaiting their own moments of transient joy. Harry was happy enough to share those stories with anyone who cared to listen, Kitty included.

The desk clerk gave Phelan a cautious and careful look when he came through the front door, drawing himself up to his full five-feet-two. Harry wasn't surprised. The two men had recognised each other at once.

They had a sort of shared history, Alfred Dyke and Harry Phelan. When he was still in uniform, Phelan had arrested Dyke three times, once for selling bootleg liquor, once for pandering, and the third time on a charge of battery against his wife, Bernice. That last charge was not what it seemed. In fact it was Bernice Dyke, easily half as large again as her husband, who had battered the hapless Alfred, working him over with a copper-bottomed skillet before calling the police to lodge a formal complaint. Since husbands were usually fair game for a charge of wife beating – and there was no doubt at all that it had always been a too common occurrence – Dyke's protests were discounted, his own cuts and abrasions disregarded. Bernice Dyke declared with passion that she had only been defending herself against her husband's vicious assault. As evidence, she displayed a bruise on the side of her head. Dyke's claim that the injury was self-inflicted, the result of a too-enthusiastic backswing with the skillet, went unheeded. As Dyke was something less than a model citizen who already had a criminal record, the judge was happy enough to add another item to his sheet.

Harry wondered now if Alfred and his Bernice were still together, or if she had moved along to other fields of marital combat. He decided not to ask. It was Guy Anthony Wilton he had come to see.

Stride almost literally ran into Major Tom Stamp on the Duckworth Street steps leading into the Court House. Stride wanted to check on Howell and schedule a second interrogation, using the new information Alex Greene had supplied. He still wasn't persuaded that Howell was good for the Rossiter murder, but it was more than interesting that there might have been a link between Rossiter and Wesley Howell.

McCowan hadn't exaggerated when he described the Major's military bearing. Stamp wasn't very tall but his demeanour gave him the impression of height. His uniform was neatly pressed, the creases on his breeches sharp enough to peel an apple. His tall leather boots glowed in the afternoon sun. Despite the heat and the fact that he was emerging from inside the Court House, Stamp was wearing leather gloves. He also carried a swagger stick.

He tapped the peak of his cap with the butt end of his stick in greeting.

"A happy accident running into you here, Eric. I had hoped that we might be able to get together with Jack McCowan while I was in town, but it seems you're fully occupied with the Rossiter case."

"Yes. I imagine we'll be at it for a while yet."

"Well, it was mostly administrative bumph that I wanted to talk with you about. Not trivial, mind you, but also not urgent. It will keep. Jack has given me a rundown on your case. I hope you don't mind, but he also let me read your progress reports."

"No, sir, I don't mind. Quite the opposite. Some of the links in the case go back to Chapel Bight, on Notre Dame Bay, and that's Ranger territory. I'm wondering if any of the names or circumstances are familiar to you."

"In fact some of them are familiar. The operative question being whether it's coincidence or relevance. In my experience, sorting one from the other is almost always a challenge. Are you familiar with the area up there?"

"No, I'm not. Everything I know about the place I've either read or been told by someone. But I take it you've been there?"

"Oh, indeed, and on numerous occasions. There's a Ranger detachment at Twillingate, across the bay and we have another at Westport on White Bay, on the other side of the Baie Verte Peninsula. Not all that far away as the raven flies, but in practical terms, long distances. I also lived in the Chapel Bight area for a time. That was back before the Great War, long before the Rangers came into existence, of course. You probably know that I was with the British Army and spent some four years in India."

"Yes, I did know that."

"Well, it's not a dark secret. I left the army after the stint in the East, and after that I worked in private industry here on the island. That's what brought me to the Notre Dame Bay area. Not my cup of tea, industry, not really, but the experience was useful. Every experience is, if you take it the right way. The time I spent up in Notre Dame Bay was especially interesting and good fun too. Great country for hiking and there's fine hunting in the area, if you know where to go. I quite enjoyed myself there. Almost like a bloody holiday, really. I might have stayed on there if the war hadn't come along in 1914. But once things got going in France and Belgium, I was back in uniform again. There wasn't really a choice."

"You say you worked in private industry in the Notre Dame Bay area? I don't suppose you might have worked for the Hurdle Company?"

"The Hurdles? No, I didn't, not for them, but I know they had some operations up there. The company I worked for was a British outfit. They were involved in mining, too, but my job was surveying work mostly. It's what I did a good part of the time when I was in India with the army. Contrary to popular fantasy, army life isn't all bang-bang and storming the barricades. A lot of it is routine day-to-day mucking about, plain as porridge and not half as nourishing. Of course, they don't tell you that when you join up, you find it out later on. And then you wonder what the hell you could have been thinking about when you signed on the dotted line in the first place. The company I worked for up Notre Dame Bay way is gone now, bought out by someone or other, I forget who. Perhaps the Hurdles, for all I know. The mining industry shuffles companies about the way most of us change socks. But to go back to your question, I did cross paths with several of the Hurdles, at different times."

"Who was that? Sir Leonard himself?"

"As a matter of fact, yes, I did meet him on one occasion. He was visiting the mine site in Chapel Bight. I was told it was his only trip to the area, at least up to that point. Sir Leonard left most of the outlying work to his son, Hubert. Now Sir Hubert, of course. I don't think he enjoyed it all that much, Hubert. Not the sort to get much pleasure from roughing it, much more the Savile Row, sherry-at-four kind of fellow. But there were compensations, I gather." Stamp laughed. "He was a randy young bugger, I was told, and the local crumpet thought he was great stuff. You wouldn't say that to look at him, especially now, but I imagine the family money and position didn't hurt his chances any. But, you know, to be honest, I've never understood what women find attractive in men. It's one of life's enduring mysteries."

"There was some special reason he was in Chapel Bight? Sir Leonard, I mean?"

"Sir Leonard? Yes, there was a special reason. It was the time they had the cave-in at the copper mine there. Sir Leonard came on up and he brought his two offspring along with him. Hubert and the daughter, too. Elizabeth? I think that's the name. Attractive girl, I thought, if a bit different. Something of an enigma, I remember thinking at the time."

"Odd that he would have brought his family to the town."

"You might say that. But having the Hurdle family there was a matter of a considerable diplomatic effort on the part of the company. Public relations I suppose is what they would call it now. Interesting how the language evolves."

"The cave-in at Chapel Bight. It was serious?"

"Serious enough. There were two men killed and at least a dozen injured, and some of them very seriously. As I was working in the area at the time and had a military background, I was asked to help organise the rescue.

We managed to get most of the men and boys out safely. Lost two of them, as I said, but they were killed immediately the shaft collapsed. Nothing we could do for them."

"When was that? The cave-in?"

"When?" Stamp thought for a moment. "It was 1911, in the early fall. I remember that part because I had been out hunting just before it happened."

"I suppose there was an inquiry into the accident?"

"Yes, there was. It was set up a few months later. I wasn't in the area at the time, but I submitted a short brief to them describing my part in the rescue. I heard it wasn't handled very well. The inquiry, I mean. These things often aren't, more especially with the situation the way it was back then. The mining industry sometimes treated men the way bad officers throw foot soldiers into the path of machine guns. I know something about both. The Hurdles paid compensation to the affected families, I was told later. But how do you put a fair price on lives and limbs lost?"

"Was the Hurdle Company to blame for the accident?"

"Were they responsible?" Stamp managed a dry laugh. "The inquiry report didn't say so, or so I was told, but inquiries are often like committees, set up to camouflage incompetence and do bugger all for the people most involved. It's an old story."

"You haven't read the report?"

"I didn't read it very closely, no, although I skimmed it. And it was a long time ago. The main finding, I believe, was that the Company had cut some corners on construction materials, pit props especially, quantity and quality both. That led to a section of the mineshaft collapsing and tons of rock falling on the men and boys working underground. To be honest, I think the Company probably was responsible. But I didn't conduct the inquiry. Someone not too far removed from the Hurdles did that. Like I say, it's an old story." Stamp peeled down the edge of his leather glove and looked at his watch. "I'm afraid I'm going to have to run, Eric. Your Chief awaits me, more administrative bumph on the menu. Well, serve me right for having leadership ambitions. I hope we can get together for another chat sometime soon, when your investigation is done with."

"I'll look forward to it, sir."

"By the way, Jack McCowan tells me you have no ambitions regarding the RCMP?"

"No, sir, I don't have any ambitions in that direction."

"I know for a fact that some of your colleagues do. Can't mention any names, of course. I gather, then, that you like what you're doing now?"

"Yes, I do."

"Stay with it, then. A man should do what gives him pleasure and avoid siren calls from ill-defined bog-holes dressed up as opportunities."

"That's very good advice, sir."

"Yes. And sometimes I even take it myself." Stamp started down the steps, then turned back. "By the way, there was a postscript to the inquiry. One that helped ease Sir Leonard and his Company off the nasty little hook they found themselves on."

"Yes?"

"I was told later on that one of the office people at Chapel Bight was cashiered in the wake of the cave-in. For incompetence, they said. From what I heard, though, he was a sacrificial lamb offered up to the gods of commerce to smooth the Hurdle family's passage through their small purgatory."

"Really? Do you know his name?"

"The burnt offering? No, I never heard who it was or if I did, I don't remember. Names aren't my strong suit, anyway. In one ear and out the other unless there's a direct connection with what I'm doing at the time. Anyway, by the time the fellow was given the boot, I had moved on to work farther down the coast. But if you're curious about who it was, you will probably find his name in the report of the inquiry. There must be a copy or two lying about someplace."

And then he was off. Stride watched as Stamp walked east down Duckworth Street. Every few paces, he slapped his swagger stick against the top of his leather boot. Then he crossed Duckworth and started the climb up Cathedral Street, on his way back to Fort Townshend.

Stride's telephone call to the Barrett Hotel missed Phelan by less than a minute. He assumed that Harry had either completed his interview with Guy Wilton, or had missed him altogether. Either way, they had agreed to meet back at Fort Townshend when they were both done. Except that now Stride had something else he wanted to do. Caleb Howell would have to wait. First, he needed to get hold of a copy of the report on the Chapel Bight mine accident. His first thought was to ask Justice McGinn if he had a copy. But that had its own set of complications. McGinn's involvement with the Hurdles had come as a major surprise. He needed to think about that.

His second choice was Grace DeJohn. She was likely to have a copy of the report. The government office that dealt with mines was a distant third choice. Stride preferred to avoid government people whenever he could. And in his experience, a private operator like Grace was more efficient at pulling out information. Also more interesting to talk to.

"Mining accidents weren't uncommon back around the turn of the century," Grace DeJohn said. "Especially with some of the smaller outfits. And they're still much too common, even now."

"Hurdle and Company Limited wasn't a small operator," Stride said.

"No, they weren't, which makes it worse. Surprising, too." She pulled open a drawer of her filing cabinet and marched her fingers across the top of the row of file folders. She found the one she was looking for and pulled it out. "When Dianne rang and asked me about Centaur, the name and the Chapel Bight location both rang a bell. I knew there was something more to the story of that mine. I guess maybe I should have followed it up, but there didn't seem to be any urgency and I didn't have the time just then. Well, you can see my problem."

She waved the file folder at a desk that was cluttered with stacks of papers and books.

"Yes, I can see you're busy," Stride said.

"I almost always am. I can't afford to turn down anything. If I did, them-that-must-be-obeyed might forget that I exist. The life of a freelance geologist in this town defines the word 'fraught.'"

"Well, maybe this won't take very long. I think I know what we're going to find."

"The predetermined outcome. The best kind of research, some would say." She sat down at her desk and shoved a stack of reports towards the back and opened the file folder.

Stride lit a cigarette and watched while she went through the report.

Grace DeJohn didn't fit any picture of a female geologist that he might have conjured up. She was small and slender, almost delicate in appearance, not pretty but attractive. Harry would have described her as bird-like. Her face and arms were deeply tanned, and that wasn't a surprise. She spent as little time in her office as she could get away with. Just now, in deference to the continuing hot weather, she was wearing a suitably feminine print skirt and white short-sleeved blouse. But a pair of high-top leather work-boots sat on a rubber mat in the corner of the office. Overhanging the boots was a clothes tree holding a pair of dungarees, a long-sleeved flannel shirt, and a broad-brimmed hat that looked a lot like a Stetson. Grace looked up and caught the direction of his gaze.

"Yes, it really is a Stetson. I bought it in the States, my last visit home."

"Do you have a horse to go with it?"

She had probably heard the line more often than she cared to remember, but she gave him a friendly smile anyway. "Not one of my own, no. But I do ride, whenever I have the chance. English, though, not western."

Stride laughed. "A gentle reply to a fairly dumb question."

"Not so dumb, if a bit short on originality." She glanced at the hat again. "Like most people, you probably think that Stetson was a Texan, one of those leathery good old boys we see up there on the silver screen, galloping around the badlands on their mustangs, poking cows, or whatever it is they pretend to be doing. In fact, John B. Stetson was a gentleman from New Jersey who started up his hat company in Philadelphia, not all that far from Chester, the town where I grew up. More Yankee than that you can hardly get."

"I didn't know that."

"You and about a billion other people. I am a fount of near-useless information." She went back to the report. A minute later she looked up. "And the occasional bit of useful stuff. You said you probably knew the name of the man who got hung with the blame for the Chapel Bight cave-in?"

"Yes. I think it was Samuel Rossiter. He worked for the Hurdles at Chapel Bight."

"The guy who was murdered? Well, that would make it very interesting for you, wouldn't it?"

"Yes, it would." Stride sat forward in his chair. "But I think you're about to tell me his name wasn't Rossiter."

"Nope, it was not Rossiter. His name was Howell."

"Wesley Howell?"

"Yes. Not the name you expected, but I see it's one you're familiar with."

"Yes, I am familiar with the name. It's come up a couple of times. And we've just arrested his son."

"Really? For the Rossiter murder?"

"Not for that, no, although we haven't ruled him out yet."

"And now, maybe you have more reason to rule him in?"

"Maybe, I don't know. But we will be asking him more questions."

She gave Stride the report, indicating the passage she had read.

Wesley Howell had worked in an office job at the Chapel Bight mine. The report described his duties as one of the people responsible for the procurement of materials for the mine site. There was an almost endless list of items involved. Mauls and spikes, picks and shovels, drums of kerosene, crates of dynamite and detonators, ore cars, and electrical generators. The list also included pit props, the wooden poles used to construct and secure the mineshaft.

Stamp had said the inquiry report had laid the blame for the cave-in at Chapel Bight on the quality and quantity of the pit props procured for the operation. The report said that they had been purchased under the authority of Wesley Howell. The report disputed, but did not dismiss outright, Mr. Howell's objections to that conclusion. Stride took a few minutes to read through other parts of the report. The writing managed to be turgid and vaporous at the same time, awash with qualifiers. It reminded Stride of a bad novel. He tried to remember who it was said the road to literary hell is paved with adverbs.

"This is about as wishy-washy as it gets," he said. "It doesn't really say anything. And it only suggests that Howell was responsible for the shoddy construction in the mine. There's no mention of criminal liability."

"That was my sense of it when I first read it a few years ago. I was researching a paper on mine accidents."

"What do you make of it all?"

"That someone cut corners on the operation is always a possibility. I wouldn't have thought it was Leonard Hurdle, though, not from what I know about him. He was more of a straight arrow than that."

"His son was also involved in the operation. Stamp said he was working at the mine site for a time. In his early days with the company, he sometimes worked outside St. John's."

"Then you might have to rule him in. You're guessing, I suppose, that the late Rossiter might have had information that would prove embarrassing to Sir Hubert?"

"It's one of a number of possibilities."

"It's tricky, though. Hubert Hurdle probably has even more political clout here in St. John's than his father had. Still, it looks like someone on-site at Chapel Bight might have been skimming money from the accounts, and the poor bastards working underground paid the price. Maybe it was your man Howell, although from what you told me on the phone, Rossiter looks like the better choice. You did say he had a senior position with the company?"

"Fairly senior."

"And he was a drinker?"

"That's what I was told."

"That can be a deadly combination. Where does this leave your investigation?"

"I'm not sure." Stride said. And he wasn't.

"You were counting on Rossiter being the man in the report who got hung with the blame?"

"Not exactly counting on it, but expecting it. It would have explained at least part of the puzzle about him. He was pensioned off, with rather a nice pension in fact, and banished to Bermuda where he ended up living most of his life."

"That's the kind of punishment almost anyone could handle."

"You fancy an exile in southern parts, Grace?"

"No, not really. Fact is, I really do like being out there in the wilderness, even with the blackflies and the predictably unpredictable weather."

"You and my father would have gotten along."

"Dianne mentioned him when she rang." Grace stood up and went to the clothes tree in the corner. She took a package of cigarettes from a pocket of the dungarees. "I'm trying to cut down. So I keep them more than an arm's length away from me."

"Does it work?"

"Not really, no. But anything's worth a try." She snapped her lighter shut and went back to her desk, trailing cigarette smoke. "I've known Dianne for a couple of years now. Maybe you knew that?"

Her tone had changed now. Stride shifted in his chair and took out another cigarette.

"No," he said. "She only mentioned that she had spoken to you about the Centaur business. I wasn't actually aware that you knew each other until then."

"I suppose not. You wouldn't have known who Dianne's friends are. Dianne and I have things in common. It helps that we're both in there, slugging it out in a man's world. For one thing, it gives us stuff to bitch about and that's always fun. Plus, I'm a transplanted American and she's married to one. That doesn't create any kind of a tight bond necessarily, but it also isn't nothing."

They looked at each other in silence for a moment that was a little too long for Stride's comfort.

"Is this leading somewhere, Grace?"

"Maybe. Would you like it to?"

He sat back and stretched his legs out in front of him. He dropped his head back studied the ceiling of her office for a moment. Then he looked at her.

"You know, I don't really mind. How well do you know Dianne? And her husband?"

"I know Dianne better than I know Marty. A bunch of us used to get together from time to time, for a meal, a picnic, a drink or three. But not so much lately. At first, Dianne said the reason was that Marty was really busy, and there's a lot of stuff still going on at the various bases around the island and in Labrador. Marty's in the supply business. He knows a few things about the comfortable relationship between industry and the military."

"Getting ready for the next war?"

"Maybe, who can say? War is good stuff for the guys who run the government and the economy, always has been. As long as you're on the winning side, that is." She looked up at him. "But don't change the subject on me."

"I wasn't. I was just asking a question."

"Alright. Anyway, I figured it out after not too long. It was obvious that something was going on. It's the little things. The way Dianne and Marty didn't touch each other any more, or at least not in the way they used to. So, being that kind of friend, I asked her what was going on."

"And she told you?"

"Yeah, she did, right flat out, like a hard smack where it really smarts." She looked at him through a veil of cigarette smoke. "People usually need to talk to someone when their life is starting to do spin-circles. How about you?

You look like the strong and obstinate type, but appearances, as the saying goes, can be deceiving. Maybe you've talked to someone too?"

"Maybe."

"Well, there you are. People are people, after all."

"Does Marty know about us?"

"I don't know what Marty knows or doesn't know. His eyesight is 20/20, but I don't know about his insight. Marty Borg comes from a rock-ribbed Lutheran clan in Wisconsin, the kind of family where sex *after* marriage is halfway frowned on. But he's been in the army since Pearl Harbor, and rumour has it there was a lot of enthusiastic screwing going on during the war, in and out of uniform. Marty might find it a challenge to locate his Eagle Scout badge these days. Smiles aside, though, t'aint really funny, McGee. But I think you've figured that out already."

"Yes, I have."

"So, what are you going to do about it? That would be the question."

Stride stood up and took his hat off the top of the filing cabinet. He leaned against the metal and brushed some dust off the brim.

"Nothing right away."

"Which is a way of saying you don't know what to do. Well, it's a tricky business, isn't it? Not that I have any personal experience, you understand." She laughed and stubbed her cigarette in the ashtray. "I think it's one of the reasons I went into the geology trade. Rocks are so much more stable and predictable than humans. Anyway, right now you have other things on your mind."

"Yes, I do."

"And thank God for that, I guess."

Stride nodded. He picked up the report and opened it again. He didn't want to talk about Dianne any longer. The report had opened at the page that listed the various people who conducted the inquiry. The chairman was a retired judge named Chalker, now long dead. The vice-chair was Robin McGinn.

"Find something else of interest?"

"It might be. Justice McGinn was the inquiry's vice-chairman."

"You look surprised. Are you?"

"A little. But there's no good reason I should be. McGinn was an up-and-coming lawyer back then. He was probably a good choice for the position."

"You sound halfway convinced it's true."

"I do what I can." Stride smiled and closed the report. "Can I take this with me?"

"Of course. But you will bring it back, right? It's my only copy."

"Yes, of course."

"I hope you're not too ticked off with me, Eric, poking into your not-so-private life and all."

"No, I'm not ticked off. And you're right. It's not all that private, is it?"

"Not any longer, it isn't. And the circle will only get wider."

As if that were news. He was halfway through the door when he turned back.

"You said you like to ride?"

"Yes, I do. Why?"

"I don't suppose you've ever done any riding at Devon Lea Farm?"

"The Hurdle place?" Grace DeJohn rolled her eyes. "I check my mail every day, hoping for an embossed invitation. But you pretty much have to be a certified Hurdle to get in there, so I've been told."

"A very private place, then."

"No doubt about that. Does Devon Lea have something to do with the Rossiter case?"

"If it does, I don't know what it is. But very private places are always interesting to people like me."

"Just because they're private?"

"For just that reason."

twenty-nine

"My guess is Wilton's family probably had money once upon a time," Phelan said. "The accent and manners were unmistakable, the tie he was wearing looked old-school to me, and his suit was tailor-made and good quality. But his shoes had been re-soled more than once, and the suit wasn't new. Pre-war would be my guess. I found myself thinking the Wilton family money might have gotten lost somewhere along the way."

The interview with Guy Wilton had been pleasant enough, Phelan said, all things considered. The "things" being that Guy Wilton was British, upper-echelon British at that, which served as a flinty contrast with Harry's background, Irish and working class.

"It fits in with him staying at the Barrett. On the other hand, he might be one of those eccentric Brits who likes to dress down, at the same time having a bank balance that would stagger a Clydesdale."

"There are people like that."

"Did he say anything to contradict Greene's story?"

"No, he didn't. It all checked out. He said he went out for a stroll late Monday night and ran into Greene on George Street. Then they went back to Wilton's hotel room and beat up on a bottle of Scotch that Wilton had brought over from England with him. He said he'd been surprised to find Greene in St. John's. He thought he was probably still in Europe, working for one of the news services."

"Instead, he's back here writing stories for the *Sunday Herald*. How old is Wilton? Greene's age?"

"Younger by at least ten years, I think. My guess is mid to late thirties."

"Greene said Wilton was in the RAF during the war. Did he say what he did?"

"He was a pilot in the RAF. He was with Ferry Command and then Transport Command, after the reorganisation. He said he'd made a dozen trips across to Newfoundland during the war. That checks out with Greene's story too. Does this take Alex Greene out of the picture?"

"Maybe. But I can't quite shake the feeling that he's in there somewhere."

"Standing in the shadows with a finger on the side of his nose?"

"You know, that almost fits."

"The stuff that Muff Conway told you about Howell is interesting. Especially the bit about Lieutenant Pryor."

"It is, but Howell was only interviewed. There wasn't any action taken and the case is closed as far as the army is concerned."

"Are you going to ask him about it?"

"If I find an opportunity to drop it on him. It might be interesting to see his reaction."

They were at the Court House now, on their way to the interview with Caleb Howell. Chesley Bavidge walked down the corridor with them, on his way to get Howell from his cell.

"You know that Howell has a lawyer, sir?" Bavidge said.

"Yes, we knew that. Abe Peddle left a message for me at Fort Townshend."

"Howell called him about an hour after you and Sergeant Phelan brought him in. We didn't even have to look up Abe's number for him. He already had it."

That wasn't a surprise. Given his background and his previous arrest, Howell would have a lawyer's number close at hand. Stride and Phelan both knew Abe Peddle well enough. In an average year, they would come up against him at least a dozen times. Peddle handled a lot of the criminal cases in St. John's, the attorney of choice on the second tier of the justice system, looking after the usual run of minor crimes and an occasional case of consequence. It was inevitable that Peddle would be known at Fort Townshend as "Dishonest Abe." Policemen, for the most part, didn't hold a good opinion of criminal lawyers. But Abe Peddle was an honest lawyer. He was no legal wizard, but he was smart and efficient, better than good at what he did.

"Peddle told me he's started proceedings to have Howell released on bail," Stride said.

"That's the gist of what he told me when he was here, sir. I thought Abe looked a little bothered, though."

"About what?"

"I think the gun was a part of it."

"Abe doesn't like guns as a general rule, and he doesn't come across hardware like a .45 during his average working week. And the other part?"

"Howell himself, I think. Abe Peddle's just a little fella, a hundred and thirty pounds of not-very-much, and with a game leg besides. Howell could have him for breakfast even on a slow day, and come back for seconds."

Stride took Bavidge's comment for what it was, the large man's assessment of someone much smaller than himself. But if Peddle had been uncomfortable with Howell, it wouldn't have been the physical difference between the two men. Abraham Stearns Peddle was as tough as they came, and his game leg was a souvenir from the war in France in 1916. Peddle and Howell had a lot more in common than Bavidge might have imagined.

Stride and Phelan took their usual positions in the interview room. Bavidge stood guard by the door, within easy reach of the prisoner.

"I'm going to ask you some questions about your father, Mr. Howell."

"My father?" Howell rubbed the stubble on his chin and looked around the interview room, first at Phelan, then at Bavidge standing by the door. "My father doesn't have anything to do with any of this. For Christ's sake, he's been dead for five years."

"I'm aware of that, Mr. Howell, but I'm going to ask you some questions anyway. I will advise you, though, that you have the right to have your attorney present. If you want him, we'll schedule the interview for later on, when Mr. Peddle is available."

Howell made a dismissive gesture.

"You can ask your questions. Lawyers don't hold your hand for the pleasure of your company. They expect to be paid. But if you ask me something I don't want to answer, I won't."

"That's understood. Your father was from Scat's Arm?"

"I already told you that."

"So you did. Are you familiar with the town of Chapel Bight? It's on Notre Dame Bay, not far from Scat's Arm."

"I've never been there, but I've heard of it."

"Tell me what you know about Chapel Bight?"

"Do I get to know what this is all about? Or are you fishing around just for the hell of it?"

"This interview is about the murder of Samuel Rossiter. Tell me what you know about Chapel Bight. Your father lived there at one time?"

"If you already know that, why bother asking me?"

"Answer the question, please. Did your father live in Chapel Bight?"

Howell sighed and stared at the ceiling. "Yes, he lived in Chapel Bight for a time."

"Doing what?"

"He worked at a mine there. A copper mine."

"He was a miner, working underground?"

"No, he wasn't a miner. He worked in the company office."

"Doing what?"

"He was a clerk." Howell put an sour inflection on the word. "He pushed paper around."

"I take it your father wasn't in charge of the office at Chapel Bight. Do you know the name of the man he worked with there?"

Howell looked away from Stride and clasped his hands together, resting them on the table in front of him. The knuckles of his right hand were badly scraped. Stride wondered what that was about. Dried blood had formed scabs over the torn flesh, but fresh blood was seeping out now as Howell clasped and unclasped his grip. As Stride watched, a small rivulet of blood trickled down the back of his hand. Howell took a handkerchief from his pocket and wiped it away. He looked at Stride.

"Alright. I think I know where this is going."

"Where do you think it's going, Mr. Howell?"

"This is how you bring Rossiter into it and try and link me up with him. Through my father."

Howell's tone was different now, more relaxed.

"Did your father work for Sam Rossiter? He was there, in the office at Chapel Bight, wasn't he?"

"You already know he worked for Rossiter, so why not stop the bullshit and just get on with it."

"We'll take it one question at a time, Mr. Howell. It's the way we do things here." Just like a clerk in an office, Stride thought. "Did your father work for Sam Rossiter?"

"Yes, he worked for Rossiter."

"And do you know the name of the company that owned the mine, the company that your father and Rossiter worked for?"

"I know the Hurdles owned it. It started out under another name, but I don't remember what it was. Maybe my father told me the name, I'm not sure. But it was the Hurdles who owned it from the start. That much I do know."

"Is the name Centaur Minerals familiar to you?"

Howell nodded. "I think that was the name. Yes, it was. I remember now."

"Did your father tell you about an accident at the Chapel Bight mine? In 1911?"

"Yes, he told me about the accident."

"Go on."

"There was a cave-in. The mineshaft collapsed and a couple of men were killed. Some of the miners were trapped underground for a while. There were injuries, too, some of them serious."

"Did your father tell you about the inquiry that was held after the cave-in?"

"Yes. He told me about that too."

"What do you know about the findings of the inquiry?"

Howell smiled. "Probably less than you do."

"Just answer the question, Mr. Howell."

"I know the inquiry report made it look like my father was responsible for the cave-in."

"Was he responsible?"

Stride waited for the reaction, but Howell only smiled once more and shook his head.

"No, he wasn't responsible."

"If he wasn't responsible, do you know who was? Did your father tell you? Was it Rossiter?"

Howell smiled.

"That would be good for you, wouldn't it?"

"Would it?"

"Sure it would. Here's how it goes. Rossiter was responsible for the cave-in, the inquiry hung the blame on my old man, and he lost his job and he had to leave Newfoundland. Then, a hundred years later, his son comes back and takes revenge for the injustice of it all." Howell laughed and slapped his hand on the table. The bleeding started again. This time he licked the blood away, then sucked at the cut on his knuckle.

"Is that what happened, Mr. Howell?"

"No, that's not what happened. And if you're really interested, I don't have a fucking clue who killed Rossiter, or why." Howell looked at his hand again. The bleeding had stopped. "My old man told me just about everything he knew about the cave-in at Chapel Bight. When it happened, everybody in the town pitched in to help, men, women, and children, digging a passage down to the men trapped underground. My old man helped too. But they didn't reach the miners until later the next day and by then, it was too late for two of the men. They were already dead."

"Alright. You say your father wasn't responsible for the cave-in. Did he say who was responsible?"

"He said it was the Company."

"Just the Company, no one in particular?"

Howell shrugged and shook his head.

"My father said it was the way they did business, the same way most companies do business. The game is to keep the costs down and keep the profits up. I know something about that. We lost good men during the war when stuff we needed didn't work properly, because the companies back in the States or in England had cut corners. It's an old story."

Howell went silent. He wasn't looking at Stride now. He seemed to be staring at a spot on the far wall. Stride thought he might have drifted back to his time in the war, years and miles away from the interview room. He took a chance.

"Tell me about Lieutenant Pryor."

"What?" The question had startled him, but he recovered almost at once. His expression went from surprised to calm, but guarded also.

"Lieutenant Weldon Pryor. You served with him in the war, here and in Europe. What happened to him?"

"Weldon Pryor. Now, there's a name from the past."

"Yes, it is." Stride repeated the question. "What happened to Lieutenant Pryor?"

"Pryor's dead. I think you already know that or you wouldn't be asking the question."

"How did he die?"

"He was murdered. In Austria, after the war ended." Howell was relaxed now. "Pryor was into the black market and he was in deep. It was big business then, and it probably still is. He came out on the short end of it, the shortest end there was."

"You were questioned in connection with his murder."

"A lot of people were questioned about Pryor's murder. It's what they do when someone gets killed, especially when an officer ends up on a slab. People like you ask questions. I learned to get used to it."

"You have a habit of being in the neighbourhood when people are murdered, Mr. Howell."

"I've been in a lot of neighbourhoods when a lot of people got killed. I was in the neighbourhood when German artillery dropped a couple of tons of steel on us in the Ardennes. I kept some of that for a souvenir, the piece they dug out of my chest. It's in a folder with my discharge papers. My medals and commendations are there too. I can show it all to you, if you like." Howell was cruising now, really comfortable. "But I forgot. You already have that folder. You took it along with you when you arrested me. Open it up sometime when you have a few minutes, take a look. You might find it interesting to read about someone who actually fought in the fucking war."

"Alright," Stride said. This wasn't his week for brilliant interviews. He looked over at Phelan, but Harry was focused on his note-taking. No comfort there. "Let's go back to Chapel Bight."

"Sure, let's do that. I don't mind."

Stride ignored the satisfied grin.

"Your father said the Company was responsible for the cave-in because they wanted to keep costs down."

"That's what he said. They shaved expenses anywhere they could, and they probably ended up cutting it too close to the line."

"The inquiry blamed the cave-in on the number and quality of the pit props used to construct the mineshaft."

"That might have been part of it. My father said that some of the wood the company purchased wasn't top quality. Maybe that was what caused the cave-in, I don't know."

"Rossiter was in charge of the office at Chapel Bight, wasn't he?"

"Yes, but he took his orders from the head office in St. John's. And there was an engineer on site at Chapel Bight. Rossiter pushed paper. He pushed paper at a higher level than my old man, but he was a paper pusher. They had other people to look after the technical work at the mine."

"You're saying that Rossiter probably wasn't responsible for the cave-in."

"I don't know whether he had anything to do with it or not. His name didn't come up when my father told me about the accident. Maybe it was just one of those things. Human error." Howell laughed. "There's a lot of it around."

"It was your father who took the blame, though. He must have been angry about that."

Howell smiled again. "I guess that would make sense, wouldn't it?"

"It makes sense to me. Are you saying your father wasn't angry about the inquiry's conclusions?"

Howell nodded. He was still smiling.

"No, he wasn't angry."

"I don't understand. Explain it to me."

"Think about it. My old man was very happy when he got that job at the mine in Chapel Bight. It was steady work, it put money in his pocket, and it got him out of the fishery. But mining was often as not a short-term thing. When the ore got played out, the mines closed. The word on Chapel Bight was that the mine had enough ore for maybe five years production, give or take a year. And when it was done and the ore was played out, it was back to the fishery for a lot of the people involved. I've never worked in the fishery, but I've heard enough about it to know I never want to. Lots like the life, but lots don't. My father was one who didn't."

"I'm not following you," Stride said. "Your father lost his job when the mine was just going into production. And you say he wasn't angry about that?"

"You didn't let me finish. After the cave-in, there was a lot of anger in and around Chapel Bight. Two men were dead, a bunch more was injured, some of them really badly, arms and legs chopped off. The situation was bad enough that Sir Leonard Hurdle brought his family up to Chapel Bight to put on a show of sympathy for the good citizens. But it pretty much backfired. The people looked at Hurdle and his crowd and they could see up close the differences between him and themselves, the kind of life they had. My father said it was almost like they were having their faces rubbed in it. The situation in the town started to get ugly."

"And that's when Sir Leonard realised he needed a scapegoat for the accident? Someone to deflect the blame from his Company and from him?"

"Like the Brits say, he heard a penny drop from a great height. It made a very loud noise."

"And your father was made the scapegoat."

Howell shook his head. "You're still not getting it, are you?"

"What, then?"

"When he saw the way things were going in Chapel Bight, Hurdle didn't know whether to shit or bake bread. They say he was a smart businessman, but he hadn't faced a situation like that before. And he didn't know what to do about it. It was my old man who saw what was needed. He made Hurdle an offer. Set up an inquiry, right there in Chapel Bight, and do it quick. Find someone to take the blame, take the heat off the Company, and off the Hurdles."

"Are you saying your father volunteered to take the blame for the cave-in?"

"That's exactly what he did. My old man didn't have much education, almost none at all, but his mother didn't raise any stupid children. He knew there was no real future for him at Chapel Bight, even if they did get the mine back into production. And if he could help it, he wasn't going back to chasing fucking codfish on the North Atlantic. So he went to Hurdle and offered himself up for the cave-in. His price was something that would get him out of Chapel Bight, out of Scat's Arm, out of Newfoundland altogether."

"A job at Haleybury School."

"That's what it turned out to be. Hurdle's son had gone to Haleybury, Hubert his name is, and Sir Leonard had friends on the board of directors."

"A caretaker at Haleybury School? It doesn't seem like much of a reward for what he did."

"Maybe from where you're sitting, it doesn't. It depends on where you come from. It's another world up there in Scat's Arm, but you wouldn't know anything about that. For my father, Haleybury was a very long step up. He had a job at a rich man's school in the States, a decent place to live, even a little bit of money in the bank. An actual bank account. You think about that. Even today, almost no one in Scat's Arm knows what it is to have a bank account, never mind what things were like in 1911. Compared to what he had to look forward to, a job at Haleybury School was a fucking paradise. As far as my old man was concerned, he thought he'd died and gone to heaven."

thiRty

Stride and Phelan drove back to Fort Townshend in silence. A couple of times Stride visited his store of profanity, but for the most part he concentrated on his driving. He didn't want to add a vehicle accident to this day's disasters. It wasn't just that he had got it wrong, that Howell had no apparent reason even to dislike Sam Rossiter, much less want to kill him. What really bothered him was the way he had given Howell an opportunity to walk all over him in the interview. He had tried to drop a surprise on him, to jolt him with the murder of Weldon Pryor in Austria, and Howell's possible involvement. Not only did that not work, it gave Howell the opening to cruise through the rest of the interview, and then drop his own surprise at the end of it.

The bitch of it was, Wesley Howell's flight to Haleybury made good sense. Life in a remote fishing outport could be brutally hard. While Stride didn't discount the fact that shared hardship and sacrifice made for strong people and solid communities, he also knew that not everyone wanted to live that way. Not if there was a choice. Stride had fled his own situation on the south coast, the tough life his father had lived, using the illegal trade in booze to lever himself into what he still considered to be a much better life. Wesley Howell had traded his own situation for a caretaker's job at Haleybury School, and in doing so, believed he had scored a personal triumph.

Caleb Howell had got one part of it wrong, though, not that it mattered in the end. Stride did know what it was like to have very little. There were times when he was growing up that his family had almost nothing, when his father had toiled with the family's survival as his only goal, and it was an outcome that was not always guaranteed. But that knowledge only more certainly hammered home Howell's main point.

The main problem now, though, wasn't Stride's wounded ego – a delicate and sometimes irritating creature – but the fact that he and Harry were back almost where they had been early on Tuesday morning when they first looked down at the pathetic crumpled figure of Samuel Rossiter in Scanlon's Lane. They were awash in information, but it was something like the harvest of fingerprints on Rossiter's liquor bottle, as much muddle as enlightenment.

Stride turned left off Bonaventure, gunned the MG across the parking lot in front of the fire station, then skidded to a halt in front of Fort Townshend, raising a large cloud of dust in the still-warm air of the late afternoon. It had little effect on his frustration level. He threw himself out of the car, slammed the door, and headed for the entrance. Then he stopped and waited for Harry to catch up. The debacle in the interview room wasn't Harry's doing. Stride had sole ownership of that.

Phelan was carrying the report of the Chapel Bight inquiry with him. He held it out for Stride.

"Grace DeJohn won't be happy if we lose this, sir."

Stride stood on the front step of the building, looking at the report. Then he rolled it into a tight cylinder and slapped it against his thigh.

"I really did think the cave-in at Chapel Bight might be the key to it all. And I was wrong."

"For what it's worth, sir, I thought so too."

"That's worth a lot, Harry. But it doesn't get me off the hook. I wanted an easy answer and there wasn't one. I screwed up." He opened the report and flipped through the pages, as if he was hoping that something useful might fall out, something that might turn events backwards, in their favour this time. It didn't happen.

"Can I suggest that a shot of rum might go down well just about now?"

"An excellent suggestion. I say we do that." He pulled the door open and followed Phelan inside.

Billy Dickson was just going off duty. He caught Stride's attention.

"A couple of phone messages for you, Inspector Stride."

"You go ahead, Harry. I'll catch up." Stride took the two slips of paper from Dickson and read them as he walked down the corridor.

When he got to the office, he closed the door behind him. Harry had already poured out two stiff shots of dark rum. Officially, drinking at Fort Townshend was severely frowned upon, but Stride and Phelan weren't the only officers to keep a bottle close at hand for emergencies.

"Anything interesting, sir?" Phelan gave Stride one of the glasses.

"Don't know, yet. One call's from Tom Butcher and the other one is from Jimmy Peach."

"We haven't heard from Jimmy for a while,' Phelan said. "Does he have something for us?"

"He probably does. He wouldn't call if he didn't. He wants us to meet with him. Maybe he'll give us our first really good news of the day."

"The usual place?"

"No, for a change he wants to meet us at Williams' teashop on New Gower Street. He says he'll be there about six-thirty." Stride drank some of his rum and read through the second message again. He picked up the phone and asked the operator to connect him with Tom Butcher. He looked at Harry. "Isn't Friday the night you get together with the Johnston clan for supper?"

"Yes, it is. But the world won't end if I don't appear. Although tonight Kitty's mother is doing a baked codfish."

"With savoury dressing?"

"And roast potatoes."

"Maybe you can go meet Jimmy and I'll take your place at the table."

"I doubt you would be able to stand it, sir. Even I find my wife's family a challenge, sometimes. We usually end up with a long and detailed discussion of family and local history."

"Point taken." He turned his attention back to the telephone. "You called, Thomas?"

"Yes, I did," Butcher said. "I wanted to ask you about Sir Leonard Hurdle. Did you tell me he died in a typhus epidemic in 1912."

"Yes. Bertie Prim gave me the information."

"The very large fellow who works at the Mercantile Association?"

"Yes. Did he get that wrong?"

"I don't know, but I am curious. When you told me about it yesterday, it didn't sound right to me, so I looked it up. I wrote a paper on infectious diseases in Newfoundland two years ago. There was a typhus epidemic in

1911, a serious one. A large number of houses were under quarantine. But there wasn't one in 1912. Is it possible Reid got the date wrong? For Hurdle's death, I mean."

"Just a second." He turned to Phelan. "Harry, do we know for sure that Leonard Hurdle died in 1912? Did you see the death record?"

Phelan put his glass on the desk and opened his notebook.

"Yes, sir, I did. And I made a note of it. It was 1912, the same year his daughter went missing. Sir Leonard died not very long after that."

"It was 1912, Thomas, there's no doubt about that. But does it have to mean anything if there wasn't an epidemic that year? Weren't there some cases of typhus most years, back then, 1912 included?"

"Yes, it has been a common enough disease. But typhus tends to occur under poor conditions of hygiene. For one thing, it's spread by lice. For good reason, it's been called both 'war fever' and 'jail fever.'"

"Not really a rich man's disease, then, is it?"

"Not as a rule, no, although the wealthy obviously aren't immune. But it isn't something you would expect for someone like Sir Leonard Hurdle."

"God's judgement for sins committed?"

"That presupposes a belief in God."

"Foiled again," Stride said. "Alright, it does look a bit odd. And just about now, I'm willing to grab onto any straw that floats by."

"I take it you've had a bad day?"

"A lousy day, if you'll forgive a rotten pun."

Butcher laughed. "I'll look into this a little further, Eric. If I find anything of interest, I'll be in touch."

Stride hung up the phone and picked up his glass.

"Butcher has some question about Sir Leonard's death?"

"He thinks maybe he didn't die of typhus. He says there wasn't an epidemic in 1912. It might mean something, or it might not."

"Maybe Sir Hubert could tell us. If we were to ask."

"Maybe he could. But I have to wonder if he would want to."

George Williams' teashop was on the east end of New Gower Street, near the intersection with Springdale. The shop had been there for as long as Stride had lived in St. John's. He found a parking spot in front and started for the door, then remembered he had left the report of the Chapel Bight inquiry on the passenger seat. He slid it under the seat, out of sight.

Stride had a nodding acquaintance with Williams, as he did with many of the shopkeepers and small businessmen in the city, the people with premises most likely to be broken into. Williams was tall and thin, something of an eccentric, but friendly enough when you got to know him. Before he went into pots of fine tea and china cups, George Williams had been in the merchant navy. Over a period of several decades, he had travelled much of the world, 'civilised and otherwised,' as he liked to put it. He had also lived in India for three years and a bit, and that, he had told Stride, was where he learned all he knew, and all he would ever need to know, about tea.

The shop was almost empty when Stride got there. Williams was at the cash, making change for a customer who was cradling a large package under his left arm. Jimmy Peach was sitting at a table near the window, his back to the wall, as was his custom. There was a woman sitting at the table with him. She was a pleasant looking woman, in her sixties Stride thought, about medium height, and solidly constructed in a way that suggested efficiency married to determination.

It was a surprise that Peach had brought someone with him to their meeting. Jimmy preferred to work alone, peddling his information, making the deal most advantageous to him. But the woman was obviously someone he knew well and was comfortable with. Jimmy was perched on his chair, grinning like an elf on a toadstool, looking very pleased with himself. It was tempting to reach down and give him a little push, just for fun. But if Jimmy was pleased, it was also likely that he had something useful to pass along. He stood up and shook hands with Stride.

"I don't think you've ever met Molly Legrow, have you, Eric?"

"No, I have not," Stride said. They shook hands. Stride pulled a chair over from a neighbouring table.

"Molly's family comes from Broad Cove, Eric, up Bay de Verde way, but she lived here in St. John's for years and years."

"I was in service here in the city for most of my life, Mr. Stride, from the time I was seventeen. My aunt was in service, too, and she found me a good position."

"Molly was with the same household for more than forty years, Eric, if you can credit it. Half a century, almost. Imagine that."

Jimmy Peach was Stride's best source of street information. Peach had contact with a wonderful variety of people in St. John's. He seemed to know something about almost everyone, the wealthy and the powerful included. He got his information from the underlings of St. John's society, the people he referred to as 'the grease in the gear-wheels' — the servants and the tradesmen, the clerks and the postmen, the butcher, the baker, the candlestick maker, the people who kept the city moving, and who kept their eyes and ears open, and took pleasure, and occasional small profit, from talking about what they saw and heard. Only some of what they told Jimmy Peach was true, of course, and one of the little man's greater talents lay in being able to winnow the one from the other, the nuggets from the nonsense. Stride and Peach had been friends for years, an association that went back to the time before Stride had joined the Constabulary, to his days as a rum-runner.

"You must have been almost like a member of the family after all that time," Stride said.

"In a way, I was. But I'm retired now, going on two years. I've moved back to Broad Cove, but I still visit the city from time to time. Of course I like to stay in touch with old friends. Like Jimmy, here."

"The family you worked for, Miss Legrow. Who were they?" Stride thought he already knew the answer.

"I went to work for Sir Leonard Hurdle and his family in 1901. It was the year the Old Queen died, God rest her soul. I will always remember that. There was a portrait of her over the mantelpiece in the dining room, and it was draped in black. It stayed there from the day she died, for a full year. Sir Leonard was like that. And after Sir Leonard passed on, I stayed with the family."

"You worked for Sir Hubert?"

"Yes, sir, I did. For more than thirty years."

George Williams arrived at the table then carrying a tray with a large pot of tea. Williams knew something about the relationship between Stride and Jimmy Peach.

"This should help you get through whatever it is you've set yourselves about." He took his time arranging the cups, saucers, spoons, as well as the milk and sugar. "If you want more, you just let me know. The kettle's always on the rumble in the back."

Molly Legrow took charge of the tea with the practised efficiency of her forty-some years in service.

"Sir Leonard liked his tea and he was quite the expert. It would take me some little while to tell you about all the teas I got to be familiar with when I was with the Hurdle family." She filled the last of the three cups. "But it's not tea you're interested in, Inspector Stride. You'd rather I talked about Mr. Rossiter, I'm sure."

"Yes, I would, Miss Legrow. I take it you knew him?"

"No, I didn't really know him, Inspector. I was only in service, so it wasn't my place to know him. But I was acquainted with Mr. Rossiter, and I saw him often enough at the house."

"So he was more than just another employee of the Company."

"Oh, yes, Mr. Rossiter was at the house quite often. Almost a member of the family, he was, much more so than myself, of course. That went back to before my time, his being close to the family, I mean."

"Was he related to the Hurdles in some way?" It was something Stride had wondered about.

"Yes, I believe he was, sir. One of the stories I was told was that Mr. Rossiter's mother was a cousin of Lady Hurdle. Not a close relative, though. She was a cousin several times removed, but there was a connection there. And I believe that's how Mr. Rossiter first came to be introduced to Sir Leonard."

"And Sir Leonard found a position for him with the Company."

"So I understand. It's not unusual for a relation to ask a favour of someone who's better off than they are. And there's nothing at all wrong with that." She smiled. "It's how I got my position with the Hurdles, after all, through my aunt knowing the right people."

"Was there more to it than that? More than Rossiter just being a distant cousin?"

"Yes, I think so. There were stories." Molly Legrow smiled. "Of course, there's always stories in big houses like that. We never wanted for things to talk about among ourselves and with the girls who were in service at other houses. One of the stories that went around was that Miss Elizabeth and Mr. Rossiter were very close, and I do believe that was true. But not in the way that was being talked about by some of those girls. They thought they heard wedding bells in the distance, but it was never like that. Miss Elizabeth and Mr. Rossiter weren't the marrying sort, you see. Not really."

"Not the marrying sort."

"No, sir. That wasn't what they were about, Miss Elizabeth and Mr. Rossiter. If you know what I mean."

"Perhaps you can tell me what you mean."

Molly Legrow stared into her teacup for a moment before answering.

"Well, I don't like to speak ill of the dead, sir, and especially not of the living." She laughed nervously. "Of course, with the dead you don't have much worry, but the living can do you a deal of harm. Miss Elizabeth hasn't gone to her reward yet, not the last time I looked."

"Anything you tell me will be kept in confidence, Miss Legrow. It will go no further."

Stride looked across the table. Jimmy Peach picked up the thread.

"That's as true as toenails, Molly. Eric's a man of his word, just like I told you. Nothing at all to worry about."

"Alright, then. What I mean is that Miss Elizabeth and Mr. Rossiter were partial to their own kind. They had no interest at all like that in each other. But it's not for me to pass judgement, whatever I might be thinking. I leave that to a higher power. Of course, Miss Elizabeth did go on to marry the Major, but that was just for appearances. And the Major was a safe enough bet for a girl like herself, or any girl at all for that matter. Anyway, Miss Elizabeth had Miss Clara Jones with her by then."

"You knew her, I take it? Clara Jones? Did you know her well?"

"I knew her as well as I wanted to."

"You didn't like her?"

"I neither liked her nor disliked her, sir. I had little enough to do with her, or with Miss Elizabeth for that matter, after Miss Jones came to live at the house."

"What was her position there? Was she one of the household staff, like yourself?"

"Miss Jones was nothing like myself and she wasn't one of the staff. She was Miss Elizabeth's companion." The emphasis she put on the word was about what Stride expected. "As far as I know she still is."

"Yes, she is," Stride said. "What else can you tell me about Sam Rossiter? Was Sir Leonard fond of him? Personally, I mean?"

"Yes, he was. We used to say that Mr. Rossiter was Sir Leonard's fair-haired boy. I know that's not really a nice thing to say about someone, it has a sort of a twist to it. But Sir Leonard and Mr. Rossiter spent a lot of time together. When Sir Leonard travelled on business, as often as not Mr. Rossiter went with him. I think Sir Leonard had high hopes for Mr. Rossiter."

"It must have been a great disappointment for him when Rossiter was caught stealing money from the Company and Sir Leonard had to discharge him."

"Stealing money from the Company?" Molly Legrow stared across the table. "Mr. Rossiter? I never heard nothing about Mr. Rossiter stealing any money, sir. And as for Sir Leonard discharging him, there was never such a thing. Mr. Rossiter was with Sir Leonard when he was stricken and he was there with him when he passed on."

"I didn't know that," Stride said. It was what Harry called a 'hello moment.' He drank some tea while he thought about what Elizabeth Cooke had told them in the interview. He wondered if Molly Legrow had any more surprises for him. "Sir Leonard died in 1912, when he was still quite a young man. What happened to him?"

"It was the typhus that took him, sir. And it's a terrible disease. Sir Leonard was sick for a long time before he died, poor man."

So that much might still be true.

"The house was quarantined, I suppose?"

"Oh, no, sir, the house in town wasn't quarantined. There was no need for that. Sir Leonard took sick at the farm."

"At Devon Lea."

"Yes, sir. The farm was quarantined, and it was at the farm that he died. After he was stricken, we never set eyes on Sir Leonard again. He never come back to the house, not until the funeral. And we didn't see him then, either. I think that was a blessing. They told us the typhus had taken a terrible effect on him."

"The other members of the family, Lady Hurdle, Hubert, and Elizabeth. Were they there as well? At the farm?"

"Hubert wasn't there, he was out of town on business when his father took ill. But Lady Hurdle and Miss Elizabeth, they were both there. And they all had to stay at the farm until the doctor said it was safe for them to leave. That was after Sir Leonard had died, of course."

"And Rossiter was there, too?"

"Yes, he was. And Miss Jones."

"I see," Stride said. A familiar line thrummed inside his head. 'I see, said the blind man, when he couldn't see at all.' And that was too close to the truth.

Then a different phrase popped up. 'A very private place.' It was what he had said to Grace DeJohn that afternoon when they had talked about Devon Lea. "You said Rossiter was already close to the family when you first came to work for the Hurdles. When did Clara Jones come into the picture? Was it in the summer of 1912?"

"Yes, it was 1912. I suppose, you being a policeman, you know that Miss Elizabeth ran away from home that summer, in July. I know the police got called in to look for her. And they found out soon enough where she was."

"She was in Chapel Bight?" It was educated guess.

"Yes, that's where it was. Chapel Bight is where Clara Jones is from."

"And when did they first meet? Was it the year before, the time of the accident at the mine in Chapel Bight?"

"That's what the talk around the house was when the two of them come back to the city with the policeman who had been sent down there to get her. And just as well there was a policeman there, because there was a terrible fuss when they came back to the house together, the two of them."

"A policeman went to get her?" She did have another surprise for him, and now another piece of the puzzle clicked into place. "Do you remember his name? The policeman who brought them back?"

"I have to think about that. I know it was an Irish name, I remember that much."

"Was it McCarthy?"

"Yes, that was his name. And I believe he was an Inspector like yourself."

"A District Inspector," Stride said.

"That would have been Seamus McCarthy," Jimmy Peach said.

Stride looked across the table. Focused as he had been on Molly Legrow, he had almost forgotten that Peach was there.

"Yes, it was Seamus McCarthy. Did you know him, Jimmy?"

"I knew about him. He had himself a nice situation with the Hurdles when he retired. He looked after Devon Lea and he lived there, too. A pal of mine who worked at St. Clare's got to know Seamus after he moved to Devon Lea. Which was a kind of a prophecy, now that I come to think about it. Himself, Seamus, he passed away at St. Clare's. He was a patient there for the better part of a month after the heart attack took him down. So, it was a comfort, I imagine, that he knew some of the people who worked there."

thirty-one

After he left the teashop, Stride thought about driving to the Johnston house to collect Harry. He could bring him up to speed on what he had just learned, discuss options with him, the theory being that two heads were better than one. But he decided against it. He still wasn't sure what to make of the new information. And anyway, it had been a long week, and Harry had earned his evening off. One of them at least should be able to sit back and relax on a Friday night.

Not that Stride minded working on a Friday night all that much. There wasn't anything else he wanted to do. That was one of the rewards for being involved with a woman who had a husband. Since meeting Dianne, he was left with many empty evenings, unable to spend time with her, and not inclined to look for company with anyone else. And if it irritated him more than he liked, it was in the end his own choice.

He also considered taking the MG for a drive into the country, down to Middle Cove, or Torbay, or Flat Rock, to walk down to the water's edge and listen to the ocean beat up on the shore. It was where he sometimes went to get away and think about things. He could take off his shoes and socks, roll up his trouser legs, walk on the beach, wade out into the shallows, and stand there gasping at the water's biting cold on his feet and ankles. *Prufrock in extremis.*

But he didn't do that either. After he said goodbye to Jimmy Peach and Molly Legrow at the teashop, he left the MG parked where it was and walked east along New Gower Street, taking his time, thinking over the new information on the Hurdles and Sam Rossiter, and Seamus McCarthy, too. In a few minutes he was standing at the corner of New Gower and Holdsworth, and he could just see the sign that hung over the door of the Admiralty. That reminded him he was hungry. The two cups of very good tea in his system were nudging his appetite. His supper tonight would be a cold beer and one of Mildred Gullage's meat pies. It wasn't baked codfish with savoury dressing and roast potatoes, but it would have to do. There were worse choices.

Hector Gullage uncapped a beer and took a glass from a shelf under the bar.

"I heard you and Harry arrested Caleb Howell this morning. That true?"

Ted Murphy was standing about ten feet away talking to a customer when Gullage asked the question. He gave Stride an anxious look. Stride reassured him with a small shake of his head.

"Yes, we did. We had reason to believe that he might have been in the neighbourhood the night Rossiter was killed. We wanted to ask him about that, so we paid him a visit at the boarding house."

"The word is he didn't like the intrusion very much."

"Word does get around."

"Yes, it does. St. John's is a small town when all's said and done. Are you charging him?"

"He's looking at a weapons charge, and it won't be trivial. Howell might be going way for a while."

"But not for murder."

"We're still thinking about that."

"I hear he has a very good lawyer working to keep him out of prison. Or at least to keep his stay down to something less than a major inconvenience. Assuming you don't go ahead with the murder charge, that is."

"Yes, I knew he had a lawyer. I had a chat with Abe Peddle this morning."

Gullage's smile carried easily across the bar.

"Abe Peddle is a good man, and that is a fact. But it would seem that Caleb Howell has taken a long step up in the world, Eric. The word is that J.V. Higgins has been brought on board ."

"Higgins? Are you sure about that?"

"Well, now, I've just given you a piece of news, haven't I? And free of charge to a good friend. Yes, that's what I was told, and not thirty minutes ago."

"A reliable source?"

"Very reliable. Caleb Howell must have some very good friends, Eric. Higgins does not toil for pocket crumbs."

"No, he doesn't."

Where Abe Peddle was the attorney of choice for the general run of miscreants charged with relatively minor crimes, John Vincent Higgins normally took only those cases that involved the upper levels of St. John's society. He divided his time between civil and criminal actions. There were many more of the former, and they provided Higgins with a very comfortable living. In real terms, he didn't need to take criminal cases at all. He took them because he enjoyed the theatre that was sometimes associated with a criminal trial.

In a week that had provided Stride with more questions than answers, and with answers that mostly raised additional questions, this latest bit of news wasn't madly welcome, but it was intriguing. And there was another interesting twitch at the line. Caleb Howell had not yet been formally charged with anything. If Higgins was taking on the brief before he knew what the actual charges were, it was likely that a substantial amount of money had already changed hands, or was promised. As much as Higgins enjoyed the drama of criminal trials, charity did not rule any part of his professional life.

Stride parked the MG on Duckworth, two doors down from Alex Greene's flat. He had telephoned Abe Peddle from Gullage's office to ask him about Higgins, but Peddle wasn't at home. Stride's next choice was Alex Greene. Greene was one of three people connected with the case who could afford to pay Higgins' fee. The other two – Elizabeth Cooke and Sir Hubert Hurdle – were not likely to be approachable. But Greene was the best bet, anyway. He had known Howell for a long time, and had seemed to be sympathetic to his situation.

"It's a good thing you rang when you did, Eric. I was about to go out. A minute later and you would have missed me."

"I apologise for the intrusion, and on a Friday evening, Alex, but I have a couple of questions for you."

"Apology accepted. I'm not in any great hurry. And, anyway, I think I owe you one for not tucking me into a cloister at the Court House." He sat in a chair facing Stride. "Can I ask if you interviewed Caleb Howell after you left here this afternoon?"

"Yes, we did."

"But I suppose you can't tell me anything about that?"

"No, I can't. Not yet. But it is Howell I want to talk to you about. By the time we interviewed him this afternoon, he had already hired an attorney. That didn't surprise me. He'd been in trouble here before, and I would have expected him to have the name of a lawyer handy."

"Abe Peddle's name is the one I heard," Greene said.

"Word does get around."

"And it's my job to stand in the way when it does. I imagine I heard about Abe around the same time you did."

"That doesn't surprise me either. Did Peddle tell you himself?"

Greene shook his head. "No, Abe wouldn't think that was appropriate. He's a stickler for protocol, and he has much respect for designated authority. I think it's probably his old army training. And, anyway, I don't often have anything to offer to him. Unless I get arrested myself, of course. But so far, so good." Greene smiled. "You said you had some questions for me about Howell?"

Stride didn't say anything right away. He looked at Greene, trying to read something, anything, in his expression. But Greene's only apparent response was curiosity.

"Have you talked with Howell since his arrest?" Stride said at last.

"No, I haven't talked to him. I thought it better not to. Why?"

"And you haven't heard anything about him in the last couple of hours?"

"No. I've been here since you and Harry left, and I've been asleep for most of that time. I didn't have to go into the *Herald* today. I had a drink, read for a while, and then I dozed off." He leaned forward in his chair, concerned now. "Did something happen to Caleb in the lockup?"

Stride looked at him a moment longer. Either Greene was playing an unusually good hand of poker, or he had no idea what Stride was getting at. He decided it was the latter.

"I've been told Howell has a new lawyer."

"Really? That's news to me. And it's a surprise. Abe's about as good a man as Caleb could get for the price."

"That has a lot to do with my question," Stride said. "You'll know soon enough who Abe's replacement is. I heard it myself from Hector Gullage when I went to the Admiralty for a bite of supper. He said J.V. Higgins is representing Howell now."

"Higgins?" Greene sat back in his chair and tented his fingers under his chin, thinking. Then he looked at Stride. "So, you thought maybe I was paying Higgins' fee? That's why you're here?"

"That is why I'm here."

"It's not an unfair assumption. My connection with Caleb goes back a long time, and in a way, I did go to bat for him when you and Harry were here. But to answer the question you haven't quite asked me yet, the answer is 'no.' I didn't know Higgins had been brought on board. And I'm not the one who will foot the bill." Greene stood up, went to a cabinet near his desk, took out a bottle of dark rum, and held it up. "News of that sort almost demands a libation. Can I interest you in one? For old time's sake? We weren't always on opposite sides of the great divide."

Stride got up and walked over to the window. He looked out for a moment, then turned and looked at Greene again. He was satisfied he was telling the truth. And a drink wouldn't be out of place. It would be useful to mend fences with Greene. And, anyway, Stride liked him.

"Yes, please. But only a small one. I may have more work to do this evening."

"Really? Are things hotting up?"

"Maybe, I'm not sure."

Greene fetched two glasses from his kitchen and poured the rum. "Can I ask if I was your only choice for Caleb's benefactor?"

"No, you weren't the only possibility."

Stride took the glass from Greene and tasted the rum. It was quality Demerara, rich and strong, just as he thought it would be.

"There can't be a lot of candidates," Greene said. "So I'm guessing one other possibility would be the Hurdle family, either Sir Hubert or his sister. Maybe both of them?"

"Yes, the Hurdles are on my list of possibles. But why do you think so?"

"A simple process of rational inclusion. They're the only other crowd with money that's connected to this case that I know about. But I take it you haven't gone round to ask them about this?"

"No, I haven't."

"I didn't think so. Sir Hubert and his sister are nowhere near as accessible as I am. Or as tolerant."

"That has something to do with it."

"Does Higgins coming on board put Caleb back in the spotlight for you?"

"As Rossiter's killer?" Stride walked across the room and sat in the chair again. "It's a curious development, sure enough, but it doesn't make Howell a better fit for Rossiter's murder. What do you think it means?"

"I don't know, and I'm as surprised as you are." Greene sat down and stretched his legs out. "Although Higgins is obviously a good choice for Howell. He's better than anyone else in town at persuading juries that black might be white, and vice versa. Caleb will need that."

"Higgins is very good, but I don't think Howell would know anything about his skills. He wouldn't have seen Higgins in full flight. I think the money is the issue here. Do you think there's a possibility that Howell has a bundle of cash stowed away somewhere?"

"I don't know that he does," Greene said.

"But you also don't know that he doesn't."

"No, I don't. But if he does have money, I'd be interested to know where he got it. He works part-time driving a truck for Len Stick. Not a source of great wealth."

"No, it isn't. And I'm also not sure how Howell might have gotten Higgins' name, or made contact with him."

"Peddle might have mentioned him. Abe is smart enough to make a referral when he has a case that looks very tough. And we both know that getting Howell off lightly after this morning's fracas won't be a walk in the park."

"No, it won't."

They sat in silence then. Stride closed his eyes and let his mind wander around the file he had on Caleb Howell. After a minute it came to rest on the picture of the four Americans in Howell's personnel file at Fort Pepperell. And on Weldon Pryor in particular.

"How much do you know about Howell's time in Europe after the war, Alex?"

"After the war?" Greene thought about that. "Some. I know more about him from before the invasion because we did an interview that time I ran into him in England, in '44. My news service published the article I wrote. Along with about a million other articles of the same kind. I still have a copy somewhere, if you ever want to see it. Why do you ask?"

"An officer in Howell's outfit was active in the black market after the war, in Germany and Austria, and it wasn't small-time. It was serious enough that it got him killed. His name was Weldon Pryor. Howell was questioned in connection with the murder."

Greene nodded. "I recognise the name. Caleb did tell me something about that."

"What did he tell you?"

"Just the bare bones, also that nothing came of it. Not for him, I mean. He received an honourable discharge from the army a year later."

"Yes, I knew about that."

"Are you suggesting now that Howell was involved in the black market with Pryor, and that maybe he came back from Europe with a sack full of money?"

"I'm not suggesting it, just mentioning it as one possibility."

"I can't help you there, Eric. If Caleb has a store of cash, he didn't say anything to me about it. But I'm not saying it isn't possible. There were any number of strange things going on over there after the war. Can I ask you a question, now?"

"You can ask."

"Has Caleb been formally charged yet?"

"No, he hasn't."

"Will he be charged with Rossiter's murder?"

"That's two questions."

"I gave you a glass of good rum. That should count for something."

"Alright. No, he won't be charged with Rossiter's murder. At least, I won't recommend that."

"Because you don't think he did it? Or because you don't have enough evidence for a trial?"

"You're up to four questions, now."

"I could pour you another rum."

"I might fall on my face, and it's too early in the evening for that." Stride drank the last of his rum and stood up. He carried the glass into the kitchen area. "To answer your question, I don't think Howell killed Rossiter. But that's between you and me. I don't want to read about it in the *Herald*."

"It will stay within these four walls. Can I say that I'm pleased to hear it, though? I don't underestimate Caleb's potential for mayhem, but I never could see him killing Sam Rossiter. I'm correct in assuming you will go ahead on the weapons charge?"

"Yes. We have all the evidence we need for that."

"Then I'll just have to hope for the best for Caleb. But you know, I'm almost looking forward to seeing Higgins in action again. It's been quite a while since he's worked a criminal trial and the man does have a certain flair. Although I imagine your feelings about him are a little more mixed? You've faced him in court, I suppose?"

"Yes, I have."

"Are you looking forward to an encore?"

"No, not really. He's better at it than I am. But that's not my principal concern just now."

"I suppose it isn't. Can I ask where you go from here?"

"No. And if you don't ask, I won't have to refuse to answer."

Stride rang the doorbell at Thomas Butcher's home on Waterford Bridge Road. He had expected Butcher's housekeeper to answer the ring, but it was Butcher himself who pulled the door open. He was dressed in a pair of baggy corduroy trousers, an open-necked flannel shirt, and a brown cardigan sweater missing two buttons.

"I take it you are to home for the evening, Thomas?"

"You take that correctly." Butcher led the way down the hallway to his study. "Hazel has the night off, as she does most Fridays. I've just finished up a cold plate she left for me. If you haven't eaten yet, I imagine I can find you something. We never lack for victuals around this place. Mrs. Goodyear has the unshakeable belief that if a man isn't at least forty pounds overweight, he is scant inches from death by starvation. Happily, it's about the only thing we disagree on."

"Thanks, Thomas, but I had a meat pie earlier at Gullage's pub."

"At the Admiralty?"

"Yes. And while I was there, Gully also fed me an interesting piece of news. J.V. Higgins has taken over Caleb Howell's case from Abe Peddle."

"Higgins? Well, that is interesting." Butcher held up a bottle of claret. "I've already made a large dent in this over supper, which you may take as a tribute to its quality. May I pour you a glass?"

Stride nodded. "A small one."

"You're planning to continue working tonight?"

"I might. I'm not sure."

"I imagine one thing you would like to know is the name of the person who's footing the bill. From what you've told me about Howell, I can't believe he could afford Higgins on his own."

"No, I don't think so." Stride tasted the wine. "This is very good. It's from Jean-Louis?"

"Yes. He brought me a selection last month. Two dozen bottles altogether. So far, this one is at the top of my list, but they're all very good."

"They usually are. To get back to Higgins and his fee, I had two possible candidates. One was Alex Greene. The Mills family is better than well off. But I've just come from Greene's place and he says he's not the one paying Higgins' fee. And I believe him."

"Your other choice, I assume, is one of the Hurdles? Or both of them, perhaps?"

"They were my other choice, yes. There's a connection between Howell and the Hurdle family that goes back to the mining operation at Chapel Bight."

"Really?"

"Yes." He gave Butcher a quick rundown of the interview that afternoon with Howell.

"Interesting enough, although it was a long time ago, and the connection is at best tenuous. Have you contacted either of them, yet? Sir Hubert, or his sister?"

"No, I haven't."

"I can't imagine how you would go about that. While we're on the Hurdles, though, I have some additional information for you on Sir Leonard. This you will find interesting."

"You still have some doubt that he died of typhus?"

"Yes, I still have doubts about that. I don't have any direct information, but the whole thing doesn't look right to me. The death certificate was signed by a Dr. Graham Stirling. The name wasn't familiar, so I looked him up. I found very little on him. What I did learn was that he was brought out to Newfoundland from Ireland in the late 1800s, on contract to the Hurdle Company."

"He was a Company doctor?"

"He appears to have been. I found no information to suggest he had a general practice anywhere on the island. Perhaps you know that our Medical Society was organised back in the 1860s? I've gone through their lists, and Stirling's name does not appear anywhere. That being the case, I would have to conclude that he was not registered in this country for the general practice of medicine."

"So, if Stirling's name wasn't on the Society's register, he might not have been a qualified physician?"

"I can't say that with any authority, but it is a possibility. Although I would prefer to make additional inquiries before I make any statement to that effect."

"Some obvious questions come to mind, Thomas. If Sir Leonard didn't die of typhus, then I have to suspect foul play might have been involved. That's my inclination, as well as my job. Is that too far a reach for you?"

Butcher lit a cigarette before he replied.

"It is a considerable reach, yes, but I can't fault your logic."

"I'll add this bit of information to the mix. I interviewed a lady tonight who was in service with the Hurdle family when Sir Leonard died. She said she was told that he died of typhus, but she also said he took sick at Devon Lea Farm, and that he died there. She said the farm was under quarantine for a long time. She also said that Rossiter was there for all that time."

"Rossiter was with Sir Leonard when he died?"

"That's what she told me. She said Rossiter was very close to the family and to Sir Leonard personally. As far as she knew he was never discharged from the Company. Apparently, he was close to Sir Leonard right up to the day he died."

"That contradicts almost everything Elizabeth Cooke told you and Harry yesterday."

"Yes, it does." Stride lit a cigarette. "At some point, and sooner than later, I will have to put the appropriate question to Mrs. Cooke."

"If I were you, I would think about that for a while. If she denies it, you will have no comeback. It's also possible your informant wasn't telling you the truth, Eric. Servants do not always love their employers." Butcher smiled. "My Mrs. Goodyear being the exception, of course."

"I think she did tell me the truth. She didn't volunteer the information about Rossiter being with Sir Leonard when he died. It came out during the interview. She hadn't rehearsed it."

"I have learned to have faith in your judgement, Eric – most of the time, anyway – but where do you go from here? If it's your lady's word against Elizabeth Cooke's, and it goes public, I don't have to tell you that it will not be a contest of equals."

"I know that. And I'm not sure where to go from here. But there is something else I want to talk to you about. It crossed my mind when you were telling me about Dr. Stirling. Something about Rossiter's autopsy."

"Yes?"

"Rossiter had a wound on his right arm, an old one, near the shoulder. You said it was a bullet wound."

"Yes, on the humerus, the proximal end. And I am satisfied it was the result of a bullet. I saw more wounds of that type during the war than I care to recall."

"You also said that if the bullet had entered his body a bit further to the right, it would have struck him in the heart."

"And we both wondered if the wound might have been intentional."

"Attempted murder, in other words."

"To give it a name. But it's all speculation, Eric. We don't know when his wound was caused, or anything about the circumstances." Butcher stood up and walked to the window. He looked out for a minute before turning back to Stride. "I'm really not very comfortable with this. Speculation is part of the game we play, you and I. We can't avoid it, and arguably it's a part of our job. But we have to walk a very careful line here."

"I know that. At the same time, though, I have to look at all the possibilities, however remote some of them might seem. If it turns out that Sir Leonard Hurdle's death wasn't from typhus, and that Rossiter was there when he died, well…"

Stride let the unfinished sentence hang there.

"But even if Sir Leonard didn't die of typhus, I'm not sure I understand how that gets you any closer to finding Rossiter's killer. They might be two unrelated events." Butcher held up his hand before Stride could respond. "I know. You're not a great believer in coincidence."

"No, I'm not."

"And if Rossiter played some part in Leonard Hurdle's death, how do you square that with the generous pension he received from Elizabeth Cooke?"

"I don't have an answer for that." In truth, he also didn't even know how to phrase the question. "But I want to ask you something else. Do you know Justice McGinn?"

"Robin McGinn? Yes, I do, but now you have lost me. Why do you ask?"

"His name has come up a few times, officially and otherwise."

"Didn't he sign the warrant giving you access to Rossiter's financial background?"

"Yes, and that's the official part. But he's also been associated with the Hurdles since early on."

"I did know that, now that you mention it. And I do know Robin fairly well. Over the years, we've worked together on any number of boards and committees. And we sometimes find ourselves at social engagements, although he's rather less of a mixer than I am. Much less, in fact."

"You say you knew about his association with the Hurdles?"

"Yes. There's nothing secret about it, even if it was a bit unusual. Sir Leonard Hurdle was, in a sense, Robin's sponsor."

"I'm not sure I know what that means."

"Robin McGinn came from very humble beginnings, Eric."

"Yes, I knew that. He told me himself the day he signed the warrant."

"He came to Sir Leonard's attention when he was a very young man, not much more than a boy, working as a labourer for one of the Hurdle affiliates down the coast. Sir Leonard knew right away that Robin was special, and he took him under his wing, so to speak. He financed his education, in fact. I believe I told you Leonard Hurdle was a generous man."

"Yes, you did. The fever wing at the General."

"Just so. He saw that McGinn had promise, and he decided to help him along. It was a decision as wise as it was generous."

"He took Sam Rossiter under his wing, too. My informant described Rossiter as Sir Leonard's fair-haired boy."

The comment took Butcher by surprise.

"What are you suggesting, exactly?"

"I'm not really suggesting anything. I'm only stating the facts as I know them, or at least as they have been presented to me. And trying to patch something together that makes sense. At the moment, it's pretty much a jumble. I'm also trying very hard not to let my imagination run loose."

"Don't try too hard. It's often the way progress is made. Only make certain you keep a stout rein on it."

Stride laughed. "I'll try."

"Whatever the history of it, Robin McGinn's career has been more than good. He has benefited this city, and the country too, in a lot of ways. But you haven't really explained why he's of interest all of a sudden. Are you hoping he can add something to our puzzlement about Sir Leonard's death?"

"He's known the family for a long time. He was involved in the Chapel Bight inquiry the year before Hurdle died. Tell me what you think, Thomas."

"Until you brought this up, it would not have occurred to me to think about it at all."

"But I can see that you're thinking about it now."

"You have caught my attention. And yes, it is possible that Robin might be able to add something to our present discussions. Do you intend to talk to him?"

"I might. There's something else. The day McGinn signed the warrant for me, he told me he had an interest in Newfoundland family names. When I asked him if he had any information on the Rossiters, he said he couldn't recall any offhand. But he said he would get back to me if he found something."

"And he hasn't done that?"

"No, he hasn't. But he must have known Sam Rossiter years ago, when they were both associated with the Hurdle Company, and both of them in Sir Leonard's good graces."

"That would seem to follow. But he gave no indication that he knew Rossiter?"

"No, he didn't. But he must have known that sooner or later we would make the connection."

"I think so, yes. McGinn does not lack for imagination."

"What do you think his reaction might be if I ask him some questions about this, Thomas?"

"I don't know, and anyway my opinion can't be used as a guide. But I don't think he will try to avoid the question. Robin McGinn is a rational and thoughtful man." Butcher smiled. "Was that vague enough for you?"

"Just about, yes."

"Now I will ask you a question. Do you think there is an actual connection between Rossiter's death and Sir Leonard's?"

"I think there is something. But I don't know what it might be."

Butcher picked up the bottle of claret and moved to pour the remainder into their glasses. Stride started to pull his glass away, but changed his mind and allowed Butcher to fill it.

"Reassure me that you are going to be very cautious with all of this, Eric."

"I will be cautious. I need to know a lot more than I know now before I actually do anything."

"I am relieved to hear that," Butcher said. He picked up his glass.

thirty-two

It had been a while since Stride had driven out into the rural area southwest of St. John's called the Goulds. The area had some of the best farmland in the region, holding onto some of the small amount of decent topsoil that was left behind when the glaciers had finished raking across the island. Devon Lea was one of several farms on Heavy Tree Road, but it differed from the others in that it was no longer a working property. McCowan had said it was a retreat for Elizabeth Cooke and Clara Jones, a place where they could separate themselves from everyone around them. Not that they would need an additional protective bulkhead to shield them from the common herd. Their money and position should have been protection enough.

Stride wasn't sure if this drive into the country reflected a lack of caution or not, although Thomas Butcher might have thought so. But Butcher was a more cautious man than was Stride, and in a way, he could afford to be. The practice of medicine had similarities to the policing trade, both of them dealing with unknowns, with threats to health, even to physical survival. It was perhaps somewhat easier to be coolly rational about the challenges of disease and debility, than with the often vague and shifting circumstances attendant on crime, especially one as serious and final as murder.

By the time Stride drove past Devon Lea Farm, the light was starting to fade. It was unlikely anyone at the farm had seen the MG, although he almost wished someone had. It might have forced his hand, even if he wasn't sure what he would then do. He continued down the road for a half-mile and then turned around, drove a little way back, and pulled over onto the shoulder. He switched off the engine and took a pair of binoculars from under the seat to take a closer look at Devon Lea.

The farm covered about thirty acres of pasture and some woodland. Beyond that was a stretch of public land, some of it covered by trees, and some of it in natural pasture. In an earlier time, when Devon Lea had supplied vegetables, milk, and eggs for the Hurdle hotel in the city, a large area of what was now open field would have been under cultivation. Now only a small part of the property was used for growing crops. A large kitchen garden was set out behind the house, and flower beds bordered the front of the house itself, and along the one side he could see.

At the back, between the house and the kitchen garden, there was a tall fence, painted white, enclosing a large rectangle of space. Within that enclosure, Elizabeth Cooke and her companion, and anyone privileged enough to join them, could relax, unseen, isolated, invisible to the world outside. Beyond the garden was a stand of balsam poplar, perhaps thirty feet tall. It hedged the property at the back, a bordering arc of tall trees. Stride thought it looked something like the wall of a fortress, shielding the house and garden from anyone who might approach across the open fields. And it wasn't a natural stand. The poplars, native to the island and usually found in greatest profusion on areas of moist rich bottomlands, clearly had been planted at Devon Lea and were thriving in the good soil of the farm. From the height of the stand, Stride estimated the trees had been set out several decades ago.

The house itself was two-storied, larger than he remembered, with gables on the upstairs windows. He guessed there might be as many as five bedrooms in the place. The house was painted white with green trim and, bathed in the still-intense light of the setting sun, it seemed almost to glow. The foundation of the original smaller house, closer to the road, had been removed completely, the only indication that it had once been there a faint depression in the ground, like a memory fading slowly.

To the left of the house was the barn, painted the traditional red, with white trim on the eaves and around the doorways and windows. The main door of the barn stood partway open, and a tortoise-shell cat sat on the step. Stride wondered if it was the same animal he had seen at the house on Winter

Avenue, brought out to the country from time to time, perhaps, to enjoy a feral interlude, and to play havoc with the local rodent populations.

Two cars, both angled the same way, more or less parallel to each other, were parked near the house. One was a black Rover sedan, similar to the car Tom Butcher drove. The other was a Morris coupe. Stride couldn't quite read the licence plate of either car, but he was reasonably certain that the Rover belonged to Elizabeth Cooke, and the Morris to Sir Hubert Hurdle. Earlier that day, he had tasked a constable at Fort Townshend with making a list of all the passenger vehicles registered to both brother and sister, as well as to the Hurdle Company.

While he stood looking at the farm, several pickup trucks and cars passed in both directions. The MG attracted the usual amount of attention, and the tall man with the binoculars did also. Some of the passing vehicles slowed so the occupants could take a closer look.

Once, while he was watching the house, he saw someone move past an upstairs window, a brief glimpse of white against the green trim of the gables. It wasn't much of a reward for his efforts, but he really hadn't expected very much. His only purpose in being here was an ill-defined need to see the place again, to take a closer look at the house where Sir Leonard Hurdle's life had ended. It couldn't even be called a fishing expedition.

After ten minutes of careful watching, nothing had happened, the only change being that the cat had disappeared from the barn entrance. He placed the binoculars back in their leather case, slid into the driver's seat, and started the motor.

Justice Robin McGinn lived alone in a large house on Pine Bud Avenue in the northeast part of the city. As far as Stride knew, McGinn had never married. The property was generally known as Harrington Acre, named for the original owner, Jacob Harrington, an English planter from Cumberland who had settled in St. John's in 1802. As the crow flew, Harrington Acre wasn't very far from Stride's house on Circular Road, but Pine Bud was as close to country as it was to city. In 1941, in a park not far from McGinn's house, the American Army had established a small tent city, Camp Alexander, where their troops were quartered until the building of Fort Pepperell was completed on the north shore of Quidi Vidi Lake.

He parked the MG on the road outside the double gates that led to McGinn's property. The gates were affixed to two massive concrete pillars, and the tall fence that ran from them around the property was made of unpainted planking, weathered now to a dull brown colour. The house was three stories tall, at least as large as Stride's, but more extensively gabled on the upstairs windows.

Stride hesitated for a moment with his hand on the latch of the gate, wondering again about the wisdom of seeking an interview with McGinn. He still had not formulated a line of questions, beyond asking McGinn to talk about Rossiter, and also about the death thirty-five years ago of Sir Leonard Hurdle. He would have to make it up as he went along. This visit had the potential to cause Stride a deal of trouble with his superiors, both McCowan and the Chief. But he had a feeling that would not happen. Robin McGinn was famous for his toughness, but there was a reasonableness about him that always seemed to come through. His was a toughness based on principle, not petulance. If McGinn decided Stride was out of line on this present foray, he would let him know, and he would seek no assistance to drive home his annoyance.

All this careful and considered logic did not prevent a fist of apprehension from knuckling against Stride's gut as he pulled open the latch.

McGinn answered the door himself. He was dressed almost formally in black trousers, a matching vest, and a white shirt and tie. The only nod to informality was a well-worn, maroon-coloured smoking-jacket made of something that might have been velvet. McGinn did not look especially surprised to see Stride standing on his front step, although he regarded him for a long moment without speaking, before stepping back to pull the door open.

Stride stepped from the vestibule into the long hallway. Light was spilling out of a room two-thirds of the way along. McGinn followed the direction of his gaze.

"I've been working." He gave Stride a half-smile. "As I think you are also."

"That is the reason I am here."

"I understand that. We can talk in the study. It's the most comfortable room in the house. It's where I spend most of my time when I'm at home."

He led the way down the hall towards the lighted room.

The study was almost as large as Stride's flat. He wondered if McGinn had renovated this part of the house to suit his personal needs, tearing down walls and creating a room that had little resemblance to the original layout. The room was filled with books set in tall bookcases that lined three of the walls. The visible portion of the wall panelling was of a dark wood, either highly polished, or one with a natural and lasting oil content. Stride had once seen an ornate mantel made of Italian walnut, more than four hundred years old, which had a lustre as rich as this.

McGinn pointed to a leather armchair, one of a matching pair that faced each other across a small rug of middle-eastern design.

"I should apologise for interrupting your evening," Stride said.

"There's no need. I well understand that you must go where and when necessary in the course of an investigation. It's still early, and in any event, I retire very late. I also rise early in the morning. I discovered long ago that I need only about four hours sleep a night. I used to think of it as an oddity, almost an ailment of some kind. Then I accepted it for the blessing it surely is. There is much I want to do in this life, and much that I enjoy doing, and good fortune has graced me with an extra four hours out of twenty-four." McGinn sat in the matching chair and crossed his legs. "You've come about the Rossiter file, I suppose?"

"Yes, and no. That file has grown a lot since we last spoke."

"I would be surprised if it were otherwise. But you say 'yes and no.' Has some aspect of the case now moved beyond Samuel Rossiter's murder?"

"I think so. One of the things we've discovered is that Samuel Rossiter was closely connected with the Hurdle family when he lived in Newfoundland. And that association continued up to the time of his death."

"And you want to ask me about that?"

"Yes. You were associated with the Hurdle family around the time Rossiter left Newfoundland for Bermuda. I'm making the assumption that you knew him, or you were at least acquainted with him."

"What you have said is correct. I did have an association with the Hurdle family at the time. And I did know Samuel Rossiter."

"Did you also know about the financial arrangements that Elizabeth Cooke had made for him?"

"Not the details, no. But I was aware that Mrs. Cooke was providing him with an income."

"You could have told me that the day you signed the warrant for me."

"Yes, I could have, and I considered doing so. But I decided it wasn't my place to intervene."

"That could be interpreted as withholding information."

"I understand that. My decision arose from my legal training, and also from my experience on the bench. Judges who intervene in investigations almost always overstep their bounds. I try to avoid doing that." McGinn held up his hand before Stride could comment. "That is a rationalisation, of course, but not, I think, an especially bad one. Married to it was the obvious possibility that Samuel Rossiter's death had nothing to do with his involvement with the Hurdle family, past or present. Or with me. In any event, I had faith that your investigation would bring the relevant facts to light. The warrants I signed for you made that a virtual certainty." He gave Stride a steady look. "Do you agree?"

"Yes. As far as it goes."

"I see. I've heard that you made an arrest this morning. You and your sergeant?"

"Yes. His name is Caleb Howell." Stride watched McGinn for a reaction to the name, but there was nothing. "The arrest was for illegal possession of a handgun. Also for assaulting Sergeant Phelan and myself. Howell knew Rossiter, and they lived in the same boarding house. But I don't happen to think Howell murdered Rossiter. For one thing, he had no motive."

"But a rough sort of fellow, nonetheless."

"Yes, he is, and I think he might be capable of murder in the appropriate circumstances. But not, I think, this murder. Is the name Howell familiar to you?"

"It's a common enough name, and names are of interest to me, as you know. But I think you're probably making reference to one Wesley Howell."

"Yes, I am. Caleb Howell is his son."

"I halfway assumed as much." McGinn looked past Stride for a few moments. "You thought there might be a connection between Rossiter's murder and the inquiry into the Chapel Bight cave-in? I recall that the inquiry found that Wesley Howell bore some responsibility for the accident. I'm assuming, therefore, that you have learned that I was vice-chairman of that inquiry."

"I have a copy of the report."

"You've read it?"

"Not closely, but I read through the summary and recommendations."

"And that brought Howell to your attention."

"That and some additional evidence."

"Obviously, you have questioned Caleb Howell about all of this, and after that you have concluded he had no reason to murder Rossiter. Perhaps you can tell me why you reached that conclusion?"

"Because I have reason to believe the inquiry was at least partly a sham, what might be called a public-relations exercise, to placate the local residents, and those who were injured in the cave-in."

"Except for those who were killed, of course. You know there were two deaths, a father and one of his sons?"

"I knew two people were killed," Stride said. McGinn was giving Stride a careful look, now, aware that he had caught him up short on the detail. He made a mental note to read the report more carefully than he had. "Do you agree with what I said about the report itself?"

"That it was a sham? Not entirely, no. Although there was a degree of calculation about it. I knew that Wesley Howell had, to use a phrase, offered himself up as a scapegoat. But the effect was rather more along the lines of giving the local people a focus for their anger."

"And deflecting it away from the Hurdle family."

"That too. I argued against that approach at the time, but I wasn't successful. In my own defence, I will say that the position of vice-chairman didn't carry very much authority. I wasn't happy with the process, nor was I entirely pleased with the outcome, even if, in the end, almost everyone seemed to gain something. Compensation was paid to the survivors and their families, and rather more than was usual for the time. Or for that matter, for the present day. Sir Leonard Hurdle was a generous man, and a basically good one at heart. Wesley Howell got what he wanted, a better situation in life. And the mine did eventually go into production, providing employment and income in an area that badly needed it."

"And Rossiter? Was he responsible for the accident?"

"Many thought so. He was the senior company person at the site. But in the end, the accident might have been just that. An unfortunate occurrence, a confluence of various factors, including human error, with no one thing standing out."

"You are comfortable with that conclusion?"

"No. I have never been comfortable with any situation where possibly preventable injury and death have occurred. But I've also learned that one has to move on. Perhaps it's a lesson you have learned as well?" Before Stride could respond, McGinn tilted his head back and closed his eyes for a moment. Then he spoke again. "Do you have another suspect for Rossiter's murder?"

"Not at present."

"Has your investigation reached an impasse, then?"

"Possibly. I am looking at additional information that has recently come to light."

"From your tone, I will guess that is one of the reasons you are here now?"

"One of the reasons. The Hurdle family keeps coming up in the investigation. We interviewed Elizabeth Cooke yesterday. She told us some things about Rossiter that are at odds with information I've since received from another source. One thing Mrs. Cooke said was that Rossiter had been discharged by Sir Leonard for theft, and that he left Newfoundland shortly afterwards."

"And your new informant has disputed that?"

"Yes, she has. She said Rossiter was with Sir Leonard when he died. An unlikely event if he had already been discharged from the Company."

"I would agree. And this person you speak of, she would be privy to such close family information?"

"I believe so. She worked for the Hurdle family for more than forty years, before and after Sir Leonard's death. She was working for the family when he took ill at Devon Lea Farm."

"Was she at the farm when Sir Leonard died?"

"No, she was at the Hurdle home in St. John's. And she was there when Sir Leonard's body was returned to the city for burial."

"And you believe this woman was telling you the truth?"

"I believe she was."

"I see."

"There is something else." Stride said.

"Yes?"

"Sir Leonard Hurdle died when he was still quite young, only fifty years old. Early on I was told he had died in a typhus epidemic. That information is on file at the Mercantile Association, and it was supplied by the Hurdle family. And that's interesting, because there wasn't a typhus epidemic the year Sir Leonard died. Also, the death certificate was signed by a Dr. Graham Stirling. But it turns out that Dr. Stirling was not registered with the Medical Society."

"You're suggesting he was not a qualified physician?"

"No. I'm only saying that he was not registered as a physician in this country. At the moment, we don't know very much about him, but I understand he was contracted to work for the Hurdle Company. You worked for the Company at about the same time, and I've been told you were also close to Sir Leonard. Were you acquainted with Graham Stirling? "

"I did meet him on one or two occasions, yes."

"Was he a medical doctor?"

"I was told that he was."

It was the kind of response that McGinn would not have tolerated in his courtroom. Stride waited for him to add something, and when he did, the words came with a subtle change in the man's posture, a kind of resigned acceptance that the discussion had moved out of his control.

"I had very little to do with Graham Stirling," McGinn said. "And I didn't know him well. I believe he had some medical training and that he was competent enough to deal with the general run of minor accidents and ailments among the Company's employees."

"But you don't think he was a qualified physician?"

"No, I don't."

"Yet he was called in when Sir Leonard fell ill, and he signed the death certificate as Dr. Graham Stirling."

"So I understand."

"Have you seen the death certificate?"

"Yes."

"Did Sir Leonard die of typhus?"

"I cannot answer that question."

"Because you don't know, or because you don't want to?"

McGinn looked steadily at Stride for a moment, then stood up and walked over to his desk. He took what looked like an address book from one of the drawers and opened it. He ran his index finger down the page, found what he was looking for, then closed the book.

"I need to make a telephone call. I'll use the phone in my office." He nodded towards the hallway. "This will take a few minutes."

It was almost dark when Stride turned onto Heavy Tree Road for the second time that evening.

It had taken McGinn ten minutes to make his telephone call. Or calls. Stride overheard him giving a number to the operator, and then McGinn had closed the door of his office. When he came back to the study, he told Stride that he should drive back to Devon Lea. McGinn declined to go with him.

Stride drove from Pine Bud to Carpasian, and from there to Duckworth, and pulled up to a Constabulary call-box. His thought was to call Harry, bring him up to speed on the evening's events, and to let him know that he was going to Devon Lea Farm. He felt a growing unease with this turn of events. He had wanted McGinn to reassure him that Sir Leonard Hurdle had in fact died of typhus, that his and Butcher's speculations had no foundation.

He sat in the MG and looked at the call-box for a minute before deciding not to call Harry after all. He didn't know what was waiting for him at Devon Lea, but if it turned out to be an embarrassing debacle, a dressing down – or worse – by one of the Hurdles, he didn't want Harry involved.

But if he was going there alone, he would take at least one precaution, however melodramatic it seemed. He got out of the MG and eased the driver's seat forward. Bolted to the chassis was the lock-box with his Colt Detective Special. He looked around to make sure that no one was watching, then took the gun from the box, and clipped the holster to his belt at the back.

When Stride arrived at the farm gate, a man was waiting there, someone he had not seen before. He was a large man, in his late forties Stride thought, and dressed in the rough gear of someone who worked the land. But there was also a look about him, an efficiency of movement that spoke to a military background of some kind. He pulled the gate open and watched as Stride drove into the yard and parked the MG beside Elizabeth Cooke's Rover. The Morris coupe was no longer there.

The main door was on the side of the house, at right-angles to the road. Elizabeth Cooke was standing in the open doorway. She stepped out into the yard when Stride got out of the MG and approached the house. If she was apprehensive about his visit, it didn't show.

"I spent a lot of time here when I was growing up," she said. "Especially in the summers, but in the winters too. My father loved this place, even more than the country house we had at the lake. What he liked most about Devon Lea was the fact that it was a working property back then. Daddy did have a romantic streak, and sometimes he could let it show, but he was very practical most of the time. Well, he had to be. There are great responsibilities attached to a large company like ours. He thought that good land should be worked, otherwise it was wasted, and he believed waste was very wrong. Especially in this country where good farmland is so limited. I'm not sure he would completely approve of Devon Lea now, a place used mostly for pleasure."

"Instead of for profit."

"That is one way to look at it. But profit wasn't what attracted him to this place. He just liked the idea of working the land. He was something of a gentleman farmer, when he had the time. But it wasn't just an affectation, he really did enjoy the farming, the hard physical work. As for being a gentleman, he got his fill of that during his week in the city. Not that he had any romantic illusions about farming, you understand. He knew it was a hard way to make a living." She gestured with her hand towards the road. "He was acquainted with all the farmers in the area. He knew their names, and the names of their children." She stepped close to Stride now. "Under normal circumstances, I would take you on a tour of the place. It's the polite thing to do, and also I like to show it to people. Some people. But we don't have the time for that tonight."

"Another occasion, perhaps."

"Perhaps. We shall have to see. I had a long talk with Robin McGinn while you were driving out here. He rang me after you set out from his house."

"I was surprised when he said he wouldn't come with me."

"I imagine you were. But Robin and I agreed it would be better if it was just the two of us to deal with this."

"Your brother won't be here?"

"No. Hubert was here earlier in the evening, but he went back to the city. And Clara went back with him."

She walked a little distance away from him and looked around the property, as if this might be the last time she would see it, or see it in the way she was used to. Stride looked around for the man who had opened the gate, but he was nowhere in sight.

Elizabeth Cooke moved towards the steps.

"We'll go inside now. It's time we got on with it."

"I want to ask you one question first." She turned and looked at him. "Did your father die of typhus?"

The reply came without hesitation.

"No, he did not."

She turned then and led the way inside, walking quickly and with determination. She led him through the house, down one hallway, then along another that took them towards the rear of the place. The house seemed even larger than it appeared from the outside, and the light was low. They turned another corner and now they were in the newer part of the house, the part, Stride thought, that had been added after Sir Leonard's death. Elizabeth Cooke came to a halt by a white-painted door and turned to speak to him.

"I will go in first. I need to make sure that it's still alright for you to come in."

She opened the door just wide enough to step into the room, and closed it behind her. Alone in the dimly lighted hallway, Stride's feeling of unease came back, edging towards fear now. He slid his right hand along his belt until he felt the holster at the back. He undid the clasp, looking around him, half expecting to see the hired man somewhere in the shadows of the hall, or standing in a doorway. But there was no one there. He was alone.

From inside the room there came a soft murmur of voices, Elizabeth Cooke's voice, and the voice of a second woman. And another sound, somehow familiar, but just beyond his grasp, a small sound tied to a long-distant memory. Then the door opened and Elizabeth Cooke stepped into the hallway. She pulled the door almost shut and leaned close to him.

"I will ask that you don't say anything. At least not right away. I will let you know when it's alright."

She pushed the door open and led him inside. A middle-aged woman in a white uniform dress stood in the centre of the room. She looked at Stride with a half-smile, not exactly friendly, but tolerant enough. She was holding something in her hands, cradling it against her chest. It took a moment before he recognised what it was, a teddy bear, light brown in colour, and made of some kind of soft, plush material. Behind the woman, almost completely hidden by her, someone was sitting in a chair, but all Stride could see were two feet wrapped in soft flannel, resting on a small footstool. Then, there came a sound from behind the woman, a sound he was able to place now, the rising, plaintive sound of a child who feels that it has been too long ignored, clamouring a wordless demand that must soon be met. The woman turned and moved towards the chair, shifting her position just far enough to the side for Stride to see who was there.

It was a man, very old, shrunken with age and decay, dressed in a white robe, and with a white woollen cap on his head. And on his face an anxious, pleading look as he reached with one thin hand for the teddy bear that the woman held out to him. He took the stuffed animal from her and pulled it close to his face, holding it with both hands. His eyes were soft now, his features relaxed. He spoke to the toy in a low and intimate tone, making sounds that were not words at all, but which were filled with meaning.

Stride stood just inside the doorway, transfixed, unable to look away from the scene before him. Then he was conscious of a pain in his throat and a pressure building behind his eyes, a fierce chill closing around him.

He felt a hand on his arm. Elizabeth Cooke spoke to him.

"This is my father, Mr. Stride. And it's alright now. He is fine. For the present, he has everything he needs."

thirty-three

Stride came awake slowly, ascending from a sleep without dreams. He had awakened only once in the night, had looked around him at the soft familiar shapes in the near-dark of his bedroom, and comforted by that familiarity, he had fallen back into another dreamless slumber.

Now he was dimly aware that he wasn't alone, that Dianne was there with him, sliding naked into his bed, her skin cool against his own. He lay on his side, his back towards her, facing the window. Neither of them spoke, the only sound in the bedroom was their measured breathing. Then, her hands were moving on his chest, then on his stomach and lower still, stroking and teasing, bringing him fully awake.

After only a few moments, he turned to meet her, taking her in his arms, burying his face in the soft cradle where her neck met her shoulder. They had still not spoken when he moved above her, entering her, starting a rhythm that built slowly, then more quickly, then rising to a sudden peak.

Afterwards, both of them spent, they lay together spoon-fashion, still not speaking. From outside he could hear the normal and unhurried sounds of an August Saturday morning. He wondered what time it was.

"You're very quiet," Dianne said. "Did something happen last night? With the case?"

He didn't answer right away.

"Yes," he said finally. And then, because his throat was dry, he coughed twice.

"I called you last night, or I tried to. But after the third try, the operator said your phone was probably off the hook. And she was right. I found it wrapped in a towel in a drawer in the kitchen."

He responded by pushing himself closer against her and covered her hand with his. After a minute, he reached for the glass of water on his bedside table and drank most of it. He looked on the table for his cigarettes and remembered he had left them in the kitchen. He wanted one, but he didn't want to get up, too comfortable to move away from her. He half-turned so that he was looking at her face. Her cheek was red where his stubble had rasped her skin during their love-making. He touched it with his fingertips. "Does that hurt?"

"Not really, no. But you do need a shave."

"I know."

"You haven't asked me what I'm doing here." She tugged at his chest hair and laughed. "I suppose I should rephrase that."

"You could. But how is it that you're here? Is Marty away?" He wasn't comfortable speaking her husband's name.

"Yes. There was a fire yesterday at the naval base in Argentia. He left last night, just after supper. He flew down in a Catalina from Torbay. He'll be there until tomorrow, assessing the damage."

"Was anyone hurt?" The question was automatic.

"I don't know. He'll probably call me later today." She looked away from him, sharing his discomfort now. She changed the subject. "Can you talk about it? Whatever it was that happened last night?"

"No, I can't. It's complicated."

"So it isn't over?"

"No," he said. "It isn't over. Not yet."

Stride and Elizabeth Cooke had stayed in the room for only a few minutes, watching as the nurse tended to the old man in the chair, talking to him, getting him water to drink, re-tying the bow on the teddy bear's neck after he pulled it loose. Watching her now, he remembered the one occasion earlier in the evening when he had seen someone wearing white move past the upstairs window of the house.

Elizabeth Cooke and the nurse discussed the complicated trivia that attended her father's situation, his clothing, his appetite, an ear infection recently cured, and other infections, once dangerous but now cleared up quickly because they had a supply of penicillin always at hand. The old man only occasionally paid them any attention, except when he wanted something, and then he made his needs known with a flurry of utterings and gestures familiar to both women. Once or twice he regarded Stride with a mild and transient puzzlement.

Whenever he could, and without being rude or intrusive, Stride looked closely at the old man in an effort to match the shrunken creature in the chair with the photographs he had seen of Sir Leonard Hurdle as he had once been, in youth and health. Sometimes he could see the resemblance, but only just. On two occasions the nurse had to reset the woollen cap on his head after he knocked it askew. On the second occasion, the cap slid far enough to one side for Stride to see a large scar on his left temple.

Then, Elizabeth Cooke suggested they should leave, and Stride quickly agreed, although the initial shock and fear had, by then, faded for him. Before they left, she knelt in front of her father, touched his cheek with her hand, and turned his head so that he was facing her. The old man's gaze moved in and out of focus, but she literally held his attention, placing her hand against his face so that he could not turn away. And there was a moment when Stride thought he saw a hint of recognition before the watery eyes wandered off once more. She leaned forward, kissed him on the forehead, stood up, and moved towards the door. By the time she reached it, the old man had pulled loose the bow on the bear's neck again, and had begun another whining plaint for the nurse to retie it.

"I imagine you could use a drink," she said when they reached the living room. "I suggest a brandy and soda. That's what I'm having."

"Yes, please," Stride said. He desperately wanted a cigarette. He took out his package and held it up, and she nodded her permission.

While she fashioned the drinks, he smoked and occupied himself by looking at the pictures on the walls. Most were depictions of English hunting scenes, horses at the gallop leaping over fences and hedges, men in red jackets, ladies in long dresses riding side-saddle, packs of hounds with anxious eyes. In one large watercolour, a fox cringed in a thicket, the lead hounds closing in for the kill.

"I've hunted in England and Ireland," Elizabeth said when she handed him his drink. It was a lavish portion, and he was grateful for that. "Never here, of course. That would be pretentious, even silly. Although we do get foxes in the henhouse sometimes. Frank Vickers takes care of it. He's killed three this year, he told me."

"That was the man at the gate, when I drove in?" McCowan had mentioned the name. "He's a nephew of Justice McGinn?"

"A cousin, on his mother's side. Frank's from the area. He's worked for us since before the war, since before your former colleague passed away, in fact. Sidney McCarthy."

"McCarthy was before my time. He had retired before I joined the Force."

"Yes, I suppose he had. Please sit down, Mr. Stride." She sat across from him in a matching armchair. "You've seen enough to know that this is a very unusual situation. I'm well used to it, of course, and Clara too. And Hubert. It's become a routine part of our lives. Something that goes on as long as this has becomes ordinary. Almost anything will if it continues long enough, even the very worst things. And this has been going on for more than thirty years."

"Thirty-five years," Stride said.

"Yes, thirty-five. Since 1912, the year my father is supposed to have died." She sipped her drink. "You know more about our family now than you knew yesterday, I think, when you came to the house. Enough that you were inspired to drive out here earlier this evening." She smiled. "Clara saw your car on the road. Can I ask who you talked to?"

"Someone who used to work for your family."

"I thought as much. Was it Molly Legrow?" She caught his reaction and held up her hand. "There's no need to answer. I just happen to know that Molly is in the city, visiting with friends. And there's no reason for you to be concerned. There will be no repercussions." She looked for a moment towards the window that faced on the yard. "You saw the scar on my father's head?"

"Yes. Did Sam Rossiter do that? I know he was here, at the farm, when your father was said to have been ill."

"Yes, Sam was here when it happened. But Sam didn't do that. My mother did."

"Your mother?"

"Yes. She tried to kill my father, and she almost succeeded. She also tried to kill Sam, and she came close to succeeding there also. Do you know anything about her? About my mother?"

"I've been told she isn't very well." 'Poor Gertrude' was the descriptive Tom Butcher had used.

"No, she is not well, not well at all. In fact, I have only a few memories of my mother as a well person."

"I was told there was a drinking problem."

"Yes, my mother had a drinking problem, and for as much of her life as I can remember. It was said she was unhappy, and I never doubted that, although no one ever said why, at least not to me. When it started, and that was before I was born, it was believed with something like religious conviction that any woman's unhappiness could quickly be resolved if only she had children to look after. A healthy dose of 'normality,' and all would be well. But I think having children only made her more unhappy." She looked away. "Never mind the effect on the agents of the supposed remedy."

"You and your brother."

"Our arrival did not effect the magical cure. I don't know that anything could have. And now my mother is so far removed from this world that there would be no point in asking her that question, or any other. But it's just possible she has finally attained a kind of happiness. At least she isn't angry any longer."

"What happened? Here, with your father, and Rossiter?"

"I will get to that." She looked at the watch on her wrist. "But it is getting late, and you're not obliged to stay and listen to a long story. Perhaps you would prefer to go back to the city now, and begin the formal process of dealing with this. Although I think you might be interested in hearing the story. To his credit, Sidney McCarthy was. Of course you knew he worked for us after he left the Constabulary?"

"Yes, I knew that. And I would like to hear the story now."

"Alright. I will start with myself, and my mother. I was never sure what my mother wanted for me. Perhaps she hoped I would be 'normal' – that word again – and settle into a good marriage, with a good man, and give her a kind of validation of her own unhappy life. But I never in my life wanted a man, good or bad, and I knew that for a certainty while I was still very young. When Sam Rossiter came on the scene, and I was very young then, I think Mummy had hopes that he and I would hit it off. And we did in a way. We had things in common, Sam and I. We enjoyed each other's company, even if he was a lot older than I was. Perhaps you know about that, too. I know Molly did."

"She did tell me about that."

"Sam and I knew the servants talked about us, of course, and that others did too, friends and family. Sometimes we went out of our way to confuse them, just for fun. That was mostly my idea, though, and I sometimes went farther than Sam liked. He wasn't as comfortable in his skin as I was in mine. But I think it is easier for a woman in a situation like ours than it is for a man. The world often expects so little of women that we can make it work to our advantage if we try. Popular ignorance casts a large shadow. There are places to hide there."

"But Rossiter managed, somehow."

"Oh, yes. Sam managed. He was more fragile than I was, but he managed. Hubert, as you may have heard, had quite a reputation in Chapel Bight, and I know that people enjoyed gossiping about him, the rich man's son and the local girls. It was a kind of entertainment. But I also know for a fact that Sam Rossiter enjoyed his time in Chapel Bight. He told me that once. But people didn't talk about that. It was a secret, or at least it was supposed to be. I can tell you it's not all that much different here in St. John's. Small minds aren't confined to small communities. Isn't it a grand world, Mr. Stride?"

He didn't have any answer for that, but one wasn't needed. He changed the subject.

"You did marry, though. Major Cooke."

"Yes, I did. And I loved Rex. Not in the way a woman is supposed to love a man, of course, but as one person loves another. And we shared the bond of personal tragedy. Rex lost a leg in the service of his country, and then he lost his career. He also lost the respect and support of comrades who should have been better than they were, or at least have behaved better towards him than they did. By the time Rex and I met, I had lost my parents, my father reduced to what you saw just now, and my mother was lost too. I was very close to my father, and losing him was terrible for me, but I discovered, to my surprise, that the greater pain was in losing the mother I never really had.

"I often think of what eventually happened as a gathering of straws, which when bundled together were heavy enough to bring my mother down, and almost everyone around her. I was one of those straws, just by being who I was. I think I was a burden for her, although we never spoke about it. We didn't know how, so we didn't try. I wish we had."

"And then you met Clara Jones."

She smiled. "An accidental meeting, you could say."

"Because of the cave-in at Chapel Bight."

"Yes. But if not Clara, there and then, it would have happened some other way, somewhere else, with someone else. But there was an immediate attachment between us, we were soul mates from the beginning. And thirty-six years on, we are still. Then almost as soon as we met in Chapel Bight, I had to come back to St. John's with my father and Hubert. Clara had responsibilities at home, her mother wasn't well, dying in fact. But the next year, I went back to Chapel Bight on my own. I didn't ask permission, I didn't even tell anyone where I was going. I just went."

"And that's when the police became involved."

"Yes. I understood why Daddy brought them into it. He didn't know where I was until after McCarthy had made the routine inquiries and tracked me to Chapel Bight. It wasn't hard to do. I wasn't trying to hide. But it was a surprise that he came to fetch me himself. It was later on that I learned his coming to get me was not an official action, that he had volunteered to do it on his own time. McCarthy, I can tell you, was a surprise to everyone. Perhaps even to himself. When he brought me home, Clara came with me. Her mother had died by then and there was nothing to hold her in Chapel Bight any longer."

"I was told that caused problems at home."

"My mother was furious, and I probably contributed to that because I was defiant and defensive. Without knowing it, or even caring very much, I had made a bad situation worse. And worse still, I had helped to make it dangerous. By then, my mother and father were antipodal, worlds apart. She was drinking heavily, possibly even more than usual. What I didn't know, what no one knew, or could even have imagined, was that she had invented a mad fantasy that my father and Sam were having an affair, that the business trips they made were excuses for them to be together. She already knew about Sam, just as she now knew about me."

"Was there any truth to it? Your father and Sam Rossiter?"

"No, it wasn't true, there was absolutely nothing to it. But that didn't matter in the end. Mummy nursed her fantasy as intensely as she did her unhappiness, and it consumed her. It all came to a head on a Friday night in early September, here at Devon Lea. Daddy and Sam had come back the night before from a business trip to Boston. The passage had been difficult because there had been a series of storms to the southwest, and the seas were very rough. Mummy had been drinking all the time they were away, fuelling her misery, and drinking more heavily as the time of their return came closer. She had already made a decision. That night she accused my father of carrying on what she called 'an unnatural liaison' with Sam. We were all taken completely by surprise. Before anyone had time to grasp what she was talking about, she produced the revolver Daddy kept in his desk, and got off three shots before anyone could stop her. The first bullet struck my father in the head, and the second one hit Sam in the shoulder. It happened in this room." She pointed with the hand that held the glass. "The third bullet went into the wall above the fireplace. It's still there, if you want to see it."

Stride got up and walked to the mantel.

"Behind this picture?"

"Yes. It's just below the hanger."

He lifted the picture from the wall and rested it on the floor. The bullet was lodged where she said it was, about two inches below the hook.

"It looks like a .32."

"Yes, it is, a Smith & Wesson. Daddy bought it one time when he was in New York. He sometimes used it to shoot rats around the barn."

"You still have it?"

"It's in my safe at Winter Avenue. Hubert wanted to get rid of it, but I didn't want to do that. I'm not sure why. I just didn't."

"Why didn't you call the police when it happened?"

"The obvious question." She placed her drink on a table and leaned forward, her elbows on her knees. "I've gone over this in my mind more times than I want to think about. My first thought was that my father must have been killed. I was standing close to him when it happened. I not only saw the bullet strike him, I heard the sound of it. And I can hear it still. Clara was the one who got the gun away from Mummy. I didn't even think about the police."

"How did Graham Stirling get into it? Was he here at the farm too?"

"No, he was in St. John's. Clara went to get him. A registered doctor was out of the question, of course. But Stirling had served with the British Army in the Crimea, in the Medical Corps, and he knew quite a lot about bullet wounds."

"It was Stirling's decision to say your father had contracted typhus?"

"He suggested it, but the decision was mine. He had seen a lot of cases when he was in the army. It meant we could put the farm under quarantine and keep people away until Daddy and Sam recovered. That's what we hoped would happen. And Sam did get better, of course, but Daddy's wound became infected and for a time we thought he would die. But it only made the damage to his brain worse. If he had died, we would have told people the typhus had killed him. But he didn't die, and then we were trapped in the story we had invented. Ironically, Sam Rossiter was the one person who did manage to escape. After what had happened here, he wanted to leave Newfoundland and settle somewhere else. I agreed to supply him with an income. It seemed little enough to do under the circumstances. "

"There was a funeral. Who is buried in your father's grave?"

"No one. Just some packets of oats and dairy feed we took from the barn. Probably very good for the soil in the long run." She managed a thin smile. "Molly must have told you it was a closed casket. We told everyone it was because of the disfigurement from the disease. No one disputed any part of it. Who would, after all? Most people believed Graham Stirling to be a real doctor, because we said he was, and because he worked for our company. No one could have imagined what had gone on here. I wonder how many would have believed it, even if we had told them?"

"I don't know," Stride said. He picked up his drink. There wasn't much left in the glass, and his head was rocking a bit from the alcohol, and from what Elizabeth Cooke had told him. She had said a lot, and she had spoken in calm and measured tones, without any great display of feeling. He wondered about that. But it was possible she had rehearsed the story over and over, against the day when it might all be found out.

"How long has Justice McGinn known about this?"

"Not from the start of it, but for quite a long time. He didn't tell you anything about that, I suppose?"

"No, he didn't."

"It's difficult, then, isn't it? Robin being a senior person in the justice system, and sitting on information of this sort."

"It was his duty to have reported it to the authorities."

"Of course it was. But to what end, I wonder? By the time Robin heard about it, the damage had long since been done. My father's life was over for all intents and purposes, and my mother was an invalid, effectively removed from ever doing harm again. At least, harm of any magnitude. Robin and I talked about it at length, and on more than one occasion. His advice was that we should do what he called 'the right thing,' bring it all into the open, bury the ghosts, and deal with the consequences. In time, it would all go away, possibly even be subsumed into something like a folk tale. Carefully managed, the story might even have brought the family a certain amount of sympathy. Hubert wanted to take Robin's advice, but I refused. As far as I was concerned, it was a family matter, our business alone. I know you probably won't agree with that, but it's what I believe. And I take full responsibility for my decision."

"Responsibility isn't that easily apportioned."

"I know what you mean. But now all of it has fallen onto your lap. What will you do, I wonder? If you do *the right thing*, there will be a great deal of disruption, not the least of which will see Robin McGinn's forced resignation from the bench, possibly with criminal charges to follow. My father will not in consequence give up his beloved teddy bear and rejoin the world of the living. And my mother, poor creature, will remain invalided and incoherent. Certainly she will never stand trial. Perhaps, in an effort to show that families like ours are not immune from punishment, she will be removed from her home and locked up in the Mental Hospital, popularly known, not so long ago as *The Lunatic*. Will you be comfortable with all of that, Mr. Stride?"

When he didn't reply, she spoke again.

"And to bring us back to where your involvement started, at the end of the day, you still won't know who killed Sam Rossiter, or why."

thirty-four

Stride sat at the kitchen table drinking tea and reading the report of the Chapel Bight inquiry. Dianne was standing by the stove holding a package of eggs in one hand and an egg-turner in the other.

"One egg or two?" she said.

She had to ask the question a second time before he looked up.

"Three."

"Three eggs? Are you sure?"

"Yes. I'm really hungry this morning. I didn't eat much last evening. Just a small meat pie and a glass of beer at the Admiralty."

"And you have been a busy boy. Scrambled or fried?"

"What?" He had already gone back to his reading.

"I asked if you wanted your eggs scrambled or fried. Pay me some attention, Stride."

"I'm sorry. I was distracted."

"That's something a woman never wants to hear from a man, especially when she's just finished making love with him."

"That was you in there, just now?"

"Maybe you'd like to wear these eggs?"

"That is an option." He got up, went over to her, and pulled her close to him. "I'm sorry, again. I was trying to be funny."

"At times you are funny, my man, but this wasn't one of them. But you are forgiven. So, scrambled or fried?"

"Fried. The last time I had scrambled eggs for breakfast, Caleb Howell tried to shoot me with a Browning .45."

"Remind me to have a word with him someday. We might find we have things in common."

He was about to say that Howell was an American, like her husband, but he caught himself in time. He went back to the table and the report.

"What are you reading?" She cracked an egg with the edge of the egg-turner, dropped it in the pan, then picked up another.

"It's the report of the Chapel Bight inquiry."

"The mining accident. You got that from Grace DeJohn, didn't you?"

"Yes. It's only on loan, though. She wants it back."

She cracked another egg and dropped it into the pan.

"Grace knows about us. Did she say anything to you about that?"

"Yes, she told me she knew." He placed a spoon between the pages of the report as a bookmark and took out a cigarette. "It sort of came up when we were talking."

"Sort of came up? You didn't tell me about that."

"I haven't seen you since I spoke to Grace. Or even talked to you, for that matter."

"No, I suppose not." She cracked the last egg and dropped it into the pan. "This will be ready in a couple of minutes. Do you like your eggs sunny-side up?"

"Yes. And I like the yolks runny."

"This is the first time we've had breakfast together."

"I know."

She took the cigarette from him and drew on it.

"It seems like an age since we were last together."

"Yes, it does. But it's actually been less than a week. You were here Tuesday night." The day of Sam Rossiter's autopsy.

"You're right, I was here then." She gave him the cigarette and went back to the stove. "What else did Grace have to say?"

"About us?"

"Of course, about us." When he didn't reply right away, she came back to the table and stood close to him, touching his hair. He pulled her closer still and rested his cheek against her stomach. "Did she say anything else?"

"Some. I asked her if Marty knew about us."

"What did she say?"

"She said she didn't know if he did or not. But I got the impression that she did know something." He looked up at her, but she was looking away from him now. "Does Marty know about us?"

"He knows I'm involved with someone. But I don't think he knows it's you, unless he's made an effort to find out. I haven't told him, and I don't think Grace would do that."

"How does it work? You and Marty?"

"You mean, how do we deal with it?"

"Yes."

"We don't sleep together any longer, if that's what you're asking."

"That isn't what I meant. Well, not entirely. How do you get through your time together? Or shouldn't I ask that?"

"You can ask. We hadn't been sleeping together – well, having sex – for a while before we got involved. You and me, I mean. Well, I think I more or less told you that the night we met. Sometimes I wondered if he was seeing someone, but I don't think that's it. I think he's just kind of drifted away from me. I don't know why. I've been told wartime marriages sometimes don't work very well."

"Did your taking a job have anything to do with it? Some men don't like that."

"That might have had something to do with it, I don't know. He didn't object to my going back to work, but he didn't seem all that enthusiastic about it, either. But whatever it is, I think it happened before I went back to work. Anyway, we don't talk very much, other than the necessary stuff, the day-to-day things. My mother told me once that an awful lot of what goes on in a marriage is just making do."

"Some marriages, anyway."

"And you'd be an expert on marriage, of course." She went back to the eggs for a moment, then looked at him. "I'm sorry. I shouldn't have said that."

"I don't mind. And you're right. My knowledge of marriage is about on a par with my piano playing."

"You don't play the piano."

"No, but sometimes I think I'd like to learn."

"And sometimes you think you'd like to be married?"

"Sometimes."

"But maybe not today."

"No, probably not today."

"Anyway, it helps that we're both very busy, also that Marty travels a lot." She turned her attention back to the eggs. Stride could see that she didn't want to talk about this any longer. "These eggs are almost done. If you want toast, you had better get at it, or these yolks will be as hard as beach rocks."

Dianne left Stride to wash up the dishes from breakfast while she took a shower. They had chatted easily enough while they ate, and they hadn't mentioned Marty again. Stride thought sometimes their relationship was a kind of mirror image of what her life might be like with her husband, the careful avoidance of certain subjects. Dianne and Marty somehow managed to get through the days of the week, without talking about the distance that had grown between them. Stride and Dianne almost never mentioned Marty, or her marriage, while being conscious of both. They made love whenever they had the chance, and enjoyed each other's company in the limited amount of time they spent together out of bed. But sex was the hinge on which the relationship turned. He had become more aware of that as the novelty had begun to wear away, and a blank spot had grown in its place. He wondered if she felt it too, and thought she probably did. Relationships that couldn't grow were likely to wither.

But he didn't want to think any more about his relationship with Dianne, not just now. He was grateful that he had other things to do. Reading the report on Chapel Bight, even washing the breakfast dishes, were good diversions. They also allowed him to take his mind off the situation at Devon Lea. That was something else he didn't know how to deal with, not yet. He propped the report up against the flour and sugar containers on the counter, and held the pages open with a heavy silver serving ladle.

His reading so far had confirmed his initial impression, that the report was badly written, and wishy-washy on details. 'Bum-fluff,' Harry would have called it. Several times he almost gave up and threw it to one side in frustration. But because he was still smarting from being upstaged by McGinn on the details of the accident, he needed to read it through, and carefully.

He looked for an indication in the writing that McGinn had made a real contribution to the report, some hint of the man's intelligence and integrity. But he found nothing significant until he got to the recommendations chapter. He read the first two, more interested now. When he finished stacking the dishes, he seated himself at the table and read slowly and deliberately through them all. There were eight in total, and they were concise and carefully written, no words wasted, the intention of each precise and clear, and they had continuity without overlap. He thought he could see McGinn's hand and mind in all of them.

And as McGinn had said, the recommendations provided decent compensation to those in Chapel Bight and Scat's Arm who were affected by the cave-in. Given the situation, that probably included at least one member in most of the families in the area. And the compensation did seem unusually generous for the time.

There were three appendices. The first listed all of the people involved in the inquiry and in the writing of the report. He recognised several of the names, including McGinn's. The second appendix listed the witnesses and the names of individuals who had submitted written briefs or comments. He couldn't find Major Stamp's name among the list of witnesses, and then remembered that Stamp hadn't been at the hearings, but had instead submitted a brief. His name was there on the second part of the list.

He turned to the last appendix, pleased that he was almost finished the reading. He scanned the names, listed alphabetically, not surprised to see that about a dozen surnames dominated. Small outports like Chapel Bight and Scat's Arm would be largely made up of related families. That made for strong communities, but when tragedy struck, as it had at Chapel Bight, it also meant that almost everyone there would have a family member affected, and the grief and loss became both widespread and closely focused.

McGinn had said that a father and son had been killed, and Stride found their names at the top of the list. He took note of the names, then started to read through the list of the people injured. He stopped and went back. He remembered then that what McGinn had said was that a father and one of his sons had been killed in the accident. Now he went back to the list of the people injured, looking for a specific name. He found it near the top of the list. He closed the report and sat back in his chair, looking through the window in the direction of Signal Hill, thinking about what he had just read.

Dianne came into the kitchen then. She was towelling her hair dry.

"You're finished reading?"

"Yes, I am." He glanced at her, then reached for a cigarette.

"You have that look." She rested one hand on his shoulder. "Did you find something?"

"Yes, I did find something. I'm going to take a shower, and then I'll have to call Harry and go out. I might be gone for the rest of the day." He placed his hand on hers. "I'm sorry. I wanted us to spend the day together."

"Can't be helped," she said. "Perhaps we'll be able to see each other later?"

"We might."

"So, is it over now? The Rossiter thing?"

"Maybe. I won't know for a little while yet."

"You don't look very happy about it, Eric. Is it something you didn't expect?"

"It was something I didn't expect," he said. "And, no, it doesn't bring me any joy at all."

Stride picked Harry up at his house on Victoria Street, and while he drove, Harry flipped through the report and read the third appendix. When he was done, he closed the report and placed it on the floor between his feet.

"It isn't anything like what we might have expected, is it?"

"No, it isn't. Assuming this actually does wrap it up for us."

"I think I might be willing to bet a shilling or two that it does," Harry said.

They were driving west on New Gower now. Stride slowed the MG as they approached the intersection with Holdsworth, then turned left. He parked just above George Street, looking down towards Water. Harry picked the report up from the floor.

"Do you suppose we need to take this with us?"

"I don't think so, Harry. Just slide it under the seat, out of sight."

There was a longer wait than usual after Harry knocked on the door of the Admiralty, but it was still a few minutes to opening time. Hector Gullage pulled the door open. He gave Stride an appraising look.

"Something must be up to bring you here this early in the day, especially on a Saturday."

"You're right, Gully, something is up."

Stride looked around the room while Phelan positioned himself a few feet to the side of the door. Ted Murphy was behind the bar drying glasses and placing them on a shelf. When he saw Stride and Phelan standing in the entrance, he stopped what he was doing, draped the towel over his shoulder, and lit a cigarette. He leaned on the bar, watching the two detectives closely.

Gullage followed the direction of Stride's gaze.

"You came here to talk to Ted?"

Stride didn't reply right away. He looked around the room again.

"No. We need to talk to Johnny Blake."

"Johnny's not here yet. What do you want to talk to him about? The Rossiter case?"

"Yes. He might be able to help us on that. When do you expect him?"

"Five or ten minutes, probably. He isn't usually late, but it's Saturday, and anyway I think he's been off his feed the past couple of days." Gullage looked towards the bar again. Ted Murphy had gone back to drying glasses. "Why don't we go into my office and you can tell me what's up. If that's okay?"

"Alright." Stride looked at Phelan. "You wait here, Harry."

Gullage closed the door and sat on the edge of his desk.

"You don't think Johnny had anything to do with Rossiter, do you?"

"In fact, I think it's likely he did. When we were here on Tuesday morning, you said Johnny knew Walter Keough from a long time ago. But you didn't say where that was. Was it here in St. John's?"

Gullage shook his head.

"I don't think so, no. I think it was down north. Walter was part of a mining crew at the time."

"Do you remember the name of the place? Where the mine was located?"

"Christ, now you're asking me something. It was the place Johnny was from, that much I do remember. I would probably recognise the name if you said it, though."

"Scat's Arm?"

Gullage shook his head.

"No, it's nothing like that."

"Chapel Bight?"

"Chapel Bight? Yes, that's the place."

"And that's where Johnny Blake is from?"

"Yes. Johnny worked the mines himself for a while, until he was crippled."

"How did he lose the foot? Was it a mining accident?"

"I think so, yes. He didn't go into details about it." Gullage walked around to the back of his desk and sat down in the desk chair. "What's it all about, Eric? What do you have on Johnny?"

"There was a cave-in at the mine in Chapel Bight in 1911. Two men were killed and a lot more were injured, some of them badly. And some like Johnny, very badly. One of the men who was killed was named Jack Blake, and I think he was Johnny's father. The other man killed was Wilfred Blake. He was Jack Blake's son."

"Johnny's brother."

"It would seem like it, yes. Sam Rossiter was working in Chapel Bight then. The Hurdle Company owned the mine. Rossiter had worked for them for years."

"That would be back when Sir Leonard ran the Company."

"Yes. Rossiter was the senior company manager at the site. Some people thought he was responsible for the accident, because he was the one in charge of purchasing. There's no way to prove that now, and it's possible the accident wasn't his responsibility at all."

"But try telling that to a man who's lost his father and brother, and had a leg amputated besides. I might be just a little pissed off myself, and you know what a calm and peaceful sort I am."

"Better than most."

"And I guess that's the road you're going down with this? You think this was a revenge killing?"

"It might have been."

"Are you going to arrest Johnny?"

"I'll wait and see what Johnny has to say for himself before we take it any further. But, yes, we might end up arresting him. Do you know where he lives, by the way?"

"Johnny? He rents a room at a place on Lower Battery Road."

"So he would normally walk past Scanlon's Lane on his way home from here."

"I guess he would. It would be the same general direction." Gullage sat forward and clasped his hands on the surface of the desk. "Jesus Christ. What a miserable, bloody business this is. Not much joy in this one for you, is there?"

"Not even the littlest bit," Stride said.

There was a knock at the door then, and Harry Phelan looked into the office.

"Blake's just arrived, sir."

"Has he said anything to you?"

Harry shook his head.

Gullage stood up and moved out from behind the desk.

"You can use the office, Eric."

"I appreciate that. Bring him along in, Harry."

Johnny Blake sat stiffly upright in a chair, holding his cane between his knees and staring at the floor. He was shy in the presence of the two detectives, two tall men standing to either side of him.

Stride wanted this over as quickly as possible and he sensed that Blake did too, so he asked the question at once, without embellishment.

"Did you kill Sam Rossiter, Johnny?"

Blake lifted his gaze from the floor and looked at Stride for only a moment before tilting his head downwards again. He nodded his head twice in affirmation.

There was a long moment of silence while Stride waited for Blake to say something. When there was nothing, he spoke again.

"Why?"

Blake still didn't answer. He continued to stare at the floor, still holding onto his cane with both hands. Stride pulled a chair over and sat in front of him. He leaned forward to capture Blake's attention.

"You're from Chapel Bight. Did you remember Rossiter from his time there, when he was working at the mine site?"

This time Blake did respond. He glanced briefly at Stride before returning his gaze to the floor.

"Yes, sir, I did. I knew him from back then. He was working there in the office."

"You worked underground at the mine, with your father and brother?"

"Yes, sir. We all worked at the mine."

"And you were all working underground the day the mineshaft collapsed?"

Blake nodded. His posture had changed now, as he seemed to gather himself even more tightly than before. Stride thought he might be revisiting the scene in his mind, the terrifying moments when the mineshaft collapsed and the men and boys underground were suddenly enveloped by darkness and fear, and the long time afterwards while they waited to be rescued.

"It must have been a surprise for you, Rossiter turning up in St. John's after all those years?"

"Yes, sir, it was. I never thought to set eyes on him again."

"You recognised him when he came here to the Admiralty?"

"Not right away. It was a long time since I saw him. He didn't look the same at all. It was later on I found out who he was."

"Walter Keough told you?"

"Yes, sir. It was Walter told me who he was. Him and Rossiter was friends."

"They were friends in Chapel Bight, back when Walter was working at the mine?"

"I don't know as they was friends, really. But they knew each other."

"Some of the people in Chapel Bight thought Rossiter was responsible for the cave-in at the mine. Did you think so too, that he was responsible for the accident that killed your father and your brother?"

Blake shrugged, then turned his head away. Stride asked the question again.

"Was that why you killed him, Johnny? Because you believed he was responsible for their deaths, and for leaving you crippled?"

Blake shrugged again, and went back to staring at the floor between his legs. He shifted the position of his hands on the cane. Stride thought he also saw another subtle change in the old man's attitude.

"I suppose so," Blake said at last.

"You suppose so?" Stride looked at Phelan.

"Yes, sir."

There was no conviction in his words. And there was something about Blake's attitude, something that didn't fit the admission. Stride looked at Phelan again to see if he was getting the same impression, and he thought he probably was. He took his package of cigarettes from his pocket and shook a cigarette loose, taking his time, watching Blake closely while he pretended to look for his lighter. There was something else, he was sure of it. He ran the bits and pieces of the case through his mind, going back to the scene in Scanlon's Lane, to Rossiter's dishevelled body, the head and throat injuries, the violence that had been visited on one old man by another. It still didn't add up for him. He was looking at Blake's hands now as they gripped the cane. The old man's hands were shaking slightly.

Stride lit his cigarette and snapped the lighter shut. And then, with a click inside his head that was almost as loud as the sound of the lighter being closed, he believed he did understand.

He looked at Blake, caught his eye and held it.

"Why were you in Scanlon's Lane Monday night, Johnny? It was late when Rossiter was killed, sometime after midnight, long after closing time here at the Admiralty. You should have been home long since. But you knew that Rossiter and Keough liked to go to the laneway to drink. You saw them leave the pub together, with the bottle that Granny Fitz gave them, and you knew where they were headed, where they would be. It was where they always went when they had a bottle. Did you go there to talk to Rossiter?"

Blake glanced at Stride, but he made no reply. Then he went back to staring at the floor between his legs.

"Did you go there to have it out with him, to tell him you remembered him from the time in Chapel Bight when your father and brother were killed?" Blake still did not respond. "I don't think you came upon Rossiter by chance on your way home. If that had been the case, you would have run into Walter Keough too. I think you waited until Keough had left, and then you decided to have it out with Rossiter, one on one. Am I right, Johnny?"

Stride thought Blake might have nodded, but he wasn't sure. It seemed there was a resigned movement of the head, a gesture of submission, but if it was there at all, it was very slight.

"You waited until Rossiter was alone in the laneway and then you confronted him." They were both looking at Stride now, the old man and Phelan together. "But I don't think you went there to kill him. That wasn't what you had in mind. I think you were angry about what happened in Chapel Bight more than thirty years ago. In your place, I know I would have been. But I think you only wanted to talk to Rossiter. I think killing Rossiter was almost as much a surprise to you as it was to him. What made you hit him, Johnny? I don't think you intended to attack him, but then you did. You hit him with your cane, and more than once. And one of those blows struck him in the throat and that was what killed him. What made you do that?"

Blake's attitude shifted again, and he was trembling. He was still staring at the floor, but Stride could see that his focus was somewhere else now, far away in place and time. Tears gathered in the old man's eyes, then rolled down his face. The intense emotion of Blake's reaction took Stride by surprise. Then, inside his head, he heard Elizabeth Cooke's words from last night.

Sam Rossiter enjoyed his time in Chapel Bight. He told me that once. But people didn't talk about that. It was a secret, or at least it was supposed to be.

Stride was almost certain he could piece it together now. He thought that Johnny Blake might have been a part of Sam Rossiter's enjoyment of Chapel Bight, and that people probably did know about it, it hadn't been a secret after all. It wouldn't have mattered a lot to Rossiter, he didn't live there, and he had a privileged position besides. But Blake did live in Chapel Bight, and if people did know about his liaison with Rossiter, it would have cost him almost as much as the accident in the mine, a permanent injury of another, perhaps crueller kind. Stride saw again the body of the old man lying in Scanlon's Lane, the trousers unbuttoned and pulled wide open. He wanted to ask Blake if Rossiter, blind drunk and deranged as well, had done that to taunt him after Blake had told him who he was. But that was something he could do later. Just now, he had neither the inclination nor the energy. They already had Blake's admission of guilt. It was enough.

thirty-five

"It's always interesting when the past catches up with the present."

It was Sunday afternoon and Thomas Butcher was picking ripe tomatoes in the garden he cultivated behind his house on Waterford Bridge Road. Butcher almost always had a good crop of tomatoes, and cucumbers too, even in a bad year. And this year had been one of the good ones. He started the seedlings in April in a glasshouse he had had constructed behind his house only a few years after he had settled in St. John's from his native Somerset. He had known before he arrived in Newfoundland that most of the plants he prized, flowers and vegetables both, would need a helping hand if he wanted to enjoy their yearly bounty. Butcher liked plants as much as he liked people, and he cared for them all with the same intense dedication.

"Trite, but true," Stride said. "And Sam Rossiter's past did catch up with him."

"Don't underestimate the importance of 'trite,' Eric. It's what sustains us a good part of the time. I have to wonder, though, if Rossiter even remembered who Blake was. But perhaps he did, at the very last, through the fog of dementia and alcohol."

"Maybe. Sam Rossiter had probably forgotten a lot of things by the time he returned to St. John's from Bermuda. If he remembered them at all, it was probably only in fragments. Forgetting who Johnny Blake was cost him the little that remained of his life."

"And it will blight what remains of Blake's, a life more blighted by tragedy and unhappiness than most of us would want to think about. It's a very sad story."

"I won't argue with that."

"No, I didn't think so. The only possible compensation being that the courts will take into consideration the tragic history of Blake's life."

"I think that's a good possibility."

"We will hope so." Butcher inspected a tomato, turning it carefully on the vine to see the underside, and decided to leave it for another day. "My Mrs. Goodyear makes a spectacular piccalilli out of green tomatoes, truly a garnish for the gods. She waits until the last few warm days of fall when there are still a lot of tomatoes left that won't ripen on the vine. Then we start picking, and for two days it's a kind of orchestrated bedlam in her kitchen. The masses of ingredients are assembled, the pots are boiled, and every inch of space becomes occupied and productive. And after that, there's the bottling, another business entirely. The atmosphere becomes positively Vesuvian."

"She puts you to work, does she?"

"Oh, indeed she does. It's actually quite a lot of fun, and I've learned to keep a supply of good wine flowing through the enterprise. If you're interested, I will invite you to join us this year. It will do you good, after your exertions of the past week, give you something less grim to think about. And Hazel puts up a first-class beef stew for the occasion, as a kind of celebration. There's always much more than we can hope to eat by ourselves."

"Let me know the day and the time and I'll be there, paring knife in hand."

"Good lad. I guarantee you'll be much the better for it." He scrutinised another tomato and added it to the harvest basket. "Not that I'm suggesting you need a great deal of improvement, you understand."

"We can all do with some improvement, Thomas."

"Equally true, and equally trite," Butcher said. He stepped back and surveyed his tomato patch. "I think that's enough for today. The hot weather has worked its magic, and we have far more than we will ever use. I'll put some of these in a bag for you to take home with you. I'll fill a bag for Harry too."

"He and Kitty will appreciate that."

"Speaking of Harry, has he said anything to you about my speculations on Sir Leonard's supposed death from typhus?"

"He asked me about that yesterday, after we had booked Blake for Rossiter's murder. He knew I had more information on it from Jimmy Peach."

"And your reply?"

"I told him it was something we weren't going to pursue any further, that the Rossiter file was closed as far as our involvement was concerned."

"He didn't really buy that, did he?"

"No, of course not. Harry's too sharp not to know when I'm making fudge. But he's also diplomatic enough to wait until I'm ready to talk about it. Happily, he trusts me not to be too bloody stupid when I make a decision, or at least not too often."

"A good sort of fellow for you to be partnered with."

"I have always thought so."

Stride held the door open for Butcher and his basket of tomatoes, and followed him into the house. He placed the basket on the kitchen counter, close to the sink.

"But what are you going to do about it, Eric? You've had a day and a bit to think about it, now."

"The obvious thing to do is to write it into my report of the Rossiter case, and let the powers-that-be make the decision."

"Jack McCowan and the Chief."

"It's the way the system works."

"I have always had the greatest respect for systems. When they stand between us and chaos, that is." Butcher turned on the tap and began filling the sink with cold water. "Speaking of systems, you're familiar with the concept of 'triage', I suppose?"

"Triage? It's the system the medical corps came up with in the First World War to sort wounded soldiers into three groups, according to the severity of their injuries."

"Full marks to you. I was a part of that, you know, both it's development and its implementation. It was a bold initiative, and not universally popular at the start. I wasn't all that sure of it myself to be honest. We established three rough groupings for the men wounded on the battlefield. One group included those with what we judged were the least severe wounds, and they were placed aside to be dealt with later, the assumption being that they would survive without immediate help. The second group was made up of the more serious cases who needed immediate attention if they were to survive. The third group included the most seriously wounded, the ones we judged would not benefit from our attentions, however hard we tried, and who would die anyway."

"But whose treatment would decrease the probability of survival for the less seriously wounded because you weren't available to deal with them."

"Just so. You can imagine it was a very difficult proposition. Assigning wounded men to categories is not easy. Some died who might have been saved, if only a different decision had been made at the sorting stage. One of my colleagues described it as the lunacy of war carried to its logically abysmal conclusion. But in the end, triage was a system that had more benefits than liabilities. On balance, we saved many more lives than we lost." Butcher turned off the tap and began placing the tomatoes in the sink. "But it was not a system devoid of costs. Every life lost is a flame extinguished forever. I can still see the faces of some of the men I might have saved. They were not just a few."

"You see a parallel with the situation I'm looking at now?"

"Oh, yes, I do. And like the triage system, it does not allow for an easy judgement. You've told me what Elizabeth Cooke said to you Friday night, after you had seen her father. I think she put the case rather well. Or at least not badly."

"From her point of view."

"Of course, from her point of view." He looked at the tomato he was holding. "There's a worm in this one, and Hazel is not an admirer of worms. Can't imagine how I didn't see that." He dropped the tomato into the trash bin under the sink. "Tell me. Do you dislike her a lot? Elizabeth Cooke?"

"Dislike her? No, in fact I don't dislike her."

"You don't?"

"No. I'll be honest and say that I actually like her. Or perhaps it's a kind of admiration, more than liking."

"That's not badly put. It's rather the way I feel about her myself."

"But my liking her, or disliking her, can't have any bearing on my decision about her and her father."

"No, of course not. Your decision has to be objective. Painful, but necessary. Not so greatly unlike the ones we had to make during the war. Do you agree there is a parallel here with the system I described?"

"I suppose I do, yes."

"Reluctantly?"

"Perhaps. But I hadn't thought about it in quite that way. It takes a bit of getting used to."

"And now that you've thought about it for all of sixty or seventy seconds?"

"Time enough, and then some," Stride said. He pulled back the curtain and looked into the yard. There was a profusion of flowers at the back, near the fence, a delicious riot of colour. It reminded him of Elizabeth Cooke's garden on Winter Avenue. He let the curtain fall back into place and turned to face Butcher. "I'm not going to do anything about it. I don't see that anyone gains if I include it in my report. It isn't a question of right or wrong. It's a question of doing the least amount of harm in a situation that has no happy, or even remotely comfortable resolution. I can't see that dragging it all into the public view, and into the courts, will benefit anyone."

"Except for a collection of lawyers, a horde of newspaper people, and at least a part of the general public. They all love this sort of thing and some of them would take a profit from it." Butcher removed the tomatoes from the water and placed them on a draining board. Then, he pulled the plug from the sink and wiped away the residue with a washcloth. "Are you going to be comfortable with this, Eric? I imagine it goes against the grain to some degree."

"Not all of the time, no. But whenever I have doubts that I've done the best thing – not the right thing, because there is no right thing – 'll think about that old man sitting in his chair at Devon Lea, holding onto his teddy bear, waiting to die, although he no longer knows there is such a thing as death. All anyone can give him now is peace and quiet. His daughter will make sure he at least has that."

"That is a bracing thought."

"Bracing enough for me."

"And your other conundrum?" Butcher took out his silver cigarette case.

"Dianne Borg?" Stride leaned against the kitchen counter and accepted the proffered cigarette. "You still haven't told me how you found out about that."

"I will only say that doctors are privy to an amazing amount of information on all manner of things. And if I know about you and Dianne Borg, it's almost a certainty that others will also, if they don't already."

"I'm all too aware of that."

"I know it's none of my business, strictly speaking, but I also know it bothers you. And, in a way, that does make it my business. Whatever the background to it all, sleeping with a married woman who is not your wife is a situation fraught with problems. As though I have to tell you that."

"No, you don't have to tell me." He gave Butcher a close look. "You speak like a man who has had some experience in this area. Do you?"

"In a way, I do, yes. And not just from the professional's point of view."

"Really? You surprise me, Thomas." Then he shook his head. "What a bloody stupid thing for me to say. Of course I'm not surprised. Rumour has it that doctors are people too."

"It's an ugly rumour to be sure, but all too true. Someday I will tell you about it, but this is not that day. Today we will talk about your situation, and I will offer well-intentioned advice that you will, if you are wise, consign to the bin labelled 'for future consideration.' And while we're doing that, I want you to help me evaluate another of Marchand's excellent clarets. Do you feel up to the challenge?"

"I think so."

"Good man. Let's have at it, then."

epiLogue

It was the usual gaggle of curious and interested onlookers, Stride thought, although he had thought there would be more people there to observe the trial of Caleb Howell. But it was a cold, dark day in late October, and the threat of snow was hanging in the air. Or failing that, an onslaught of freezing rain, a meteorological blessing known locally as *sliver thaw*. The popular opinion had it that St. John's was about to pay the price for a long and unusually hot summer. Nature, it was said, was re-establishing the balance of punishments and blessings.

The charge against Howell, brought about after much negotiation between the Crown Prosecutor and J.V. Higgins, was possession of a dangerous weapon. In this case a handgun, specifically a .45 calibre Browning semi-automatic pistol. J.V. Higgins had successfully argued against a charge of assault on the two officers involved in Howell's arrest. He pressed home the point, more than once, that Howell had been in a deep sleep when Stride and Phelan had come into his room at the Burridge house, and he had only been defending himself against what he saw as two strange, and very large men who had not properly identified themselves to him. It was, Higgins maintained, an unfortunate incident, but one that could be understood if the Crown Attorney would place himself in Mr. Howell's position.

For his part, the Crown Attorney acknowledged that intelligent compromise was at the heart and soul of the justice system. He also knew that he did not want to do battle with Higgins in open court on the matter of Howell's state of mind and awareness when he had – as Higgins and Howell both maintained – been rudely awakened from a deep sleep, and had acted at the behest of the conditioned reflexes drilled into him during his army training.

The Crown Attorney also knew he would have his hands full enough arguing for the reduced charge of possessing a dangerous weapon. He knew too well that Higgins would trot out a brightly coloured dissertation on Howell's gallant service in the cause of freedom and democracy, his life-threatening chest wound, and the cumulative trauma of having lost so many beloved and treasured comrades in the fight against Nazi tyranny. The court would be reminded that Caleb Howell was, in truth, a child of Newfoundland, one of their own, the only son of native-born Newfoundlanders of humble origins who had sought a better life for themselves and their son in the United States.

And so it went. Stride had never seen Higgins in better form than he was on the occasion of Caleb Howell's trial. As Alex Greene had pointed out, it had been quite some time since Higgins had worked a criminal trial, and it appeared that the prolonged rest from that special arena had only allowed his well-honed skills to regenerate to full rhetorical flower. And to Stride's considerable surprise, Higgins was uncommonly polite to both him and Harry when they took the stand, praising their service records with the Constabulary, even offering warm congratulations on bringing the Rossiter case to a swift and successful conclusion.

Stride and Phelan both stayed on to await the judge's verdict in the case – Higgins had opted for trial by judge alone – and Harry didn't think they would have to wait very long. Mr. Justice Thomas Hollett was presiding and, as a veteran of the First World War, he was known to be sympathetic to anyone who had survived what he called 'the ordeal of fire.' An acquittal wasn't a realistic probability, but Stride thought it likely that Howell was looking at only a minimum amount of time behind bars, possibly even a suspended sentence combined with a fine.

While they waited for Justice Hollett to reappear and deliver his verdict, Stride glanced quickly around the courtroom at the various spectators who had stayed on. Only a few of them remained. Alex Greene had been there throughout the trial, and now he was sitting on the opposite side of the room, two rows back, writing in his notebook. When he caught Stride's eye, he raised his hand in greeting, then cupped his fingers in an approximation of a drinking glass. Stride smiled and nodded his agreement. Now that it was almost all over and done with, both the Rossiter case and Howell's trial, he was looking forward to a quiet drink or two with Greene. Perhaps he would take the opportunity to ask him why he was in St. John's working for the *Sunday Herald*, when he had the background and education for higher pursuits.

Then the Court Clerk appeared, calling for all in the courtroom to rise for the entrance of Justice Hollett. The judge wasted no time in delivering his verdict. Howell was found guilty on the charge of possessing a dangerous weapon. Stride was not really surprised when he was given a six-month suspended sentence, and assessed a fine of one hundred dollars. It was all over in a very few minutes. J.V. Higgins, neatly attired in the standard dress of a barrister, black vest under a black jacket and gown, and with neck tabs on his white shirt, enthusiastically shook hands with Howell. Alex Greene was next in line to offer his good wishes. The two spoke together for a minute, and then Greene moved towards where Stride and Phelan were sitting.

"I guess it's about what we expected," Phelan said.

"Yes," Stride replied. "I wonder what Howell will do now? If he'll stay on in St. John's, or pack his bags and go back home."

"I suppose it depends on where he thinks home is these days. Maybe he's back here to stay."

"If he is, we might have occasion to make his acquaintance again."

"We might, at that, sir. It's always nice to have something to look forward to. As the saying goes: 'No work, no job.' But I imagine he'll behave himself for a while. I'll count on not hearing anything about him for at least a day or three."

"There's still that one loose end, though. We still don't know who picked up Higgins' fee. I don't like loose ends, but I don't know how we might tie that one up."

"Abe Peddle didn't know?"

"No, he didn't. He was just as surprised as we were when Higgins took over the brief. And he has asked around. No one knows, or if they do, they're not saying."

"Maybe it's just one of those things that we will never find out."

"A mystery, you mean?"

Phelan laughed.

"Yes, one of those."

"That's the kind of word that sells papers," Greene said. He was sitting behind them now. "Which mystery is that you're talking about? Something I can base an article on?"

"It might be. The matter of Higgins' fee. And if you can find out who paid it, I will buy you a drink."

"Only one? I should have thought that sort of information would be worth more than a single libation."

"Two drinks, then."

"Well, that is more like it." Greene looked at his watch. "Speaking of which, I calculate that the sun is well over the yardarm now."

"It's not even two o'clock yet, Alex. The sun, even if we could see it, has a long way to go before it gets anywhere near the famous yardarm."

"I was thinking of our shared ancestral homes, actually. It's definitely past six in England and Ireland."

"Ah," Stride said. "Now that you've clarified the issue, I agree we should probably be on our way."

They stood up and made their way from the courtroom, with Greene walking in front. They paused in the foyer to pull on coats, hats, and scarves.

Caleb Howell watched them leave, and then he shook hands one more time with his attorney. Higgins picked up his briefcase, patted Howell on the shoulder and he left also, the hem of his silk gown billowing in his wake. Up at the bench, the Court Clerk was tidying up after Justice Hollett, who had a habit of making complicated doodles on a legal pad during the proceedings and almost always neglected to take the pad and pencil with him when he departed.

After the Clerk had gone, there were only two people left in the courtroom, Caleb Howell and a tall man in his early thirties who had sat through the trial in a corner at the back, slumped down in his chair, well removed from the rest of the observers. Now he stood up and met Howell at the door that exited the courtroom. The two men shook hands and paused in the foyer where they pulled on overcoats, gloves, and hats in preparation for the bitter wind that awaited them outside.

"Don't know as I'll ever get used to this kind of weather, Caleb."

"The trick is to wear a lot of clothing and not go outside unless you have to," Howell said. "Anyway, we survived two winters in Germany and Austria, and we'll survive this too. At least no one is shooting at us this time." Then he laughed. "Not yet, anyway."

His companion looked at him for a moment, and then he laughed also.

When he heard the sound of laughter, the constable standing inside the Court House entrance turned and looked at the two men. He recognised Caleb Howell at once as the man who had just stood trial in courtroom number one. He looked at Howell for a moment, then turned his attention to the man standing with him. After a moment he looked away because he didn't want to seem to be staring, but then he looked at him again. The constable was interested and a little intrigued because the man looked different from Howell somehow, different in fact from everyone standing in the foyer. There was just something about him. Howell's companion wasn't aware he was being looked at, so the constable continued to watch him until Howell pushed the door open and the two men stepped outside.

The constable continued to think for a minute or two about the man who had left with Caleb Howell. As a policeman, he had been trained to observe people, to take note of any unusual characteristics. Now he was trying to put his finger on just what it was about the man that had caught his attention. His first thought when he saw him was that he looked something like Joe Louis, the reigning heavyweight boxing champion, the man the sportswriters had nicknamed the 'Brown Bomber.' But that didn't make any sense, because the man with Howell was a white man, there was no question about that.

The constable thought about it for a few moments longer and then gave up the exercise. He looked at his watch and saw that it wasn't quite two o'clock yet. He muttered a mild oath under his breath. It was more than an hour yet before he could go downstairs for a mug of hot tea and a cigarette. And that was a pain, because just now he really wanted a smoke.

During the writing process I consulted a variety of sources in an effort to ensure historical accuracy for the narrative: Arthur Fox's *The Newfoundland Constabulary* (Robinson Blackmore Printing & Publishing Ltd., Newfoundland, 1971); Peter Neary's *Newfoundland in the North Atlantic World, 1929-1949* (McGill-Queen's University Press, Montreal & Kingston, 1988); Paul O'Neill's *The Oldest City – The Story of St. John's, Newfoundland* (Boulder Publications Ltd., Portugal Cove-St. Phillip's, Newfoundland, 2004); Harold Horwood's *The Newfoundland Ranger Force* (Breakwater Books, St. John's, Newfoundland, 1986), A.B. Perlin's *The Story of Newfoundland* (The Guardian Press, St. John's, Newfoundland, 1959), E.R. Seary's *Family Names of the Island of Newfoundland*, Corrected Edition, edited by William Kirwin (McGill-Queen's University Press, Montreal & Kingston, 1998), and Wendy Martin's *Once Upon A Mine: Story of Pre-Confederation Mines on the Island of Newfoundland* (Special Volume 26, The Canadian Institute of Mining and Metallurgy, Printed by ANLO INC., Westmount, Quebec, 1998.)

The communities of Scat's Arm and Chapel Bight, Newfoundland, and Seaward and Haleybury, New Hampshire exist only in the author's imagination.

Thomas Rendell Curran

was born in St. John's, Newfoundland in 1939. He was
educated at Holloway School, Prince of Wales College,
Memorial University of Newfoundland, and the University of
Toronto. For more than twenty years, he was a senior researcher
and writer with the Parliamentary Research Branch in Ottawa.
Undertow was shortlisted for the *2003 Arthur Ellis Award for Best
First Novel*. He currently lives in Ottawa.

Also by Thomas Rendell Curran

UNDERTOW
AN INSPECTOR STRIDE MYSTERY

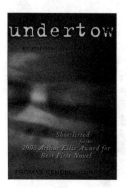

While investigating two unsolved murders in 1947,
Inspector Eric Stride of the Newfoundland Constabulary
finds that his own life is in danger.
The first installment in the *Inspector Stride Series.*
Shortlisted for the 2003 Arthur Ellis Award for Best First Novel.

ISBN 1-55081-193-2 / $ 19.95 PB / 6 X 9 / 384 PP

Praise for *undertow*